EDGE
—OF—
MADNESS

A Zach Templeton Thriller

Keith Hoar

Second Edition

Zhetosoft Publications

Published by: Zhetosoft Publications

Edge of Madness is a work of fiction. Names, characters, places, and events are either the product of the author's imagination or are used fictitiously. Any resemblance to actual events, locales, organizations, or persons, living or dead, is entirely coincidental and beyond the intent of the author.

1. Nuclear submarines -- Fiction. 2. United States military and government -- Fiction. 3. USS Providence (ship) - Fiction. 4. USS San Juan (ship) - Fiction. 5. Terrorist bombing - Fiction.

ISBN(13): 978-0-9994590-2-7 (hardback)
ISBN(13): 978-0-9994590-0-3 (paperback)
ISBN (13): 978-0-9994590-1-0 (e-Book)

Other books by Keith Hoar

<u>NOVELS</u>:

RAGE

<u>NONFICTION:</u>

DECEIVED The Assault of Revisionist History

This book is dedicated to my incredibly dedicated and patient wife who graciously put up with long hours and many weekends when I left her abandoned while I disappeared into my office, typing furiously like a madman. Her meticulous review of numerous revisions of this book aided greatly in producing a final manuscript devoid of spelling and grammar errors. Without her faithful love and support and constant encouragement this book would likely have never been completed.

"This is an evil among all things that are done under the sun, that there is one event unto all: yea, also the heart of the sons of men is full of evil, and MADNESS is in their heart while they live, and after that they go to the dead."

Ecclesiastes 9:3

Edge of Madness

Cast of Characters

UNITED STATES ADMINISTRATION
Paul Cantwell, President of the United States
Arthur Mead, Vice-President of the United States
Matthew Tyler, National Security Advisor
James Sandberg, Director CIA
Michael Shuff, Director FBI
Frank Porter, Deputy Director, FBI National Clandestine Service
Richard Howland, Director, Bureau of Alcohol, Tobacco, and Firearms
Mark Bradfield, US Senator, State of Oklahoma
Fleet Admiral Douglas Bennington, Chairman Joint Chiefs of Staff
William Danvers, General of the Army
James Radford, General of the Air Force
Andrew McCune, Marine Corp Chief of Staff
Colonel Craig Elmont, OPSDEPS Staff Liaison Officer
Brigadier General Samuel Worthington, Operations Deputy, US Army
Rear Admiral Michael Eads, Operations Deputy, US Navy
Major General Ethan Cook, Operations Deputy, US Air Force
Brigadier General Alan Stockton, Operations Deputy, US Marine Corps
Sergeant Wilbur Solis, Pentagon Police

NATIONAL MILITARY COMMAND
Vice Admiral Harlan Beckwith, Director, Joint Staff
Rear Admiral Charles Hadley, Director of Naval Intelligence
Captain Aaron Carpenter, Staff Aide
Captain Ronald Whitfield, Staff Duty Officer for CNO
Kip Johnson, Gulfstream G550 Pilot

DIA COMMUNICATIONS CENTER
Captain Robert Prescott, Senior Watch Officer
Commander Owen Patterson, Records Section
Eugene Williamson, FBI Special Agent
Andrew Tiner, FBI Field Agent (aka Aronoff Porubsky)
Benjamin Slater, FBI Field Agent

COMSUBLANT (Commander, Submarine Force Atlantic)
Lieutenant Commander Paul Davis, Command Duty Officer
Lieutenant James Chetham, Staff Duty Officer

USS SAN JUAN - SSN 751
Commander Steven Richards, Commanding Officer
Lieutenant Commander Edgar Dixon, Executive Officer
Lieutenant Franklin Bishop, Weapons Officer
Lieutenant Alfred Patterson, Engineering Officer
Quartermaster First Class Gregory McCain, Qmstr. of the Watch
Radioman First Class Tim Bentley, Message Center Supervisor
Sonarman First Class Roy Carter, Sonar Supervisor
Engineman Second Class Mike Hall, Duty Helmsman
Engineman Third Class Kent Green, Duty Planesman

USS PROVIDENCE - SSN 719
Commander Samuel Chandler, Commanding Officer
Lieutenant Commander Leroy Graham, Executive Officer
Lieutenant Edwin Harris, Weapons Officer
Lieutenant Thomas Flanigan, Navigation Officer
Lieutenant David Brinker, Assistant Weapons Officer
Lieutenant Conroy Sullivan, Engineering Officer
Lieutenant Jg. Kyle Johnson, Electrical Division Officer
Lieutenant Kent Madoc, Communications Officer
Master Chief Engineman Michael Mazetti, Chief of the Boat
Chief Radioman Kenneth Barton, Radio Division Chief
Radioman First Class Daniel Sabatino, (MAINCOMM) Supervisor
Radioman Second Class Brett Easley, CRYPTO Operator
Radioman Second Class Albert Benson, Broadcast Operator
Radioman Third Class Mike Hall, Radio Checker
Quartermaster First Class Timothy Wilson, Qmstr. of the Watch
Sonar Technician First Class Randy Jenkins, Sonar Operator
Engineman Second Class Marvin Connaly, Duty Helmsman
Machinist Mate Second Class Carl Hill, Duty Planesman
Hull Technician Second Class Ben Whitman, Rescue Diver
Hull Technician Third Class Andy Baldwin, Rescue Diver

SUBMARINE DEVELOPMENT SQUADRON 12
Lieutenant Carl Franks, Staff Duty Officer

US NAVY AMPHIBIOUS ASSAULT TEAM TWO
Lieutenant Conrad Moore, Team Leader
Senior Chief Gunner's Mate Robert Tucker, Weapons Specialist
Boatswains Mate First Class Brian Draper, Team Member
Machinist Mate Second Class Miguel Sanchez, Team Member
Engineman Second Class Scott Hardman, Team Member

US NAVY SQUADRON ONE, AZORES
Lieutenant Commander Glen Ewing, Command Duty Officer

NEW MEXICO LAW ENFORCEMENT
Juan Moralles, Sierra County Sheriff
Alberto Ramirez, Sierra County Deputy Sheriff
Robert Morgan, Troop Commander, State Patrol

CIVILIAN CHARACTERS
Zachariah James Templeton, Owner – Microwave Services
Angie Templeton, Zach Templeton's Wife
Bill Morrison (aka Josek Krizova), CIA Operative
Sergei Karadnya, CIA Operative
Leuka Sokołowski, Undercover CIA Operative
Paul Duniven, Exec. Vice-President, Government Procurement Services
Da'ud Amin Bahar, Radical Extremist
Khalil Jawdah Amari, Radical Extremist
Abdul Suhaib Hadad, Extremist Proselyte
Norman Glover, Retired Undercover CIA Operative
Henri (Frenchie) Boulee, Hired Assassin
Angus McDonald, Hired Assassin
Mike Branford, Captain Marine Vessel – Sea Princess
Captain Tom Grantham, Commercial Aircraft Pilot
Marvin Spangler, Outside Maintenance Technician, NRAO
Jamison Rhodes, Maintenance Manager, NRAO

Author's Note

The U. S. Navy, as well as civil aviation, uses the letter "Z" (phonetically pronounced "Zulu") to refer to the time at the prime meridian. The U.S. time zones are Eastern ["R", "Romeo]; Central ["S", "Sierra"]; Mountain ["T", "Tango"]; Pacific ["U", "Uniform"]; Alaska ["V", "Victor"], and Hawaii ["W", "Whiskey"]

The U. S. Navy coordinates operational time at multiple locations around the world by using the time designation - Zulu. Zulu Time is the same as the old time designation known as Greenwich Mean Time (GMT).

Greenwich Mean Time (GMT) is the time at the Prime Meridian (the reference line or starting point determined to be the transit circle at the Royal Observatory in Greenwich, London) or 0° longitude.

After 1972 GMT was no longer used as a time standard. Since then, UTC(Coordinated Universal Time) is the time standard commonly used across the world. The world's timing centers agreed to keep their time scales closely synchronized - or coordinated - therefore the name Coordinated Universal Time. Also note that UTC is NOT affected by changing seasons.

In this book, you will find Zulu Time used for all sections involving maritime, military operations, or scenes in Europe.

This novel is set in various locales in the United States and in other countries. Seemingly incorrect grammar that is contained within quotes may reflect broken English this is used by some foreign characters. For example: "I not see you in long time." Would be typical speech for someone who has a poor command of the English language.

Thank you for taking the time to read **Edge of Madness**, Book 1 in the Zach Templeton Thriller Series, and, hopefully, the next book, **RAGE**, in the Zach Templeton series. The author is very grateful for fans of his books, and would love to correspond with readers like you. Sample prologues and/or the first chapter of current and upcoming books can be viewed on his author website at www.Zhetosoft.com. You are welcome to reach out to the author through his personal email address at author@zhetosoft.com.

Keith Hoar

PROLOGUE

Friday, March 20 - 10:58 a.m. Eastern Daylight Time
North Calvert Street
Baltimore, Maryland

Paul Duniven would be dead in two minutes. Was he the target or was it for no other reason than he was in the wrong place at the wrong time? Or was it that he was in the right place at the wrong time? Those questions would never be answered. History would only record that he died at precisely 11:00 a.m. Eastern Daylight Time.

The forty-one-year-old executive vice-president of Government Procurement Services, Inc. was walking toward Baltimore's Penn Station, on his way to a meeting in Washington, DC, to discuss serious issues affecting a government contract his company was overseeing.

Waiting to cross North Calvert Street, Duniven was standing less than twenty feet from Abdul Suhaib Hadad. For the past two years, nineteen-year-old Hadad had listened intently to the radical extremists in his neighborhood. His mind had become so saturated and influenced by the hate-filled rantings of his mentors, he had lost touch with reality. He no longer dreamed about the things other nineteen-year-olds dreamed about. His sole desire was to become a martyr for his new-found cause. The marvelous glory he would receive for sacrificing himself was all he thought about. That image of glory filled his mind as he waited for the signal that would ignite the fifty pounds of high explosives lining the vest hidden under his heavy coat.

Paul Duniven never saw or felt a thing. He simply ceased to exist. Storefronts were blown out and windows were shattered for five blocks in all directions.

Local law enforcement, the Bureau of Alcohol, Tobacco, and Fire Arms, and the FBI sifted through the debris for days looking for evidence that would lead them to the perpetrator or perpetrators of the despicable act.

Two tiny scraps of the detonator, too burnt and mangled to provide any usable information, were all that was found. Hadad was identified using surveillance photos and a small bone fragment embedded in a shredded piece of the vest he had been wearing.

Hadad's mother, Amsah, was horrified when she was told her only son had blown himself up. She argued with the FBI, insisting her son would not do such a thing. Amsah was unable to tell the FBI agents anything because Hadad had been very careful to never mention the extremist names in his mother's presence.

Numerous interviews and many hours of research only yielded a tenuous link to a group of dissidents in Europe. The extremists had been meticulous in eliminating any evidence of their connection to Hadad. After Hadad left his apartment for the last time, someone planted phony travel documents where they would be easily found. The extremists sought no credit for the bombing as it was not their plot. Someone else had provided the explosives, the detonator, the exact location, and the phony materials, promising to pay them a very large sum of money.

The first time Hadad showed up at one of the meetings, he was quickly identified as a naïve and eager follower. Da'ud Amin Bahar and his accomplice Khalil Jawdah Amari skillfully molded the gullible Hadad using fanatical rhetoric and promises of glory to come. They felt absolutely no guilt over using the immature teenager. He was nothing more than a tool to be used in their war with the infidels.

The day after Hadad blew himself up, Da'ud Amin Bahar called the number that had been included with the explosives. Bahar was uneasy but the promise of money, a lot of money, overrode his anxiety.

"Hello. What do you want?" a distorted voice asked.

"It is done," Bahar answered.

"Everything? The materials as well?"

"Yes. Everything."

"When I am certain, the money will be transferred."

Before Bahar could ask how soon the money would arrive, the connection went dead.

The man who provided the explosives felt no remorse whatsoever for the lives that had been snuffed out. He would rather not have sent those seventeen people to their deaths, but when you were about to orchestrate the death of millions, a few more really did not matter.

CHAPTER ONE

Zachariah James Templeton (Zach to close friends and family) was bone tired. More tired than he had ever been in his entire life. Not just physically tired, he was emotionally drained.

Overwhelmed, he gave in to the frustration rising inside him. Snatching the papers he had been poring over for the last three hours, he hurled them off his desk. The papers swirled in the air and floated to the floor in wild disarray. Rubbing his tired, gritty eyes, he glanced at the digital clock sitting on the corner of his desk. It was nearly midnight and he had to meet his wife, Angie, at the airport for a flight to Miami in just six short hours.

No matter how much time and effort he put into trying to solve the problems plaguing the Department of Defense (DOD) microwave system, his company's prime client, not only could he not come up with an answer, he did not even have a clue where to start. The DOD was demanding a resolution, and soon, but he had to get home and get at least a few hours of sleep before meeting his wife.

The DOD procurement office had made explicit threats that they were going to cancel their contract with his company if the problems were not corrected soon. Without the DOD contract, his struggling company would be doomed. Owning his own business had been his lifelong dream. From its inception, the company had consumed an increasing portion of his time and energy. Despite his best efforts, his dream was dying right before his eyes.

Adding to the immense strain he was under; his marriage was teetering on the brink of collapse. Three months earlier Angie had moved out and

3

said she wanted a divorce.

After Angie moved out, Zach spent every moment he possibly could with her, or more truthfully, every moment she would allow. He often worked late into the night to compensate for the time spent with Angie. He was determined to save his company and his marriage.

Angie's decision hit Zach like a steamroller. They had been madly in love from the first day they met. Zach was certain of that. They loved the same foods, the same books, the same recreational activities. They agreed on nearly everything except the importance of church. Zach attended occasionally at Angie's urging. He sat and listened but it just did not have the same draw for him as it did for her. What had happened to the deep love they had shared? Another question that Zach could not answer.

The tremendous emotional strain and the long hours were affecting him both mentally and physically. He was becoming increasingly irritable and was having trouble concentrating. His life was in shambles. It was at moments like this he considered giving up. But he could not just give up. There was far too much at stake.

Only Zach knew the reason he was so driven to succeed and be respected. It was deeply personal and impossible for Zach to talk about. If forced to admit the truth, Zach knew he was trying to convince himself as much as anyone he was a success. Success would be a substitute for the affirmation he never received from his father. He believed his father loved him, but never once had he heard his father say that he was proud of him.

Five years earlier, on a beautiful, clear day, Zach's parents had sailed from San Francisco on their beloved sailboat Tipsy, lovingly named after his Aunt Clara's habit of over-imbibing during family gatherings. His parents disappeared without a trace. No one ever knew why. The authorities assumed the sailboat had some kind of mechanical problem and had sunk without a trace. After agonizing weeks of waiting, Zach was forced to accept the fact his parents were gone. A profound emptiness settled upon him, knowing the affirmation he longed for would never come. Unconsciously, he transferred that longing into his craving to succeed and be respected.

Pushing his chair back from the desk, he stood and stretched to relieve the pain and stiffness in his muscles, the result of sitting so long. He glanced at the papers strewn about the floor. Simply too exhausted to care, he shrugged, turned his back on the mess, and headed for the door.

As he closed the office door and shoved the key into the lock, he stared at the company name and logo stenciled on the door, remembering how satisfied he had felt the day the painter completed the sign. He had been so enthusiastic and full of hope the day he started Microwave Services Inc. Sadly, that hope soon faded as the demands on his time and energy drove a wedge between him and Angie. He desperately wanted to open up to her and share the pain of past events. Every time he tried to open up to her, he simply could not bring himself to explain to her why the company was so important.

Was he going to have to give up his dream and walk away from the company he had struggled so hard to start? Would that be the ultimate price he would have to pay to prove to Angie she was the most important thing in his life? Would he be able to walk away from his lifelong dream?

Zach hoped and prayed he would not be forced to make that choice. Deep down inside he already knew how he would choose. Zach locked the door and headed for the elevator completely unaware of the horror that lay ahead.

* * *

Monday, March 23 - 1700 Eastern Daylight Time
USS Providence, SSN 719, (Los Angeles class submarine)
US Naval Submarine Base, Groton, Connecticut

Commander Samuel Chandler hurried down Pier Seven toward the last-minute activity in progress on the deck of *USS Providence*. He glanced at his watch. *Providence's* crew had less than one hour to complete their final preparations and get under way.

Commander Chandler rushed up the aft gangway, turned aft toward the national ensign, and saluted smartly. He turned and saluted the Officer of the Deck then hurried down the aft access hatch.

"Attention. Officer on deck," Radioman First Class Daniel Sabatino announced, recognizing the Commanding Officer of the boat stepping off the bottom of the aft ladder. "Good morning Captain," Sabatino said.

"As you were," Commander Chandler called out. "Get these provisions stowed quickly. We're due to get under way in less than one hour."

"Yes, sir. We're just finishing up, sir," Sabatino answered.

"Very well," Commander Chandler acknowledged as he exited the mess deck and headed forward.

"Okay, men. You heard the Captain. Let's get this stuff stowed. On the double," Sabatino hollered.

Chandler entered his cabin and pulled the door shut. The next thirty minutes passed quickly while he busied himself finishing up last-minute paperwork. He shoved the papers he had been working on into a wall safe, exited his cabin, and hurried toward the command and control center, the nerve center of the boat.

Upon arriving at the command and control center, he stepped up on the one-foot high platform in the center of control, known as the Conn, and turned toward the Chief of the Boat, "COB, is the boat ready to get under way?"

"Aye, aye sir. Everything is stowed and secure. Power plant is online, all systems indicate green, and all maneuvering watches are manned and ready," Master Chief Michael Mazetti responded.

"COB, assign lookouts to the bridge," Chandler instructed.

"Aye, aye sir." Master Chief Mazetti turned toward the two lookouts who were standing nearby and barked orders. The two lookouts responded immediately, scrambling up the ladder to their lookout positions on the sail bridge.

"Mister Graham you have the Conn. I'm going topside to the sail bridge."

"Aye, aye Captain," Lieutenant Commander Leroy Graham, *Providence's* Executive Office, responded crisply.

Commander Chandler climbed the ladder behind the lookouts and took his position on the sail bridge for the process of getting underway. He leaned over and watched as the crew members on deck preparing to cast off the mooring lines. Pride filled his mind as he surveyed the sleek, black boat. He took a deep breath and smiled. He loved the ocean, but even more he loved the sense of fulfillment that came from commanding one of the most powerful warships in the world. Not just for the awesome power of destruction it carried, but also for the satisfaction derived from commanding the best trained crew of any ship in the United States Navy.

USS Providence, commissioned on August 4, 1984, the fourteenth Los Angeles class nuclear powered attack submarine, had been built by the Electric Boat Division of General Dynamics Corporation in Groton, Connecticut. *Providence* was one of the most advanced undersea vessels of its type in the entire world. Her stated mission was to hunt down and destroy enemy surface ships and submarines. The three hundred sixty foot, sixty-nine-hundred-ton ship was extremely well equipped to accomplish that mission. Faster than her predecessors and equipped with highly accurate sensors and weapon control systems, she was armed with sophisticated Mark 48 ADCAP anti-submarine torpedoes and Tomahawk cruise missiles. Fully manned, *Providence* carried a total crew of one hundred forty-five; fourteen officers and one hundred thirty-one enlisted men, all very highly skilled specialists.

Providence was previously home-ported in San Diego, California. After a two-year overhaul in Kittery, Maine, her homeport shifted to Groton, Connecticut, where she became the lead boat of Subron12 (Submarine Squadron 12), attached to Submarine Group Two. It was from that homeport *Providence* prepared to sail on her latest assignment to keep the oceans of the world safe.

Commander Chandler did indeed have much to be proud of. He was *the* officer the Navy had selected to shoulder the responsibility of commanding one of the most lethal killing machines ever devised by man.

Commander Chandler heard the crew complaining and saw their disapproving glances as he passed them on the boat. The crew was very distressed after learning their shore leave had been cut short. For unknown reasons, COMSUBLANT (Commander, Submarine Force Atlantic) had ordered *Providence* to get underway earlier than scheduled. Commander Chandler just accepted it as part and parcel of being the world's peacekeeper.

Commander Chandler's attention focused on the final preparations for what he thought was just another routine patrol.

* * *

Tuesday, March 24 - 0500 Eastern Daylight Time
Navy Executive Corridor
Pentagon – Corridor 9, E Ring
Washington, D.C.

"Soon. Very soon. They would be dead. They would all be dead," thought Vice Admiral Harlan Beckwith as he approached the door to the Pentagon. Smiling slightly, he pushed the door open. Yes, very soon the vengeance he longed for, the vengeance he dreamed of, the vengeance he lived for would finally be his.

Beckwith headed down the E-Ring Corridor, his footsteps echoing loudly as he hurried down the deserted corridor. Despite the early hour, there was much activity in the Pentagon, mostly concentrated in the underground communications and intelligence sections. Passing the intersection with Corridor Ten, he turned right and walked down Corridor Nine, the Navy Executive Corridor.

He shoved his security access badge into the card reader next to the door to his office. Deep in an underground bunker, a massive computer searched the Pentagon's information center database for his security clearance level. With a loud clunk, the electronic locking mechanism withdrew the locking bar. Beckwith pulled the door open and walked across the small interior office of his deputy assistant, stopping in front of the door to his personal office. He thumbed an access code into the cipher lock mounted next to the door. Once again there was a metallic clunk as the electronic mechanism accepted his access code and withdrew the locking bar.

Walking across the room in the semi-darkness, he switched on a small brass desk lamp. He unbuttoned his uniform jacket and hung it over the back of the chair. The soft glow from the lamp illuminated the shiny, brass name plate sitting on the front edge of the desk that read Director, Joint

Staff.

The Chairman of the Joint Chiefs of Staff had personally selected Admiral Beckwith, a three-star, senior Navy officer, to assist in managing the Joint Staff activities. Under the Chairman's direction, Admiral Beckwith assisted other JCS members in carrying out their responsibilities.

The Chief of each branch of military service appoints an operations deputy who works with the Director, Joint Staff, as part of the Operations Deputies or OPSDEPS in the world of military acronyms. The OPSDEPS members meet to consider issues of lesser importance or to review major issues before they reach the Joint Chiefs of Staff. The Director, Joint Staff is the only OPSDEPS member that is officially a part of the Joint Staff.

Beckwith had sacrificed much to rise to the high-level, Pentagon assignment he currently occupied. During his career in the United States Navy, he had endured many long separations from his family, serving in faraway places. His stellar rise up the ranks had been due, in part, to his graduation from the United States Naval Academy at the top of his class. At the pinnacle of an exemplary career, he was slated to soon receive his fourth star. Despite that, Beckwith felt no sense of accomplishment or satisfaction. There was no longer any purpose in his life except the blind rage and all-consuming desire for revenge that boiled deep inside him.

A horrifying incident four years earlier had robbed him of his entire family. Beckwith had been assigned as Commander, Navy Region, Europe, billeted in Naples, Italy. It was a rare overseas assignment where his family had been allowed to accompany him. He and his family had been in Italy less than six months when a radical Chechen terrorist annihilated himself and twenty-two other people.

On a cool spring day, while he was busy with administrative duties related to the arrival of a U. S. Navy carrier task group, his wife and two daughters had decided to go shopping along the Spaccanapoli, a long, straight, narrow street, bisecting the old, historic center of the city of Naples from east to west. Spaccanapoli literally meant "Naples splitter" since viewed from above, it seemed to divide the city in half. The street, officially named Via Benedetto Croce, starting at the Piazza Gesù Nuovo, was the main promenade for tourists; lined with many interesting churches, shops, and other historic buildings. On most days, the Spaccanapoli was literally teeming with tourists and locals searching for souvenirs and bargains.

On the ill-fated day the terrorist had chosen to detonate his vest, crammed with high explosives, Beckwith's wife and two daughters were standing less than ten feet away, according to the investigators. However, it was never more than an opinion because the horrific blast had literally obliterated everything within two hundred feet. All that was recovered were some small scraps of clothing and a few bone fragments, later identified through DNA analysis. His beautiful wife, Janie, and his two adorable girls, Gabriel and Amy, were gone in an instant.

There had not even been enough left of his family to bury. A small memorial service was held in Richmond, Virginia, mostly for his wife's parents' sake. Beckwith was left completely alone, being an only child. Both his parents were dead and he had long ago lost contact with his few distant relatives. The Navy had granted him an extended leave to grieve. The two weeks following the memorial service were absolute agony for him as he wandered around the large house they still owned in a suburb of Washington, D.C. He ate very little and drank too much, sleeping on the living room couch to avoid entering the bedroom he and his wife had shared. Never once had he so much as opened the door to his daughters' bedrooms. He seldom left the house and talked to no one.

The overwhelming grief ate at him like a cancer. Adamantly refusing to talk to anyone, his grief grew deeper and deeper, finally morphing into a white-hot, burning fury. At the end of the third week, he realized he would soon have to return to duty. Through sheer willpower, he pushed the burning anger just below the surface. The single thing that drove him was a growing desire for revenge. Without that hope for revenge, the rage smoldering inside him would have consumed him. As the last day of his extended leave arrived, a plan for revenge had formed in his mind.

Beckwith sat in his dimly-lit Pentagon office and stared at the photograph of his wife and two girls stolen from him on that dreadful day. Sliding open the center drawer of his desk, he pulled out an old Bible, which showed the wear that only came from years of frequent handling. He laid it on the desk and opened it to the book of Ecclesiastes. Slowly he read the verse he had read hundreds of times before, his finger tracing the words as he read. As he reached the middle of the verse, he began reading aloud, ". . . the heart of the sons of men is full of evil, and MADNESS is in their heart while they live, and after that they go to the dead."

Beckwith reached out and picked up the photograph of his wife and daughters, ever so gently caressing the smiling faces. No matter how hard he tried to forget, the gut-wrenching images from the day they were murdered were indelibly burned into his mind, inescapable, impossible to ignore. Images just as raw and vivid in his mind as the day the horrendous event had occurred.

His mind seethed with hatred for the evil that had murdered his family. Not only the man directly responsible but for anyone remotely associated with him. Only an evil born out of madness would deliberately murder innocent women and children.

Exacting revenge only on the Chechen rebels would be like picking at a scab on a leg infected with gangrene. It would be pointless and would only spread the putrid disease. The source of the disease was the country that funded the rebels and provided them weapons, instigating them to greater violence. It was more than a disease. It was a horrible cancer eating away at the world. It must be stopped. He vowed he would be the one to stop it.

Four long years his tortured soul had hungered and cried out for righteous revenge. That longed-for revenge was the only thing keeping his grief at bay. A grief so painful and crushing he could not even speak of it. A brilliant military career destroyed by one despicable act of violence.

He gently set the photograph back on the desk and read the Bible verse again, silently mouthing the words. As he closed the Bible and laid it back in the drawer, he promised himself he would "send them to the dead", no matter the cost.

CHAPTER TWO

Tuesday, March 24 - 0920 Zulu
Ostravské Muzeum
Masarykovo Náměstí 1, Ostrava, Czech Republic

Josek Krizova (known as Bill Morrison until he had assumed his current identity) strolled through the Ostravské Museum looking at the paintings, sculptures, and various displays, nervously glancing at his wrist watch. Ten minutes remained before the pickup, hastily arranged the previous afternoon, was to occur.

Josek's contact had been unable, or perhaps unwilling, to tell him anything definitive. The only comment had been that no sacrifice was too great to obtain the materials. Bill struggled to calm his nerves. In this part of the world, there were always eyes watching. It was imperative he not look nervous or he might attract undue attention.

Something had to be terribly wrong. Everything about the meeting violated the strict security protocol under which he worked. Not only was the meeting to be in a crowded public place, it was to take place in broad daylight, and it was much too close to the residence hotel in which he lived.

Bill could not imagine what could be so important that it would justify compromising two years of preparation and more than a year of hard work spent infiltrating the dissident group which was growing rapidly and becoming increasingly violent. It would not be long before it became a very real threat to the tenuous peace that existed in central Europe.

Afraid to loiter inside the museum any longer, he exited the museum on the Masaryk Square side of the plaza. Strolling slowly over to an empty bench he sat down. He opened the newspaper he was carrying and pretended to read, his eyes darting frequently around the plaza looking for anyone suspicious. Everything seemed normal. Old men in animated conversations, perhaps arguing over politics or religion. Families with small children coming and going. Young couples entwined in each other's arms, enjoying the early morning sun.

Bill sat for several minutes then got up, folded the newspaper, and placed it under his arm. Turning right, he casually strolled down Velká street. Continuing for several hundred feet, he turned left on Solná street and walked past the monument. Satisfied no one following him, he again selected an empty bench and sat down. He pulled the newspaper out from under his arm and laid it on the bench beside him.

Less than two minutes passed before a very overweight man walked up and sat on the other end of the bench.

"Południe, słońce w południe dobry," the fat man said.

"Tak. Czuje się dobrze na mojej twarzy," Bill answered.

Upon hearing the expected response, the fat man laid his newspaper on top of the one Bill had placed on the bench. "To dobry dzień na spacer mój przyjaciel," he said as he got up and walked away.

Bill watched as the fat man walked down the street and disappeared. Bill picked up both newspapers, shoved them under his arm, and walked east on Solná street. Halfway past Masaryk Square he stopped and leaned against a trash receptacle. The newspaper passed to him by the fat man was folded around a large manila envelope. He slipped that newspaper under his jacket and discarded the one he had been carrying. Heading in the opposite direction, he again walked past Masaryk Square, but this time he turned south on Strelnicni street, continuing south to the next intersection and then west on Pivovarská street.

Knowing he would have to be extremely careful during the next few hours, he decided to find a café and get something to eat. After that he would spend several hours going from bar to bar. He dare not risk returning to his apartment until he was absolutely certain no one was following him.

As he meandered around the city, he had great difficulty resisting the urge to open the envelope. With every step, the lump under his arm needled his curiosity. He desperately wanted to rip open the envelope and examine its contents. Whatever was inside the envelope had to be incredibly important to justify the extreme risk he had just taken.

Over the next few hours as he traveled a circuitous route past sleazy bars and taverns, Bill's mind conjured up all manner of dreadful conspiracies that would be revealed when he would finally be able to safely look at the contents of the envelope.

It was fortunate indeed that Bill had no idea what remained hidden in the envelope he was carrying. Had he known, the shock and terror on his face would have been impossible to hide.

* * *

Tuesday, March 24 – 9:30 a.m. Eastern Daylight Time
Oval Office
West Wing - Whitehouse
Washington, D.C.

President Paul Cantwell paced briskly back and forth in front of the three large windows that formed the south wall of the Oval Office. He stopped and turned toward the four men already seated on the opposite side of the Resolute Desk. About to buzz his personal secretary, Cantwell looked up as National Security Advisor Matthew Tyler was ushered into the office.

"Sorry I'm late Mr. President," Tyler offered, panting and out of breath.

Cantwell did not answer, simply pointing to the remaining empty chair. As soon as Tyler took his seat, Cantwell began, "Gentlemen, I want to know what you know about the bombing in Baltimore. Now!"

Richard Howland, Director of the Bureau of Alcohol, Tobacco, and Firearms, was the first to speak. "Mister President, so far we know very little. All that we have recovered to this point are two small fragments of what we assume was the detonator and a small scrap of a vest containing an embedded bone fragment. I say *assume* because the fragments are so burnt and mangled we can't be certain. The scrap of the vest is already at the lab. DNA analysis should be running as we speak."

FBI Director Michael Shuff opened the notebook laying in his lap, retrieved a photograph, and slid it across the desk to the President. "After viewing images from surveillance cameras in the area, we believe this is the perpetrator. His name is Abdul Suhaib Hadad, nineteen years old, lived in a small apartment on East Madison Street in Baltimore. A search of his apartment turned up evidence of recent travel to the Czech Republic. We also found some literature linking him to a subversive group."

"Has anyone taken credit for the bombing?" Cantwell asked.

"Not as yet," Shuff answered, glancing at CIA Director James Sandburg.

"Our undercover sources have informed us this group has been exhibiting increasingly violent tendencies. However, so far it has only been threats and rhetoric," Sandburg added.

Shuff continued, "We questioned Hadad's mother extensively. She was adamant her son would never commit such an atrocity. We are convinced she knows nothing. Hadad must have been careful to conceal his relationships. That is all we have at this time."

Cantwell stood, placed his palms flat on the desk, and leaned forward. "That's it! That is all you have?"

"Mister President, it has only been three days," Shuff protested.

"Three days is an eternity," Cantwell shouted. "What if they're planning another attack? What then?"

Cantwell turned and looked directly at Frank Porter, Deputy Director of the FBI's National Clandestine Service. "I don't suppose you know anything either."

"We have tried to contact our undercover agent, but there has been no response as yet," Porter answered.

Cantwell slumped down in his chair. "Not good enough gentlemen. Not nearly good enough. The public is outraged and they are demanding answers. They want to know how this could happen. I agree with them. I want to know what happened!" The five men cringed as President Cantwell nearly screamed the last sentence.

"Get out! Go learn something," Cantwell roared as he reached for the phone.

The men scrambled out of their chairs and hurriedly left the Oval Office. They rushed toward their respective offices, hoping they could do as the President had instructed. All the men, except for Deputy Director Porter. As soon as Porter exited the White House, he dug a cell phone out of his pocket and dialed a number from memory.

Not waiting for the other party to speak, Porter said, "He is fuming." He ended the call, dropped the phone back in his pocket, and continued on his way.

CHAPTER THREE

Tuesday, March 24 – 12:47 Eastern Daylight Time
Paisano's Restaurant
558 23rd Street South
Arlington, Virginia

Admiral Harlan Beckwith dabbed at the corners of his mouth with a red cloth napkin, dropped it on the empty plate, and leaned back in his chair. He was absolutely stuffed. *Pasta Carbonara*, his favorite Italian dish, was a heavy choice for lunch, but he was feeling good. In just three days, the bombing in Baltimore had created sweeping outrage in the United States and a widespread demand for retribution. Not just from the general public but also in all levels of the government.

The outrage was palpable. The mood of the country bristled with anger. In numerous cities, large crowds gathered, demanding immediate retaliation against those responsible for the cowardly act. Beckwith's plan was working perfectly. The country's rapidly growing hostility adding the fuel necessary to launch his plan.

Beckwith glanced at the check and dropped several bills on the table. He exited the restaurant and headed back to his office to finish preparing the documents he would need later.

* * *

Tuesday, March 24 - 2210 Zulu
28 Říjná 16
Ostrava, Czech Republic

"My God!" Bill Morrison gasped as he stared at the photographs and documents spread out before him. Bill had been on a deep undercover assignment for two years; a mission which required extreme discipline and control. A mix of emotions welled up in his throat; fear, terror, panic, and anger. Hot, burning anger raged deep within as he stared at one face in particular, a face he knew well, a person whom he would have entrusted with his life. Until that instant.

A faint glow from a small table lamp was the only light illuminating the ratty, decaying apartment. A worn, rotting carpet revealing many years of foot traffic covered the floor; large areas of paint on the ceiling and walls were peeling and stained with grime from years of neglect. One bare table sat under the lone window. A threadbare, mildewed couch sat in the middle of the room and a small dining table and two chairs sat in the corner, the only evidence anyone inhabited the dismal apartment.

Bill was bent over the dilapidated dining table haphazardly shoved into one corner of the single room apartment. The rickety table rocked back and forth on uneven legs as he shifted his weight in the hard wooden chair, his mind recoiling at what he saw. He shook his head as he reread the handwritten message scrawled across the corner of one of the documents.

One by one he reexamined the photographs, pushing them directly into the dull beam of light that shone out from under the dirty shade perched atop the single bulb lamp. He desperately wanted to disbelieve what he saw. It could not be true. It must not be true! The longer he looked at the photographs, the deeper the fear and anger grew in the pit of his stomach. Perhaps he could discount the documents, but not the photographs. He simply could not deny the face staring back at him.

Bill knew he had to expose the conspiracy revealed by the materials scattered on the table. If he did not, the world's very existence would be threatened. He would have to act immediately and with extreme care. Bill was not naïve, having been in the intelligence field long enough to know it was not a matter of "if" the people behind this evil conspiracy found out the information was in his possession. It was a matter of "when" they found out; and when they did, there would be nowhere he could hide.

The instant his gaze fell upon the photographs, his life changed forever. Bill knew only one person in the entire world that could help him expose and, hopefully, stop the conspiracy. An old comrade he had not seen for years was the only one he could trust to get him to the right person. But would his old friend help? His old friend had been allowed to believe he had died in the jungles of Southeast Asia. How was he going to explain what he had done? The lies? The lives that had been sacrificed? Bill shuddered as he contemplated confessing his role in the vile alliance he had fallen into, narrowly escaping with his life. Despite the outcome, how could he justify the things he had done. Would his old friend forgive him? He hoped so. The future of the world would depend on it.

Bill was startled by a slamming door in the hallway. He reached up and switched off the lamp, listening intently. Loud footsteps. Coming closer.

There was movement in the dim light seeping in under the door. Someone stopped directly in front of the door. As quietly as he could, Bill crept over beside the door, slipping his hand under his jacket. His fingers closed around the knurled grip of his 9mm automatic. Barely breathing, he waited.

CHAPTER FOUR

Tuesday, March 24 - 2021 Eastern Daylight Time
Anchorage north of Cat Caye
Bimini, Bahamas

Zach Templeton leaned against the forward rail on the starboard side of the Marine Vessel *Sea Princess*. Zach was average height and not as thin as he had once been. As evidenced by his thinning hair, he had inherited his father's baldness, something he desperately hoped he would be spared. He was painfully aware of his appearance, even when nobody was there to notice.

How calm and serene everything seemed as he gazed across the calm water. "Yeah, right..." he muttered under his breath. He had to admit things were a lot better than they had been for most of his life. No more midnight launches into cold, dark water from the pitching deck of a submarine. No more covert reconnaissance missions, or swimming up leech-infested rivers to save some downed pilot. No more slogging through steamy jungles to eliminate something or someone. No more parachuting into third world countries to do something the local government would not do and probably would not like if they found out. Many times, he had thought of writing a book about his career, but who would believe it. Besides, the CIA would never allow him to publish it. Despite the dangers he had lived through, here he was forty-six years old with his life in shambles.

The wind ruffled his thinning hair as he stared blankly across the azure green water. In the distance, he could see the waves gently lapping on the beach of Cat Caye. Three days earlier Zach, his wife Angie, nineteen other passengers, and five crew members had sailed out of Miami harbor for a week-long SCUBA diving trip aboard the *Sea Princess*, an eighty foot, single-masted sailboat.

The transit across the Gulf Stream had been relatively smooth. Far smoother than anyone had expected. A week earlier, a minimal hurricane had passed through the southern Bahamas; and finally, the weather had settled and the seas were glassy smooth.

Deeply troubled by recent events, Zach was worried about his microwave service company. Microwave Services, Inc. was struggling because of severe interference problems plaguing the company's prime contract, the Department of Defense "Microwave Communications and Signaling System". Two weeks earlier the interference had become so bad, the Department of Defense Procurement Office threatened to cancel their contract with his company if the problems were not corrected soon. So far, extensive testing had revealed absolutely nothing out of the ordinary.

Zach had sacrificed much to realize his dream of owning his own company, more than he could ever have imagined when he started the fledgling service company three years earlier.

The biggest sacrifice of all was the reason for the hurriedly arranged SCUBA trip. Three months earlier Angie had moved out and told Zach she wanted a divorce. Zach was devastated. He knew there were problems but he had failed to realize the problems were that serious. His company and the issues it faced consumed so much of his concentration and energy. His marriage was dying right before his eyes and he did not see it happening.

For three long years, the business had consumed him. He had assumed Angie understood why the business was so important to him and why he needed so desperately to succeed. The need to succeed was so clear to him, but he failed completely to grasp the fact that Angie did not feel or understand that need.

Zach's careful planning and sacrifice had failed to consider one vitally important fact. His dream was not Angie's dream. Angie had been against the idea from the very beginning. When Zach quit his full-time job to start the company, she did her utmost to support him. Despite her best efforts, she became tired of sitting at home alone wondering what mountain top he was at this week or what radio site he would be at next week. Most of all she became tired of taking second place in Zach's life.

After Angie moved out, Zach worked diligently to make time to spend with Angie, despite his company's growing problems. He worked long, tiring hours at the office when they weren't together. After an evening with Angie, Zach would often return to the office, trying to keep the struggling company afloat. Often, he spent the entire night doing billing, creating proposals, calculating payroll, scheduling. All the things the office manager he could not afford to hire should have done.

Zach drove himself to near exhaustion, but he refused to let himself stop. He was as determined to save his marriage as he was determined to save his company. No matter how hard he drove himself, there were nights, sitting bleary eyed at his desk and unable to concentrate, it seemed as if he must choose between his marriage and the company. It was at those times, he felt most alone. It was as if some malevolent force was determined to destroy him. No matter how many hours he labored trying to identify the source, the DOD interference problems just got worse. No matter how many hours he spent talking with Angie, he failed to undo the feeling of bitterness and neglect she felt. Nothing he did seemed to matter anymore.

Must he make a choice between the woman he loved and his life's dream of building a successful company? If he did choose, was it already too late to save his marriage or his company?

Zach had arranged the SCUBA vacation with the hope he would be able to convince Angie how much he loved her and explain why salvaging his company was so important. He also intended to tell Angie about some of his missions as a Navy SEAL. He was convinced if she knew about his past and the demons he was running from, she would understand why he was so driven.

One of the crew members yelled at the captain as they completed the process of setting the sailboat's anchor. The sudden noise startled Zach and broke his train of thought. He turned and watched the final activities of the crew as they secured the boat for the night.

Pushing himself away from the rail, Zach headed aft, intending to go below and convince Angie to come up on deck so they could talk while waiting for the sunset. He took several steps and stopped short when Angie emerged from the main salon. He watched her intently as she made her way along the gently rolling deck.

He marveled at how beautiful she was; a beauty that improved with time. Even though she had reached middle age, she still looked incredible. Long, slender legs, beautiful auburn hair that turned golden in the sunlight, beautiful blue eyes, and just enough freckles to give her an impish schoolgirl look. The feature that captivated Zach most was her enchanting smile. When she smiled, there was a sparkle in her eyes and a softness to her face that held Zach nearly spellbound. No matter how many times he looked at that face, the love in his heart never faded.

He loved her more than he ever had. A thousand times the same questions raced through his mind. What had happened? How could such love and commitment just cease to exist? No matter how many times he heard Angie say she did not love him anymore, he could not get himself to believe it. Or was it just that he refused to accept it?

Zach raised his arms to embrace Angie but she sidestepped him and continued past where he was standing. She leaned against the rail and looked out across the water toward Cat Caye.

"Beautiful, isn't it," Zach said.

"Sure is," Angie replied.

"Enjoying the trip so far?" Zach asked as he moved beside her, gently laying his hand on her arm.

"Of course, I'm enjoying the trip," Angie responded, a tinge of irritation in her voice. "You know how much I like diving, Zach."

Zach started to say something but stopped. He removed his hand from Angie's arm and just stared across the water.

"What do you want, Zach?" Angie asked. She knew Zach well enough to know when he was holding back.

"It's only about fifteen minutes or so before sunset. Why don't we wait for it and talk," Zach suggested. "There are some things I want to say."

Angie turned and looked at Zach. "I'd really rather not. I'm really tired. I think I'll turn in early tonight. I just came up to see what the weather was like."

"Sure. Okay. I understand. I..." Zach stammered, disappointment obvious in his voice.

"Zach, we've been over this and over this," Angie blurted out. "There just isn't any point in discussing it anymore. Let's just enjoy what is left of the trip. Can't we just let it go?"

Before Zach could respond, Angie turned and headed aft. She walked straight to the ladder that led down to the main salon and disappeared below without looking back.

Zach stood motionless for several minutes not knowing what to do next. He could not go below. That would just cause more tension. Completely deflated and not knowing what else to do, he meandered aft and stopped at the stern ladder used to retrieve divers. Grabbing the bucket used to rinse photographic equipment, he sat it upside down on the deck. He sat down on the bucket and leaned against the back of the air compressor enclosure. The *Sea Princess* had swung around on the anchor rope and aligned itself into the light wind blowing from the East, causing the stern to face due West. Zach looked up at the incredible sunset painting itself across the Caribbean sky.

Too bad Angie had not stayed on deck for the sunset, Zach thought to himself. It was going to be spectacular.

One of Zach's favorite pastimes was to sit and watch sunsets. For Zach, it was a time of peace, a time of quiet, an enchanted time, a time when dreams were formed. It was a time of day that belonged to neither light nor dark, as the sun slid slowly below the horizon and the sky faded into muted shades of pink, crimson, vermillion, violet, magenta, and gray. It was a mystical time nestled between day and night.

As Zach gazed up at the sky, he realized that his life was just like the sunset. His life was in an "in between" place, a place between light and dark. Between the love and acceptance he so fiercely wanted and the rejection and loneliness he so desperately feared.

The battle of his life lay just ahead but Zach decided he was not going to just lie down and give up. He would fight. He would never give up if there was the slightest glimmer of hope that he and Angie could recapture the love they once had.

As the sun slid below the horizon, the bright, warm shades of pink and gold faded to the cold, gloomy shadows of darkness. Zach pushed himself up and headed for the ladder to the main salon. About to start down the ladder, he stopped and turned, taking one last look at what was left of the sunset. All that remained was a faint glow on the horizon, a tiny sliver of reflection shimmering across the water. How small and alone he felt as he gazed up at the vast heavens. He shivered and went below.

Once down the ladder, he made his way to his and Angie's berth by the glow of a small night light. A strict rule aboard the *Sea Princess* demanded that all common area lights were turned off no later than thirty minutes past sunset. One lone light was on in the far port side berth. A single diver scribbled in what appeared to be a dive log.

As quietly as he could, Zach slipped into the berth and pulled the curtain closed. Angie was already asleep. He lay there listening to the sounds of her slow rhythmic breathing. They had been up early that day and it had been a long day of diving. He, too, was soon asleep, lulled by the gentle rocking of the boat.

As tired as he was, dreams, horrible dreams, came quickly. He slept fitfully as he battled one ferocious enemy after another. Zach awoke with a start, breathing hard, drenched with perspiration. The dream seemed so real. He was shaking. Careful to avoid waking Angie, he slipped out of the berth and went topside to get some air.

Zach sat alone in the dark for a long time, trying to reason with himself, but he could not shake the feeling of impending doom that hovered over him like a dark cloud. He tried to convince himself it was just due to the stress of his marital problems coupled with the problems his company was having. But there was something deeper; something inside him that refused to be dissuaded.

Perhaps it was the instincts he had developed during his service as a Navy SEAL. Whatever its source, the feeling was too unsettling, too real to simply be cast aside.

CHAPTER FIVE

Wednesday, March 25 - 0130 Zulu
28 Říjná 16
Ostrava, Czech Republic

Sudden movement in the light coming under the door, Bill held his breath and waited. He jumped when something hit the floor. Whoever was standing in front of the door reached down and picked up the object from the floor. Bill heard what sounded like the jangling of keys as the person tried to insert a key into the lock several times.

Bill jerked the 9mm automatic out from under his jacket and thumbed the safety off. He heard a man swear as he made another attempt to insert a key into the lock. It sounded as if the man was drunk. The man swore again and staggered down the hallway. More muffled sounds. A door slammed. Bill listened intently for several minutes and heard only silence. He returned to the table, sat down, and switched the lamp on.

Bill thumbed the safety on and returned the automatic to its holster. He leaned back in the chair and pulled a handkerchief from his pocket, wiping beads of perspiration from his forehead. The sudden scare made him acutely aware of the risk he was taking. He replayed the events of the last few hours in his mind to determine if he had missed anything.

Just minutes earlier, he had slipped into his apartment and quietly pulled the door shut. Carefully he had felt his way across the dark room to the single window and had pulled the window shade down. As an extra precaution, he had also pulled the curtains together to make certain no one could see in.

Stumbling over one of the chairs, he made his way to the table in the corner of the room. He switched on a small table lamp and sat down. Still under his jacket was the large envelope that had been passed to him by a fat, sloppily dressed man he did not know.

The previous afternoon, during his routine, weekly meeting with his normal contact, he had been passed a message containing detailed instructions regarding the hastily arranged meeting. After the highly unusual meeting, Bill had spent several hours going from bar to bar, as instructed, watching for any sign that he was being followed. Finally, satisfied no one was watching him, he had returned to his apartment, making numerous detours along the way. Only something very serious could have justified such a breach in security protocol.

Bill's hands had trembled as he opened the large, manila envelope. There had to be something extremely important inside the envelope. As he tipped the envelope up, two one-page documents and five photographs slid out onto the table. He had quickly read the handwritten message scrawled across the corner of one of the documents and then scanned the documents. Then he had spread out the photographs.

Bill's attention returned to the present and the crisis he faced. He continued to stare at the photographs. Bill recognized two of the other four faces in the photographs from the various intelligence materials he had been required to memorize before embarking on this assignment. He had been ready to dismiss the information he had stumbled across several weeks ago because it was too shocking to be believable. Convinced the information was false, concocted to deliberately mislead anyone that uncovered it, he had ignored it. But now the undeniable proof laid on the table before him.

It was obvious the photographs had been taken with an extremely good surveillance camera. The detail was crisp and the images were crystal clear. The final piece of the puzzle had fallen into place. The nightmare he believed inconceivable turned out to be real.

There was no doubt in Bill's mind what his next step must be. It was imperative this information get to Washington as quickly as possible. The materials laying before him were far too vital to trust to the normal intelligence channels. He would have to sacrifice the hard work of the past two years and deliver the materials himself.

Bill had been sent to Ostrava in the Czech Republic over a year earlier after two full years of preparation. He had learned to speak the language fluently and had been taught the country's history, its art, and its music. His identity had been flawlessly contrived. Absolutely no one would have guessed he was not a Czech citizen.

The instant he had arrived in Ostrava, a hatred of the city began to build. For fourteen long months he had labored, establishing himself with the local dissidents. The city of Ostrava was not simply ugly—it was spectacularly, unforgettably ugly. The embodiment of an idea carried to an irrational extreme. Ostrava, where the Czech Republic, Poland, and

Slovakia met, was the crucible that forged the unbridled desires of Eastern European communism for two generations. It had been populated according to a master production plan, the days of its residents regulated by the screeching of factory whistles and the monotonous clanking of machinery.

Ostrava was known by many as *The Black City*. Abandoned mine shafts, smokestacks belching grit and grime into the air, mountainous heaps of slag, the faces of men and women, eyelids caked with a fine black dust, acquired from long days spent laboring in the coal mines, and children who coughed incessantly. Such images were the portraits of the city and citizens of Ostrava.

At the core of Ostrava's crisis was a problem also familiar to America: acute, cancerous deindustrialization, with its resultant social crime and irresolvable unemployment. After two generations of unprecedented peace and plenty, the brilliant success story of Western Europe was sliding fast into the nightmare of abandoned central cities and an embittered underclass of discarded human beings.

Investments were to be made elsewhere. The final irony would be that the men and women of cities like Ostrava, who had braved half a century of life in the cold, dark shadow of oppressive communism, were to be discarded. They would end up in the same graveyard as their abandoned, decaying factories.

It was the rapidly growing dissidence, created by a sense of abandonment and lack of purpose, that worried senior officials in Washington and ultimately had led to Bill's assignment.

Bill had gained the trust of several of the most prominent dissidents. The intelligence value of his undercover position was enormous, but it would have to be sacrificed. Nothing was as important as the information that lay scattered on the table in front of him.

Bill had tried to sleep but he had managed only to catnap, his mind flooded with thoughts of being captured and the information in his possession being lost. He tossed and turned, wrestling with the musty, tattered blankets. No matter how hard he tried, he could not relax enough to sleep.

Distressed and bleary eyed, Bill sat up and looked at his watch. It was still early. Far too early to go out on the street and use a pay phone. He retrieved a cell phone from a secret compartment under the table. The risk was enormous but he simply could not wait any longer. He punched in his emergency contact's number and pressed send.

After five rings, a sleepy voice answered, "Hello."

"Leuka, this is Jozek. Why are you sleeping? The day is wasting. It will be a nice day for a stroll."

Leuka was instantly awake upon hearing the prearranged emergency phrase. His comrade, Jozek, needed an immediate extraction plan. The final sentence instructed Leuka that not even their superiors were to be informed of the extraction. Something must be terribly wrong to require such action. Leuka shivered, pulling a blanket up around his neck. "Yes, old friend, I agree, it will be a good day for a stroll."

Leuka looked at the clock beside his bed. It read 5:20 a.m. He did some quick math in his head. He estimated it take him at least five hours to make the necessary arrangements. "I meet you in park by the fountain at 11:00."

"Good. See you then, Leuka."

Bill turned off the cell phone and returned the documents and photographs to the envelope. He got up from the table and began gathering personal items. What he didn't take with him would be abandoned. Anything that could possibly reveal his identity would first be destroyed, then discarded

The next few hours would be crucial to his flight from the Czech Republic. He would do everything within his power to minimize the risk of detection and capture but a quick exit was critical. If he didn't get the information to the right people quickly, the world as he knew it could cease to exist. The future of world was in his hands. Failure was unacceptable. He would do whatever was required to complete his objective.

CHAPTER SIX

Tuesday, March 24 - 2151 Eastern Daylight Time
Navy Executive Corridor
Pentagon - Corridor 9, E Ring
Washington, D.C.

Vice Admiral Harlan Beckwith, in a crisp, starched uniform, walked up to the Defense Protective Services security desk and shoved his ID badge across the counter.

"Working late sir?" the security officer asked offhandedly, holding up the badge and comparing the photo on the badge to the face in front of him.

"Yeah, never ends in this business," Beckwith answered.

Satisfied with the identity of the officer standing in front of him, the security officer shoved the ID badge back across the counter and pressed the electronic door release. Admiral Beckwith picked up the ID badge, pushed the door open, and stepped into the space between the outer door and the inner security door. Hearing the outer door latch, he pressed his palm on the identity scanner and inserted his ID badge into the card reader. A thin bar of light scanned his palm from top to bottom. Several seconds passed as the massive computer deep in the Pentagon's information center searched for his security clearance level and matched the scanned image of his hand print to the one stored in the its data bank. The "Access" indicator turned green and the bolt on the inner security door withdrew with a loud clunk.

He pushed the door open, feeling a faint breeze on his face as he stepped inside. The breeze was created by the overpressure maintained at all times inside the inner core of the building. The overpressure provided positive proof all electronic emission seals were secure. The sensitive and highly classified work being done inside the space demanded absolutely no electronic signals of any kind escape.

Admiral Beckwith held the ID badge in his hand as he walked down the hall, coming to a door marked *Restricted*, where he again jabbed his ID badge into a card reader. For the second time, the massive computer searched its memory banks for the proper clearance level. The electronic lock released and he opened the door and walked into the room. Because he spent so much time on the opposite side of the Pentagon, he had appropriated a small, unused space, turning it into an alternate office.

Admiral Beckwith closed and locked the door. He clipped the badge to the lapel of his uniform jacket as he walked over to the desk and retrieved an electronic device from the bottom drawer. Carefully, he passed the wand shaped device over all surfaces of his desk, the phone, the desk lamp, the framed photographs of the President and Chairman of the Joint Chiefs of Staff, the seams around the door jam, the heat register along the wall; every conceivable place where a listening device could be hidden. Even though it was extremely unlikely anyone could plant a listening device in an ultra-secure area, he was not going to take any chances. He had not attained his rank by being stupid or sloppy.

Satisfied the room was free of listening devices, he walked back over to the desk, and returned the scanning device to the drawer. From his pocket, he retrieved a smaller device resembling a small flashlight except it had a dark blue lens. Switching on the device, he knelt down on one knee and directed the faint, purplish beam of light toward the upper left corner of the lower right desk drawer. A vivid orange line appeared across the gap between the desk frame and the drawer. The thin, gossamer filament he had placed across the gap the last time he had been in the spare office would have been invisible without the black light that made it glow as if it was on fire. The filament still in place provided positive proof no one had tampered with the drawer.

He thumbed a five-digit code into the cipher lock and opened the drawer. Lifting several documents out, he carefully arranged them on the desk. After a quick scan of the documents, he picked up the phone, switched on the scrambler, and dialed a number from memory. All outgoing calls were logged but it no longer mattered. By the time anyone analyzed the list and determined anything was suspicious, it would be too late. All the cell phones he had acquired for this project were cheap burner phones that had been purchased in different states using false identities. Any attempts to trace the usage from any of those phones would fade into hopeless dead ends.

After two rings a male voice answered, "This is Sam."

"Is the last site active?"

"Yeah, two days ago. Caused some false interference just like before.

The manager at the government site made a big stink. He's threatening to go to the GAO if the maintenance company doesn't get it fixed soon."

"What about the technician?"

"He's stupid. A real whiner. Can't be trusted."

"Silence him immediately. What about the man you have inside the procurement office?"

"I'm not sure. I think he may be getting cold feet."

"With what I pay you I expect you to be certain! Find out and let me know. Tonight!"

"Yes sir. Tonight."

The connection went dead. He replaced the handset on the phone and took a deep breath. "No need to panic," he told himself. Everything was in place just as he had planned it.

He examined the maps indicating the geographic sites he had selected, the false communications intercepts to be planted, and the expertly crafted intelligence documents that would set his plan in motion. Everything was perfect. He unbuttoned his uniform jacket and opened the false seams on both sides. The maps with the access codes required for final activation of the plan went in the left side. The false intelligence documents went in the right side. He pressed the closures together, smoothed the seams flat, and re-buttoned the jacket. The false communications intercepts would be planted on his way out of the building.

A smile crept onto his face. After four years of dedication, hard work, and preparation, the culmination of his plan for revenge was within reach. Finally, the evil men were going to pay. Just a few more days and the final pieces of the plan would fall into place and nobody would be able to stop it. Not the President, not his advisors, not even the armies or navies of the world.

He reached out and picked up the gold-framed photograph of his wife and two daughters. How he had loved them, but that seemed so long ago. It felt like a lifetime had passed since the terrorist's bomb had exploded and leveled an entire city block. He hadn't even had bodies to bury, only memories. The love that had once filled his heart had soured and transformed into hate and visions of revenge. Only sheer willpower had prevented him from going insane. With great determination, he controlled the burning rage, using it to fuel his one desire. Revenge. Sweet, gratifying revenge.

There would be no escape for those responsible for the murder of his wife and daughters. The blinding rage deep in his soul had become the sole purpose of his existence. Retribution was at hand. No price—not even the sacrifice of his own life or even his country—would be too high to achieve the vengeance he so desperately sought.

Gently, he set the photograph back on the desk, adjusting its position so it aligned perfectly with the other objects sitting on his desk.

After he closed the drawer and reset the cipher lock, he walked to the door, unlocked it, and headed for the communications center. Soon the false communications intercepts would be planted and nobody would be able to stop the retribution.

CHAPTER SEVEN

Wednesday, March 25 - 1023 Zulu
28 Říjná 16
Ostrava, Czech Republic

Making several sweeps around his apartment, Bill Morrison made certain not even the smallest shred of evidence was left behind. No mementoes, no clothing, nothing. He intended to leave the apartment exactly as it was the day he first walked in.

What food was left in the dilapidated refrigerator was discarded in the trash bin at the end of the hallway. Opening every cupboard door, he carefully examined the contents. The only items remaining were the few cracked and chipped dishes provided when he moved in.

He checked each drawer in the decrepit dresser. After selecting a change of clothes and a few toiletries and stuffing them into a duffel bag, he removed each drawer and dumped everything remaining into a bag to be discarded.

Making one last circuit around the apartment, he carefully inspected every inch. Satisfied he had left nothing behind, he laid the apartment key on the dresser, grabbed his duffle bag, and left the apartment.

Bill walked the six blocks to the university line bus stop as quickly as he could. He took a seat on the empty bench and waited for the next bus, his eyes constantly surveying the street for anyone suspicious. Ten minutes passed before a battered bus roared up the street. Holding his breath, he stepped through the cloud of thick black exhaust billowing out from under the bus. He dropped the required fare in the coin box and took a seat three rows from the front. Riding along deep in thought, he wondered what sort of plan his contact had arranged for his departure.

Bill reached up and tugged at the cable to signal the driver he wanted off at Listopadu Street, the next stop. He got off and walked one-half block to the Areal tram stop.

As the tram approached, Namesti Republiky (Republic Square), Bill got up and took a position in front of the closest door. A large number of passengers got off the tram because Namesti Republiky was the closest stop to Ostrava's central bus station.

Bill headed for the fountain in the center of the square. Breathing a sigh of relief as he rounded the fountain, he saw that his contact was already seated on a bench beside the fountain.

"Hey Leuka, beautiful morning," Bill said as he walked up and sat beside him.

"Yes, my friend," Leuka replied.

"It will be a good day for a stroll," Bill said, repeating the code phrase from their previous conversation.

"I agree, but you certain?" Leuka asked, a puzzled look on his face. "Sorry, my English not good."

Bill knew Leuka must be concerned because of the suddenness of his request. Eyes sweeping the surrounding area to be certain no one was within earshot, Bill said, "Leuka, believe me, it is absolutely necessary. That is all I can tell you."

"I make all necessary arrangements. When you wish to execute?" Leuka asked.

"Right now, this very minute!" Bill answered.

Leuka picked up the folded newspaper lying on his lap and placed it on the bench beside Bill. "I suspected. You find details inside paper. On final end, my nephew meet you. He can be trusted. Come. I have car waiting."

Bill pushed himself up from the bench. For a brief instant, his eyes caught sight of a man on the opposite side of the square looking directly at them. He followed Leuka as they headed toward the tram stop.

"Wait up, my shoe's untied," Bill said as they reached the edge of the square. As he kneeled, pretending to tie his shoe, he glanced quickly in the direction of the man he had noticed. His suspicion was confirmed. The man had gotten up and had started to follow them. Seeing them stop, the man pretended to stop and look at some pigeons feeding on the sidewalk.

"Don't look back. Someone is following us," Bill said softly as he straightened up and continued walking. "Where are we headed?"

"Tram to main station," Leuka whispered back.

As they continued walking toward the tram station, Bill's brain worked furiously, formulating a strategy to either lose or eliminate the man following them. "We have to lose the tail. Any ideas Leuka?"

"Ah, ah," Leuka stammered. "If we go past tram station and through tunnel, maybe we jump him on other side."

Bill thought for a moment. "I guess we don't have a lot of options. I'll take the left side, you take the right."

Bill and Leuka walked past the tram station and into the tunnel next to the tram station. As they neared the center of the tunnel, two men in animated conversation passed them.

Bill's mind recoiled in fear when he felt the cold, hard steel of a gun barrel jabbed roughly into his ribs.

"If you make wrong move, you die here, right now," a guttural voice snarled in his ear.

CHAPTER EIGHT

Wednesday, March 25 - 0712 Eastern Daylight Time
Defense Intelligence Agency Communications Center
Pentagon - Washington, D.C.

Vice Admiral Harlan Beckwith inserted his ID badge into the Defense Intelligence Agency card reader. As soon as the electronic latch disengaged, he pushed the door open and walked up to the counter where the senior watch officer, Captain Robert Prescott, was seated.

"May I help you sir?" Captain Prescott asked.

"Any unusual or suspicious activity during the overnight watch?" Beckwith asked.

"Yes sir, two intercepts came in late last night. Sometime after twenty-three hundred I think," Prescott replied.

"I'll need to see them," Beckwith instructed, sliding his ID badge across the counter.

Prescott picked up the ID badge and studied it carefully, lifting the badge up and comparing it to the Admiral's face. Satisfied, he reached under the counter and pressed the electronic door release.

Beckwith pushed the door open and walked to one of the secure cubicles used for studying intelligence documents. Following close behind, Prescott laid a sealed document folder with a border of bright red diagonal strips labeled "Top Secret" on the desk.

"Have these been to analysis yet?" Beckwith asked.

"No sir, they have not. Is there anything else you need sir?"

"Don't think so. If there is, I'll give you a shout."

"Yes sir," Prescott acknowledged.

Beckwith broke the seal on the folder and pulled out the documents. When he saw the two documents he had carefully planted the night before, he smiled, quickly scanning the attached preliminary analysis summary. Perfect. Absolutely perfect. The false intelligence documents had aroused exactly the concern they were meant to. Admiral Beckwith spent a few more minutes in the cubicle to make the senior watch officer think he had fully studied the documents. He exited the cubicle and walked over to the senior watch officer's desk.

"Captain, I need to use a secure telephone."

"Certainly," Prescott replied as he got up and led Beckwith to what looked like a combination between a sound proof booth and a phone booth.

Beckwith stepped in and pulled the heavy door shut. He dialed a number and waited.

"Hello," a sleepy voice answered.

"Colonel, this is the Director. We have a priority incident," Beckwith announced.

"Any details?" Colonel Craig Elmont, the OPSDEPS staff liaison officer, asked, instantly awake as he sat up in bed and switched on a bedside lamp.

"Not on the telephone, Colonel. I need to meet with OPSDEPS."

"Yes sir. Do we need the entire security council?"

"No. Just the senior OPSDEPS members for now."

"How soon sir?"

"I'd like to have them assembled no later than zero nine hundred."

"Yes sir," Elmont answered. "I'll start making the notifications right now. I'll contact you when everyone is in place."

Beckwith hung up the phone and walked back over to the information counter. "Captain, I'll need to take these with me."

"Yes sir. Just sign the custody log," Prescott replied, pushing a clipboard with a custody release form on it across the counter.

Beckwith entered the document reference numbers on the log. He signed and dated it, then slid the clipboard back to Colonel Prescott.

Beckwith dropped the documents in the security case he was carrying and locked it. "Good day, Captain," he said as he left the communications center and headed for his office adjacent to the OPSDEPS briefing room.

* * *

Wednesday, March 25 - 0902 Eastern Daylight Time
OPSDEPS Briefing Room
Pentagon - Washington, D.C.

Vice Admiral Beckwith sat at his desk going through a mountainous stack of overnight message traffic. He placed the last document back on the stack. It was all routine traffic and contained nothing that would warrant further analysis.

He glanced at his watch and reached for the phone just as the pager lying on the corner of his desk started to buzz and dance around. He picked up the pager and pressed the display button. The code in the display window indicated the OPSDEPS members were seated and waiting for him in the briefing room. He got up, put on his uniform jacket, and walked next door to the briefing room.

A Marine guard stationed at the briefing room door saluted and opened the door.

"Good morning, Director," Colonel Craig Elmont said, pulling out a large swivel chair at the head of the table.

"Thank you, Colonel," Beckwith said as he took his seat and slid his chair up to the table. As Director of the Joint Staff he served as chairman of the Operations Deputies, or OPSDEPS, in the world of military acronyms.

The OPSDEPS staff currently seated in the briefing room was composed of the Director, Joint Staff, appointed by the Chairman of the Joint Chiefs of Staff, and operations deputies appointed by each of the other Service Chiefs. It was the OPSDEPS's charter to consider issues of lesser importance or to review major issues before they were passed up to the Joint Chiefs. Except for the Director himself, no one else in the briefing room was part of the Joint Staff.

The Director surveyed the room and noticed that several of the OPSDEPS members had just arrived and were still conferring with their senior aides. He waited as Colonel Elmont, his senior aide, filled his coffee cup. Tapping his cup with a spoon, he waited for the other members to conclude their conversations.

"Gentlemen, there is a priority issue. We need to get started," the Director commanded. "Colonel, place a couple of carafes of coffee on the table."

As soon as Colonel Elmont had done as instructed, Beckwith continued, "This is a sensitive issue. All aides and junior staff leave the room please."

The OPSDEPS members waited while their aides and junior staff members grabbed their briefcases and left the room. Beckwith tapped Colonel Elmont on the arm as he was about to leave.

"Tell the guard absolutely no one is to enter this room until we are finished," Beckwith instructed.

As soon as Beckwith heard the door close, he picked up the security case sitting beside his chair, thumbed in the combination, and removed the documents. "These are extremely sensitive and cannot be copied. You will have to take turns reviewing them," he said as he slid the documents to the OPSDEPS member immediately on his left.

First the documents went to Brigadier General Samuel Worthington, Operations Deputy, US Army. General Worthington was a field combat soldier as evidenced by the chest full of ribbons pinned on his uniform jacket. The Bronze Star with combat-V and oak leaf indicating a repeat award, and the Purple Heart with two oak leaves indicating two repeats sat at the top of the array of ribbons. He watched as General Worthington began to review the first of the two documents. The General's dark eyes flashed rapidly back and forth across the document. The General's eyebrows raised as he digested the information. He spent less than thirty seconds examining the first document before passing it on to the next member.

Seated next was Rear Admiral Michael Eads, Operations Deputy, US Navy. Rear Admiral Eads, tall and thin with light sandy hair, a Naval Academy graduate, was a line officer who had commanded several submarines prior to his selection for flag rank. His assignment immediately prior to being selected as Operation Deputy had been Chief of Staff for COMSUBLANT, Commander, Submarine Forces, Atlantic. His reaction mirrored that of General Worthington. Comprehension and shock came quickly as he scanned the documents and passed them on.

Third to receive the documents was Major General Ethan Cook, Operations Deputy, US Air Force. General Cook was Beckwith's age, plus ten to twelve years with salt-and-pepper grey, thinning hair and an unlit pipe in his mouth. General Cook was older than the other members, having started his military career as an enlisted man. Upon reaching the rank of Airman, First Class, he applied to and was accepted into the NESEP program. He spent three years at the University of Arizona graduating with honors and a degree in aeronautical engineering. After completing pilot training school, his rise up the ranks had been exemplary. After becoming too old to be an active pilot, he served in various staff and command billets. Once selected for flag rank, he served as Air Wing Commander at Ramstein Air Base in Germany and finally as senior staff at the Air Combat Command, headquartered at Langley Air Force Base, Virginia. His reaction upon scanning the documents mimicked the first two members as evidenced by bulging jaw muscles as he clenched and unclenched the pipe between his teeth.

Lastly, the documents went to Brigadier General Alan Stockton, Operations Deputy, US Marine Corps. General Stockton, no more than five foot seven, with closely cropped, brown hair, was, like General Worthington, a combat soldier. His eyes were pale blue and cold as ice. A pencil thin scar ran from the bridge of his nose to the bottom of his right cheek bone. His chest bristled with ribbons, marksmanship badges, and presidential unit citations, many bearing one or more oak leaves indicating repeat awards. Only a glance was necessary to see he was extraordinarily fit. His career had started as a second lieutenant in a field infantry unit, gravel agitators, or cannon fodder as they were jokingly referred to. He was often referred to as a Marine's Marine by those that had served with him, having proven himself gallantly in battle time after time, as evidenced by the Navy Cross and Silver Star displayed in the first-row ribbons. Several rows from the top was the Purple Heart with gold oak leaf indicating five awards. He switched the ever-present, un-lit stub of a cigar from one side of his mouth to the other but never displayed the slightest hint of a reaction as he scanned the documents and passed them back to Beckwith.

Beckwith had watched intently as each OPSDEPS member examined the documents in succession, carefully assessing their reactions to verify the documents he had crafted had produced the desired results. He was certain they had except for General Stockton. No one ever knew what that man was thinking.

Beckwith slid the documents back in front of himself and began his overview. "These documents were received in the Defense Intelligence Agency Communication Center last night shortly after twenty-three hundred. They have not been through analysis as yet. I felt they represented too urgent a threat to allow them to run through normal channels so I picked them up this morning and arranged this meeting. I believe these documents tie into the intercepts we received two days ago. I expect you will concur they indicate a much greater threat than we had originally theorized. Comments gentlemen?" Beckwith asked, leaning back in his chair.

"Do we have any other intel, or satellite imagery perhaps?" General Worthington asked.

"No satellites feeds at this time. They are currently positioned on other areas. The assets we have in country are all quiet expect for one," Beckwith replied, lifting a third document out of the security case, handing it to General Worthington. "Pass this document around, then I'll continue." Again he waited as each member read the document and passed it on. That document produced raised eyebrows as had the first two. There were expletives muttered as each member read through the text. Even the generally stoic General Stockton was heard to mutter, "Holy Christ!" under his breath.

"I suspected you'd all feel the same way I did when I first read through that message," Beckwith said.

"You know what this means!" Admiral Eads exclaimed.

"I certainly do," Beckwith answered. "The entire east coast defense system is in jeopardy of being compromised." Admiral Eads started to say more but Beckwith silenced him with a raised hand and continued. "I already know what your question will be and the answer is no. We don't have confirmation on this but I believe we can trust the source and I believe we have to act and act quickly."

"Couldn't we have a satellite repositioned and wait for some more information or at least get some intel from our in-country assets?" General

Cook questioned.

"I don't believe we can afford to wait," Beckwith replied. "Repositioning the satellite will take a full day or more, considering the time to get the required approvals and waiting for the bird to pass over the region. Waiting for intel would take even longer. I might add there has not been any contact with the assets in that area for over a week. My source over at CIA informed me that there is no trace of the assets. He thinks they have likely been eliminated," Beckwith said with extra emphasis, knowing full well the assets had been eliminated, because he had ordered it.

Beckwith saw their startled faces. His plan was working perfectly. Nobody said a word. The OPSDEPS members just stared at him.

"Okay, here's what I expect to happen. It's obvious this must go to the Joint Chiefs and then on to the full Security Council. Each of you go back to your office and draft a response to this threat and meet me back here in ninety minutes," Beckwith instructed.

"No," General Worthington responded. "That's unrealistic, sir. We would need at least two to three hours to prepare a practical response to a threat this large."

"I understand that General, but the real world is not as accommodating as we would like it to be," Beckwith countered. "There simply is not any more time available. I will start running tactical simulations and then I will incorporate your responses into a final plan. I want to present that plan to the Joint Chiefs no later than thirteen hundred."

Fidgeting in their chairs, the others members were about to speak out but Beckwith silenced them again. "Gentlemen, you are wasting time. There will be no more discussion. If we do this wrong, the cost will be enormous," he said as he closed his time planner and zipped it shut. He watched as the other members gathered their materials and stood to leave.

"By the way gentlemen, this is to be considered need to know only. Do not discuss it with anyone except your senior aide and only if you need their direct assistance in preparing your response. The lid is on tight. If I hear that any of this information leaked out, I will personally see to it the source's career ends immediately. And gentlemen be certain that is not an idle threat," Beckwith warned. "Any questions?"

As expected, there were no questions. Beckwith watched as the OPSDEPS members filed out of the briefing room. Only one more detail and the plan would be complete Beckwith thought to himself.

CHAPTER NINE

Wednesday, March 25 - 1158 Eastern Daylight Time
White House Situation Room
Washington, D.C.

Vice Admiral Harlan Beckwith took a deep breath, straightened his uniform jacket, and entered the White House situation room. He walked directly to his position at the end of the long conference table and took his seat. All key decision makers, except one, for the most formidable military force in the world were seated and awaiting his presentation. As he sat down, the senior staff aide picked up the telephone and spoke quietly into the receiver. Everyone in the room stood as the President entered the room and took his position at the head of the conference table.

"Are we ready?" President Paul Cantwell asked as he sat down.

"Yes sir," Beckwith responded. "There is a folder in front of each of you containing intelligence documents that were received in the DIA communication center last night around twenty-three hundred hours. I will give you a few minutes to scan the documents before I continue."

Just as he had done during the briefing with the OPSDEPS members, Admiral Beckwith watched intently as the members of the National Security Council broke the security seals on their respective folders and studied the documents. At the head of the long conference table was President Cantwell with the Assistant to the President for National Security Affairs on his immediate left. Seated behind the President, not directly at the table, were the President's Chief of Staff and Senior Counsel.

Vice-President Arthur Mead was seated immediately on the President's right followed by the Secretary of Defense, Secretary of the Treasury, and the Director of the CIA. On the left side of the table, after the Assistant to the President, was the Chairman of the Joint Chiefs, Fleet Admiral Douglas Bennington, followed by the rest of the Joint Chiefs, General of the Army, William Danvers, General of the Air Force, James Radford, and Marine Corp Chief of Staff Andrew McCune.

Only the Chairman of the Joint Chiefs was a member of the National Security Council, but the presence of the remainder of the Joint Chiefs had been requested by Beckwith when he spoke with the President's chief of staff to arrange the emergency meeting. Their concurrence and support for the military aspect of his plan would be crucial.

Beckwith saw that everyone except President Cantwell had finished viewing their copy of the documents. No one spoke as they waited for the President; not out of courtesy but rather, desiring not to be the target of the President's superior intellect and arduous questioning. President Cantwell was a Rhodes scholar, keenly short of patience. He was extremely demanding of his advisors and military leaders, possessing a "take no prisoners" demeanor. Many had witnessed the agonizing distress of those foolish enough to be drawn into a debate with him unprepared.

President Cantwell finished viewing the documents and laid them on the folder in front of him. Looking squarely at Beckwith, he asked, "What is the source of these documents?"

"The best asset we have, ahhh…, had in the area Mister President. See the mark in the very lower right corner of the first two documents? There is no doubt as to the source," Beckwith responded.

"Why did you say had?" Cantwell asked.

Beckwith had prepared well for the meeting and did not hesitate before responding. "There has not been a single response from any of the assets in the area for nearly four days. We can only assume they have been compromised and are likely dead. I have been informed two agents were sent in to confirm and they also have not been heard from. They are now eighteen hours overdue for their check in time."

"Have the documents been confirmed?"

"No sir. Direct confirmation would be difficult without the assets that are missing. However, as you can see from the ancillary document, we have every reason to believe the threat is valid."

"Are you telling me we should commit resources based on these unconfirmed documents?" Cantwell demanded, the challenge in his voice obvious.

Beckwith had to suppress a smile because the President's response was exactly what he had expected. Taking a deep breath, he continued, "Yes sir. That's exactly what I and the Joint Staff propose we do. Each Operations Deputy came up with an almost identical response. Independently, I might add. I allowed them to view the master documents and then tasked each of them to develop an appropriate response. The proposed response I am going to present is a summation of their scenarios with some additions of my own."

Beckwith nodded at his aide in the rear of the room and got up from his chair. He walked over to the large display in the front of the room as the aide dimmed the lights and switched on the LCD projector. "I know time is short so I will be brief," Beckwith said as he slipped a laser pointer out of his shirt pocket and began the presentation.

Beckwith's presentation was flawless, lasting slightly over eleven minutes. "Colonel, lights please," Beckwith said as he finished and returned to his seat.

As the room lights came up, Beckwith could tell everyone in the room, the President included, had been impressed with the presentation. They seemed to be especially impressed considering the documents had been received only thirteen hours earlier. What the attendees did not know was that Beckwith had been working on this presentation in his mind for weeks. The documents were perfect and no one, except for their alleged source, could deny their genuineness. Beckwith knew that could never happen because the elimination of the alleged source had been ordered by himself and had been confirmed.

"Gentlemen, if this plan is approved, it will be designated Operation Brushfire," Beckwith said with as much dramatic effect as he dared. "Are there any questions?"

The only one to speak was President Cantwell. "I know we can reposition satellites to get updated imagery but that would take eighteen to twenty-four hours. Per the plan you detailed Admiral, the movement of tactical assets will need to happen before that. Am I correct?" Cantwell asked.

"Absolutely correct Mr. President," Beckwith replied. "I spoke with COMSUBLANT earlier. There is a Los Angeles class attack submarine from New London that can be re-tasked for this mission. Necessary stores have been loaded and she is preparing to get under way."

Turning to his left, the President looked at the Joint Chiefs. "Do you all concur with the Admiral's plan gentlemen?" They all nodded agreement.

"Very well. Make it happen and keep me informed," Cantwell said as he pushed his chair back and left the room.

"*Now, the real fun begins,*" Beckwith thought to himself as he gathered up his materials and stuffed them into his briefcase.

CHAPTER TEN

Wednesday, March 25 - 1132 Mountain Daylight Time
National Radio Astronomy Observatory
Socorro, New Mexico

Marvin Spangler steered the pickup he was driving into the space marked "Maintenance Only" behind the National Radio Astronomy Observatory's main building. He had just returned from completing some routine maintenance at one of the far antennas on the western arm of the radio telescope. Suffering from a miserable headache and feeling somewhat nauseated, he slammed the pickup's door and hurried toward the entrance to the maintenance office.

Marvin absolutely hated his job. For over a year he had been working for the NRAO (National Radio Astronomy Observatory) as an entry level electronics technician, performing whatever menial, odd jobs his moron of a boss felt like assigning him. He hated the long drive to work every day, but he needed the job so he tolerated it and put up with a boss he despised.

Marvin was assigned to outside maintenance on the VLA (Very Large Array) radio telescope operated by the NRAO. It was the largest "Array" type radio telescope in the world, located approximately sixty miles west of Socorro, New Mexico. The radio telescope array was composed of three arms shaped like a "Y," each arm extending twenty-one kilometers from the center. Each of the individual array arms was composed of twenty-seven movable antennas, twenty-five meters across.

Eager to get a promotion and be transferred to the inside technician staff that operated and maintained the signal processing and analysis equipment, Marvin had spent many hours studying the design and operation of the telescope. If he could land the promotion and transfer, he would not have to work outside in the dreadful heat anymore. During his study, Marvin had learned the observatory's main focus of research was in the area called very long baseline interferometry.

That very long and confusing term simply meant the signals from all the individual antennas were combined to make them look like one single, large antenna. The radio telescope in New Mexico was then connected to radio telescopes on other continents by simultaneously recording their outputs using extremely accurate atomic clocks. The net effect was a single radio telescope that appeared to be thousands of miles across.

An extensive search had been undertaken to find a site that satisfied all the requirements for building a "large array" radio telescope. During his study, Marvin learned the telescope required a huge, isolated, flat desert to reduce radio interference. It also needed a relatively high altitude, a dry climate to reduce the effects of the atmosphere, and a latitude low enough to observe a large part of the celestial sphere.

The topography and climate at the NRAO site were nearly perfect. The altitude at the center of the antenna was nearly seven thousand feet and rainfall averaged a mere ten inches per year. In addition, the mountains on all sides formed a large valley, creating a very effective screen against man-made radio frequency interference.

In his current frame of mind, Marvin could not care less how ideal the conditions were. As far as he was concerned, those ideal features created a very inhospitable place for humans to work.

Marvin walked into the break room and sat down at one of the tables, resting his head in his hands. He was exhausted and felt absolutely miserable. Not only soaked with sweat, he had a splitting headache, the result of drinking too much the previous night. Suffering from a miserable hangover, he was feeling very sorry for himself.

Manager of Maintenance, Jamison Rhodes, his boss, walked into the break room, making an already horrible day even worse. Rhodes had been looking for Marvin for over an hour and was in one of his usual foul moods.

"You've got work to do," Rhodes yelled at him. "What are you doing loafing around here in the break room?"

"I just got back from working on the far antenna of the western arm," Marvin replied in self defense. "I'm tired and I don't feel good,"

"I don't care how you feel. Maybe if you stayed off the booze you wouldn't feel so bad."

Marvin opened his mouth to answer but thought better of it, forcing himself to let it go. He could not afford to rile his boss and risk jeopardizing the promotion he desperately wanted.

Seeing Marvin was not going to answer, Rhodes continued, "Have you completed the weekly check of the microwave system yet? It was supposed to be done two days ago. The observatory depends on that system. I want that check completed today, before you clock out. Do you understand me?"

"Yeah, I understand," Marvin croaked. "I'll start on it right after lunch,"

"No, you'll start on it right now!" Rhodes shouted.

"Okay, okay. I'll go start on it right now," Marvin grumbled, pushing himself back from the table. His head throbbed with excruciating pain as he stood. It was going to be a very, very long afternoon.

"If only that stupid jerk would just leave me alone," Marvin whined as he headed for the microwave equipment room at the far end of the building.

Marvin's head hurt so bad he was having trouble focusing his eyes. Surely this had to be more than just a hangover Marvin thought. He had endured many hangovers and never had he felt this bad. All he could think of was getting through the day so he could go home and climb into bed.

Pulling a large ring of keys from the clip on his belt, he unlocked the door to the microwave equipment room. He pushed the door open and stepped inside. Leaning against the wall, a wave of nausea washed over him. Taking a couple of deep breaths, he tried to focus his mind on the job he had to do. He decided to finish the microwave check as quickly as he could. In spite of what his idiot boss thought, he would take the rest of the day as a sick day.

Marvin was startled when the alarm annunciator went off. The shrill, piercing squeal of the annunciator made him want to scream. The alarm was not particularly loud, but it's high pitched squeal aggravated Marvin's headache, producing a blinding pain behind his eyes. His only thought was to silence the piercing screech.

Ripping the front cover off the inbound microwave link, he tossed it aside and scanned the bank of channel group cards to determine what was producing the alarm. The master signaling channel indicated it was offline. Unable to tolerate the ear-piercing screech of the alarm any longer, he reached up and pulled the annunciator card out.

Silence. Marvin breathed a sigh of relief. His frantic effort to locate and silence the alarm left him weak and shaking. Another violent wave of nausea washed over him. He knew he was going to be sick, feeling the hot, burning vomit rising in his throat. Swallowing hard, he tried desperately to gain control of his cramping stomach. His stomach cramped again, the bile again rising in his throat. Knowing he was about to lose the battle, he reached down and pulled the master signaling channel card out of the card rack.

"There, that will shut the stupid thing up. Forget the whole blasted mess," Marvin moaned, as he slammed the door open and sprinted for the bathroom.

Marvin never returned to the microwave system. After spending twenty minutes in the bathroom vomiting, he was simply too weak to return to work. He staggered down the hallway, stopping beside the receptionist's desk.

"Martha, I'm really sick," he said, leaning against the wall to keep from falling down. "I'm going to go home and go to bed."

"Mr. Rhodes stopped by my desk several minutes ago looking for you. Again, I might add!" Martha warned, glancing up from her keyboard.

"What did he want?"

"I don't know. He seemed more angry than usual. You better check with him before you leave."

"I don't care. Tell Mr. Rhodes to go ...."

Marvin stopped himself. It would have been a monumental mistake to complete the thought begging to escape from his lips. He took a deep breath and continued, "Just tell him I'm sick and I'm going home."

Dropping the keys to the maintenance pickup on Martha's desk, Marvin staggered down the hallway and went out the door leading to the employee parking area. He stumbled over to his car and unlocked the door. Before he could climb inside, he doubled over and sank to one knee, coughing and gagging for several minutes. There was nothing left in his stomach. Marvin pulled out a handkerchief and wiped his mouth, slowly standing up. Using the steering wheel for leverage, he dragged himself inside the car. In spite of the heat, he sat there shaking, racked by violent chills.

Once the chills passed, Marvin started the car, backed out of his space, and drove out of the parking lot. The master signaling channel he had disabled never even entered his mind. One single, solitary thought consumed him; getting home, taking some aspirins, and climbing into bed.

CHAPTER ELEVEN

Wednesday, March 25 - 1700 Eastern Daylight Time
USS Providence, SSN 719
US Naval Submarine Base, Groton, Connecticut

"Cast off the forward and stern mooring lines," Commander Samuel Chandler shouted. The forward and aft crewmen each released the last loop of line from the mooring cleats, tossing the lines to waiting support crew standing on the pier. As soon as the lines were free, Chandler picked up the microphone for the 7-MC, "Helm, Bridge, all back slow."

"Bridge, Helm, all back slow, aye."

The long, black boat shuddered and slowly slipped away from the pier, sliding backwards into the Thames river. "Helm, Bridge, all stop," Chandler ordered as the bow of the boat passed the end of the pier.

"Bridge, Helm, all stop aye."

Two large tugs had been standing by to assist *Providence*. As soon as the *Providence's* bow cleared the pier, the tugs moved into position. One positioned itself against the port side of the bow while the other positioned itself against the starboard side of the stern. The tugs throttled up their massive engines, the river water erupting into foamy, green swirls as the large propellers chewed up the water.

The opposite forces of the tugs pivoted *Providence* clockwise in the river until *Providence's* bow was pointing down river toward the open water of the Atlantic ocean.

"Helm, Bridge, ahead slow. Make turns for three knots," Chandler commanded.

"Bridge, Helm, ahead slow. Make turns for three knots, aye."

"Helm, Bridge, right five degrees rudder. Steer course one-seven-five."

"Bridge, Helm, right five degrees rudder. Steer course one-seven-five, aye."

The channel in the Thames river was extremely narrow and required careful piloting to not run aground or hit one of the bridge pilings as they passed under the Gold Star Bridge. The tugs would follow closely to assist, if necessary, until *Providence* was safely beyond the mouth of the river and in deep water.

The short trip down the Thames River was uneventful as Commander Chandler did a flawless job of piloting the boat. He turned and saluted each of the tug commanders as they withdrew and headed back up river. "Helm, Bridge, ahead one third. Make turns for eight knots."

"Bridge, Helm, ahead one third. Make turns for eight knots, aye."

"Sonar, Bridge, how's it look?" Chandler asked.

"Bridge, Sonar, no contacts at this time," Sonarman First Class Randy Jenkins responded.

"Helm, Bridge, left standard rudder. Steer course zero-seven-one."

"Bridge, Helm, left standard rudder. Steer course zero-seven-one, aye."

Providence rolled slightly as it turned to port.

"Bridge, Helm, steady on course zero-seven-one, making turns for eight knots," the helmsman reported several minutes later.

"Very well," Chandler responded.

Commander Chandler loved this part of getting underway, especially when the sun was behind the boat and low in the evening sky. The sun's rays shining across the water made everything gleam like gold. He remained on the sail bridge for the first hour, until *Providence* was well beyond the sight of land.

A light fog began to roll in from the north. It was time to submerge the boat and turn toward Point Bravo, nothing more than a designated point on the chart, slightly north of the Kelvin Seamount. Upon reaching Point Bravo, Chandler would open *Providence's* sealed orders and, hopefully, gain some insight into the reason behind their early sailing.

"Shift the watch belowdecks. Prepare to dive," Chandler ordered, waiting as the two lookouts unstrapped themselves and scurried down through the hatch. He followed the lookouts down the ladder, pulled the lower bridge hatch shut, and spun the locking handle until the hatch lugs engaged.

Chandler entered the control room and stepped up on the platform. "I have the Conn," he announced.

"I have been relieved," Lcdr. Graham responded, stepping off the platform.

"All stations, Conn. Prepare to submerge the boat."

The Quartermaster looked up from the nautical chart on the navigation table in front of him. Glancing at the boat's fathometer, he called out, "Seven hundred fifty fathoms beneath the keel."

"Green board Captain," the Chief of the Watch reported.

Satisfied *Providence* was ready in all respects, Chandler rotated the periscope until it lined up along the boat's longitudinal axis. He pressed his cheek against the eyepiece and peered through the scope. "Dive, Conn, submerge the boat to one-eight-zero feet," he ordered over the 7-MC.

The Diving Officer signaled the Chief of the Watch who shouted, "Dive, Dive.", mashing the boat's diving alarm twice, the distinctive ahhh-oooghh-aaahh, ahhh-oooghh-aaahh of the klaxon echoing throughout the boat.

The Chief of the Watch opened the valves to the main ballast tanks, allowing seawater to flow through the grates in the boat's keel. *Providence* gradually sank into the ocean as it achieved negative buoyancy.

Engineman Second Class Marvin Connaly, one of the two assigned planesmen, eased the diving planes forward and watched the bubble rise in the diving indicator. He pulled back slightly as the bubble passed two degrees and watched as the bubble stopped dead-on at three degrees, a smile of satisfaction creeping across his face. It was Connaly's third patrol. He had become proficient in all systems on the boat, qualifying for his "Dolphins" halfway through his second patrol.

"Deck's awash," Chandler reported as *Providence* pitched slightly downward and slid beneath the cold waters of the Atlantic Ocean. When the waves passed over the boat's bow, the air escaping from the ballast tanks shot geysers up into the air.

"Passing six-zero feet," Connaly announced as *Providence's* sail slipped below the surface.

Finally, the waves washed over the periscope and *Providence* disappeared completely from sight. Chandler folded the handles of the periscope up, rotated the periscope locking ring, and lowered the periscope into its storage well.

Providence slowed its descent into the cold, dark water, leveling off at one hundred eighty feet. "Level at ordered depth," Connaly called out.

"Very well," Chandler answered.

"Sonar, Conn, any contacts?"

"Conn, Sonar, No contacts sir."

"Quartermaster, Conn, give me a sounding."

"Conn, Quartermaster, depth to keel is seven hundred sixty-five fathoms.."

"Sonar, Conn, are there any thermals?"

"Conn, Sonar, there's a distinct thermal layer at two hundred ten feet."

"Dive, Conn, three degree down bubble. Make your depth three hundred feet."

"Conn, Dive, three degree down bubble. Make your depth three hundred feet, aye."

"Mr. Graham, I need a course to Point Bravo."

Lcdr. Graham bent over the navigation chart, picked up a protractor, and made a quick check. "Course to Point Bravo is one-one-eight degrees Captain."

"Helm, Conn, right standard rudder. Come to course one-one-eight," Chandler ordered.

"Conn, Helm, right standard rudder. Come to course one-one-eight, aye."

"Helm, Conn, all ahead two-thirds. Make turns for fifteen knots."

"Conn, Helm, all ahead two-thirds. Make turns for fifteen knots, aye."

"How long to Point Bravo Mr. Graham?"

Lcdr. Graham picked up a pair of dividers and measured the distance from their present position to Point Bravo. He made a quick calculations on a pad of paper. "One hour and ten minutes to Point Bravo based upon our current position and speed."

"Very Well. Mr. Graham you have the Conn."

"Aye sir. I have the Conn."

Chandler turned toward Master Chief Mazetti, "COB, join me on the mess deck for a cup of coffee."

"Yes sir," Mazetti responded, following the captain as they headed toward the mess deck.

Chandler grabbed two coffee cups from a tray and pointed to the far booth. As they sat down, Chandler held up his cup to signal the mess specialist they needed some coffee. Interrupting his preparations for the evening meal for those not on watch, the mess specialist rushed over to fill their cups.

"See that we are not interrupted," Chandler ordered.

"Yes sir," he answered.

"COB, it looks like we may be developing a morale problem. I have heard some of the crew complaining and I've gotten some pretty dirty looks. I want you to head this off before it gets any worse."

"I've seen it also sir, but I don't think it's anything to worry about. The men will settle down as soon as they get busy with their duties. This is the finest crew in the submarine fleet sir. You can't really blame them for being upset. Our last patrol was a long one. The men expected more time to spend with their families. Leaves were canceled. A lot of plans were ruined. I think the crew is doing quite well considering."

"I understand the crew's frustration COB, but I want to be certain their frustration does not affect their performance. As soon as I open our orders and we establish our patrol route, I think we should have some drills to make certain the crew is sharp."

Chandler and Mazetti discussed the particulars of the drills they felt would be necessary and ways of improving the crew's morale. When they returned to the Conn, *Providence* was fifteen minutes from Point Bravo.

"Mr. Graham, anything to report?" Chandler asked.

"No sir. No contacts, all systems functioning normally," Lcdr. Graham replied.

Chandler walked over to the navigation table and examined the navigational chart to check on the boat's progress. He continued watching until it was verified that *Providence* was on station at Point Bravo.

Chandler looked over at Lt. Thomas Flanigan, the boat's navigation officer and waited. "Sir, Kelvin Seamount bears two-seven-zero relative, range one thousand yards," Lt. Flanigan answered crisply.

"Very well. Mr. Harris, you have the Conn. Mr. Graham come with me," Chandler ordered.

Providence's Weapons Officer, Lieutenant Edwin Harris, stepped up to the Conn, "Aye aye Captain. I have the Conn."

Chandler and Graham, *Providence's* Executive Officer, headed for the Captain's cabin to open their patrol orders. Graham sat and waited as Chandler opened the wall safe, took out the packet marked "SECRET", and laid it on the desk. "Go ahead Mr. Graham," Chandler instructed.

Graham picked up the packet, broke the seal, and dumped the contents onto the desk. Chandler quickly scanned the enclosed patrol route and orders. He pushed them over to the XO, waiting for his response. No change of expression was evident on the XO's face.

"The men are not going to like this," Chandler said.

"That's an understatement sir," Graham replied. "It was bad enough when their shore time was cut in half. Another extended patrol to the Mediterranean is not going to be well accepted."

"The men are trained professionals, Mr. Graham. I expect them to act that way. I have already spoken to the COB about the growing morale problem. I expect you to work with the COB to head off any potential problems."

"Aye sir. I'll speak with him immediately," Graham answered. "Will there be anything else sir?"

"No, nothing else."

Chandler and Graham returned to the Conn.

"Mr. Harris, I have the Conn," Chandler said, steeping up on the platform.

"Aye aye sir," Lt. Harris replied.

"Mr. Graham, indicate in the ship's log that the patrol orders were opened and verified at twenty-two forty-five Zulu, then plot an easterly transit course for us."

Graham hurriedly made a notation in the ship's log, stepped over to the navigational chart and compared their current position to the standard west to east transit courses. Then he plotted an intercept course to the closest one. "Course one-three-six degrees for fourteen hours which will put us at the end of the New England Trough, then course one-six-nine degrees for the easterly transit sir."

"Helm, Conn, right standard rudder come to course one-three-six."

"Conn, Helm, right standard rudder come to course one-three-six, aye," EM2 Connaly answered.

When the words "transit course" were spoken, eyebrows raised all over the control room. The crewmen knew only too well what those words meant. They were on their way to an extended patrol on the other side of the world. Angry glances flashed between several of the crew members. Glances that did not go unnoticed. Mr. Graham had been watching for signs of hostility when the course was announced, knowing it was going to be a difficult patrol.

Chandler motioned Mr. Graham over to the bridge, turned away from the control center, and spoke in hushed tones. "Keep the men sharp. There is something very peculiar about this patrol. I picked up a hint of something when I talked to COMSUBLANT this morning. They claim it's just a routine shifting of resources, but I don't believe them. Don't say anything to the men. Just be alert."

Chandler turned back toward the control center, "Mr. Graham, you have the Conn. I'm going to my cabin to finish some paperwork."

"Aye aye sir," Graham answered. "I'll tell Sonar to keep a close watch for any contacts. I'll put the best men we have on the section tracking party. You will be informed the instant we pick up any contacts sir."

"Very well," Chandler replied as he turned and headed for his cabin. For some reason, he just could not shake the unsettled feeling nagging at him As he walked forward to his cabin, he tried to convince himself it could possibly be something he ate because he had not felt very well all day. He made a stop in the galley and waited as the duty mess specialist filled a carafe with hot coffee, then he proceeded on to his cabin.

He entered his cabin and shut the door. After he filled the cup his son had given him for his birthday with the hot, steaming brew, he set the carafe on the desk. *"The World's Greatest Dad"* was stenciled on the side of the cup in bright, bold letters. The cup rekindled pleasant memories of his birthday, less than a week earlier. He loved his family very much and did everything he could for his children, but it was difficult when he had to be away from them for such long periods of time. In keeping with Naval Academy tradition, no matter how much he loved his family, the Navy came first. Always.

He slid the top drawer of the desk open, grabbed a bottle of antacid tablets, and shook two tablets out into the palm of his hand. Popping them into his mouth, he chewed them as he dug through the stack of paper on his desk. He reached down and undid the hook on his trousers and leaned back in his chair. He really did not feel well. *"Maybe if I lay down for a while,"* he thought.

He got up from his chair and laid down on his bunk. Hoping a few minutes of sleep might help, he switched off the cabin light and closed his eyes.

It seemed as if he had just closed his eyes but, in actuality, he had been asleep for over thirty minutes when he heard someone shouting his name. Slowly his mind returned from the dream he had been having. Someone from the radio room was shouting his name.

"Captain. Captain," the voice called out again as someone banged loudly on the cabin door.

"Enter," Chandler stammered as he switched on the light and sat up on the bed. "What is it?" he asked as Radioman Second Class Albert Benson stepped in and came to attention.

"Flash traffic sir," Benson answered.

"Well, let's see it," Chandler growled.

"It's Eyes Only sir," Benson replied.

"Very well. Let's go," Chandler answered as he slid off his bunk and waited for the crewman to exit.

Radioman Second Class Benson, with Commander Chandler following close behind, hurried to the radio room as fast as was possible in the restricted spaces of a submarine passageway. "Eyes Only" traffic could only mean something serious was brewing. They entered the radio room and Chandler grabbed the microphone for the 7-MC. "Conn, Radio, this is the Captain. Take the boat to periscope depth. We have flash traffic. As soon as we reach periscope depth, extend the UHF radio mast."

"Radio, Conn, periscope depth right away sir," Lcdr. Graham replied.

"Dive, Conn, ten degree up bubble. Take us up to periscope depth smartly."

"Conn, Dive, ten degree up bubble. Come to periscope depth smartly, aye."

Before the XO had completed the ordered depth change, Chandler walked over to the communication control display unit and typed in his user code and password. It was against patrol orders to stay at periscope depth any longer than necessary. He wanted the radio equipment ready as soon as they reached periscope depth. Nervously he waited, watching the communications link "acquire" indicator.

"Come on. Come on," he urged as he waited. "Bingo," he exclaimed when the communications link "acquire" indicator changed from red to green. He punched in the necessary commands to download and decipher the message from the satellite. The screen indicated the message had been decoded and authenticated.

"Gentlemen I'll have to ask you to leave the room."

As the last crewman left the radio room, Commander Chandler punched in the command to display the message on the screen. He studied the brief message closely, reading it several times. The last paragraph of the message jumped off the screen at him. Something extremely ominous must be happening. He read the message one last time, making a mental note of the location contained in the instructions. He printed a portion of the message and stuffed it in his pocket.

"Conn, Radio, flash traffic received. Take the boat back down to patrol depth," Chandler ordered. Before Lcdr. Graham could respond, Chandler threw open the radio room door. "Make a hole!" he shouted as he ran toward the control room.

Several crewmen literally had to dive out of the way as Chandler ran up the passageway toward the control room. "Mr. Graham, I have the Conn," he puffed, out of breath, running into the control room. "What's our position?"

Graham glanced quickly at the navigational chart, "Looks like we're about three nautical miles southwest of the New England Seamount sir."

Chandler looked at the chart and made a quick course computation in his head.

"Helm, Conn, ahead full make turns for twenty-five knots."

"Conn, Helm, ahead full make turns for twenty-five knots, aye."

"Helm, Conn, left full rudder. Come to course zero-four-zero.

"Conn, Helm, left full rudder. Come to course zero-four-zero, aye," EM2 Connaly answered.

Connaly rotated the rudder to the full position. "Wow, something big must be up," Connaly whistled to the crewman sitting beside him.

"Yeah. We sure did a quick about face," the other maneuvering watch laughed.

Chandler waited for the course change to be completed.

"Conn, Helm, making turns for twenty-five knots."

"Conn aye."

"Conn, Helm, my rudder is left full, passing zero-nine-zero degrees."

"Conn aye."

"Mr. Graham, once we're safely clear of the seamount, plot a new course line with a new heading of zero-zero-six. Tell me if we have any problems at our current depth.

"Conn, Helm, my rudder is left full, passing zero-six-zero degrees."

"Conn aye."

"Captain, course looks good. Ocean depth is well below our current depth for the next four hundred twenty miles until we reach the George's Bank Shelf," Graham answered from the navigation station.

"Very Well."

"Conn, Helm, my rudder is left full, passing zero-five-zero degrees."

"Conn aye."

Chandler fidgeted as he waited for the course change to be completed. A glance around the bridge revealed many eyes staring at him. He knew they wondered what had made them suddenly change course, but for now they would have to be kept in the dark.

"Conn, Helm, steady on course zero-four zero."

"Conn, aye. Mr. Harris you have the Conn. Maintain present course and depth for twenty minutes. Verify we are clear of the seamount, then turn the boat to zero-zero-six. If any unusual contacts appear, find me immediately. Mr. Graham with me. Now!" Chandler barked.

Chandler headed for his cabin with Graham running along behind. When they reached the captain's cabin, Chandler held the door open and waited for Graham to enter.

"Sit," Chandler directed as he pulled the portion of the flash message he had printed from his pocket and laid it in front of Lcdr. Graham.

"Do you know the reason for the sudden change of patrol route or what the package is?" Graham asked.

"No. The message did not elaborate. It did, however, say that the remainder of the patrol will be classified on a strict need to know basis," Chandler answered. "That is all we know at this point. Return to the Conn and keep us on course to the coordinates detailed in the message."

As Graham left, Chandler picked up the printed message and fed it into the shredder.

CHAPTER TWELVE

Wednesday, March 25 - 1920 Eastern Daylight Time
Anchorage north of Cat Caye
Bimini, Bahamas

Clutching a cup of steaming, hot coffee in one hand, Angie Templeton carefully climbed up the ladder from the main salon and stepped out onto the deck of the Marine Vessel *Sea Princess*. Turning toward the bow, she saw Zach leaning against the front of the horseshoe staring off into space. Hesitating, she put her free hand on the salon cover to steady herself on the gently pitching deck. She was truly sorry for the way she had treated Zach the previous evening, but she had simply not wanted to go over the same issues again.

As she stood there staring at the only man she had ever loved, she was filled with a deluge of conflicting emotions. Guilt, sorrow, anger. Even love, perhaps? She did not hate Zach. She did not even dislike him, but she did not love him anymore. Or was she trying to convince herself she did not love him anymore? Was it just guilt that filled her heart, she wondered, staring at Zach. She knew Zach was under tremendous pressure and she did not want to add to his trouble, but she refused to lie to him.

Zach always argued with her and made it a joke whenever she mentioned it, but she thought he was a very handsome man. So what if his hair was thinning a little and graying at the temples. Maybe he was not the lithe, agile combat soldier he once had been. Standing there, clad only in swim trunks, his body still bore the evidence of years of conditioning. The past few days in the Caribbean sun had bronzed his body quite nicely. Yes, he was quite attractive, she thought.

The previous evening, after leaving Zach standing on the deck, Angie had gone below to their berth. Laying there waiting for sleep to come, she made a mental list of the things she liked about Zach. There were many things to like: his honesty, his integrity, his quick wit, his fairness, and his strict code of conduct. Most of all she was impressed by his devotion to friends and family. "He has so many good qualities why can't I love him?"

she asked herself over and over.

"What went wrong? Am I just as guilty for the emptiness and tension between us? Am I just jealous because "the business" got more time than I did?" Unanswered questions swirled in her mind as she cried silently, tears seeping from the corners of her eyes, soaking into the pillow. She had longed for Zach's strong arms around her, for the feeling of safety and comfort it would give her, but she had refused to give in. That would have been unfair to Zach. Exhausted by a full day of diving, Angie's feeling of emptiness and sorrow had given way to sleep.

Returning from her daydream, she looked forward and watched Zach for a few moments. She really did feel sorry for him. Matching the swaying motion of the boat, she started forward to watch the sunset with him.

"Hey Zach," she called out as she approached the spot where he was standing.

"Huh?" Zach responded, turning to see who had called out his name. "Oh, Angie. I'm glad you came up on deck. It's going to be another great sunset. I promise I won't say a word. Let's just sit and enjoy it."

"Zach, I'm really sorry about last night," Angie apologized. "I was really exhausted and I just didn't want to go over the same old issues. You know. We always end up at the same point. I don't ...."

"It's okay, really," Zach interrupted. "I understand. I just have trouble trying to control my need to fix our problem," Zach said, emphasizing the word "fix". He reached up and brushed a few loose strands of hair off his forehead and continued, "The purpose of this trip was to allow both of us to relax and unwind. I shouldn't have even brought it up. We're here to enjoy the sun and make holes in the ocean."

Angie laughed at Zach's comment about making holes in the ocean. "It's so beautiful here Zach. It's going to be really hard to go back to work. I wish we could stay here forever," she said as she gently laid her hand on Zach's arm.

Zach shivered imperceptibly, electricity coursing through his body from the mere touch of Angie's fingers on his skin. Gooseflesh covered his arms, a smile spreading across his face.

"What?" Angie asked, noticing the smile on his face.

Zach did not answer. He just continued to stare across the azure water with a smile on his face.

"What are you thinking about?" Angie probed, sensing his detachment.

For a long moment Zach did not answer, then he said, "No, it's not important."

"Come on Zach, tell me," Angie coaxed.

He turned and looked at her, "You really want to know what I was thinking about?"

"Yes, I do," she said a little anxiously, fearing she might be opening

Pandora's box.

He suppressed a laugh, as though what he was going to tell her was silly. His left arm came up and he pointed across the water, "See the beach over there on Cat Caye? I was thinking of a moonlit night, water lapping at the sand, a gentle breeze. You and me wearing nothing but sand. Remember?"

Angie looked at Zach whose face was now filled with a huge, silly grin like the Cheshire Cat. "Oh, Zach. Of course I remember," she said as she stepped closer and put her arms around him, overcome and momentarily helpless against the desire welling up inside her. She never could resist Zach's smile and the little dimple that formed only on the left side of his face.

"This is good. Really good," Zach chuckled as his arms encircled her and he held her tight. He continued to hold her tight for several minutes, enjoying her softness and the warmth of her breath on his neck. He reached up and cradled her face in his hands and kissed her ever so gently. He felt Angie respond and give in to his kiss. Zach had no idea how long the kiss lasted, only that he felt very empty when it ended.

"Zach, I...," Angie quavered.

"Don't worry about it. No apologies. No questions, No excuses. Let's just enjoy it," Zach said before she could continue.

Angie complied and did not say a word, a gentle sigh escaping from her lips as she rested her head on Zach's shoulder, dreaming of a better time. A time when their love for each other had been the only thing that mattered.

Minutes passed as neither one said a word, simply enjoying the closeness and the soft Caribbean breeze. Still in each other's arms, the sun slipped below the horizon and lit up the western sky as if it were on fire. Zach tapped Angie on the shoulder, "Hey beautiful, look at the sunset."

"Wow, it's beautiful," Angie blurted out.

"Certainly is," Zach agreed.

"Zach do you," Angie started.

"Shhhhh," Zach said as he kissed her again, not as gently as before. Angie did not pull away but she did not respond as she had before. Zach felt sad and empty, realizing the fleeting moment between them had passed. "Well, we have another full day of diving tomorrow. I guess we should go below and fill in our log books. We should call it a night," Zach said, releasing his hold on Angie and letting his arms drop to his side.

"Yeah, I guess you're right," Angie agreed. She too felt sad that the fleeting moment of closeness had passed.

Zach and Angie went below, grabbed their dive logs from the shelf above their bunk, and sat down at the centerboard. They spent twenty minutes discussing and filling in details about each of the day's four dives: location, time at depth, water temperature, visibility, currents, and types of fish or coral they had seen. After all the details had been entered, they signed and dated each other's dive logs. Zach stowed the log books while Angie took her turn in the main salon's only head.

When Zach finished his turn in the head and climbed into their bunk, Angie dog eared a page in the book she had been reading and placed it on the shelf.

"Zach, up on deck, I ahh…. I ahh…. I don't want you to get the wrong idea. I don't believe anything between us has changed," Angie said, propping herself up on one elbow.

"I don't intend to analyze it. Let's just accept it for what it was and let it go at that," Zach replied.

"See, that's exactly what I mean," Angie said, picking up on the defensive tone that had crept into Zach's voice.

"What do you mean?" Zach demanded.

"You immediately got defensive. I could hear it in your voice," Angie answered.

"Angie, I love you and I want us to be together. How did you think I would react?" Zach snapped, his frustration obvious.

"I'm sorry. I shouldn't have said anything. We always end up right here at the same issue," Angie offered in defense. Zach was upset and quiet. Angie could always tell by the ripple by his ear as he clenched his jaw. She continued to press the issue, "Zach I know you're upset and…."

"You bet I'm upset," he interrupted, giving in to his rising frustration. "The woman I love doesn't want to live with me anymore. My company's in serious trouble and I think I'm going to lose the DOD contracts. If that happens the company will fail."

"I didn't realize the company's troubles were that bad," Angie responded. "I am sorry you are having so many problems, but I think you're lying to yourself Zach. I don't think I'm as important to you as you think I am. You're just afraid of being alone. Every time we argue it always boils down to something involving the company."

"What do you think I should do?" Zach pressed. "When we return home, should I close the doors and fire everyone? What would I do for a living then, huh? Answer me that." Zach was angry and speaking without thinking about the consequences of his words. Before Angie could respond, he continued, "Probably be the best thing anyway. I'm convinced someone is sabotaging the systems. And then, I get a phone call from some stranger that knows way more than he should. Even threatened me and everyone around me."

"What are you talking about? Why would someone threaten you?" Angie questioned.

"Angie, forget what I said. You've got to let this go. I slipped. I shouldn't have said anything," Zach pleaded. "I won't let you get involved in this. I have to deal with it myself."

"No Zach. I want to know more," Angie demanded.

"I'm not going to tell you anymore. I can't," Zach protested. "Let's just pretend I got angry and said something stupid. Again! That's not hard to believe. Is it?" Zach held up his hand and then pressed his finger to Angie's lips, signifying no more was to be said. A sudden chill ran down Angie's back. Never before had she seen that cold, hard look in Zach's eyes.

Zach knew he had to defuse the situation quickly, before Angie got more worried or suspicious. "Please Angie, I beg you. Do not mention this to anyone. I am going to take care of it as soon as I get back to the office. I promise you that. I give you my word. Promise me. Angie, I want to hear you say it."

Angie stared at Zach. What was Zach involved in? Could she make a promise regarding something she knew so little about? All kinds of wild ideas were spinning through her mind.

"Angie promise me," Zach demanded.

"Okay, Okay, Zach. I promise. But only if you tell me more," Angie replied.

"Absolutely not," Zach declared. "It might put you in too much danger. Not until I know more. You're just going to have to trust me on this. Subject closed!"

Angie had seen that look of stubborn determination before. There would be nothing to gain by asking Zach any more questions. She knew he had said all he was going to.

"I'm going to go topside. I need to calm down," Zach said as he lifted the blanket and slipped out of the berth. He leaned back into the berth, cradled her face in his right hand, and kissed her cheek. "Trust me. I can handle this," he said as he slid the curtain closed and disappeared up the ladder.

Zach sat alone in the dark for a long time, emotionally drained by the roller coaster ride of emotions he had experienced the last few days. For a brief moment he had felt on top of the world when the woman he loved had responded to him. Then he plummeted to the depths of despair and loneliness as she pushed him away yet again. Even worse, he had gotten angry and told her things she should not know. The horrible feeling of impending doom that had settled over him the past several weeks was growing worse.

"What on earth do I do now?" he asked himself over and over as he sat there in the dark.

CHAPTER THIRTEEN

Wednesday, March 25 - 2017 Eastern Daylight Time
Office of Director, Joint Staff
Pentagon – Corridor 9, E Ring
Washington, D.C.

Vice Admiral Harlan Beckwith sat at his desk going over routine intelligence traffic and operational dispatches. His eyes widened as he scanned the document he had just lifted from the stack. Dropping the document, he punched the intercom button on his phone. "Colonel Elmont, you still there?" he hollered, anger bristling in his voice.

Colonel Dennis Elmont cringed as he answered, picking up on the angry tone in Beckwith's voice, "Yes sir. Just about to walk out the door."

"My office. Now!" Beckwith shouted.

"Holy Cow. What now?" Elmont muttered, grabbing his notebook and heading for Beckwith's office. A glance at his watch only confirmed how tired and ready to go home he was. Summoned to the office early, he had already been there for more than thirteen long hours.

Elmont walked up to Beckwith's door, rapped twice, and waited.

"Enter."

Elmont hurried over to the desk, came to attention, and said, "Yes sir."

"Have you seen this op order?" Beckwith asked with a menacing tone, sliding the piece of paper across the desk.

Elmont picked up the document, quickly scanned it, and checked the receipt stamp on the lower right corner. "Yes sir. I logged it in two hours ago. It looks like a routine repositioning of Navy patrol assets sir."

"Oh does it?" Beckwith yelled, getting up and coming around the desk. He stood beside Elmont, pointing at the paper. "What is that right there?" he questioned, jabbing his finger at the second line in the header.

"Oh, God!" Elmont gasped. "I completely missed that."

"Yeah, I guess you did," Beckwith sneered sarcastically, ripping the document out of the Elmont's hands. "Get on the phone and find out the reason for the change of patrol route," Beckwith ordered. He looked up and saw that the Colonel had not moved. "Now!" he barked.

"Yes sir. Right away sir," Elmont answered as he came to attention, did an about face, and rushed out of the office.

"Good Lord," Beckwith complained as he dropped the document on his desk and slumped back into his chair. His perfect plan had run into its first potential obstacle.

In less than three minutes, the intercom on Beckwith's desk buzzed. He punched it and spoke without waiting, "Well, what did you find out? Who altered the patrol route and why?"

"I called the Operations Desk at COMSUBLANT and asked for the CDO," Elmont replied. "I asked for the justification and source of the patrol route change. The CDO informed me that he did not have that information. I asked to talk to his superior, but he told me not to bother. All intelligence regarding *Providence* has been restricted. I informed him that you had requested the information, but he said it didn't matter. There's nothing more I can do sir."

"Very well. I'll make the call myself," Beckwith said as he slammed the phone down. Grabbing a phone index, he selected the letter he wanted and pressed the release tab. He ran his finger down the list until he located the number he wanted. He punched in the number and waited.

"Chief of Naval Operations, Captain Ronald Whitfield speaking," the duty officer answered.

"This is the Director, Joint Staff. Is he in?"

"No sir. He left over an hour ago."

"Well, how about his assistant?"

"No sir. He left ten minutes after the CNO did."

"I guess you'll have to help me then, Captain. I presented a plan to the Joint Chiefs, to which they concurred I might add, for the movement of some Naval units to monitor a developing situation. *Providence* is a critical part of that plan and I need to know why her patrol route was altered."

"Just a minute sir," Whitmore said as he put the line on hold. Beckwith drummed his fingers on the desk impatiently, soft jazz playing in his ear.

It was nearly five minutes before Captain Whitmore took the line off hold and answered, "Sir, the orders for *Providence* have been sealed."

"I already know that," Beckwith barked into the phone. "By whom and under what authority?"

"Sir, I can't tell you that," Elmont replied. "All I can tell you is that it had to be an outside agency because the orders aren't here. They were signed out under secure escort."

"What? That's not SOP Captain," Beckwith yelled, his voice rising in volume.

"Sir, it won't do you any good to yell," Elmont responded. "There's nothing more I can tell you. It is sealed. It's a black op."

"Very well," Beckwith growled and hung up.

Beckwith was troubled by this new development because it could jeopardize his entire plan. The perfect plan he had crafted so meticulously. A plan he had spent the last four years dreaming about. A plan that had become his entire reason for existence. If he did not do something soon, it might unravel right before his eyes.

Left with no other alternative, He decided to remove the one last remaining threat to his plan. He picked up the phone and dialed a number from memory.

"Yes," a male voice on the other end answered.

"I need you to do one last thing then I want you to disappear forever," Beckwith said.

"I'm listening," the man replied.

"There's one name left on your list. I want him eliminated immediately and I would prefer it if he didn't turn up for at least several days," Beckwith instructed.

"That will cost more. The risk is great."

"After the job is done, I will pay you three times the amount we agreed to. Is that satisfactory?" Beckwith asked.

"Absolutely. I will be in touch." The line went dead.

Beckwith hung up the phone and straightened the papers on his desk. The man he had spoken with was pure evil and driven solely by money. Beckwith believed he would murder his own grandmother if the price was right, but he really didn't care because the man was a necessary part of the plan he had dreamed about day and night. Getting up from the desk, he put on his uniform jacket and left his office to put the next step of his plan into motion.

CHAPTER FOURTEEN

Thursday, March 26 - 0919 Zulu
USS Providence, SSN719,
44°20'N, 52°48'W
Northern Edge of Desbarres Canyon

The phone in Commander Chandler's cabin rang. He picked up the receiver and answered, "Yes. What is it?"

"Sir, sonar has picked up a narrowband contact bearing zero-four-seven." Lcdr. Graham replied.

"On my way," Chandler responded, already rising from his chair.

Chandler ran down the passageway and rushed into the control room. "I have the Conn," he announced, stepping up on the platform.

"Aye sir," Lcdr. Graham acknowledged, stepping down and assuming his position beside the control deck.

"Quartermaster, Conn, give me a sounding," Chandler barked into the 27-MC, still slightly out of breath.

Quartermaster Of The Watch, Quartermaster First Class Timothy Wilson looked at the long, ragged trace of the fathometer sounding on the ocean floor far below. "Conn, Quartermaster, depth is falling away to port sir. Current depth is three hundred plus fathoms," Wilson replied.

"Sonar, Conn, range and bearing to new target?" Chandler requested.

"Conn, Sonar, designate contact Sierra six-three, bearing zero-six-seven, range slightly over fourteen thousand yards. Contact is still too faint to classify," Sonarman First Class Jenkins answered without taking his eyes off of the sonar screen.

"Sonar, Conn, any indication he knows we're here?" Chandler asked.

"Conn, Sonar, none sir. Contact has been steady on course two-seven-six. No change in aspect since we picked him up sir," Jenkins answered.

"Notify me the instant anything changes," Chandler instructed as he turned and looked over at the navigation officer. "How far are we from the Grand Bank shelf Mr. Flanigan?"

Providence's navigation officer, Lt. Thomas Flanigan studied the chart mounted on the navigation table for a few seconds then turned and answered, "Approximately sixteen hundred yards Captain."

Chandler thought for a moment then ordered a course change. "Helm, Conn, right standard rudder. Come to course three-three-eight."

"Conn, Helm, right standard rudder. Come to course three-three-eight aye."

"Sonar, Conn, any classification on that contact yet?"

Sonarman Jenkins leaned even closer to the bright, green sonar screen and made several adjustments. The bright green streaks and specks on a darker green background were unintelligible gibberish to the untrained eye, but Jenkins was one of the best in the entire Navy at his job. He leaned back and rubbed his tired, strained eyes. "Conn, Sonar, sorry sir. The signal is just too faint and noisy. I can't hold a clear signal long enough for the classification software to make a positive ident."

"Very well," Chandler answered. *Providence* was silently sliding through the icy, North Atlantic water at five hundred eighty feet, hugging the southwestern edge of the Grand Banks Shelf that ran Northwest to Southeast south of the Island of Newfoundland. The Grand Banks Shelf descended to a depth of over seventeen thousand feet at the northern edge of the Sohm Abyssal Plain. The contact *Providence* was tracking was seven miles northeast of the shelf's edge. The shelf must be blocking the contact's signal Chandler thought to himself.

"Dive, Conn, no angle on the bow planes. Ease us up to two hundred feet slowly," Chandler ordered, keeping his finger over the 7-MC transmit button.

"Conn, Dive, no angle on the bow planes. Ease up to two hundred feet slowly aye," MM2 Carl Hill responded as he pulled back on the diving planes ever so slightly.

"Helm, Conn, slow to five knots," Chandler ordered to reduce the acoustic flow noise the boat would make as it slid through the icy water. He wanted a classification on that contact quickly.

"Conn, Helm, slow to five knots aye."

Chandler waited impatiently as the depth indicator slowly climbed from five hundred eighty feet to two hundred feet.

Even before the planesman could respond that he had leveled the boat at two hundred feet, Chandler's finger had already depressed the 27-MC transmit button. "Sonar, Conn, anything on that contact yet? I don't want to keep the boat at this depth any longer than absolutely necessary."

"Conn, Sonar, our depth change helped. The signal is clearing. I'm getting something. The signal is weak but steady. Contact's bearing moving slowly to port," Sonarman Jenkins answered, waiting for the computer to compare the contact's acoustic signature to those stored in its memory. "Classification coming in now sir. It's Russian sir. Kirov class battlecruiser.

The computer classifies it as the *Pyotr Velikiy*. No doubt about it sir."

The Kirov class of Russian warships was built as part of "The Russian Heavy Missile Cruise Ship Project" in the Baltic Shipyard in Saint Petersburg, Russia. Kirov class cruisers provided the Russian Navy the capability to engage large surface ships and to defend the Russian fleet against air and submarine attacks.

Kirov class battlecruisers bristled with armament and sophisticated weapons systems, armed with twenty Granit (NATO designation SS-N-19 Shipwreck) long range, anti-ship missiles, installed under the upper deck. Kirov class battlecruisers also carried the S-300F Air Defense Missile System, consisting of twelve launchers and ninety-six vertical launch, air defense missiles. The missile system was deadly accurate, integrated into the ship's combat systems and able to download target data directly from the ship's sensors.

Kirov class battlecruisers were well protected by an air-defense gun system. The gun system provided defense against a wide range of precision weapons including anti-ship and anti-radar missiles, air bombs, aircraft, and small naval ships. The gun system could engage up to six targets simultaneously, firing at a rate of one thousand rounds per minute.

A deadly threat to *Providence*, was the Kirov's sophisticated anti-submarine warfare systems. A Kirov class battlecruiser carried twenty Vodopad-NK anti-submarine torpedoes which could be launched from ten torpedo tubes and two anti-submarine and anti-torpedo rocket systems. However, the most deadly threat of all was the fact that a Kirov class battlecruiser was outfitted to carry up to three Kamov Ka-27PL (NATO codename Helix) helicopters equipped for anti-submarine warfare, each equipped with surface search radar, sonobuoys, dipping sonar, and magnetic anomaly detectors.

"Good work Jenkins. Notify me if anything changes," Chandler acknowledged. He pressed the transmit button for the 27-MC again and continued, "Helm, Conn, slow to three knots."

"Conn, Helm, slow to three knots aye."

Chandler stepped down from the control deck and walked over to the navigation table. He leaned over, examined the chart, and asked, "What's our current position?"

Lt. Flanigan took a pencil and made a mark on the chart. Chandler studied the chart for a few seconds then pointed with a ruler to a point on the chart close to the edge of the Grand Banks Shelf where the water was just over one thousand feet deep.

"Right there," Chandler said. "I want to be right there waiting when the Russian cruiser approaches the edge of the shelf. We will have deep, open water to port if we need to run plus our systems work better in deep water."

"Plot a course to the edge of the Laurentian Trough," Chandler directed as he returned to the control deck.

Lt. Flanigan grabbed a straight-edge and compass and made some hurried measurements. "Maintain present speed. Course three-two-seven for five minutes, then course three-one-one for three minutes, then course three-three-zero for eight minutes. That should put us eight hundred yards from the southern end of the trough," he announced.

"Very well Mr. Flanigan," Chandler ordered the course changes Lt. Flanigan had calculated. Each leg timed precisely to avoid the dangerous ridges near the edge of the Grand Banks Shelf. The ocean floor rose gradually for several hundred miles northward from the seventeen thousand foot deep Sohm Abyssal Plain, then rose rapidly the last several miles before leveling out to the three hundred foot depth of the Grand Bank shelf.

Eighteen minutes later the sleek, black boat passed two hundred feet above the last ridge and approached the edge of the Laurentian Trough. "Sonar, Quartermaster, give me a sounding," Chandler requested as the last leg was completed.

"Conn, Quartermaster, depth to keel is twelve hundred fifty feet."

"Dive, Conn, one degree down bubble. Make your depth two hundred eighty feet."

"Conn, Dive, one degree down bubble. Make your depth two hundred eighty feet aye."

MM2 Hill gently eased the diving planes forward. *Providence* pitched slightly downward, sliding deeper into the icy, dark waters in wait for its prey. Chandler watched as the digital depth indicator slowly clicked off the depth change.

"Helm, Conn, all stop," Chandler ordered as soon as the boat leveled off at the requested depth.

"Conn, Helm, all stop aye."

Chandler thumbed the transmit button of the 1-MC again and announced, "Man battle stations torpedo. Rig for ultra-quiet. All hands, dead quiet. I don't want our Russian friends to know we're here."

All non-essential activity stopped immediately upon the captain's announcement. Anyone that spoke did so in hushed tones. In the sonar room all eyes were glued to the bright green sonar screens, watching for the slightest indication of a course change for the contact they were tracking.

"Weapons, Conn, load tubes one and two but do it quietly. Flood the tubes but leave the outer doors closed," Chandler ordered, remaining vigilant because he had been given reason to believe *Providence* might be fired upon. The crew would be required to function at the very peak of their abilities because a Kirov class battlecruiser was a very formidable foe.

The last paragraph of the flash traffic message received earlier and signed by the Chief of Naval Operations himself and approved by the

President of the United States made the *Providence* truly lethal. He replayed the message in his mind, "In the event of an attack on *Providence*, threatened or otherwise, by any foreign power, the Commanding Officer, *Providence*, is authorized to use whatever self-defensive measures are deemed necessary and appropriate. Use of preemptive action is hereby authorized."

"Conn, Weapons, load tubes one and two aye," Lt. Edwin Harris, *Providence's* weapons officer, answered. Harris turned and instructed his men to load two Mark 48 torpedoes into tubes one and two. "Extra caution men. Let's get those fish in there quickly, but do so quietly," he added as he stepped over to monitor the loading process.

Slightly less than six minutes later, Harris stepped to the 27-MC, "Tubes one and two loaded. Tubes flooded. Outer doors closed," he reported.

"Conn, aye."

Chandler looked around the control room and noticed nervous glances being exchanged between some of the crew members, mostly from the more junior members of *Providence's* crew. The experienced crew members had been through the deadly cat-and-mouse, catch-me-if-you-can, games that went on between the United States and Russian navies many times. Everyone sat absolutely still. Deathly quiet. Waiting. Only an occasional hushed whisper between crewmembers broke the tense silence. "*Nothing to do now but wait for our Russian friend*," Chandler thought as he also stood there waiting.

Seconds turned into minutes as everyone waited. The soft hum of the air handlers as they pumped air scrubbed of its carbon dioxide back into *Providence's* atmosphere was the only sound that could be heard, except for an occasional cough muffled by a T-shirt or handkerchief. *Providence* hovered silently, undetectable, in the icy, dark water.

"Conn, Sonar, new contact, submerged, designate contact Sierra six-four. Bearing two-five-eight, range eight thousand yards!" screamed Sonarman Jenkins' excited voice.

Before Chandler could respond, the excited voice filled the control room again, "Conn, Sonar, change in aspect ratio contact Sierra six-four, increase in speed."

"Sonar, Conn, report course of new contact. Where did he come from?" Chandler asked.

"Conn, Sonar, I don't know sir. The new contact just suddenly appeared. He had to have been sitting dead in the water sir. Track is too new. We don't have a course or speed as yet," Jenkins replied.

"Give me something quick. We can't just sit here," Chandler snapped into the 27-MC.

Thirty seconds passed as the men in the sonar room frantically tried to determine the course and speed of the new contact. "Best estimate, new contact course one-nine-eight, speed eighteen knots. Contact Sierra six-three course is one-six-three, speed twenty-five knots."

"Conn, Sonar, two new contacts breaking away from the *Pyotr Velikiy*! Active sonar sir. We're being pinged!" Jenkins shouted into the 27-MC.

Five miles to the north of *Providence's* position, two Kamov Ka-27PL helicopters had launched from the deck of the *Pyotr Velikiy* and were racing in the direction of *Providence* at top speed, just thirty feet above the surface of the water. Two miles outbound from the *Pyotr Velikiy* one of the helicopters slowed and dropped its "dipping sonar" pod into the water and immediately switched on its active sonar. The other helicopter continued flying toward *Providence's* position.

For a brief instant Commander Chandler stood frozen. "They had to have known we were here!" he exclaimed. "But how could they? They had stayed submerged and they had been extremely careful," he asked himself as his mind churned, hurriedly devising an escape plan.

As Chandler reached for the transmit button, the 27-MC barked to life again. "Conn, Sonar, close aboard splashes, starboard side! Sonobuoys! First pass north to south. They'll have a solid fix on us in seconds!" the excited voice shouted.

Chandler pressed the 1-MC transmit lever, "Man Battle Stations Torpedo."

Another announcement over the 27-MC reverberated throughout control, "Second pass, port side. More splashes!"

Providence would pass right through the sonobuoy field. The only thing *Providence* could do would be to split the distance between the rows of sonobuoys and slow down to reduce the acoustic noise generated by the engine and propeller.

"Helm, Conn, ahead slow, make turns for five knots. Left full rudder, come to course two-six-four," Chandler ordered. Not waiting for a reply, he continued, "Dive, Conn, fifteen degree down bubble, make your depth four hundred fifty feet."

"Conn, Helm, ahead slow, make turns for five knots. My rudder is left full, coming to course two-six-four."

"Conn, aye."

"Conn, dive, fifteen degree down bubble, make my depth four hundred fifty feet aye."

"Conn, aye."

Everyone in the control room grabbed something to steady themselves as *Providence* healed over to port and the deck pitched precariously forward.

Chandler's action was designed to silently slip away from the sonobuoy field and put some distance between *Providence* and the Russian ships and, hopefully, lose them completely beneath a thermocline. If his action was successful, *Providence* would go deep and fast and fade off their sonar screens.

The 27-MC barked to life yet again, "Additional splash in the water, bearing one-zero-nine."

Before Chandler could respond, the 27-MC screamed again, "Conn, Sonar, high speed screws! Torpedo in the water, bearing one-zero-nine, range twelve thousand yards!"

For a fraction of a second the image of a coffee cup bearing the inscription *"World's Greatest Dad"* popped into Chandler's mind. Would he ever see the little boy that had given him that cup again? The image vanished as quickly as it had appeared as Chandler's attention returned to the desperate situation at hand.

"ALL AHEAD EMERGENCY!" Chandler yelled into the 7-MC.

CHAPTER FIFTEEN

Thursday, March 26 - 0945 Zulu
USS Providence, SSN719,
44°29'N, 54°06'W - South of Laurentian Trough

"Conn, Helm, answers all ahead emergency."

"Conn aye," Commander Chandler barked as he contemplated his next move to avoid the torpedo screaming toward *Providence*. Chandler's mind churned furiously, analyzing all available data. *Providence's* speed, top speed of Russian torpedoes, distance from the incoming torpedo. "GOOD LORD!" Chandler exclaimed. They had less than eight minutes before the incoming torpedoes would slam into *Providence*.

"Sonar, Conn, what is the bearing and course to incoming torpedo?"

"Conn, Sonar, torpedo bears zero-four-seven, course two-one-eight."

"Track the time to impact," he shouted to Lcrd. Graham who was holding on to the navigation chart table for support.

"HARD RIGHT RUDDER, COME TO COURSE ZERO-THREE-EIGHT!" Chandler shouted, beads of perspiration beginning to glisten on his forehead. "HANG ON!" he yelled as *Providence* rolled violently in the opposite direction.

"Right hard rudder, come to course zero-three-eight aye," EM2 Connaly cried out as he twisted the rudder from full left to hard right.

Commander Chandler counted off the seconds he had estimated it would take to intersect the torpedo's inbound track.

"Sonar, Conn, bearing to torpedo?"

"Conn, Sonar, torpedo bears three-one-three."

Chandler waited and watched the second hand race around the face of the stopwatch he was holding.

"Sonar, Conn, bearing to torpedo?"

"Conn, Sonar, torpedo bears three-zero-one."

"Weapons, Conn, launch the port countermeasures, NOW!" Chandler bellowed.

"Conn, Weapons, port countermeasures away," Lt. Harris answered as his hand mashed the launch button. Two large decoy canisters shot out from *Providence's* port side. The canisters immediately filled the water with the sound of millions of bubbles. Hopefully the clamor of the bubbles and the wall of disturbance they created would capture the attention of the incoming torpedo's sonar and acoustic sensors.

"HELM, CONN, RIGHT EMERGENCY RUDDER, CONTINUE RIGHT TO ONE-ONE-EIGHT," Chandler yelled, hearing the tell-tale hiss and vibration of the countermeasure launcher.

"Dive, Conn, twenty degree down bubble, make your depth eight hundred fifty feet."

"Conn, Dive, twenty degree down bubble, make your depth eight hundred fifty feet aye," the planesman answered, shoving the diving yoke forward.

All maneuvering watches, according to SOP, were belted into their positions. The sudden, violent maneuvers did not affect them. But many other crew members, especially those caught off guard by the suddenness of the course and depth changes, were knocked from their feet. Other crew members that were able, grabbed at the flailing bodies as they slid forward, down the highly pitched deck.

Chandler's intention was to throw up the countermeasures on the torpedo's exact inbound track and go deep perpendicular to the torpedo's track. If the torpedo's reported track was correct and if his timing was spot on, his actions should mask *Providence's* radar image as she went deep. It would not take very long to determine whether all the "ifs" were correct.

"Call off time to impact Mr. Graham?"

"Three-minutes, fifteen seconds sir."

"Conn, Dive, passing three hundred feet."

"Conn, aye."

"Conn, Helm, steady on course one-one-eight."

"Conn, aye."

"Two minutes, forty-five seconds," Graham called out.

"Conn, Dive, passing four hundred feet."

"Conn, aye."

"Two minutes, fifteen seconds," Graham called out.

"Conn, Dive, passing five hundred feet."

"Conn, aye."

"One minute, forty-five seconds," Graham called out.

Everyone in the control room waited silently, the final seconds ticking off before impact.

CHAPTER SIXTEEN

"One minute, thirty seconds to impact," Lcdr. Graham called out.

"Sonar, Conn, what type of torpedo is it?"

"Conn, Sonar, it's definitely Russian. Computer says VA-111."

"Sonar, Conn, Russian? Are you certain?" Commander Chandler questioned, shocked a Russian submarine would fire on them without provocation.

"Conn, Sonar, absolutely sir. The VA-111 is a super-cavitating torpedo. Computer confirms with ninety-nine percent certainty."

"Conn, Dive, passing six hundred feet."

"Conn, aye."

"One minute to impact," Graham hollered.

"Rig for impact!" Chandler shouted as he grabbed the railing around the periscope tower and braced himself for the impact he hoped and prayed would not come.

"Thirty seconds to impact," Graham shouted.

Providence was not going to be able to outrun the incoming Russian VA-111 torpedo. The speed of the VA-111 far exceeded that of any other standard torpedo, supposedly capable of incredible speeds in excess of two hundred knots, the result of super-cavitation. The torpedo, in effect, flew in a gas bubble created by the outward deflection of water due to its specially shaped nose cone and the expansion of gases from its engine. In actuality, the VA-111 was more of an underwater rocket than a torpedo. Worst of all, the VA-111 torpedo carried a four hundred sixty pound warhead.

Providence's only hope was that the torpedo would be fooled by the massive wall of bubbles created by the countermeasures canister. Even so, *Providence* had not had enough time to create a safe margin of distance from the countermeasures. If the torpedo detonated on the countermeasures, the impact might still be deadly. In *Providence's* favor, the torpedo was closing from above. Hopefully, the torpedo would be fooled and target the countermeasures. If so, the angle of attack and the ship's double hull might be enough to absorb the impact. If not, a close aboard explosion would breach *Providence's* pressure hull. If even one of its compartments flooded, *Providence* would be doomed. Even an emergency blow of the main ballast tank would not create enough buoyancy to reach the surface.

"Ten seconds to impact," Graham announced.

The torpedo's pings could now be heard through Providence's hull, the volume of the pings increasing in intensity as the torpedo raced across the remaining distance. Fear gripped the crew of *Providence* as they waited in silence, broken only by the periodic pings of the incoming torpedo.

"IMPACT!" Graham screamed.

Everyone in the control room cringed and held their breath, bracing themselves for the expected impact at any second.

"Conn, Dive, passing seven hundred feet."

"Conn aye"

"Impact plus ten seconds," Graham called out.

"Conn, aye."

Five seconds later a thunderous shock wave pounded *Providence*. It was as if Thor himself had slammed the hull with his gigantic hammer, sending an earsplitting roar reverberating through every compartment of the boat. *Providence* rocked violently as the shock wave engulfed the full length of the boat. EM2 Connaly wrestled with the helm controls, battling to keep the boat from pitching over as the boat rolled violently to starboard.

A look of utter horror spread across Connaly's face when he saw the attitude indicator's needle climb to fifty-seven degrees. If *Providence* over-rotated on its longitudinal axis and the sail rolled past the center of gravity, she would roll completely over and the boat would be doomed. If *Providence* rolled to sixty degrees, it would be impossible to stop the roll. Connaly fought mightily to suppress the urge to slam the helm control in the opposite direction of the roll. Doing so would overwhelm the control systems and he would lose control for certain. He continued to push the control yoke in the opposite direction as hard as he dared, his gaze riveted on the attitude indicator. Fifty-seven degrees... Fifty-eight degrees... Fifty-nine degrees...

CHAPTER SEVENTEEN

Thursday, March 26 - 1043 Zulu
USS Providence, SSN 719,
44°26'N, 53°39'W

EM2 Connaly swore under his breath, pushing harder on the control yoke. Fifty-nine degrees... Fifty-nine degrees... The roll angle had stopped increasing and was holding. No upward movement. Fifty-eight degrees... Fifty-seven degrees... Fifty-six degrees... Fifty-five degrees... He had won. *Providence* was again under control and beginning to right herself. A number of the crew members picked themselves up, having been thrown to the deck by the violent maneuvers.

"Conn, Sonar, enemy torpedo locked onto and targeted the decoys. No other high-speed contacts at this time."

"Sonar, Conn, aye. Get me an identification of the contact that fired the torpedo and get me a range and bearing!" Commander Chandler screamed. "Let me know the instant you have a steady track." He continued barking orders without waiting for a response from anyone, "Dive, Conn, zero degree bubble. Hold us at this depth for now. Helm, Conn, ahead slow make turns for five knots. All departments report damage."

Once the immediate threat from the incoming torpedo had passed, Chandler ordered the boat to slow down for two reasons. First, it would make the boat quiet and nearly impossible to detect and second, he wanted to give sonar time to determine a range and bearing to the contact that had fired the torpedo. Once the range and bearing had been determined, the fire control technicians could develop a firing solution to the target and feed it into the Combat Control System.

"Damage Control, Conn, small leak in the forward torpedo room has been sealed," a voice crackled from the 4-MC. "No other leaks reported. Minimal damage. Offline systems are being reinitialized now. All systems should be back online within two minutes."

"Conn aye."

The damage reports were far better than he hoped. No serious system damage and there had been no serious leaks, the most dreaded fear of a submariner. Two crew members had broken bones, but the remaining injuries were limited to bumps and bruises and a few minor cuts. Several electronic systems were offline due to the shockwave, but, as damage control had reported, the duty operators were already in the process of rebooting those systems and bringing them back online.

"Helm, Conn, left full rudder come to course zero-one-five." Chandler cursed to himself as he began planning the exact details of his attack.

"Conn, Helm, left full rudder come to course zero-one-five aye," EM2 Connaly answered.

"Conn, Sonar, torpedo track indicates it was fired by contact Sierra six-four," Sonarman Jenkins announced over the 27-MC.

"Conn aye. Designate Sierra six-four as Master One."

"Weapons, Conn, develop a firing solution on the submerged target as quickly as you can. We're coming around to open a better track. Be ready to fire the instant we get a solid range and bearing. I want two torpedoes fired five seconds apart, passive approach, slow speed until eight thousand yards, then go active. I'm going to turn and point before firing," Chandler ordered.

"Conn, Weapons aye. We'll be ready Captain," Lt. Harris answered. Harris stepped over and briefed the fire control technician team on the captain's orders. The fire control technicians as well as *Providence's* Mark 1 Combat Control System were ready except for the input of the final range and bearing. Everyone in the torpedo room was ready and eager to shove two fish down the throat of whoever had attacked them.

"Dive, Conn, five degree up-bubble. Make your depth three hundred feet."

"Conn, Dive, five degree up-bubble. Make your depth three hundred feet aye," Connaly replied.

Commander Chandler reminded himself to stay cool while he waited for *Providence* to get in a better position and for the Sonar room to get a solid track. "Be calm. I've got plenty of time. It will take them at least ten to fifteen minutes for them to determine they missed," he whispered to himself. "Wait till we get closer to their stern arc. There will be less chance they'll hear the launch transients when we fire the torpedoes. I don't want them to see it coming."

"Conn, Helm, steady on course zero-one-five."

"Conn aye."

"Conn, Dive, level at three hundred feet."

"Conn, aye."

Chandler waited as the seconds ticked off. *Providence* was still rigged for ultra quiet. The crew was angry and they were focused. The most lethal, killing machine in the world now had one singular purpose. The swift and total destruction of their attacker.

"Conn, Sonar, contact Master One bearing zero-four-one. High frequency lock. Good aural tone. Good bearing. No change in track. Computer identifies the contact as a Russian Akula class submarine," Jenkins reported excitedly.

"What? Are you certain?" Chandler gasped. "Why would a Russian submarine launch an unprovoked attack on a U.S. warship?"

"Absolutely certain sir. The computer gives it a ninety plus percent probability. Classifies Master One as the K-391, *Bratsk*," Jenkins acknowledged.

"Very well. Good work Petty Officer Jenkins."

Everything was preceding as Chandler had planned. He would maintain their present course for another six minutes then he would turn in for the kill. He checked the contact's range and bearing twice more as the minutes slowly ticked off. Exactly six minutes later he made one last check.

"Sonar, Conn, last range and bearing check."

"Conn, Sonar, contact Master One range nine thousand six hundred yards, bearing steady at zero-four-one, course one-two-seven, speed eight. Good firing solution," Jenkins answered.

"Conn aye. Helm, Conn, right standard rudder. Come to course zero-four-one. Slow to three knots."

"Conn, Helm, right standard rudder. Come to course zero-four-one. Slow to three knots aye."

As *Providence* steadied up on the ordered course, Chandler alerted the crew. "All departments firing point procedures, contact Master One, Tubes One and Two," he ordered. "Weapons, Conn, open outer tube doors. STAND BY TO FIRE!"

"Conn, Weapons, outer doors open. Primary weapon, tube one. Secondary weapon, tube two. Tubes one and two ready in all respects. Firing solution set and locked."

"FIRE!" Chandler yelled into the 27-MC.

Lt. Harris' hand mashed the firing control for tube one. "One... two... three... four... five," he counted out loud. His hand mashed the firing control for tube number two.

Providence shuddered twice as the big Mark 48 ADCAP torpedoes punched out into the ocean in search of the contact that had been loaded into their electronic brains. Throughout the boat the crew heard the dull thuds as the torpedoes left the tubes.

"Conn, Weapons, both torpedoes under guidance."

"Conn aye. Arm the torpedoes."

"Conn, Weapons, torpedoes armed, sir."

Crew members in the Sonar room watched on their screens as the torpedoes bored menacingly through the water, on their low speed setting, deep and very quiet, sonar in the passive mode, listening only. Trailing out behind the torpedoes were the thin, super strong, electronic guide wires, through which the torpedo guidance officer could send course corrections into the electronic brains, located just behind the deadly warheads.

The first one and one-half miles of the journey took three minutes and forty-five seconds. At that point the first torpedo established contact to starboard and was ready for the final phase of its attack. A few seconds later the first torpedo reported active contact and began transmitting its lethal, short pings. The guidance officer released the first torpedo and cut the guide wire followed a few seconds later by the second torpedo.

"Conn, Weapons, torpedoes one and two report active acquisition, released to auto-home," reported Lt. David Brinker, the Torpedo Guidance Officer.

"Conn aye," Chandler acknowledged, a slight smile creeping onto his face.

Providence's two Mark 48 torpedoes quickly adjusted course, accelerated to fifty-five knots, and bore down on the black hull of the *Bratsk* with chilling disregard for the lives on board. The *Bratsk*, moving southeast at eight knots, had been oblivious to the incoming threats until the two torpedoes went active. Excited screams filled *Bratsk's* control room as the two inbound contacts were reported. Evasive maneuvers and countermeasures were ordered but they were completely ineffective because the two racing Mark 48s crossed the remaining two thousand yards in approximately twenty-four seconds.

The first of *Providence's* torpedoes crashed into the *Bratsk's* hull forty feet behind the sail and exploded with terrifying force. The explosion ripped a five foot hole in the pressure hull, by itself a mortal wound. Five seconds later the second torpedo smashed into the hull just thirty feet from the bow of the *Bratsk*. The second torpedo exploded and ripped the entire forward section off as the *Bratsk's* own torpedoes detonated. No one on board the *Bratsk* survived for more than a few seconds as the frigid water of the North Atlantic surged through the gaping holes in the hull. Icy water roared throughout the ship smashing equipment and crewmen alike as it dragged the dying ship to the ocean floor thousands of feet below.

Inside *Providence*, Chandler heard the unmistakable double bang as the two Mark 48s struck their target. For almost a full minute sonar operators listened to the lonely, chilling echoes of secondary explosions as the *Bratsk's* hull collapsed from the pressure of the ocean as it plummeted downward toward its dark, icy grave. The Russian ship would never be seen again. *Providence's* attack had been so swift and skillful there was no possibility the crew would have been able to send any kind of signal. It would be many hours or even days before the *Bratsk's* escort ships determined for certain she was lost.

Feeling nothing personal about the task he had just completed, Chandler remained icy cold in the face of the death he had just meted out, recognizing, and fully accepting, the demands of his country. Demands he carried out faithfully. If the situation demanded, he was fully prepared to die carrying out those duties, as was every other member of *Providence's* crew. But that day it had been someone else's turn to die.

Lcdr. Graham was the first one in the control room to speak. "Captain, shall we go after the surface contact?"

"No. I don't think that would be prudent," Chandler advised. "It would be difficult to get close enough with the anti-submarine helicopters searching the area. I think we should depart the area and phone this in once we are safely clear of the area,".

He believed they had been extremely fortunate to escape the attack and something was not right about the way the Russian Akula had fired upon them. Why had they fired on *Providence* without the least provocation. How had they known where *Providence* was? Too many unanswered questions. The incident definitely needed to be phoned in.

"Helm, Conn, left full rudder. Come to course two-one-zero. Ahead standard. Make turns for twelve knots. Dive, Conn, ten degree down bubble. Make your depth nine hundred fifty feet," Chandler ordered. He would take *Providence* deep and clear the area before returning to periscope depth to report the attack.

"Conn, Helm, left full rudder. Come to course two-one-zero aye. Ahead standard. Make turns for twelve knots aye."

"Conn aye."

"Conn, Dive, ten degree down bubble. Make your depth nine hundred fifty feet aye."

"Conn aye."

Providence passed through a halocline at three hundred ten feet and became virtually invisible, descending into the inky blackness of the Sohm Abyssal Plain. In the Russian battlecruiser's control room, sonar picked up the explosions and then both contacts simply vanished. The battlecruiser's crew had no idea if the American submarine had been sunk or if it had escaped. Their search would be fruitless because *Providence* was long gone and the Akula class submarine, *Bratsk,* was resting on the bottom of the ocean.

When he was certain *Providence* had evaded the surface ship, Chandler turned the boat over to Lcdr. Graham and went to his cabin to draft a message to send to COMSUBLANT. He sat down at his desk and slid a blank piece of paper in front of him. Incredibly tired from the tension, he leaned forward and rubbed his temples. A splitting, stress headache had developed at the base of his skull, a result of the massive amount of adrenaline his body had pumped though his veins during the past thirty minutes.

He deliberated for several minutes then picked up a pencil and composed the message very carefully:

YYYY DE XXXX 012/34
YYYYXXXX RUCBXXX3456 17118855-UUUU-RMFRSUU.
ZNR UUUUU
P 104518Z JUL 14
FM: USS PROVIDENCE SSN719
TO: COMSUBLANT
BT
CLAS //N01950//
1. USS PROVIDENCE ATTACKED SOUTH OF LAURENTIAN TROUGH
2. SUBMERGED TARGET CONFIRMED, RUSSIAN AKULA CLASS SUBMARINE, K-391, BRATSK
3. NO KNOWN REASON FOR ATTACK
4. NO PROVOCATION GIVEN
5. SUBMERGED CONTACT DEAD IN THE WATER
6. SECOND SURFACE CONTACT CLASSIFIED, KIROV CLASS CRUISER, PYOTR VELIKIY.
7. ANTI-SUBMARINE HELICOPTERS LAUNCHED FROM CRUISER, DROPPED SONOBUOYS AND DIPPING RADAR
8. TORPEDO AVOIDED, USING EVASIVE MANEUVERS AND DECOYS
9. FIRED TWO MARK 48 TORPEDOES
10. TARGET KILL CONFIRMED BY PRIMARY AND SECONDARY EXPLOSIONS AND BY HULL POPPING AS CONTACT BROKE UP AND SANK
11. INTEND NO FURTHER ATTACK ON ESCORT SURFACE SHIP(S)
12. DEPARTED AREA, AWAITING FURTHER INSTRUCTIONS
13. WILL RE-CONTACT AT DESIGNATED INTERVAL(S)
BT
2019

Chandler returned to the control center, resumed command, and waited until *Providence* was safely out of range of the Russian battlecruiser and its helicopters. He ordered *Providence* to periscope depth. In the radio room, the Task Group Operator (TGO) accessed the satellite and sent the flash message traffic in less than thirty seconds. Five seconds later *Providence* was back on its way deep, becoming invisible in the cold Atlantic waters. The message transmission was completed at 0655, Eastern Daylight Time. At 0736 Eastern Daylight Time Matthew Tyler, the President's National Security Advisor, nearly had a coronary when he was aroused from a sound sleep and was handed the message.

"HOLY MOTHER OF GOD!" he shrieked as grabbed his clothes and hurriedly got dressed. Visions of World War Three swirled in his mind as he sprinted out the door and headed for the Defense Intelligence Agency Communications Center.

CHAPTER EIGHTEEN

Thursday, March 26 - 0809 Eastern Daylight Time
Outside the Whitehouse Situation Room
Washington, D.C.

Outside the entrance to the Whitehouse Situation Room in the basement of the West Wing, Matthew Tyler, the National Security Advisor, paced nervously back and forth, waiting. He had called Vice Admiral Beckwith as soon as he had reached the Defense Intelligence Agency Communications Center and had signed out the hardcopy of the flash message handed to him thirty minutes earlier.

He stopped pacing and stiffened when he noticed Vice Admiral Beckwith sprinting down the hall. "In here Admiral," he shrieked as he grabbed Beckwith's arm, directing him into the empty office.

"What is it?" Beckwith asked as Tyler shoved him through the doorway.

Tyler held up his hand to silence Beckwith as he turned and locked the door. "Here, look at this!" he instructed.

He watched Beckwith as he read the flash message. He could see the Admiral's eyes flitting back and forth across the page.

"What the ... When did this come in?" Beckwith exclaimed adding just the right amount of excitement he thought the National Security Advisor would expect.

"A little over thirty minutes ago, Admiral," he answered.

"We'll need the full security council and the Joint Chiefs on this one," Beckwith advised, looking at his watch. "This was received at ten forty-five Zulu and the next comm check by *Providence* should be at twenty hundred Zulu, less than seven hours from now. We obviously will not be able to meet and have an update for the next comm check ...," Beckwith paused. "Ahh ... the second comm check will be zero seven hundred Zulu on Friday. Still doesn't give us much time."

"There's no way on Earth we can get the full council and chiefs together and draft a response by then," Tyler said.

"I agree," Beckwith responded. "I'll notify my team and we'll get started on a preliminary response. I'll make certain we have something for *Providence* by the second comm check."

"Agreed," Tyler replied, unlocking the door. "I'll go notify the duty watch officer to start making the calls and you get your team started."

Tyler pulled the door open and waited for the Admiral to leave the office. Tyler turned right and hurried toward the duty watch officer's desk while Beckwith turned left and headed for the spare office he used to prepare for special meetings.

Beckwith could not help but smile as he pushed the door open and exited the building. He had been worried when he had no choice but to reassign *Providence* and order her to put to sea early, but the timing had worked out perfectly and he would be able to draft the exact response he wanted. "Nobody will be able to stop me now," he whispered under his breath.

* * *

Thursday, March 26 - 0830 Eastern Daylight Time
White House Situation Room
Washington, D.C.

Vice Admiral Harlan Beckwith and National Security Advisor Matthew Tyler waited impatiently as the last two of the Joint Chiefs filed into the Situation Room and took their respective seats. The Whitehouse Situation Room, not the spacious war room packed with glitzy equipment that many people think it is, is actually a small suite of rooms, with a conference room at its core. The conference room is eighteen feet square with seating for twenty-four people. One high-ranking official once called it, "uncomfortable, unaesthetic, and essentially oppressive." However, for the President and his advisors, it is absolutely vital to national security.

The mission of the Whitehouse Situation Room is to provide current intelligence and crisis support to the security council staff, the National Security Advisor, and the President. In effect, the Situation Room is a twenty-four/seven, one-stop repository for the sensitive information flowing into and out of the White House. It is also the conduit through which most communications, especially classified information, passes.

The Joint Chiefs' service aides filled coffee cups and left the room. As the aides left, the door was closed and a security guard stepped in front of the door to make certain absolutely no one entered.

As in their previous meeting, all members of the Joint Chiefs had been invited to the emergency meeting of the National Security Council because of the military involvement contained in the materials to be discussed. The last attendee, President Cantwell, had been invited due to the seriousness of the threat. Any change to the United States' defense readiness condition (DEFCON) status would require his authorization.

As soon as the door was closed, Beckwith's senior aide placed a sealed folder in front of each of the meeting attendees. Beckwith and his aide conferred in hushed tones and then the senior aide also left the room.

"Gentlemen you may open your folders," Beckwith announced.

Everyone slid their hand under and broke the black and white, diagonal stripped security seal. There was much shifting in seats and murmurs under their breath as the documents were read.

Beckwith stepped to the front center of the room and addressed the assembled group, "Gentlemen the message in your folders was received less than one hour ago. As you recall, less than twenty-four hours ago we met in this room and discussed the worsening threat in central Europe. We all agreed and committed to the repositioning of communications satellites to gather additional intelligence. Additionally, we committed to the repositioning of military assets to counterbalance the threat in the event a quick response became necessary."

Before Beckwith could continue, President Cantwell interrupted, "Admiral, do we have any new imagery from the satellites?"

"Only some very preliminary images which have not been fully analyzed as yet sir," Beckwith answered. "The satellite re-tasking was completed less than two hours ago. It will likely be several hours before we have definitive output from the analysis section. Also, the area where the attack took place is on the very periphery of the re-targeted area visible to the satellites."

Before anyone else count interrupt, Beckwith punched the button on a small remote in his left hand. The lights dimmed and a detailed map of the North Atlantic Ocean appeared on the front wall of the Situation Room. Beckwith withdrew a small laser pointer from his pocket and focused the beam of red light on a cluster of icons representing Russian ships. "Gentlemen, this is very early, raw imagery from the satellite as it was repositioning. It shows a group of Russian ships, two cruisers, the *Ochakov*, a Kara class cruiser, the *Pyotr Velikiy*, a Kirov class cruiser, the *Bezuderzhny*, a Sovremenny class guided missile destroyer, the *Vorovsky*, a Krivak III Class Anti-Submarine Warfare Frigate, and, we believe, at least one Akula class submarine. These ships were in close proximity to the area where *Providence* was attacked. We feel this group is the likely perpetrator of the attack on *Providence*."

Beckwith paused and looked around the room. Assured he had everyone's attention, he continued. "There is also intelligence indicating a number of additional Russian ships are preparing to leave port. The frenzied activity in those ports would seem to suggest the sailings will be earlier than planned. The incident involving *Providence*, this new information, and the information we discussed yesterday clearly indicates a rapidly escalating, and ominous threat. Gentlemen, I suggest we raise the threat level and move our forces to DEFCON 2."

Fleet Admiral Douglas Bennington, seated half way down the table spoke up, "Admiral Beckwith, have we had any further contact with *Providence?*"

"No sir. We did not have time to meet before *Providence's* first scheduled comm check. The next comm check is ..." Beckwith paused and looked at the large clock on the wall. "At twenty-two hundred Eastern Daylight Time. We have just under twelve hours before the next comm check, Admiral Bennington. I and the OPSDEPS team agree we should immediately move all forces to the increased level of readiness. The team further agrees we should contact the *Providence* and turn her back toward the Russian convoy with orders to closely track their movement while waiting for other assets to arrive in the area. Based on the unprovoked attack, we believe Commander Chandler should be given preemptive launch authority."

This time it was General of the Army, William Danvers that interrupted. "Admiral, surely you can't suggest that we turn a submarine commander loose with the authority to shoot at anything he wants to."

"Yes, General, that is most assuredly what I suggest we do!" Beckwith shot back at the General. "Commander Chandler is one of our most experienced sub commanders. And I might remind you that less than two hours ago he and his crew were fired upon by that Russian convoy. An unprovoked attack I might add."

"We can't be certain of that," Danvers said.

"Who else do you suppose it was General? There aren't any other ships within five hundred miles of that area," Beckwith responded, sarcasm dripping from his voice.

"Hold on gentlemen," President Cantwell interrupted, knowing that Admiral Beckwith and General Danvers didn't much care for each other and had had confrontations on numerous occasions in the past. Cantwell would not allow the meeting to turn into a power struggle between them. "I think we need to focus on the situation at hand. Admiral Beckwith, do we have any intelligence that would indicate a reason for this seemingly unprovoked attack?"

"Absolutely nothing sir," Beckwith answered.

"Well then, I concur with your suggestion to raise the alert level of our military forces, however I believe DEFCON 3 is sufficient. I also concur that *Providence* should be directed to track the Russian convoy. I want it made clear to Commander Chandler *Providence* is to maintain a safe distance from the Russian convoy and to track their movements only."

Beckwith was about to interrupt, but a raised hand from President Cantwell silenced him. Cantwell continued. "I want every available analyst we can find assigned to review the latest data coming in from the satellites."

Cantwell turned and looked directly at the Director of the CIA, "And I want you to turn up the heat on every contact you have in Central Europe. I want to know what is going on and I want to know yesterday! Do I make myself clear?"

"Absolutely, Mr. President," Michael Ellwood, Director of the CIA responded.

"Anything else?" Cantwell questioned, his attention returning to Admiral Beckwith.

"Yes sir," Beckwith answered without hesitation. "The language in *Providence's* message indicates the submerged contact was waiting in ambush for them. That being the case Mister President, there must be a very high level leak somewhere in our organization. I recommend knowledge of this incident be limited to a strict need to know basis."

"So ordered," Cantwell agreed. "Gentlemen, this information is not to be shared with anybody outside this room without my direct approval. Admiral Beckwith be certain to pass the word to OPSDEP that they are not to discuss this incident with anyone."

Everyone in the room jumped to attention as the President pushed his chair back and stood up. "I expect frequent updates Admiral Beckwith," he said as he turned and left the room.

Beckwith swore under his breath. He had been certain his plan would be accepted without any changes. President Cantwell's resistance could possibly delay his plan by several days. A delay was simply unacceptable. He would have to bring other contingencies into play sooner than he had planned.

CHAPTER NINETEEN

Jamison Rhodes walked up to the maintenance division receptionist's desk and asked, "Where is that lazy bum Spangler?"

"He called in sick this morning, Mister Rhodes," Martha answered. "Didn't you get my message?"

"No, I didn't get any message," Rhodes snapped. "I've been too busy. Haven't been to my desk since I came in. Did Spangler say anything about the job I assigned him yesterday?"

"No, not a word. Just said he's still sick and wouldn't be in today."

"Get that idiot on the phone right now," Rhodes bellowed.

Mr. Rhodes stood there strumming his fingers on the desk while Martha searched the card file for Marvin's home phone number. She dialed the number and waited.

Marvin was startled awake by the ringing of the phone. He still had a ferocious headache. His head hurt so badly he could hardly focus his eyes. As he reached for the phone, he knocked the lamp off the night stand.

He had to be suffering from more than a hangover, having been up half the night vomiting. In addition, he was fighting horrible chills. He picked up the phone, swallowed hard to fight back another wave of nausea, and answered weakly, "Hello."

As soon as Marvin answered, Martha handed the receiver to Rhodes. "Spangler, this is Jamison Rhodes. Why didn't you come in this morning? You have an important job that must be completed today."

"Sorry, sir," Marvin whispered. "I'm really sick. I've been up half the night and I have a splitting headache."

"I don't care what your problem is. I expect you here in an hour. If you don't finish that job by the end of the day you're fired. Do you understand me Spangler?" Rhodes yelled at the receiver.

"Spangler, did you hear me? Spangler, answer me!" Rhodes screamed, the veins along his temples bulging.

Marvin had not heard a word Rhodes screamed at him because he had given into the latest wave of nausea and had run for the bathroom.

Rhodes' face was beet red, the veins in his neck purple and distended, when he slammed the receiver back into its cradle. Martha was afraid he was going to have a stroke right on the spot. In her mind, there was little doubt one day his terrible temper would get the better of him.

"Martha, where is Kent Monahan working today?" Rhodes asked angrily.

"I believe he is working somewhere on the south arm of the antenna," Martha replied, offering no more information than what Rhodes asked for.

"Call dispatch and have them contact him on the radio. Tell him to drop whatever he is doing and come to my office immediately."

Rhodes turned and headed off down the hall toward his office before Martha could answer. Rhodes walked into his office and slammed the door so hard several items fell off the bookcase standing beside the door.

"Morons. I'm surrounded by morons," he complained, slumping down in the chair behind his desk. "How, can I be expected to run a maintenance department full of morons?"

Marvin was deathly sick. There was little doubt in his mind he had triggered his ulcer again with his drinking as he was now vomiting blood. His doctor had warned him repeatedly he would kill himself someday if he did not stay away from alcohol, but at this point Marvin just did not care.

Two weeks earlier he had agreed to hide some specialized electronic circuits at two microwave sites. The two men frightened him but he desperately needed the money and he was to be paid quite well. His idiot boss continually refused to recommend him for a raise, so he justified the sabotage in his mind. Three days ago the men had paid him another visit. He had become even more frightened when they had warned him in no uncertain terms of the danger if he talked to anyone.

Marvin was as weak as a kitten, having vomited blood on his last two trips to the bathroom. Holding on to the rim of the toilet, he struggled to get to his feet, far too sick to notice the figure slipping up behind him. The individual, dressed completely in black, grabbed him by the back of the neck and smashed his head against the rim of the toilet with such force the porcelain toilet bowl cracked completely to the floor.

The force cracked Marvin's skull. He jerked and quivered for a few seconds, then lay motionless. The hooded figure bent over and placed two fingers on Marvin's throat, feeling for a pulse.

The hooded figure straightened up, pulled a cell phone from his pocket, and pressed a speed dial button.

"Yeah," a male voice on the other end answered.

"The stupid imbecile has been silenced."

"Are you absolutely certain? There had better not be any more screw ups or you will be next. Do I make myself clear?"

"Absolutely."

The hooded figure ended the call and stuffed the cell phone back in his pocket. Stepping over Marvin's lifeless body he slipped out the bathroom window.

"How stupid. People should learn to lock their windows," the figure laughed as he pushed the window closed. He slipped off the black ski mask and disappeared without raising anyone's attention.

Rhodes sat at his office desk rubbing his temples, another stress headache building at the base of his skull. The headaches were coming a lot more frequently.

He jumped when the phone rang, the sudden movement causing a large stack of paperwork to slide off his desk. The papers hit the floor and scattered across the floor. "What now," he growled as he reached for the phone. "This is Rhodes," he hissed into the receiver.

It was his boss, the director of site operations. "What are the results of the microwave system check I asked you to complete yesterday?" he asked.

"The check hasn't been completed yet," Rhodes answered in defense. "The technician I assigned to the job went home sick yesterday and didn't come in this morning either."

"Do you have only one technician that can handle a job that simple?"

"No sir. I already have a replacement technician on the way."

"I want that job completed by the end of the day even if you have to do it yourself. Notify me the instant it has been completed."

The line went dead. Mr. Rhodes dropped the receiver into its cradle, the veins in his temples bulging, his headache intensifying rapidly.

"That's it!" he bellowed as he got up from his desk. "Mr. Spangler is fired as of right now! I will not tolerate that idiot's incompetence any longer!"

He walked to the door, jerked it open, and stomped down the hall toward the receptionist's desk. He stopped at the receptionist's desk and bellowed, "Martha, call Human Resources and tell them to terminate Spangler immediately. No notice, no severance, no nothing. Then call Spangler and tell him he can report to Human Resources for his final pay check whenever he feels up to it."

He turned back toward his office, stopped for several moments, then turned back toward Martha's desk. "Has Kent Monahan called in yet?"

"No. Dispatch has not called back," Martha replied, again offering only the information Rhodes asked for. When he was in one of his moods, the less said the better.

"Morons, all morons," he muttered as he threw up his hands, turned the opposite direction, and headed for the far end of the building. He turned his head and shouted over his shoulder, "If anyone calls, I'll be in the microwave equipment room. I'll do the blasted microwave check myself."

Stopping at the test equipment storage locker, he gathered all the test equipment he would need and headed for the microwave equipment room. He unlocked the equipment room door, propped it open, and pushed the cart he had loaded with test equipment into the room.

As he stepped in front of the microwave equipment rack, he noticed the alarm annunciator card had been pulled out. He pushed the annunciator card into the card socket, immediately setting off the alarm. Two racks lower he saw that the master signaling channel card had also been pulled. He pushed the channel card in but the alarm did not stop.

It was obvious that Spangler had deliberately disabled the entire alarm circuit. Far worse, the alarm had been disabled all night. He hoped nothing serious had happened during the night. If it had, his boss would have his head.

He reached up and pulled the alarm annunciator card out to silence the alarm. Picking up the phone, he punched in the number for dispatch.

"Dispatch. This is Alvarez. May I help you?" a heavily accented voice at the other end answered.

"This is Rhodes. Were there any microwave system problems reported on the overnight shift?"

"Just a minute sir. I'll check last night's log," Alvarez stalled, flipping through the pages in the log book. "Ah, yes sir there it is. The operations office at Alamogordo reported there was no response on the master signaling channel at twelve forty-seven hours yesterday."

"Are you certain about the time? Why wasn't I notified?"

"Yes sir, the time is correct. There's also a note in the log book indicating MSI's field engineer was testing the system. I imagine everyone assumed he had the channel interrupted to test signal levels."

"Everyone assumed!" Rhodes spat into the phone. "Is there an entry in the log indicating MSI's field engineer called to say he was taking the signaling channel off line?"

Alvarez hesitated. Everybody in the Outside Electronics Department was keenly aware of Rhodes' hair trigger temper.

"Well, is there?" Rhodes asked again.

"No."

"Mr. Alvarez, you know the procedure as well as I do. I am to be notified if there is an unexplained outage of any kind. How would you describe that outage, Mr. Alvarez?"

"I ahh… ahh… I guess it's unexplained," Alvarez answered sheepishly.

"Yeah, I guess it is!" Rhodes yelled. "Hold on a minute," Rhodes said. He walked over to the microwave system, pushed in the master signaling channel card, and returned to the phone. "Call Alamogordo and ask them to test the signaling channel. Then call me back at extension two-eight-nine."

"Yes sir. Right away sir," Alvarez responded.

"How can people be so unbelievably stupid?" Rhodes growled as he returned to the microwave system. He didn't know how much longer he could take this stress. His department's overall performance had been deteriorating for months. If it got any worse he would be finished. During their last weekly staff meeting, his boss had warned him further deterioration would not be tolerated. This fiasco would likely be the final straw.

He leaned against the equipment rack, his headache raging. But he refused to let it affect him. He would not go home sick like that gutless wimp Spangler had.

He pulled the master signaling card out of the rack, sliding it into an extender card, thereby allowing him access to all the circuits and test points on the channel card. The phone rang as he was about to connect an oscilloscope to test the input signal level.

He grabbed the receiver, "What did you find out from Alamogordo? Did the retest work?"

"No sir. Alamogordo says the signaling channel is still out," Alvarez answered.

"Has anybody heard from MSI's field engineer? His name is Hargrove I believe."

"No sir. Not a word. I even asked the duty operator at Alamogordo. He checked his log clear back to eleven hundred hours yesterday. Says there is absolutely no reference to a Mister Hargrove or the microwave system on his end. I also tried contacting him via the order wire circuit on the microwave system. Still no response"

"Call the Desert Sands Motel in Socorro and ask if anybody there has heard from him. Do it now on another line. I'll hold on this line. This is critical. I need an answer now."

He stood there for several minutes rubbing his temples with his free hand, listening to the elevator music coming from the earpiece.

Alvarez came back on the line. "No one at the motel has seen him since early yesterday morning. The front desk said he did not pick up his messages last night or this morning. Sounds suspicious to me."

"Yes, I agree," Rhodes replied. "Call Alamogordo and have them alert the Air Police. Have someone backtrack the tower sites starting from their end. Tell them to find out which tower site Mister Hargrove is working at and radio it in. Call me back at this extension the instant you hear anything."

CHAPTER TWENTY

Jamison Rhodes tested the signaling channel circuitry thoroughly and found absolutely nothing wrong at the NRAO location, which meant there had to be something wrong with the circuitry at one of the microwave tower sites. He was in the process of disconnecting the test equipment leads when the phone rang.

He lifted the receiver from its cradle and answered, "Rhodes."

"Sir, uh, I just got off the phone with Alamogordo," dispatch operator Alvarez said, his voice wavering. "Mister Hargrove is dead."

"What? You've got to be kidding!" Rhodes stammered. "When? How did it happen?"

"The sergeant I spoke with said someone found his overturned vehicle early this morning. The state patrol thinks he drove off the road sometime yesterday, late morning or early afternoon is their best guess. They said the Bronco he was driving rolled several times. The coroner said the preliminary cause of death appeared to be severe head injuries."

Rhodes was utterly stunned, "Good God, just what I need. Another catastrophe to deal with. Get me the number for.... Never mind. I'm going back to my office. If you get any additional information, call me there."

Rhodes did not even bother to finish disconnecting the test equipment. He locked the door to the equipment room and hurried down the hall, yelling at Martha as he rushed past her desk, "Get MSI's office on the phone right away. Buzz me in my office as soon as you reach them."

He walked into his office and fell into his chair. "Why me? Why is all this happening to me?" he asked himself, blood pounding in his temples like a giant bass drum. Feeling dizzy, he knew had to calm down. He could not let this job continue to get to him. It was a lousy job and not worth the aggravation.

The intercom on Rhodes' desk buzzed, "Mister Rhodes, MSI is on line two."

He snatched the receiver from its cradle, "This is Jamison Rhodes at the National Radio Astronomy Observatory. Is Zach Templeton there?"

"No. Mister Templeton is vacationing in the Bahamas," Miss Janine Wilmot, MSI's receptionist, answered. "He won't be back until late tomorrow afternoon. May I help you?".

"We've got serious trouble here. Have you spoken with anybody from the New Mexico State Patrol?" Rhodes asked.

No, I haven't. Is there some reason I should have?" Miss Wilmot asked, becoming fearful of what the answer might be.

Rhodes took a deep breath, "I hate to break the news this way, but someone has to tell you. The New Mexico State Patrol found Fred Hargrove dead this morning. Apparently he drove his vehicle off the highway and rolled down a steep embankment. He was pronounced dead at the scene."

He waited for several moments and when Miss Wilmot did not respond he continued, "Miss Wilmot are you there?"

"Yes, I'm here. I just can't believe it. I just spoke with Fred yesterday morning," answered a disbelieving Miss Wilmot.

"Did Mr. Hargrove have any family?" Rhodes asked.

"Yes, a wife, Rachael. They didn't have any children. I don't know how I'm going to tell her. They were so much in love. She is going to be devastated."

"Did Mister Hargrove say anything about the microwave system? Did he indicate anything was malfunctioning and, if so, what may have been wrong?"

"He said was he was going to recheck the last three tower sites. He told me he planned to finish all three sites and catch an early flight home."

"Well, something is still seriously wrong with the system. The entire master signaling channel is off line. Mister Hargrove never reported anything to our dispatch center or to Alamogordo's operations center. It doesn't make any sense. Unless the system failed after he left the tower site at Monticello. The state patrol said they found him about two miles east of the tower site."

He was about to describe the accident but thought better of it, sensing Miss Wilmot was already upset enough and there was nothing to be gained. "Do you think you can catch Mister Templeton before he boards his flight to Tulsa? I need to talk with him as soon as possible."

"I can try, Mister Rhodes. The sailboat they are on is due to dock at the marina in Miami sometime before nine a.m. Friday morning. Their flight is scheduled to leave Miami at eleven forty-nine a.m. Where can Mister Templeton reach you if I catch him?"

"Tell him to call my office at the observatory. I'll be here. I'm really sorry about Mister Hargrove. Thank you for your help Miss Wilmot."

Rhodes hung up on his end and the line went dead, but Miss Wilmot just sat there with the receiver pressed against her ear, tears streaming down her cheeks. She laid the receiver back in its cradle and grabbed her purse from under the desk, retrieving a tissue and dabbing at her eyes.

"How am I going to tell Rachael?" she wondered out loud. The thought of telling Rachael Fred was dead filled her with dread, but she knew she had to do it. It would not be right to allow her to hear such ghastly news from a stranger. It needed to be done immediately before someone from New Mexico called.

She picked up the receiver and punched in the extension number for the map storage room. "Monica, come to my desk right now," she sobbed into the phone.

Upon hearing the sobs, Monica came running out of the map storage room and rushed up to Janine's desk. One look at Janine's tear stained face and she knew something was terribly wrong. "What's the matter Janine?"

"I just got a call from Mister Rhodes at the National Radio Astronomy Observatory. He told me they found Fred dead this morning," Janine sobbed.

"What happened? Does anybody know?" Monica asked.

"The New Mexico State Patrol said they found him early this morning in an overturned vehicle close to one of the microwave tower sites."

"That's awful. What can I do to help?"

"Watch the phones. I've got to go tell Rachael. Don't say anything to anybody until you hear from me."

"Please tell Rachael how sorry I am," Monica called out to Janine's back as she disappeared through the office door, heading for the elevator.

Janine ran across the parking lot, unlocked the car door, and slipped into the seat. She sat there dabbing at her eyes as she went over in her mind what she was going to say to Rachael. "Oh God, help me get through this," she pleaded as she started the engine and headed for Rachael's house.

CHAPTER TWENTY-ONE

Thursday, March 26 - 1611 Zulu
Rebiechowo Airport
Gdansk, Poland

Bill Morrison walked into the airport terminal building and quickly surveyed the interior. He located a restroom and splashed some cold water on his face. As he reached for a paper towel to dry his face, the gun in his duffle bag clunked against the porcelain sink. He had completely forgotten about the gun in his rush to the airport.

Carrying a gun into an airport was a really bad idea. Left with no other choice, he had to discard the gun. He ripped three paper towels from the dispenser and dried his face and hands. Glancing around the restroom and finding it to be empty, Bill pulled the gun from the duffle bag and quickly wrapped it in the wet paper towels. He stuffed it as deeply as he could in the trash barrel on his way out.

"Now what do I do?" Bill asked himself. He had enough cash in his pocket to go anywhere he wanted, but where? It would be impossible to get the documents he was carrying where they needed to go without help. Contacting his normal contact was out of the question. Someone outside the "agency" was what he needed. But who? Who did he know that had sufficient contacts and influence to help him escape his current predicament. A sudden insight flashed through his consciousness like a streak of lightning. He did know someone with the influence and contacts required. Bill walked past the ticket counters, past several newsstands, a snack shop, and a duty free liquor store. Bill selected a seating area overlooking the airport ramp and picked the most isolated seat he could find. His location gave him full view of everyone as they passed by. He carefully scrutinized the activity in the airport until he felt assured he had not been followed.

Bill fished a small, badly worn notebook from a zippered pocket of his duffle bag. Flipping through the pages, he scanned for the name of the one man he could trust, someone from the records section at the Pentagon. He called the man and begged him for the home contact number of someone he had not talked to in a very long time. Bill waited, listening to the tapping of keys followed by silence. More tapping of keys. More silence. Bill scribbled a number down as the man read it from his computer screen.

Bill thanked the man profusely and instructed him to tell absolutely no one of their conversation. Taking a deep breath, he punched the number into his cell phone and waited, extremely worried about the response he felt certain the call would evoke.

After four rings, an unexpected female voice answered, "Hello."

"Is he there?" Bill asked, not wanting to reveal anything without being certain he was talking to the right person.

"Yeah, just a minute," the female voice mumbled, her mouth full of food.

Muffled voices and the clinking of silverware. A male voice, tinged with irritation because of the mealtime interruption, answered, "Yeah, what?"

"Dah-he-tih-hi," Bill spoke slowly and deliberately into the phone.

"Huh? Is this a joke? Who is this?" the male voice demanded.

"Dah-he-tih-hi, Chin-di, Lha-Cha-Eh," Bill repeated, adding two additional code words.

"Yes, I'm listening," Commander Owen Patterson responded.

"Tse-Gah, Ah-Nah, Dibeh-Zazzie, Bi-So-Dih," Bill spoke slowly and distinctly, using code words from the Navajo language because it was an undecipherable code, being an unwritten language of extreme complexity. Its many dialects, made it virtually unintelligible to anyone without extensive exposure and training. The Navajo language had no alphabet or symbols, and was spoken only on reservations of the Southwest United States. One estimate claimed less than three dozen non-Navajos could understand the language.

The Navajo code was used extensively by U.S. Marine divisions during World War II to transmit secure telephone and radio messages. It was used in every assault the U.S. Marines conducted in the Pacific. In all that time the code was never broken by anyone.

It was for that reason Navy SEAL Team Four, of which Bill had been a member, used the code for situations requiring extremely secure communications. Only a handful of SEAL team members, less than five in actuality, had been trained to use it. That handful, including the man Bill was talking to, had used it extensively for emergency extractions. Bill used the code, knowing it would get the man's attention and it would verify his identity.

"Yes, I get it," Patterson acknowledged. "You can be one of only two people. Which are you? No, wait," he said, pushing his chair back from the table.

"I'm going to take this in the other room dear. Hang up for me when I get there," he said to his wife as he walked toward the doorway. He walked into the den and switched on the light. "I've got it," he hollered, pushing the door closed.

Patterson waited until he heard the click of the receiver being replaced. "Okay, go ahead. Which one are you?"

"Little Bear," Bill said, waiting for a response.

"Not possible. He died in an ambush in the jungle years ago."

"The only other soul that knows the code is Na-Hash-Chid and I'm not him. You know that," Bill declared.

"How is that possible? I saw ...."

Bill interrupted, "I can't explain now. Just believe it."

"Okay, say I believe you. Why are you calling me after all this time?"

"Is it safe to talk?" Bill asked.

"This is my personal residence. The line is not secure," Patterson replied.

Bill shrugged. "I guess I don't have any choice. I'm in serious trouble. I'm working deep cover and have uncovered a level four threat. I have documents that absolutely must get to the right people. My normal channel has been compromised. I've been ambushed three times. Someone is leaking information. I have no one else I can trust."

"I don't know if I can help you," Patterson objected, not certain he wanted to get involved.

"You absolutely have to!" Bill pleaded into the phone as loudly as he dared. "There is more at stake here than you can possibly imagine. Thousands will die if you don't help me, maybe more!"

"Thousands? Come on! Surely, you can't ...."

"Listen to me!" Bill demanded, cutting Patterson off. "I swear on the graves of all those we lost from Team-Four. You are the only one that can help me. I need someone to provide back channel support. You know, off the record support."

"Are you crazy?" Patterson protested. "You call me out of the blue and expect me to believe some wild tale about a level four threat. If I do what you ask and get caught, my career is over. And I would probably go to prison."

"If you don't and I get caught, you will likely find yourself standing right smack dab in the middle of World War Three," Bill snapped angrily. He hoped to avoid revealing any information but it looked like it was time for him to play a trump card. A very big trump card. "Do you know Vice Admiral Harlan Beckwith?"

"Of course I know him," Patterson answered. "He's the Director of OPSDEPS, advises the Joint Chiefs."

"Well, I have a photo of him meeting with several members of a violent, and extremely dangerous, group. They are well funded, expertly trained, and fanatical in their desire to destroy the United States. I am dead serious when I tell you I believe they have the ability to do just that," Bill added.

"Come on," Patterson repeated. "We've analyzed dozens of such threats. They all turn out to be nothing more than noisy posturing by demented fanatics. I don't doubt the group you speak of is dangerous, but World War Three? Get a grip."

"Get a grip you say!" Bill blurted out, deciding it was time for desperate measures. "This group may be fanatics, but demented, no. Noisy posturing, not hardly. Have you heard of Operation Brushfire?"

Patterson gasped. "Where did you hear that? There are less than a dozen people in the world that are supposed to know about that. Its new and its hot."

"Same source as the photo. Somebody is feeding information to this group. If the number of people cleared on the operation is as small as you say, then the leak is very high. Wouldn't you agree?" Bill added sarcastically

"Yes. What's your point?" Patterson asked.

"My point is that we can trust no one. I need your help to get the documents I'm carrying to someone I can trust. There is no one else that can help me?" Bill pleaded.

"Okay, you convinced me. But I'll need some time to put a plan together," Patterson answered.

"Time is something I have precious little of," Bill exclaimed. "I need something now! I will call you back in ten minutes. I at least need the beginnings of a plan,"

Patterson did not answer. His mind searching through the list of contacts he knew, searching for a name, someone, anyone that he could trust implicitly, someone who had authority to accomplish what was required. He was still deep in thought when Bill interrupted him, "Are you still there?"

"Yes. I'm coming up blank. I need time. Call me back."

"Ten minutes. I cannot emphasize enough how serious this is. Be very, very careful who you talk to," Bill said as he ended the call.

Bill sat for a few seconds studying the activity within his field of vision. No quick, furtive glances in his direction. No faces peeking over a newspaper or magazine. He got up and strolled over to a food kiosk adjacent to the main terminal. Bill ordered a medium, mocha latte. He slipped a cardboard ring around the cup to insulate his fingers from the hot liquid and returned to the same seat.

Steam curled up and fogged up the lenses of his glasses as he blew across the hot liquid. He watched and waited impatiently for ten minutes to pass.

Seconds seemed like hours as waited. He sipped the hot, chocolaty, coffee mixture. He watched. He waited. Throngs of passengers clutching all manner of bags and packages hurried to catch their flights. People milled around the security entrance that led into the gate area, waiting for relatives to arrive from far away cities. A typical day in a busy airport. But it was anything but typical for Bill.

Precisely ten minutes from the time he ended his previous call, Bill flipped his cell phone open and pressed redial. On the very first ring Commander Patterson answered. "Yes?" he said with a questioning tone.

"Little Bear," Bill replied.

"Okay. I called in a favor. A *really* big favor," Patterson emphasized. "I don't have the final details yet but I have you covered for the next fifteen hours. Timing is going to be critical. You must be at the Port of London no later than zero six hundred Friday. You will receive the rest of your instructions from a man at the pier. Do you think you can make that?"

"Sounds pretty tight, but if everything goes off without a hitch I can make it," Bill replied.

"The cargo ship's name is *Przeznaczenia*, berthed at pier twenty-three. Your contact's name is Rajmund. He will have the rest of your instructions," Patterson advised. "I must warn you. This is the only chance you will get. I took immense risks. If you don't make it on time, or if you get caught, I won't be able to help you. You will be completely on your own."

"Understood," Bill acknowledged. "Oh, I need you to contact one other person."

"Way ahead of you," Patterson said calmly. "I expected as much. I already have someone trying to locate him."

"Thanks, I owe you," Bill said.

"Yes, you certainly do," Patterson agreed as he ended the call and busied himself with the task of completing arrangements for a ghost from the past, someone he thought to be long dead. When he talked to Rajmund, a preliminary, high-risk plan had been discussed. They both felt it might work but there were large obstacles that would require precise orchestration. The plan would require committing some very large assets, all outside the normal chain of command. It was not going to be easy to keep the details quiet.

Bill had been fully prepared for the fact that he would get only one chance. When you called in favors at such a high level, you could not expect any more than that.

Bill flipped the phone shut and removed the battery cover. He flipped the battery out and bent the contacts back and forth until they broke off. From this point on he would be on his own. On the way to the ticket counter, he dropped the destroyed cell phone in a trash bin.

At the British Airways ticket counter he waited in line only to learn there were no seats available on any flight either to London Heathrow or London

Gatwick. The same outcome occurred at the next three ticket counters he tried. Only two ticket counters remained. Starting to get worried, he stepped in line at the LOT Polish Airlines ticket counter and waited.

When Bill's turn came, he stepped up to the counter and asked for a ticket on the next flight to London. Bill breathed a sigh of relief when the ticket agent informed him there was one remaining seat on LOT flight 5831, departing in forty-five minutes. The ticket agent informed Bill the ticket price was one thousand two hundred eighty-one Euros. Under normal circumstances, Bill would have refused to pay over sixteen hundred US dollars for a short four and one-half hour flight, but these were not normal circumstances. He paid for the ticket with cash and ran for the gate.

CHAPTER TWENTY-TWO

Thursday, March 26 - 1549 Eastern Daylight Time
Submarine Force Atlantic (COMSUBLANT)
Building Three, Naval Submarine Base
New London, Connecticut

Lcdr. Paul Davis, command duty officer for Submarine Development Squadron Twelve, looked up from the book he was reading upon hearing the door to the communications center swing open. He quickly straightened in his chair and sat at attention seeing a chest full of ribbons and the two bright gold stars on the shoulder boards of the officer walking up to the counter.

"May I help you Admiral Hadley?" Davis asked after a quick glance at the name plate pinned slightly above the right breast pocket of the admiral's uniform jacket.

"Yes you may Mister Davis," Rear Admiral Hadley replied. "I have a highly classified flash message that must go out immediately."

"Ahh... Yes sir," Davis answered somewhat puzzled as it was outside SOP (standard operating procedure) for an admiral to hand deliver message traffic.

Hadley noticed the hesitation and confused look on Lcdr. Davis' face. "I know this is not SOP, Mister Davis, but it is critically urgent and absolutely must go out immediately. In addition, it is classified at the highest level, marked as "eyes only". I hand carried it to minimize the chances of it being leaked."

Hadley placed a small attaché case on the counter and thumbed in a four-digit cipher code. He opened the case, removed the message, and split the security seal on the message folder. "You will hold the message face down with the safety screen in place and slide the message into the communications scanner," Hadley instructed. "You will cover the message sheet with the safety screen as it exits the scanner. You will then return the message to me."

"Yes sir. I understand sir," Davis answered.

Davis walked over to the opposite wall of the communications center and fed the message sheet into the communication scanner keeping it covered exactly as instructed. The message sheet disappeared into the machine as the optical sensors read the characters and stored them in the machine's internal memory. Once the entire message was read, the control and routing codes were checked and verified for accuracy. An electronic version of the message was then transmitted to the appropriate transmitting circuitry for the destination identified in the message.

The screen on the scanner flashed "Complete" as the message sheet exited the machine. Davis reached down and held the security screen over the message sheet.

"Mister Davis, clear the transmit history for that message from the scanner," Hadley ordered.

"But sir, I... ," Davis started to say.

"I know what SOP says Mister Davis," Hadley interrupted. "I am giving you a direct order to delete the history of that message. I will assume full responsibility."

"Yes sir," Davis acknowledged as he selected the message history from the menu options. He scrolled through the entire list, selected the last message entry, and pressed "Clear". Against his better judgment, he pressed "OK" on the confirmation screen and all history of the message just sent was deleted from the machine's memory. Something seemed very wrong, but you simply did not argue with a two-star admiral.

Davis turned around and returned the message to the counter. He handed the message back to Hadley who placed the message back in the security folder and slipped it inside the attaché case. He closed the case and spun all digits of the cipher lock several times, making certain it was securely locked.

Hadley reached inside his uniform jacket and retrieved a small leather wallet from an interior pocket. He flipped it open and held out his security credentials for Davis to see. Lcdr. Davis' eyes widened when he saw the DNI (Director of Naval Intelligence) designation in the middle of the ID badge.

"You will forget all details of this event Mister Davis. I was not here. There was no message sent. There was no message erased," Hadley advised.

Davis started to say something but Hadley continued before he could get a word out, "Mister Davis, I repeat. I was not here. There was no message sent. There was no message erased. If a single word of this gets out, your career is over! Do you understand me?" Hadley said looking Davis directly in the eyes.

"Yes sir. Understood sir," Davis acknowledged.

"I am very glad Mister Davis because I do not make idle threats. I would hate to see you end up as an ensign on a destroyer somewhere in the

Persian Gulf," Hadley threatened as he turned on his heels and left the communications center.

Davis sat down and took a deep breath, visibly shaken. There was definitely something strange going on but he decided that whatever it was, he was not going to jeopardize his career over it.

"Message. What message?" he laughed to himself as he returned to his book.

* * *

Thursday, March 26 - 2002 Zulu
USS Providence SSN 719
Somewhere in the mid-Atlantic

Commander Chandler was sound asleep and snoring softly. He had taken two aspirins and had laid down to catch a short nap. He and the crew were still adjusting to the "at sea" change to Zulu time. Exhausted after the sudden attack and sinking of the Russian submarine, he had fallen asleep quickly, dreaming about an upcoming vacation. In spite of being sound asleep, the announcement blaring from the 1-MC jolted him awake.

"Alert One! Alert One!" echoed throughout all compartments of the boat.

Chandler sat upright in bed, struggling to clear the sleep from his mind. Fifteen seconds later someone pounded on his cabin door.

"Captain, Captain," Radioman Third Class Mike Hall, the duty Inbound/Outbound Radio Traffic Checker, shouted as he banged on the captain's cabin door. Hearing no reply, the duty radioman banged on the door again and shouted, "Captain. Captain."

"Yes. What is it?" Chandler called out through the closed door.

"Sir, this is the duty traffic checker. We have emergency EAM traffic on the long wire antenna," Hall shouted through the closed door.

"Wait one while I get dressed," Chandler replied, grabbing his shirt from a clothing hook beside his bunk. He buttoned the shirt, hurriedly stuffing the tail into his trousers. He threw open the door and shouted at the waiting radioman, "Let's go."

Together they ran forward heading for Control. Hall ducked into the radio room and Chandler continued on toward Control.

"I have the Conn," Chandler barked.

"Aye aye sir," Lcrd. Graham replied.

A few seconds later the officers not on watch arrived in Control. Officers were assigned in pairs to decode incoming Emergency Action Messages (EAMs). Lt. Brinker, Assistant Weapons Officer, and Lt. Jg. Kyle Johnson, Electrical Division Officer, formed decryption team one.

Decryption team one stopped and waited outside the Op Center, a small room adjacent to the radio room.

Radioman Chief Kenneth Barton, Radio Division Chief, peered through a small window in the door, recognizing the two officers waiting outside. He opened the door and allowed them into the cramped space. Lt. Brinker entered the combination into the safe containing the EAM codebook and jerked the door open. He withdrew the codebook and handed it to Lt. Jg. Johnson.

Barton stepped out of the Op Center into the radio room, ripped the EAM from the radio room printer, and returned a few seconds later with the EAM in his hand.

"EAM message sir," Barton announced, handing the piece of paper to Brinker.

A single three letter sequence of letters appeared on the paper. Brinker slowly read off the letters using the phonetic alphabet with Johnson looking over his shoulder, "ECHO – TANGO – FOXTROT." Together, they looked through the codebook to determine what action the EAM called for. Johnson returned the codebook to the safe while Brinker headed for Control.

"Captain, we have an EAM requesting *Providence* to break patrol orders and proceed to periscope depth to receive emergency flash message traffic," Brinker announced.

Chandler grabbed the 1-MC to make an announcement to the entire boat, "This is the Captain. We are going shallow to receive flash traffic. Rig the boat for ultra-quiet."

"Helm, Conn, all ahead slow. Dive Conn ten degree up bubble come to periscope depth smartly," Chandler ordered.

"Conn, Helm, all ahead slow," EM2 Marvin Connaly answered.

"Conn aye."

"Conn, Dive, Ten degree up bubble. Come to periscope depth smartly," the diving watch answered.

"Conn aye."

Chandler waited as the change in depth ticked off on the digital depth display. "XO you have the Conn. Maintain current depth and heading," he ordered as the boat reached periscope depth. "I don't want to stay at this depth longer than absolutely necessary. As soon as the flash traffic has been received and verified, I will instruct you to take the boat back to patrol depth."

Without waiting for a reply, Chandler stepped off the platform and ran for the radio room. As he stuck his head into the radio room, he looked over at the senior radioman. "Is the message complete and verified?"

"Just completing now sir," the radioman replied. "Starting verification."

Twenty seconds passed as the communications control computer compared the cryptographic control codes embedded in the message just received to those stored in its internal memory.

"Message verified sir."

"Very well. Print it," Chandler ordered. As soon as the printer stopped, he ripped the paper from the printer and began to read. A puzzled look came over his face as he read to the end of the message .

"XO, take the boat back to patrol depth," Chandler ordered. "As soon as we are back at patrol depth, turn the Conn over to Lieutenant Flanigan. Then meet me in my cabin."

Chandler turned and faced the crewmen on duty in the communication center. "Gentlemen, there was no message received here tonight. Anyone who says one word will find himself chipping paint on an oiler for the rest of his career. Do I make myself clear?"

Chandler looked directly at each man and waited for an acknowledgment. Satisfied they all understood, he folded the message in half, stepped into the passageway, and headed for his cabin.

Chandler poured himself a cup of coffee and waited the five minutes it took the boat to return to patrol depth. One minute later, Mister Graham knocked on the door.

"Enter," Chandler instructed.

Chandler unfolded the top portion of the message and slid it across the small desk to Mister Graham. The second half of the message had been removed and placed in Chandler's top desk drawer. "Well, Mr. Graham, what do you think?" Chandler asked.

Graham took a deep breath. "Sounds like something big is brewing sir," he answered. "Did the message say who or why?"

"I cannot tell you that. The remainder of the message was very explicit. I am to tell the crew, including the officers, only what is absolutely necessary," Chandler said.

"We're going to have to tell the department heads something sir," Graham responded.

"Only what's necessary XO. Round up the department heads and we'll meet in the wardroom in ten minutes. Tell them personally and quietly. No announcements on the internal communications system. Strict secrecy." Chandler ordered.

"Aye aye sir," Graham acknowledged as he left the Captain's cabin and headed for the control room.

Graham located each department head and personally notified each one there was a meeting with the Captain in the wardroom in ten minutes.

When Graham and the department heads entered the wardroom, Chandler was already seated at the head of the table waiting. He motioned to the empty chairs indicating they should be seated. "Coffee gentlemen?" he asked, waiting as the mess specialist filled the cups of all those wanting coffee. When the mess specialist finished, the Captain followed him to the door and closed and locked it behind him. Returning to the head of the table, he sat down.

Chandler surveyed the faces of those seated at the table: Lcdr. Graham, Executive Officer; Lt. Edwin Harris, Weapons Officer; Lt. Conroy Sullivan, Engineering Officer; Lt. Kent Madoc, Communications Officer; and Lt. Thomas Flanigan, Navigation Officer. The expression on their faces suggested they were eager to find out what had drawn them away from their normal duties.

Chandler took a sip of coffee from his cup then began, "Gentlemen, what I am about to tell you is to stay in this room. The crew can be told only what is absolutely necessary for them to perform their duties. Is that understood?"

When all department heads had given their assent, he continued, "It seems we have been diverted from our previous patrol orders to make an off the record pickup somewhere close to the mid-Atlantic Ridge. I am not allowed to give you any more details except that we have been ordered to secure the package and return it to Norfolk Naval Station as fast as possible. In addition, we have been ordered to maintain absolute radio silence. There are to be no more regular comm checks."

"What kind of pickup?" Lt. Harris asked.

"You will know when the time comes Mister Harris," Chandler answered. "I cannot give you any more details at this time. Each of you will be given only the details you need in order to complete this mission. That is all I'm going to say. I want the crew on heightened alert. Tell them I was not satisfied with their performance during the last drill. Schedule some extra drills and see that their performance improves. This meeting is concluded gentlemen."

The department heads pushed their chairs back and jumped to attention.

"Dismissed," Chandler barked while motioning at Graham. He unlocked the door and waited for the other officers to leave the wardroom. "Find Petty Officer Jenkins and send him to my cabin immediately."

"Aye aye sir," Graham answered as he left the wardroom and hurried toward the Sonar room.

Chandler returned to his cabin and poured a glass of water from a carafe sitting on his desk. He had not even taken a swallow, when he heard three raps on the bulkhead.

"Enter," Chandler shouted.

Sonarman First Class Randy Jenkins entered the cabin and came to attention in front of the Captain's desk, "Reporting as ordered sir."

"At ease Petty Officer Jenkins. Pull the door shut and sit down. I need your help," Chandler said, handing a piece of paper to him. "Do you recognize that frequency?"

"Yes sir. It's on the low end of the Low Frequency Coherent Source sonobuoy frequency band," Jenkins answered. "But nobody uses those sonobuoys anymore Captain."

"Very good Jenkins," Chandler remarked. "Now, what I'm about to say absolutely goes no further than this cabin. You are not to share this with anyone. Do you understand?" Chandler asked as he reached out and retrieved the piece of paper from Petty Officer Jenkins' hand.

"Yes sir," Jenkins acknowledged.

"In approximately one hundred ten to one hundred twenty hours, give or take, we should receive a signal on that frequency. I want you to be on the lookout for that signal. When you pick it up, find me. No one else, just me," Chandler instructed.

"Yes sir. Anything else sir?" Jenkins asked.

"No. That's all. You're dismissed," Chandler responded.

"Aye aye sir," Jenkins replied. He came to attention, did an about face, and exited the cabin.

On his way back to the sonar room, Jenkins wondered why in Heaven's name there would be a sonobuoy in the middle of the Atlantic ocean transmitting on an old, unused frequency. And why was it so hush-hush? Probably just part of an exercise he concluded. One thing he did know was that it was going to mean little or no time off. He had just come on watch and was scheduled to go off in six hours. The captain had instructed him to tell no one, which meant he alone would have to monitor the equipment looking for the strange frequency.

Having been in the Navy for over ten years, he was getting used to such events. "Oh well, it's not just a job it's an adventure," he exclaimed sarcastically as he shrugged his shoulders and headed down the passageway toward the sonar room.

CHAPTER TWENTY-THREE

Friday, March 27 - 1048 Eastern Daylight Time
Miami International Airport
Miami, Florida

Zach sat in stony silence, staring at the passing scenery as the taxi he and Angie were riding in headed toward Miami International Airport. The anger that agitated him the previous day had cooled somewhat, but still smoldered beneath the surface, requiring only the slightest provocation to fan it into full flame once again.

He and Angie had not participated in any more dives after their blowup the previous afternoon. At four ten p.m. the previous day *Sea Princess* cleared Bahamian customs at Cat Caye and departed for the return trip to Miami.

Zach and Angie did not speak a dozen words to each other after leaving Bahamian waters. Zach stayed up on deck until he was certain Angie would be asleep. As *Sea Princess* entered the edge of the Gulf Stream, the waves increased in height and the boat began to pitch considerably. Zach took two motion sickness tablets and waited another fifteen minutes before going below. As carefully as he could, he slipped into the bunk and pulled the sheet up to his waist. The motion sickness pills combined with the exhaustion from a full week of diving put him to sleep quickly. Awakening at six thirty a.m., he concentrated on clearing US customs and packing for the return trip to Tulsa, only speaking to Angie when it was absolutely necessary.

As the taxi sped along Dolphin Expressway toward the airport, Zach replayed the events of the past week in his mind. It had been an enjoyable dive trip, but it had utterly failed its main purpose. So much tension existed between him and Angie, they could never relax and enjoy being together. Maybe Angie was right. Perhaps the trip had been a mistake. Was it foolish to think they could forget all that had happened in the past? Was their marriage really over? He loved her so much he could not bear the thought of spending the rest of his life without her. But, on the other hand, he also could not stand the constant tension. Depression settled over him like a dark cloud.

"Zach, you're awfully quiet," Angie prodded.

"Just thinking about the past week," Zach answered. "I had hoped we would have time to talk and maybe work out some of our problems. But there was always someone around. The boat was rather cramped and we didn't have any real privacy. I'm sorry. I guess I should have known it would be a mistake."

"Zach, there you go again. It was a great week. It was great to get away from the grind at the office. I really do appreciate your effort. I know it was difficult for you to take time away from the company." Angie turned, looked directly at Zach, and continued, "Zach, I know you don't want to hear this but I think we are better off apart. We always end up in the same place."

Zach was about to respond but the taxi pulled up to the departing passengers section of the airport. The taxi driver got out and unloaded their luggage from the trunk. After he finished setting their bags on the curb, Zach stuffed several bills into the driver's hand.

"Good day mon," the driver said as he got in the taxi and sped off in search of his next fare.

Zach picked up the large dive gear bag and the large suitcase leaving only one small duffle bag for Angie to carry. Struggling with the heavy bags, he headed for the automatic door.

"Zach!" Angie scolded. "I'm not helpless. I could carry the suitcase."

"Okay. I'll trade you," Zach responded, setting the suitcase down and taking the duffle bag from Angie. Together they headed for the automatic doors and the coolness inside the terminal. Once inside, they proceeded to the closest seating area. Zach stood perfectly still for several seconds staring at the wall. After spending a week on the sailboat, with its constant rolling from side to side, his equilibrium had become disrupted. Back on solid ground, he felt as if the building was swaying slowly back and forth.

Zach stood there with a funny look on his face. "Angie, do you feel as strange as I do? I would swear the building is swaying back and forth. I wonder how long this ...,"

"Shhh. Zach, be quiet," Angie interrupted. "I think you're being paged."

Zach stopped talking and listened. Several seconds later the message repeated. "Departing passenger Zach Templeton please pick up a white courtesy telephone for an emergency message."

Zach scanned the ticketing area trying to locate a white telephone. Angie tapped on Zach's shoulder, pointing to his left. There was a white telephone approximately thirty feet to his left. He walked over to the telephone, picked up the receiver, waited for an operator to answer, then spoke into it. "This is Zach Templeton. You have a message for me?"

"You have a message to call your office immediately. It's urgent," a female voice advised.

Zach replaced the receiver in its cradle and returned to where Angie was waiting. Shrugging his shoulders he said. "I'm supposed to call the office. They said it was urgent. I'll only be a minute." Zach knew the look on Angie's face. No doubt she felt this was just another proof his business was more important to him than she was. He intended to discuss it with her as soon as he found out what was so urgent.

He dug his cell phone out of his bag and dialed his office. The connection completed and he heard ringing on the other end.

"Good morning. "Microwave Services. May I help you?" a female voice answered.

"Janine, this is Zach. Your message said it was urgent. What's up?"

Janine started to answer but began sobbing. She stopped and started again but the words would not come.

"Janine, calm down. What's the matter?"

"Oh, Zach, I'm so sorry. Fred's dead!" Janine wailed into the phone.

"What? You can't be serious. He's in New Mexico."

"Mister Rhodes from the Observatory called yesterday. He said the New Mexico State Patrol found him dead in an overturned vehicle. I had to tell Rachael. Zach it was just awful."

Zach stood there frozen. He did not know what to say. What he was hearing could not possibly be true. It had to be a horrible dream. "Janine tell me this isn't true."

Zach was stunned. He turned and stared at Angie. The shock building inside him must have shown in his face because Angie realized instantly something was very wrong. In all their years together the look spreading across Zach's face was like none she had ever seen.

"Janine, are there any more details?," Zach inquired.

"Fred's body is still in New Mexico. Rachael wants you to take care of the arrangements. She's in no condition to take care of herself let alone make funeral arrangements," Janine sputtered between sniffles, dabbing at her eyes.

"Absolutely," Zach answered without hesitation. "Any other details I need to know about?"

"That's all I know right now. Oh, wait, there is one other thing. Mister Rhodes demanded that you call him the instant you got this message. Something about the master signaling channel being off line."

"Janine, clear my schedule for all of next week. I'll see if I can rewrite my ticket and fly directly to New Mexico. I'll call you when I have the flight arrangements. Read me Mister Rhodes' phone number."

Zach pulled a small notebook from his bag and wrote the number on it as Janine read it to him. He said goodbye and ended the call.

He stood there, dumbfounded. His friend of many years dead. How could life be so cruel? Fred was the only true friend he had ever known. Together they had survived hazardous missions as part of an elite Navy SEAL team. His only friend dead and he had not been there. "*This can't be happening,*" his mind screamed over and over.

He returned to where Angie was waiting. He walked up to her and just stood there unable to speak. He felt paralyzed. The grief he felt was more intense than he could ever have imagined he could feel. As with all people who lose someone close, Zach's first reaction was denial. His mind refused to accept the fact that his best friend was gone. He would wake up and it would all be a horrible nightmare.

Angie was becoming worried. "Zach, what on earth is the matter? You look like you've just lost your best friend. Zach, talk to me."

Zach stood there like a zombie. Angie stepped directly in front of him. No longer able to hold back, tears rolled down his face and dripped onto his shirt. Angie grabbed his arm and led him to an empty section of seating and made him sit down. "Zach talk to me. Tell me what's wrong."

"Angie, Fred's dead," he blurted out.

"Oh, Zach, I'm sorry. My comment..... I didn't..... ," She stammered not knowing what to say.

"It's okay. You couldn't have known. Angie, I just can't believe it. Fred's gone. What am I going to do?" he whimpered.

Angie had never seen Zach like this before. The face looking up at her was the face of a frightened little boy. The tears continued to roll down his face. His eyes pleading for comfort she was not certain she could or should give him. But she just could not ignore him sitting there with such pain evident in his face.

She reached out and pulled Zach to her. "Oh Zach, I'm so sorry."

She held him tight and said no more. She knew words would not ease the pain he was feeling. She knew only that he and Fred had served together in a special forces unit, but they had always refused to talk about it. Zach had been ecstatic when he was finally able to convince Fred to join his company. Fred's technical expertise had helped Zach get his struggling company out of trouble. But she had sensed there was much more than that. Zach changed as soon as Fred joined the company. He seemed less stressed and a little less worried about his company's future. She was very worried how he would react to Fred's death.

She too was deeply saddened. Fred had been a good friend to them both. And poor Rachael. How must she feel? They would go see her the instant they got back to Tulsa.

She felt Zach move. He straightened up and asked for a tissue. Angie dug in her purse, found a tissue, and handed it to Zach. "When is the funeral?" she asked.

Zach dabbed at his eyes, trying to compose himself. "Not set yet. Janine said Rachael asked me to see to the arrangements. She said Rachael is in no condition to handle them herself. Fred's body is still in New Mexico. Seems there's something wrong with the microwave system too. I'll try to rewrite my ticket and fly straight to Albuquerque."

"Zach, do you have to?" Angie asked. "I don't want to face Rachael alone."

"I really have to Angie. I'll have to make arrangements to have Fred's body shipped home. And I will have to make a quick check of the system. I told you about the problems we have been having. We've been getting increasing pressure from the Department of Defense to identify and correct the problems. I wish I didn't have to but there's simply no other way," Zach offered in defense.

"Yeah, I guess you're right," Angie answered. "Go get your ticket changed and I'll dig some things out of the luggage for you."

"Angie, I....," Zach started to say something but Angie cut him off.

"Zach, it's okay. Hurry. Go get your ticket changed. The sooner you get there the sooner you can come home."

Zach turned, located the American Airlines ticket counter, and rushed off to get his ticket changed. Angie rummaged through their luggage locating some personal items she thought Zach would need for his trip. She emptied the small duffle bag she had been carrying and stuffed Zach's items into it.

Zach raced back, out of breath. "Angie, they're holding a flight for me. I've got to run."

"I put some things in this bag for you. I hope I got everything you'll need."

"I appreciate it," Zach replied. "If I need anything else, I'll just buy it there if I can't do without it. Angie, I love you. I promise I'll return just as quickly as I possibly can." Zach bent down and kissed Angie and ran off in the direction of his flight's departure gate.

Zach turned and hollered over his shoulder, "Can you pick up Pablo at the kennel? I'll pick him up at your apartment as soon as I get back."

"I'll be glad to Zach. It will be fun to have him. See you when you get back," Angie shouted toward Zach's disappearing back.

Angie watched him until he disappeared from sight. She was becoming increasingly worried about Zach. He was under tremendous pressure. The increasing problems his company was having, their marital problems, and now he had lost his best friend. He had been trying so hard to change. She knew he was working very long hours on the days they were not together to allow him to spend more time with her. She respected Zach very much, but she just did not love him anymore.

"*Why can't I love him?*" she wondered. She had asked herself that question over and over, but had not come up with an acceptable answer.

Her mind switched to the upcoming meeting with Rachael. What would she say? She sat there alone deep in thought as she waited for the flight to Tulsa, her mind switching back and forth between their marital troubles and the dreaded meeting with Rachael.

Panting, sweat dripping down his face, Zach raced up to the departure gate and handed his ticket to the flight attendant. She tore off the flight coupon, returned his seat assignment card, hustling him through the jetway door. The instant Zach was on the aircraft, one of the flight attendants closed and secured the hatch as the other one escorted him to his seat. He had not even set down when the aircraft lurched as it was pushed back from the gate. Zach half fell into the seat and quickly buckled his seat belt and settled in for the long flight to Albuquerque.

CHAPTER TWENTY-FOUR

Friday, March 27 - 1110 Eastern Daylight Time
Navy Executive Corridor
Pentagon – Corridor 9, E Ring
Washington, D.C.

The phone on Vice Admiral Harlan Beckwith's desk rang, interrupting him as he labored over the task of completing manpower projections and budget estimates for the upcoming fiscal year.

He dropped the highlighter he had been using and picked up the receiver, "Yes. This is Admiral Beckwith."

"Admiral, *Providence* is seven hours overdue for the last required comm check," Lt. James Chetham, Staff Duty Officer for COMSUBLANT, advised.

"What?" Beckwith bellowed. "Seven hours. Why wasn't I notified of this sooner?"

"I don't know," Chetham answered. "The communications notice was just now delivered to the duty office."

"Is there any mention of a reason for the noncompliance?" Beckwith demanded.

"Nothing sir," Chetham replied. "Just that she is overdue. Nothing else."

"Very well," Beckwith snarled. "Contact the source of the communication notice and see what you can find out. Let me know the instant you have anything."

Beckwith swore out loud and slammed the receiver back into its cradle. He slammed his fists on the desk and swore again. Everything had been going according to plan and now this. He had given explicit orders *Providence* was to answer comm checks at specified time intervals. If they did not respond within seven hours of the designated time, something must be terribly wrong.

Beckwith decided not to wait for the COMSUBLANT Duty Officer to call back. A long delay could seriously jeopardize his carefully orchestrated plan. He picked up the receiver and punched in the number for Submarine Development Squadron Twelve.

"Submarine Development Squadron Twelve duty office," Lt. Carl Franks answered.

"This is Vice Admiral Beckwith."

"Yes sir," Franks snapped.

"Lieutenant Franks, I understand *Providence* is seven hours overdue," Beckwith announced. "I am trying to ascertain why I was only notified ten minutes ago."

"Admiral, there were no special instructions attached to *Providence's* patrol orders," Franks explained. "The scheduled communications checks, or lack thereof, would have been discussed as part of the morning analytics meeting per SOP sir."

"Are you certain of that Lieutenant?" Beckwith challenged.

"Yes sir. Absolutely," Franks asserted. "I have the patrol orders right here in the duty office binder sir. I am looking at them right now. There are no special instructions Admiral."

Admiral Beckwith swore under his breath. "Sir?" Franks questioned.

"Well, are there any incident reports or comments regarding why *Providence* is overdue for her last comm check?" Beckwith asked, irritation evident in his voice.

"No sir," Franks replied. "Other assets in Squadron Twelve answered their scheduled comm checks. All communications equipment is in working order and protocols are being followed implicitly."

"Very well," Beckwith conceded. "If you get any updates, call me immediately."

"Yes sir," Franks agreed.

Beckwith slammed the receiver down and swore even louder. He was certain he had attached instructions for augmented updates to the patrol plan. Anger and frustration seethed inside him. If *Providence* failed to answer by the next scheduled comm check, he would have to alter the timeline drastically. That would mean initiating the final pieces of the plan far sooner than intended

He decided he dared not wait to see if *Providence* answered her next comm check. He would begin the final execution of his plan early. After four long years of dreaming, hungering, and planning, he refused to be thwarted by anyone or anything.

Beckwith slipped a prepaid cell phone out of his pocket and punched in a number from memory.

In the office of the CIA's Deputy Director of Clandestine Services, a cell phone buzzed in the pocket of a suit jacket hanging on the coat rack. Deputy Director Frank Porter jumped up from his desk, locked the door, then fished the cell phone out of the jacket pocket.

On the sixth ring Deputy Director Porter answered, "Yes, Mr. Green. This is Victor."

"Are you able to talk?" Beckwith questioned.

"Yes," Porter acknowledged.

"There has been an issue. I need you to move up the time table," Beckwith said.

"No. It's too soon," Porter replied. "The risk would be enormous."

"I don't care!" Beckwith roared. "The final message is to be transmitted in seven days. Is that clear?"

"I don't think that can be done," Porter answered.

"I determine what can and cannot be done!" Beckwith raged into the receiver, his face turning red with anger. He was a three-star admiral used to having people jump when he gave orders. His hand shook as he continued, "You will do exactly as instructed. Need I remind you what would happen to you if I reveal what you are up to?"

Not waiting for a response, Beckwith continued, "You would spend the rest of your life in prison. I have been meticulous. There is absolutely no way anyone could tie me to any of this."

Beckwith waited. No reply came. "Well. What is your answer?"

Porter knew he had no alternative, at least not at that moment. "I will do as instructed. The final message will go out in seven days. I repeat my warning. The risk is enormous and I cannot be responsible if something goes wrong."

"You had better make certain nothing goes wrong," Beckwith threatened. "If anything does go wrong, it will be your neck on the line. If there are any leaks whatsoever, silence them immediately."

The line went dead. Porter flipped the cell phone shut and dropped it on the desk. Leaning back in his chair, he considered how he could comply with the Admiral's orders and not end up in prison for the rest of his life.

He would need help from agents he could trust. However, it was not so much a matter of trust. It was more a matter of fear. They were in as deeply as he was and they would also go to prison for the rest of their lives. He picked up the cell phone and began making calls to set up a meeting.

CHAPTER TWENTY-FIVE

Friday, March 27 - 1117 Central Daylight Time
Flight 1034,
34,000 feet above West-central Mississippi

Zach dozed fitfully as the aircraft flew west toward its intermediate destination of Dallas, Texas, his head resting against the window of the aircraft. His breathing was labored and small beads of perspiration glistened on his forehead. In his dream, he was thousands of miles away.

Zach was slogging through waist deep water in a slow moving jungle stream. He and other members of one of the Navy's elite SEAL teams had been inserted into a country in southeastern Asia under cover of darkness. Their off-the-record mission was to locate and neutralize two members of a government faction that intelligence sources had determined was an unacceptable threat to the security of the entire region.

The mission had not felt right from the beginning, but Zach always followed orders and left the decision making to the generals and politicians. Zach, a classic soldier, adamantly believed in following orders. But still, there had been an unsettled feeling about the mission. Something had felt very, very wrong from the outset.

Zach heard the sound of heavy equipment. He stopped and made a hand signal to the man behind him who repeated the hand signal to the man behind him and so on until all team members had been warned. Zach pointed to Fred Hargrove and motioned for him to follow. They were going on ahead to reconnoiter the situation.

He and Fred moved approximately thirty yards further downstream when the scream of incoming mortars ripped through the jungle silence. They dove for the closest cover they could find. The sound of exploding mortar shells was deafening. After the first volley of mortar shells landed, he and Fred tried to make their way back to the rest of the team but it was impossible. The peaceful jungle had erupted into a firestorm. The only smart course of action was to find cover and stay there, but they could not just ignore the rest of the team.

They moved back toward the other team members, picking the best cover they could find. It seemed unlikely that anyone could have survived, but they had to be certain. Once again, the air was filled with shrieking mortar shells.

One shell landed not more than twenty feet from their position. Hot, searing pain ripped through Zach's left shoulder, having been hit by a piece of shrapnel from the exploding shell. It felt as if the entire left side of his body was on fire. He collapsed and fell into the mud.

Fred, following close behind Zach, had been shielded from the mortar shell's blast by Zach's body. He made his way over to Zach's semiconscious form and screamed in his ear, "We have to get out of here. The rest of the team is gone. It's just you and me. We have to get out of here. NOW!"

Fred dragged Zach into the stream, putting as much distance between them and the firestorm as possible.

After moving one hundred yards downstream, the jungle fell eerily silent. Fred stopped and listened, hearing muffled voices, too far away to make out what they were saying. Whoever had ambushed them was checking for survivors.

He grabbed Zach and continued downstream being careful to make as little noise as possible. He had to put more distance between them and the ambushers before he could check on Zach's wounds. Several hundred yards further downstream Fred saw a dense clump of trees overhanging the stream. It would make a good hiding place while he tended to Zach's wounds.

He struggled to get Zach and himself out of the stream and into the clump of trees. He ripped Zach's shirt open and examined the wound. The wound did not look too bad. Nothing major had been hit by the shrapnel and the bleeding was only moderate. He poured antiseptic powder on the wound and covered it with a field dressing.

"How you holding up Zach?" Fred asked.

"Okay. Hurts a lot. Feels like my shoulder is on fire," Zach answered through gritted teeth.

"We need to sit tight for a while," Fred whispered. "If they don't know how many of us there were, we may be able to sneak out of here after it gets dark."

Fred offered Zach a drink of water from his canteen. While Zach drank from the canteen, Fred looked back upstream with his binoculars. He saw nothing.

For several minutes, Fred continued watching the jungle foliage for movement and the surface of the stream for telltale ripples. He could see smoke rising. There was sudden movement. Fred only caught glimpses through the dense jungle foliage. A lot of movement, but no one coming their way.

Suddenly, there was movement in the trees surrounding them. A dozen enemy soldiers with AK47s pointed at them. In an instant, their situation went from grim to hopeless. They were going to die.

Zach awoke with a start, sweat streaming down his face. It took several seconds for the dream to fade and for him to realize where he was. The nightmare had been so vivid, so real. Just like it always was. No matter how many times he had that same nightmare, it always seemed real.

"Are you alright?" the passenger seated next to him asked.

"Yeah, I'm fine. Just a bad dream," Zach answered. "Excuse me. I need to go to the lavatory and splash some cold water on my face."

The passenger got up and let him into the aisle. Zach made his way to the aft end of the aircraft and entered the lavatory on the left and locked the door. Leaning over the sink, he splashed cold water on his face. He stood there for a long time, water dripping from his face.

Why couldn't he shake that horrible, recurring nightmare? It was not even true to the actual events. The enemy soldiers did not find them. He and Fred escaped that night. Over the next three days they managed to make their way back to the insertion point and retrieved the SCUBA gear they had buried. That night when it got dark, they slipped into the surf and swam two miles offshore. Actually Fred swam and Zach was dragged. Fred activated their locator beacon and suspended it in the water. A short fifteen minutes later, the submarine rescue team hauled them onboard.

Maybe he felt guilty that he and Fred had escaped the firestorm when everyone else on the team had been killed. He had been in charge of the mission and he felt guilty because everyone did not return. Had they not been careful enough? Had they made too much noise? How had the enemy known where they were?

He had asked himself those same questions a thousand times. Each and every time the answers were exactly the same. Yes, they had been careful. No, they had not made too much noise. And there was no way the enemy could have known where they were. But the enemy had known! How? How had they known?

A gnawing suspicion that the team had been sacrificed just would not go away. But why?

When he and Fred were debriefed, they had been told that all records regarding the mission had been purged. They were ordered to never mention the mission to anyone, ever. Simply put, the mission never existed. They were warned that the slightest mention of it would bring serious repercussions. Officially, Zach's injuries were attributed to a botched training exercise.

Several weeks later, Zach and Fred had discussed the events privately. It was obvious they had been part of a dirty mission. Nobody was supposed to have returned from the mission. They both had suspicions who had been responsible, but they could not prove any of those suspicions. To save their careers, they had made a pact neither of them would discuss the mission with anyone without the other's knowledge and approval.

Zach pulled a paper towel from the dispenser and dried his face. He wadded the paper towel up and dropped it into the waste slot. Standing there in the lavatory reminded him of standing in the head on *Sea Princess* on the last day of the dive trip when he had opened the capsule that had been passed to him by an unknown diver. The capsule contained a warning that did not make sense.

Zach shook his head and exited the lavatory and returned to his seat. He sat there going over the events of the past few weeks in his mind, trying to find anything that would give the cryptic warning some credibility. No matter how many times he went over the past few weeks he could not come up with anything to justify such a warning. What was happening? His company was on the verge of collapse, his marriage was nearly over, his best friend was dead, and now this. He life was spinning out of control.

The captain's voice came over the PA system advising passengers to return to their seats and fasten their seat belts in preparation for landing at Dallas/Ft. Worth International Airport.

CHAPTER TWENTY-SIX

Friday, March 27 - 1415 Eastern Daylight Time
CIA Headquarters
Langley, Virginia

Three men sat in an interior office of the CIA headquarters building talking in hushed tones. Deputy Director of National Clandestine Services Frank Porter, Special Agent Eugene Williamson, and Field Agent Andrew Tiner were discussing an extremely sensitive issue.

As a routine precaution, the entire room had been swept for listening devices and no one was allowed to make written notes of any kind. The issue being discussed was so sensitive no written evidence was permitted.

"Something is very wrong out there," Porter declared. "Three people are dead, an agent is missing, and a key player in New York has disappeared. Gentlemen, I need answers and I need them now!" He waited. There was no response from either of the other two men.

"Did you hear me?" Porter asked, the volume of his voice rising.

"Yes sir," Williamson responded. "We really don't know very much. We have five field agents working the case. None of them have been able to turn up anything. Whoever is behind this is very slippery. There hasn't been a single usable lead as yet."

"Not acceptable Gene," Porter threatened. "Need I remind you of what we are dealing with?"

"No sir. I know what's at stake," Williamson affirmed. "One of our agents in New Mexico was able to strike up a conversation with a fat deputy sheriff at the local bar. Seems the local authorities don't have a clue as to what really happened. They are likely going to rule the MSI man's death an accident. We all know it wasn't but there is absolutely no evidence to indicate otherwise."

Porter turned and looked directly at Field Agent Andrew Tiner and asked, "What does Mister Templeton know?"

"We believe he knows nothing," Tiner answered. "He and his wife just returned from a SCUBA diving trip in the Bahamas. He changed his tickets

121

at Miami International and flew directly to Albuquerque. He can't possibly know anything."

"You had better be certain of that Agent Tiner," Porter warned. "Your career and your life depends on it. Select two additional agents and fly to New Mexico tonight. Follow Mister Templeton day and night. I expect a verbal report every day or sooner if there is anything unusual. You know the number. Take a scrambler with you. I don't want any more leaks. Understood?"

"Yes sir," Tiner replied. "We'll be on the first flight I can arrange. I'll check in as soon as we arrive and locate Mister Templeton."

The other two men waited for Agent Tiner to leave. Once the door was closed, Porter got up and locked it. He returned to his desk and sat down. He looked directly at Agent Williamson.

"How much does Tiner know?" Porter asked.

"Only what he needs to know," Williamson answered. "The same with all the other field agents. No one knows more than is absolutely necessary."

"Dear God, I hope you're right!" Porter exclaimed. "It looks like the entire project may be unraveling. We may have no choice but to shut it down. Are there any other loose ends that I should know about?"

"Don't think so. But I don't see how we can stop it now," Williamson objected. "The equipment is all in place. The first phase has already started. Are you willing to tell Mister Green that we are going to shut the project down?"

Porter did not have to answer that question. They both knew the man they answered to would never agree. He was driven by blind rage and hatred and would accept nothing other than the full conclusion of the plan. It had gone much too far to be stopped.

They had been instructed to never use Mister Green's real name. If the project failed, they would take all the blame. Their careers would be over and they would spend the rest of their lives in prison. The project had to be successful, no matter the cost.

Porter took his glasses off, laid them on the desk, and rubbed his tired eyes. He was so tired and stressed it felt as if his eyes were full of sand. He hoped this would be over soon. Slipping his glasses back on, he looked at Agent Williamson, "What do we have on Mister Templeton?"

Williamson retrieved Zach's service record from his briefcase and scanned through the pages. "His service record indicates he served in the Navy, the last eight years as a SEAL. Joined the Navy when he was seventeen. Took early retirement with nineteen years and two months of active service. He received two Bronze Star medals with combat V, three presidential unit citations, and the Navy Cross. He is a weapons expert, a martial arts expert, and has been trained in demolition and guerilla warfare. Wait a minute; something's odd here. A page has to be missing. There's a nine month gap and his last set of orders aren't here. No matter. Probably just didn't get added before his discharge."

"I wouldn't want to meet this guy in a dark alley," Williamson added.

"Do you think he could be recruited?", Porter asked.

"No way! Absolutely not!" Williamson replied, continuing to thumb through the service record. "This guy is honest-to-goodness hero material. No way you could ever recruit him."

"Pick two of your most trusted operatives and send them to New Mexico," Porter instructed. "Provide them with FBI credentials and tell them to carry no other identification. Have them watch Agent Tiner and Mister Templeton. If it looks like either one is on to anything, tell them to make contact with Mister Templeton and find out what he knows. If he knows anything, and I mean anything, silence him and Agent Tiner as well."

"You can't be serious!" Williamson protested, looking up from Zach's service record, disbelief evident on his face. "There have been too many bodies already. Two more will raise too much suspicion."

"What choice do we have?" Porter snapped. "We have to keep a lid on this for at least another few days. After that nobody will be able to stop it and we will be gone. They will just have to find a way to make it look accidental."

"But, I don't....."

"I don't want to hear any of your lame excuses," Porter interrupted. "Just do what needs to be done."

Williamson had heard that tone before. Further argument would be futile. He dropped Zach's service record on the desk, walked to the door, and waited for Porter to unlock it.

"I'll contact you when the job is complete," Williamson said as he pulled the door shut.

Field Agent Tiner exited the building and walked to the parking lot. He unlocked his car and got in, scanning the parking lot to see if anyone was watching. Satisfied no one was watching, he started the engine of his bright red Porsche 911, backed out of the space, and squealed the tires as he roared out of the parking lot.

Tiner laughed to himself at how easily the Americans had been fooled. Tiner was the offspring of two Russian agents that had been planted in the United States many years earlier.

When Andrew was born, his parents gave him an American sounding name and saw to it that he was educated in the best schools. His real name was Aronoff Porubsky; a name they used only in absolute privacy.

Aronoff's parents drove him hard to excel at whatever he did; to always be better than the Americans. From the time he was little, his mind had been saturated with the political rhetoric of communist hardliners. He had learned his lessons well, becoming a true, hard-line communist, despising all

Americans and their decadent way of life.

Aronoff drove for several miles then pulled into the parking lot of a convenience store and parked in the back. Certain no one had followed him, he pulled an object that resembled a cell phone from a secret compartment in his briefcase. He punched in a series of numbers and waited for someone to answer.

" Privyet," the voice on the other end answered.

"Levka, it is me, Aronoff."

"I have been waiting. What have you found out?"

"The silly American fools do not suspect a thing," Aronoff sneered. "They think I am nothing more than a junior field agent and not a very good one at that."

Levka laughed. "Good. Very good Aronoff. Glasnost has made the American fools sloppy. What is next?"

"I am being sent to New Mexico," Aronoff answered. "I have been instructed to watch the man from the communications company. They are afraid he may know something."

"But what of Anatoly?" Levka questioned. "I thought he was to make this communications man disappear."

"Yes, that's true Levka," Aronoff conceded. "I have not heard from Anatoly. Something has gone wrong but it does not matter. I have already made the code changes. It was so easy Levka. Every time I look at those American fools I want to laugh."

"Yes Aronoff, next time we are together, we have good laugh," Levka chuckled. "We have played Americans like piano. Do zvidaniya, my good friend."

"Do zvidaniya, Levka," Aronoff acknowledged as he switched the phone off and replaced it in the secret compartment.

He scanned the parking lot again. Nobody was watching. He steered the red Porsche back onto the highway and headed for his apartment to pack for the trip to New Mexico.

CHAPTER TWENTY-SEVEN

Friday, March 27 - 1509 Mountain Daylight Time
Albuquerque International Airport
Albuquerque, New Mexico

Flight 1395 landed, taxied across the tarmac, and pulled up to the jetway for gate twenty-seven. A mix of travelers streamed out of the jetway door and into the airport concourse. Men and women dressed in business suits returning from meetings with clients. Vacationing families with children in tow. Elderly people returning from family visits. And Zach.

Zach watched as travelers met with waiting parties. There were limousine drivers holding signs with names on them. Families waiting eagerly for loved ones. He hated arriving at airports. There was never anyone waiting for him, painfully reminding him of how empty his life felt. He wondered if anyone noticed there was no one to meet him. Did anyone wonder why he was alone. No! They could not possibly have any idea what a shambles his life was at that moment.

Zach had no luggage except for the duffle bag Angie had hurriedly packed for him while he changed his ticket. He stared at the overhead signs and located directions to the rental car agency.

He walked down the concourse and entered the main terminal area. All rental car agencies were on the terminal's lower level. At the bottom of the escalator, he turned left and walked to the far end of the terminal, next to the last baggage carousel. Zach stepped up to the counter and asked, "Do you have anything available? I don't have a reservation."

"Just a minute and I'll check to see if we have anything," the agent replied. The agent tapped some keys on her terminal and waited for the computer to answer. She tapped several more keys and said, "Ah, yes. But all we have left are full size. Is that all right?"

"That'll be just fine," Zach answered. "I'll need it for two, maybe three days."

"What form of payment will you be using?" the agent asked.

Zach laid his credit card on the counter and pushed it toward the agent.

The agent took the credit card, ran it through the card reader, and waited as the computer authorized Zach's credit card.

"Where will you be staying Mister Templeton?"

"The Desert Butte Motel in Socorro," Zach answered.

The agent keyed in the motel's name and pressed the key to print the contract. The agent ripped the completed contract from the printer and shoved it in front of Zach. "Initial the circled areas here and here and sign at the bottom."

Zach did as instructed and pushed the contract back to the agent. The agent took the contract and separated the copies. She stuffed Zach's copy in a folder and grabbed a set of keys from the peg board behind her. She handed the folder and keys to Zach.

"A white Lincoln Towncar," the agent announced. "You will find your car in space three-eight-seven, up one level on the north side of the terminal. Have a great stay, Mister Templeton."

"Thanks," Zach said, grabbing the contract and keys. He turned and followed the signs to the rental car parking area, stopping at the information booth to ask for directions to his car. The attendant pointed out where the Towncar was parked. Zach declined the map that was offered as he had been to Albuquerque often and knew the route well.

Zach unlocked the Towncar and threw his duffle bag in the back seat. He slid into the front seat, started the engine, and turned on the air conditioner full blast. Once the air conditioner was blowing cold, he shut the door, backed out of the space, and headed for the rental lot exit.

Zach exited the rental car parking lot, turning right onto Sunport Boulevard. As he drove west on Sunport Boulevard, a gray Jeep Cherokee pulled out of an adjacent parking area and dropped in several cars behind Zach's Towncar. Zach turned left onto the entrance ramp for Interstate 25. Merging into the light south bound traffic, he settled in for the long ride to the National Radio Astronomy Observatory.

The observatory was approximately one hundred thirty miles from the airport which would take him slightly over two hours. He used the time to try to sort out the events of the past few weeks. Zach set the cruise control at seventy-two. Switching the air conditioner fan to medium, he settled in for the long trip to the observatory.

The driver of the light gray Jeep Cherokee did likewise, staying only close enough to Zach's Towncar to keep it in sight.

One hour later Zach took Exit Number 150 for Socorro. He stopped at the end of the exit ramp and turned right onto Highway 60. The driver of the Jeep Cherokee picked up his cell phone, punched a speed dial key, and waited for someone to answer.

"Yeah," a male voice answered.

"This is Frenchie. Looks like he's heading for the observatory. We're going to wait here and pick him up when he comes back."

"Is that wise?", the voice on the other end asked.

"All he was carrying when he arrived was a small duffel bag," Frenchie explained. "No test equipment of any kind. There's not much traffic out that way. I don't want him to get suspicious."

"Okay. It's your call. You know the risk. The people in New York will bury you if you lose him!"

"Yeah, I know," Frenchie said. He flipped the cell phone closed and dropped it on the seat beside him. He pulled into an abandoned gas station, turned around, and headed back for town.

Stopping at a little restaurant on the south side of the highway, he said "Let's grab something to eat while we waiting for our friend to return."

Frenchie and his not too bright associate walked into the restaurant and selected a booth with a view of the highway. "Keep your eyes on the highway," Frenchie told Angus. "I don't want to miss our friend if he changes his mind and comes back to town."

Zach drove the remaining forty-seven miles to the observatory deep in thought. He turned off the highway onto the observatory access road and drove past the line of large antennas. He drove up to the observatory administration building and parked in one of the visitor parking spaces.

He entered through the observatory's main door and walked up to the receptionist's desk. "Zach Templeton to see Jamison Rhodes," he announced.

"Mister Rhodes is expecting you," the receptionist answered. "His office is down the hall, third door on the right. Go on in. I'll let him know you're on your way."

Zach glanced down at the name plate on the desk. "Thanks Martha," he said as he headed for Mister Rhodes' office.

Zach was about to knock on the door when it flew open. "Mister Templeton, glad you're here. Come on in," he said, offering his hand to Zach. They shook hands, Rhodes pointed Zach to a chair.

"Sit down Mr. Templeton," Rhodes directed. "Make yourself comfortable. I'm sorry about your friend, Fred Hargrove. Everybody here was shocked when they heard the news. Have you spoken with the authorities yet."

"No. I drove straight here from the airport," Zach answered.

"The State Patrol asked me to have you contact them as soon as you arrived," Rhodes said. "I'll have Martha call them right now."

Rhodes buzzed Martha's desk and told her to call the troop commander at the State Patrol office in Albuquerque and put it through to his office.

It was not long before the phone on Rhodes' desk buzzed. He picked up the receiver, listened without saying anything, and handed the receiver to Zach. "It's the State Patrol," he advised. "Troop commander's name is

Robert Morgan."

Zach's conversation with the State Patrol was short. He agreed to meet the troop commander at the Sierra County Sheriff's Office in Truth or Consequences the next morning at eight thirty a.m.

"Okay Mister Templeton. Let's get down to business," Rhodes began.

"Does anyone have any idea what the current microwave system problem could be?" Zach asked. "When I spoke with my office this morning, Janine said something about the master signaling channel being off line."

"What do you mean does anyone have any idea what's wrong?" Rhodes fumed. "That is what your company is contracted to know. We've had nothing but problems since your company installed the microwave system. I want that blasted system fixed and I want it fixed now!"

Zach had heard about Rhodes' hair-trigger temper but he had never experienced it firsthand. He could see this meeting was not going to be pleasant. "Mister Rhodes, I assure you I will do everything humanly possible to correct the problems with the master signaling channel," Zach offered in defense. "I intend to correct that tomorrow, if the State Patrol will release the test equipment Fred had with him. And provided the test equipment still works."

"It had better be corrected by noon tomorrow!" Rhodes bellowed. "My boss in Washington has threatened to fire me if these problems are not corrected soon."

"The master signaling problem is not the same as the earlier problems you reported," Zach shot back. "We think the recurring problems are being caused by some kind of external interference. It's so sporadic it's impossible to identify the source of the interference."

"I don't want to hear any excuses," Rhodes demanded. "I just want the system fixed. Do you understand Mister Templeton?"

"Yes, I understand," Zach answered. There was a lot more Zach wanted to say but it was not the time. More questions would just make Rhodes more angry.

"If the system is not one hundred percent functional by the end of next week, I'm going to call the Department of Defense office and instruct them to cancel your contract," Rhodes threatened. "I have more important things to do than baby sit a maintenance contractor."

"Yes sir," Zach replied as he got up to leave. "Anything else?"

"Call me the instant you have the signaling channel working. I'll be here most of the day tomorrow," Rhodes shouted.

"You can count on it," Zach promised, pulling the door shut.

Zach walked down the hall and stopped at Martha's desk. "What's with Mister Rhodes," he asked.

"Nobody knows," Martha answered. "He's been like that for weeks.

Everybody thinks he's going to have a stroke. I don't think anybody would care though. Everybody hates him."

Zach asked for the direct phone number to Rhodes' desk so he could call him when the system was corrected. Martha wrote the number on a small piece of paper and handed it to Zach.

Zach climbed into his rental car. All he could think about was getting to the motel, grabbing something to eat, and then a drink. A very large drink. Angie would not approve, but considering the circumstances he just did not care. After the drink, a long soak in the motel's hot tub. *"What a horrible way to end a vacation,"* Zach thought to himself as he slipped the Towncar into gear and started the boring return trip to Socorro.

CHAPTER TWENTY-EIGHT

Saturday, March 28 - 0515 Eastern Daylight Time
Wisconsin Avenue,
Georgetown, Maryland

Vice Admiral Beckwith was startled out of a sound sleep by the ringing telephone on the night stand beside his bead. Wrestling with the covers to get a hand free, he switched on a lamp and snatched the receiver, "This is Admiral Beckwith."

"This is Lieutenant Franks, Submarine Development Squadron Twelve Duty Office," Lt. Carl Franks announced.

"Yes. What is it?" Beckwith asked.

"Sir, you asked to be updated regarding comm checks by *Providence*," Franks answered.

"Yes I did," Beckwith affirmed. "What do you have?"

"*Providence* is one hour overdue for the zero seven hundred Zulu comm check," Franks replied. "That makes three consecutive comm checks she has missed sir."

Beckwith shook his head in disbelief. His most important asset had not been heard from for over thirty-six hours. Something was seriously wrong.

"Are the other Squadron Twelve assets still responding to their scheduled comm checks?" Beckwith questioned.

"Yes sir. Right on schedule," Franks affirmed. "All communications systems are functioning correctly."

"Has anyone tried to contact *Providence* on the long-wire antenna?" Beckwith asked.

"No sir," Franks responded. "There is no radio traffic scheduled for *Providence*."

"What?" Beckwith barked.

"Per *Providence's* patrol orders, all communication is to be initiated by *Providence* only sir," Franks countered. "Any non-routine communications would require flash traffic authorization."

Beckwith's anger flared and he was about to scream into the receiver but he stifled the urge, knowing the Lieutenant was correct. He would have to initiate the flash traffic request in person. When he arrived at COMSUBLANT headquarters, he would determine what other available assets could be redirected.

"Lieutenant, I will initiate a flash traffic request myself," Beckwith declared. "I will be leaving my residence in about thirty minutes. Call me on my cell phone if there are any updates regarding *Providence*."

"Yes sir," Franks replied.

Beckwith dropped the receiver in its cradle. He sat there for several minutes deciding what to do next. Another change of plans would definitely be required. He swung his legs out from under the covers and sat on the edge of the bed while digging in the night stand drawer. He pulled out an untraceable cell phone and punched in a number. He waited while a phone on the other side of the ocean rang and rang and rang. After twelve rings, he slammed the phone shut. He flipped the phone open again and punched in the same number.

On the sixth ring a voice answered, "Yeah."

"This is Raul. I'm looking for Alberto. I have an important message for him."

Recognizing the prearranged identification, the voice on the other end answered, "Go ahead, I am listening."

"Have you located the man and the documents?" Beckwith asked. "I believe Jozek was the name you mentioned."

"No. We no find him," the voice answered. "Somehow he managed to kill Grzegorz. Then he disappear like ghost."

Beckwith continued, shaking his head in disbelief, "You must find him."

"I have many contacts," the voice replied. "All looking for him. I call when anybody find him."

"See that you do the instant you have any sightings," Beckwith growled, slamming the cell phone shut.

"Good Lord!" Beckwith exclaimed out loud. "The whole blasted plan is falling apart!"

He dug around in the night stand drawer again and pulled out a small device slightly larger than a pack of cigarettes and inserted it between the wall outlet and the land-line phone. After a wait of fifteen seconds, a light on the device turned green, indicating the scrambler circuits were functioning. He dialed a number and waited.

On the fifth ring a sleepy voice answered, "Hello."

"Plug in the scrambler," Beckwith ordered.

After another fifteen second delay, the distorted, metallic voice of Deputy Director Porter answered, "Okay, the scrambler is active."

"There is another change in plans," Beckwith advised. "The final message has to go out in three days."

"No, not possible!" Porter objected. "The change to seven days you requested was risky enough. There is simply no way we can move the final message up three days."

"As I said before, you will do exactly as I say," Beckwith snarled.

"If we move the final step up that much, we risk alerting the microwave service company," Porter argued. "Their senior technician was found dead two days ago. The owner of the company is in New Mexico now. Any more changes and he will know it is something more than equipment problems."

"What?" Beckwith sputtered. "Dead? Where? How?"

"The two men I had watching the technician were careless," Porter offered in defense. "He spotted them as he was coming out of the equipment building. One of the men is a stupid ignoramus that doesn't seem to know his own strength. He hit him with a homemade equalizer and cracked his skull."

Beckwith tried to interrupt but Porter continued, "They said they had no choice. They put him in his rental car and pushed it off the road and down a steep embankment. The local Sheriff's office is going to rule it an accident."

"You stupid moron!" Beckwith roared. "They were only supposed to watch him. What if they left evidence behind."

"They assured me they were extremely careful," Porter answered. "They had gloves on the entire time. They put all the panels back on the microwave equipment and locked the building door. To be safe, they grabbed the guy's camera and all the film he had."

"For your sake, it had better be ruled an accident," Beckwith warned. "Is anybody watching the owner of the company?"

"Yes," Porter replied. "The same two men"

"Do you think that is wise?" Beckwith asked. "Sounds like they can't be trusted. We can't afford any more screw ups."

"No choice," Porter replied. "They are the only resources I have in New Mexico. I have an agent on the way there now. Someone we can sacrifice if and when the need arises, I might add."

"If the owner of the service company suspects anything, and I mean anything, silence him immediately," Beckwith ordered.

"Do you …,"

Beckwith cut off Porter, "I don't want to hear any more of your whining. Just do what I tell you."

"I don't think that is wise," Porter insisted, in spite of the Admiral's warning.

"Not another word!" Beckwith screamed. "I am going to say this only once. If he suspects anything, kill him."

Beckwith continued without giving Porter a chance to respond, "If you fail to follow my orders, I promise you I will personally put a bullet in your brain! Is that clear enough for you?"

Beckwith slammed the receiver down. He unplugged the device and reconnected the phone line directly to the wall socket. He hurriedly got dressed and headed for COMSUBLANT headquarters.

CHAPTER TWENTY-NINE

Saturday, March 28 - 0825 Mountain Daylight Time
Sierra County Sheriff's Office
Truth or Consequences, New Mexico

Zach pulled up in front of the Sierra County Sheriff's Office and got out of his rental car. He opened the sheriff's office door and walked in. A very fat man in a blue uniform shirt sat behind the counter, his shirt stretched so tightly it looked as if the buttons would fly off at any moment.

Zach walked up to the counter and waited for the man to notice him. A silver name plate bearing the name Alberto Ramirez was pinned just above the man's right pocket. To Zach's surprise, a gold badge was pinned above his left pocket.

In spite of the grief weighing him down, Zach had to suppress a snicker. In his mind he had a comical image of the fat deputy trying to chase down a fleeing criminal.

Deputy Ramirez finally looked up and noticed Zach, "May I help you señor?"

"My name is Zach Templeton," Zach replied. "I'm supposed to meet the sheriff and the troop commander from the State Patrol."

"Yes. Sheriff Moralles said he was expecting you. I will let him know you are here."

The deputy buzzed the sheriff and told him Zach had arrived. "Mister Templeton, the sheriff said he will be out in a few minutes. Have a seat. Can I get you a cup of coffee?"

"Yes, that would be great."

The deputy struggled out of his chair and waddled over to the coffee pot in the corner of the room. "How do you take it?" he asked.

"Black, one sugar."

The deputy dropped one sugar cube and a stir stick into the cup and waddled over to where Zach was sitting. When he came around the corner of the counter, he made an even more laughable sight. The gun hanging from his belt looked like a child's toy next to the enormous stomach hanging over his belt.

"Just finished perking before you walked in," Ramirez beamed as he handed the steaming cup to Zach.

Zach took the cup and blew on the surface of the coffee to cool it. He took a small sip. It was strong and quite good. "It's great," Zach hollered out to the deputy.

Several minutes passed. Zach was edgy. He fidgeted in his chair, eager to get the ordeal over with. A mountain of details still needed his attention. Most important of all, he still had to make arrangements to get Fred's body released and shipped home. He had called Angie the previous evening from the motel and asked her to call the local American Legion post and have them make preliminary funeral arrangements.

In addition, the master signaling channel was still offline and needed to be reset. He also wanted to see if he could find any clues that might reveal the cause of the interference plaguing the DOD microwave system.

Zach waited, finishing the coffee the deputy had given him. He fidgeted. Finally, out of patience, he got up to ask the deputy if it was going to be much longer. Just as he reached the counter, Sheriff Moralles opened his office door, walked over to where Zach was standing, and offered his hand.

"Good morning. I'm Sheriff Juan Moralles. Sorry to keep you waiting so long."

"Good morning Sheriff," Zach answered. "Can we get started? I have a ton of things to take care of."

"Certainly, come on in to my office. Just a few routine questions. Shouldn't take long."

Zach followed the sheriff into his office. The sheriff was tall and muscular with dark olive colored skin. His uniform was crisp, perfectly ironed, with razor sharp creases. He carried himself very straight with an air of authority. No doubt this man was a professional, in sharp contrast to the deputy seated out front.

Zach walked into the office and noticed someone already seated on the right side of the sheriff's desk. Crew cut, yellow stripe down the legs of his blue trousers, and a "Smoky the Bear" hat laying in his lap. No doubt it was the State Patrol troop commander he had spoken to the previous day.

"Mister Templeton, this is Troop Commander Robert Morgan," Sheriff Moralles announced. "The State Patrol is in charge of the investigation. I'm only involved because the accident happened here in Sierra County."

"First, let me offer my condolences for the loss of your friend," Commander Morgan said. "The questions we have are just routine. Would you like another cup of coffee before we get started."

"Sure. I could use another cup," Zach answered. "I didn't take time to grab breakfast this morning."

The sheriff picked up his phone and buzzed the deputy, "Alberto could you bring a pot of coffee in here please."

A few seconds later the deputy tapped on the door. The sheriff opened the door and took the pot of coffee. Cups were filled. Everyone was ready.

"Mister Templeton, did Mister Hargrove have any reason he would commit suicide?" Morgan asked.

"What? Absolutely not!" Zach shot back. "He and Rachael had just purchased a new house in Tulsa. They were extremely happy. He wouldn't even think about such a thing!"

"How can you be so sure?" Morgan questioned.

"Fred and I were members of a Navy SEAL team. When you face death with someone you get to know that person very well. No. Not even a chance. Fred wouldn't do that. I would stake my life on it."

Morgan opened his notebook and produced a sheet of paper. He handed it to Zach and asked, "Do you recognize the handwriting?"

"Yes. It Fred's handwriting," Zach stated. "But something is different. It's extremely shaky and hard to read. Where did you find this?"

"The coroner found it clutched in Mister Hargrove's hand," Morgan replied. "He said he had to pry his hand open to get it out."

"Maybe he wrote the note after he had the accident," Zach offered. "He loved Rachael very much. It would be just like him to try to leave her a note. He called her every day when he was out of town."

"Did they have any financial problems that you know of?"

"No. None whatsoever!" Zach protested. "They didn't have any children. He worked for the CIA after he left the Navy and was paid quite well. They were very comfortable financially. There is simply no reason Fred would want to commit suicide."

"I'm sorry Mister Templeton. I have to ask these questions. It's standard procedure. I doubt if someone that had decided to commit suicide would drive their vehicle off the side of a road. However, the note does seem kind of odd though. The coroner said he couldn't be sure if Mister Hargrove died instantly. There is a possibility he died some time after the crash."

"Fred always carried a notebook in his pocket," Zach added. "May I see the original note?"

Morgan opened his notebook again, retrieved a small plastic bag, and handed it to Zach.

Zach examined the note. "It looks like the kind of paper that would come from a small notebook. Did you find a notebook in the vehicle?"

Morgan scanned the accident report and the coroner's report. "I don't see a notebook listed but that doesn't mean there wasn't one. The accident investigators don't always list every item."

"May I have a copy of the note for Rachael?", Zach asked.

"I don't see anything wrong with that," Morgan answered.

Zach handed the original note back to Morgan who then handed it to the sheriff.

"Sheriff, make a copy of this please," Morgan directed. "The copy I made is not very legible. Maybe your copy machine will make a better copy."

"Was there any camera equipment?" Zach questioned. "Fred was an amateur photographer. He sometimes took his camera equipment on trips."

Morgan again scanned his reports. "No. There isn't any camera equipment listed.

Zach lied to Morgan, knowing that Fred never went anywhere without his camera equipment. He was not exactly certain why he lied. Something did not feel right. The mysterious diver, the message in the capsule warning of danger, and now Fred's death. The events of the past few days made Zach extremely suspicious.

"Where is Fred's rental vehicle?" Zach asked.

"In the county impound lot behind the building," Morgan replied.

"May I see it," Zach requested.

"Certainly," Morgan replied. "As soon as we finish here,"

The sheriff returned with the note and the photocopy. He handed the original note to Morgan and the photocopy to Zach. Zach folded the copy and put it in his pocket. He would study it in detail later.

"Sheriff, you were at the scene. What is your opinion of the accident?" Morgan asked.

Sheriff Moralles leaned back in his chair and thought for several moments then answered, "My official opinion is that it was an accident. Several of the tires were flat. It looks to me like he had a blowout and couldn't maintain control and left the highway and rolled multiple times. There is no way of knowing how long he was there before a rancher spotted the vehicle. None of the mechanical systems on the Bronco were damaged in the crash. They all appeared to be in good working order."

"I agree," Morgan added. He took the investigation report from his notebook and wrote accidental as the cause and signed the report. "I'll notify the coroner he can release the body immediately," he said to Zach, handing the accident investigation report to the sheriff.

"Now we can go have a look at the vehicle Mister Templeton," Morgan advised.

They walked through the building and exited out the back door. Zach walked over to the crumpled Bronco and circled it several times. He looked inside but saw nothing out of the ordinary.

"Where is the test equipment and Fred's toolbox?" Zach asked as he turned around and faced the two men.

"The equipment is inside to protect it from the elements. Not that we ever expect any rain," the sheriff joked. "The equipment is a little beat up. Don't know if it still works. We didn't even turn it on. Nobody here would know if it was working if we did."

"May I take the equipment?" Zach asked. "There are some problems with the microwave system Fred was here working on. I came straight here from Miami. My wife and I had just returned from a SCUBA diving trip when I was notified of Fred's death. I'll need that equipment to test the system and make any necessary repairs."

The sheriff looked at Morgan. "Sure. Just have Mister Templeton sign the release forms," Morgan said.

Morgan left. Zach and Sheriff Moralles returned to the office. Zach sat while the sheriff rounded up the necessary forms.

"Sign here and here," Moralles instructed. "That's it. The equipment is yours Mister Templeton."

"I still need to make arrangements to have Fred's body shipped home. Is there a mortuary you could recommend?" Zach asked.

"That's easy," Moralles answered. "There's only one. Jorgenson Mortuary. Down the street, three blocks, on the left. Owner's name is Bill Jorgenson. Tell him I sent you."

"Thank you," Zach offered as he left the sheriff's office. He drove his car around to the side door and loaded the test equipment, Fred's laptop computer, and the toolbox into the trunk of the rental car. Zach got into the car and drove down to the mortuary.

Zach met Mister Jorgenson, the mortuary owner, and made all the necessary arrangements to have Fred's body shipped back to Tulsa. Jorgenson agreed to contact the American Legion post commander and provide him with the flight number and arrival time. He assured Zach that Fred's body had been handled with the utmost care and respect and that it would leave late that afternoon.

Zach left the mortuary and headed for the microwave tower site near Monticello. Something was very wrong. Fred never went anywhere without his camera equipment. Zach was getting tired of nothing but unanswered questions. He wanted answers. He needed answers. He promised himself that he would not rest until he found some.

CHAPTER THIRTY

Zach spent most of the trip to the Sanchez tower site near Monticello thinking about the final funeral arrangements he would need to make when he returned to Tulsa.

Zach pulled up to the gate that led to the Sanchez tower site. He unlocked the gate and drove far enough up the access lane to allow him to close the gate. He closed the gate and pushed the padlock closed. Normally he would just hang the padlock on the chain, but today he felt edgy and decided he would feel much better knowing the gate was locked. He drove up the lane and stopped in front of the equipment building.

Zach grabbed Fred's toolbox from the back seat and went inside and completed some cursory equipment checks. Nothing seemed visibly wrong according to the system indicators. After removing the front panels from both sets of receivers and transmitters, he saw no alarm indications of any kind. That was not possible. If the master signaling channel was offline, there would definitely be an alarm indication. Something was very odd indeed.

He decided to put the master signaling channel card on an extender board so he could troubleshoot the problem. He opened the toolbox and began searching for the extender board in the jumbled contents of the toolbox. When he pulled the extender board out, hidden underneath it was a single roll of film. Zach picked up the roll of film and examined it. It was definitely exposed film, but there had been no camera equipment in Fred's vehicle. Why would Fred have exposed film in his toolbox but no camera? Zach did not like the feeling growing inside him.

Desperate to get the problem fixed quickly, he returned to the equipment rack and pulled the master signaling channel card out. Once the extender card was in place, he pushed the master signaling channel card into it. He turned on the frequency selective levelmeter and tuned it to the correct frequency for the master signaling channel.

When Zach placed the levelmeter's probe on the channel board's test point, a small piece of rolled up paper fell on the floor. He picked up the tiny tube of paper and unrolled it. Fred's handwriting was clear and unmistakable. The small scrap of paper contained only three words. Zach stared at the paper for several minutes, grief returning as he stared at the words and thought about his old friend.

Unable to make sense of the message, Zach pulled his wallet out and placed the scrap of paper under his driver's license for safe keeping and returned his attention to the channel card.

A close examination of the board revealed a copper trace had been deliberately cut. Zach removed the master signaling channel card, retrieved a battery powered soldering iron from Fred's toolbox, and repaired the trace. He replaced the master signaling channel card. Still no alarm. He pulled the channel group card. Carefully inspecting it, he found the power lead to the LED indicator had been cut. Zach repaired the cut power lead and replaced the channel group card.

Any lingering doubt that Fred's death had not been an accident was fading fast. The trace on the circuit board had been deliberately cut to disable the signaling channel. There could be no doubt Fred had deliberately disabled the system in such a way to be certain he would find the note.

Zach plugged a portable, lineman's phone set into the jackfield and signaled the dispatch office at the National Radio Astronomy Observatory.

"Dispatch, Barnes speaking," the duty operator answered.

"This is Zach Templeton from Microwave Services. I'm at the Sanchez microwave site near Monticello. I just repaired the master signaling channel. Do you show a clear board at your location?"

"Yes, Mister Templeton. All indicators are green. Anything else?" the operator asked.

"Indicate in the logbook the time of repair and leave a message for Mister Rhodes," Zach instructed. "I am going to complete a quick alignment test and then I am going to return to Tulsa on the first flight I can catch. Inform him I will be unavailable until Wednesday due to Mister Hargrove's funeral."

"My condolences, Mister Templeton," the duty operator offered. "Too bad about your friend. I will see that Mister Rhodes gets the message as soon as he calls in. Is there anything else I can do for you Mister Templeton?"

"No. But thanks for asking," Zach acknowledged as he disconnected the phone set from the jackfield.

Zach set up some additional test equipment to precisely monitor the system's output frequency. Fiddling with the test equipment controls, he tried to get the display to stabilize. No matter what adjustments he made, the signal just would not settle.

He could not afford to spend a lot of time completing the tests so he decided to get Fred's laptop and record the test data for later analysis. He returned from the car with the laptop and turned it on.

Shaking his head in disbelief, he stared at the screen. The screen was bright blue with a yellow box in the center. In the yellow box a message in bold, red letters declared, "This computer is infected with ANTHRAX! The hard drive is being sterilized."

Zach frantically punched at the power button, knowing it was probably too late. He waited for thirty seconds then turned the laptop back on. An error message blinked on the screen, "Bad or missing command interpreter". Zach knew the damage had already been done.

"Holy ....," Zach stifled the expletive he desperately wanted to scream at the blinking message. Angie really disliked it if he swore. He was genuinely trying to stop using such language. "What else can go wrong?" Zach moaned as he slammed the laptop shut.

He sat down on the toolbox and considered what to do next. The virus could not possibly be an accident. Zach had personally installed virus protection software on all their communications computers and laptops several months earlier and Fred only used the laptop for field work. There could be no doubt the virus had been deliberately planted on the laptop and that Fred had been murdered.

There could be only one reason. Fred must have learned something that someone did not want known. Something serious enough to kill for. The events of the past several days replayed in Zach's mind as he tried to make sense of his friend's death.

If all those events were related, Fred must have stumbled onto something big. If that were true, it meant he must also be in danger.

Zach hurriedly disconnected the test equipment and replaced all the microwave system covers. There was not enough time to pack the test equipment for shipment back to the office, so he just piled it in the corner of the building. Zach had a very unsettled feeling in the pit of his stomach. Something gnawed at his subconscious, making him feel as if he was overlooking some piece of a puzzle. He needed to get back to Tulsa so he could reexamine all the test data that had been gathered.

He turned the lights off, slammed the door, and verified it was locked. He jumped in his rental car, started the engine, and raced down the access lane toward the main road. A quick stop to open and close and then relock the gate and he was on his way to Albuquerque and a flight back to Tulsa.

After Zach came down out of Monticello Canyon and the highway straightened out, he set the cruise control just above the speed limit. Arriving at the airport, he quickly dropped off the rental car and caught the shuttle bus to the airport.

Zach rushed up to the ticket counter and purchased a ticket for the next flight to Tulsa, scheduled to depart in just fifty-five minutes.

Zach's haste to return to Tulsa, likely saved his life. The agents sent to watch him, and silence him if necessary, arrived at the airport just as he was boarding his flight.

During the flight to Tulsa, Zach had time to dwell on Fred's so-called accident. He pulled the roll of film he had found in Fred's toolbox out of his pocket and rolled it around in his fingers. Staring at the film canister, he wondered if the photos inside would shed some light on the unanswered question swirling around inside his head.

Someone had murdered Fred. Of that he was certain. That meant he would need to be very, very careful. He promised himself he would find out who was responsible for Fred's death. And he would see to it they paid dearly.

CHAPTER THIRTY-ONE

Saturday, March 28 - 1420 Eastern Daylight Time
CIA Headquarters
Langley, Virginia

Deputy Director Frank Porter sat at his desk attempting to wade through the stacks of memos and surveillance reports threatening to overflow his desk. He was unable to concentrate and was falling behind on his normal tasks since his last encounter with Mister Green. Porter was deeply worried, not just because of the threat Mister Green had made, but because the scheme he was involved in seemed to be imploding. If the agents he dispatched to New Mexico failed, it would mean prison for a very, very long time.

Porter jumped and sloshed coffee on his chin and down the front of his shirt when the cell phone is his pocket buzzed unexpectedly. He yanked the cell phone out of his jacket pocket and flipped it open. "Porter. I hope you have some good news," he exclaimed, dabbing at his shirt with a couple of tissues.

"No sir," Agent Williamson stammered, swallowing hard, knowing the tongue lashing that was about to come. "I have not heard anything from the agents I sent to watch Templeton and Agent Tiner."

"What?" Porter shrieked. "It has been twenty-four hours. They must be there by now."

"Yes sir," Williamson answered. "Their flight was scheduled to arrive there around nine p.m. local time."

"Has Agent Tiner reported in yet?" Porter asked.

"No sir," Williamson gulped. "I have not heard from him either. He has simply disappeared"

"What kind of kindergarten are you running?" Porter fumed. "Contact them immediately and get a status report. Call me back as soon as you know what is going on. Can you handle that?"

"Yes sir," Williamson replied, knowing that the less said the better.

Porter slammed the cell phone closed and swore. What was happening? The whole operation was falling apart.

He decided to not wait for that idiot Williamson. He flipped open the cell phone and dialed Agent Tiner's cell phone number. He waited. The voice mail system picked up immediately after the first ring. Porter slammed the cell phone closed and swore again.

"What kind of incompetent idiots do I have working for me?" Porter growled.

Any further work on the mountain of paper sitting on his desk would be hopeless. He was far too angry and agitated to concentrate. For fifteen long minutes he just sat there staring out the window. The cell phone vibrating and dancing in a circle on the surface of his desk got his attention.

He picked it up on the second ring. "Porter. What have you got?"

"Ahh … Ahh …," Williamson stammered, afraid to continue.

"Come on. Out with it," Porter demanded. "I don't have all day."

"I am afraid I have bad news," Williamson choked, summoning the courage to continue. "I could not reach either of the agents I sent. All I got was their voice mail, so I called the Albuquerque office to see if they knew anything."

Porter waited for Williamson to continue. Seconds passed. Exasperated, he barked into the phone, "Well, is that it?"

"No sir. The Albuquerque office said two FBI agents were found murdered in their hotel rooms. Shot twice in the back of the head, execution style." Williamson blurted out.

Silence. Porter sat there stunned, speechless.

Williamson waited. Desiring to get the shouting and screaming over with, he asked, "Sir?"

"Any details we should be worried about?" Porter asked. "Are you certain they cannot be traced back to us?"

"No details sir," Williamson replied, surprised there was no screaming from Porter. "The Albuquerque office said the local authorities have no leads whatsoever. The two men I selected were off-grid. I assure you their fingerprints are not recorded anywhere. The local authorities will assume they are undercover FBI."

"I hope you're right," Porter conceded. "Stay close to your phone. I'll be in touch."

Porter flipped the phone closed and dropped it back in his jacket pocket. He swiveled his chair and stared out the office window, a vacant look on his face. Five minutes passed. He got up from the chair and pushed it up to the desk.

"That's it! This operation is over! Mister Green can make all the threats he wants to. I'm going to pull the plug," he muttered as he headed for the door.

* * *

Saturday March 28 - 1705 Eastern Daylight Time
Submarine Force Atlantic (COMSUBLANT)
Building Three, Naval Submarine Base
New London, Connecticut

Vice Admiral Beckwith pushed open the door to Submarine Force Atlantic headquarters. He walked down the hallway to the Submarine Development Squadron 12 duty office and stuck his ID badge into the security card reader. After a few second delay, the electronic lock clunked as it withdrew the locking bolt. Beckwith pulled the door open and stepped in.

Lcdr. Paul Davis, command duty officer, for Submarine Development Squadron 12, turned around from the file cabinet he had been stuffing folders into. He quickly straightened to attention when he saw the three bright gold stars on the shoulder boards of the officer approaching the counter.

"May I help you Admiral?" Davis asked.

"Yes you may Mister Davis," Beckwith answered, pulling a leather wallet out of his inside jacket pocket. He flopped it open, and held it in front of Davis. "There is a situation developing in the mid-Atlantic and I need to know what assets are available."

"Yes sir," Davis exclaimed, realizing who was standing in front of him. "Just a list or do you need to know current positioning data?"

"I need current positioning data for all Squadron Twelve assets," Beckwith replied.

Davis pressed a button under the counter to release the door to the squadron's communication and control center. "Right this way sir."

Beckwith pushed the door open and followed Davis down a short hallway and into the communication and control center. The two radiomen on duty nearly had a heart attack when they saw a three-star admiral walk into the room. Immediately dropping what they were doing, they jumped to attention.

"As you were," Beckwith directed.

Beckwith walked over to the situation display and studied the positioning of the various squadron assets. Unable to make out the small characters describing each asset he looked at one of the duty radiomen, pointed to a spot on the display and asked, "Can you expand the display right there?"

"Yes sir," the radioman responded, typing in a command on the keyboard in front of him. "Is that enough sir?"

"A little more please," Beckwith responded.

The radioman typed in another command. Beckwith watched as the icons on the display grew larger and the underwater topography became more distinct. He studied the positions of the assets for several minutes.

"When is the next comm check for the *Toledo*?" Beckwith asked.

Davis studied a chart on the wall opposite the display board, then answered, "The *Toledo* had its last comm check just over an hour ago sir. Their next scheduled comm check is eighteen hours from now."

"How about this one?" Beckwith asked, pointing to a different icon.

Davis bent over the display board and consulted the chart. "That is the *Georgia* sir. Next comm check is twenty hours from now."

"Are there any assets with a comm check in less than twelve hours?" Beckwith questioned.

Davis directed the radioman to highlight all assets with a comm check due in less than twelve hours. The radioman typed in a series of commands. Beckwith watched as a bright green circle appeared around three assets. He studied the positions of the three highlighted assets relative to the point he was interested in.

"This one," Beckwith said pointing at one of the glowing icons.

"That is the *San Juan* sir. Comm check is due at 0810 Zulu, ten hours from now", Davis advised.

"That will have to do. Follow me," Beckwith said as he turned to leave the communication and control center.

"Good job gentlemen," Davis called out to the duty radiomen as he turned and followed Beckwith down the hallway and into the duty office.

Beckwith exited the duty office and stood in front of the counter. He pulled a communications order from his briefcase and laid it in front of Davis.

"Mister Davis, this communications order is to be sent to the *San Juan* marked Operational Immediate and scheduled for the next comm check," Beckwith said.

"But sir …."

"I know Mister Davis," Beckwith interrupted. "The situation is urgent and demands special handling."

"Very well sir," Davis acknowledged, taking the communications order and placing it in the "Priority Action" folder. He watched Beckwith exit the squadron office. There was definitely something peculiar going on. Two admirals requesting special message handling in just three days.

Davis tagged the latest message for priority processing, called for a duty runner, and returned to his task at the file cabinet. Fifteen minutes later, he heard the duty office door open again. He turned and to his utter amazement he saw another senior flag officer standing at the counter.

"Good evening, Mister Davis," Rear Admiral Charles Hadley said. "Do you remember me?"

"Yes sir, I do," Davis answered.

"I have an urgent EAM message for USS *Providence*," Hadley announced, leaning across the counter, displaying his DNI badge. "It must go out immediately. Same processing as before. I was not here. There was no message."

"May I speak freely sir?" Davis asked.

"You may Mister Davis," Hadley affirmed.

"Something peculiar is going on sir," Davis remarked, hoping he was not climbing out on a limb and jeopardizing his career. "Three emergency communications requests with absolute secrecy delivered by senior flag officers in just three days is highly unusual to say the least sir."

"What do you mean?" Hadley questioned. "I have only been here twice. Who delivered the third request?"

"Vice Admiral Beckwith," Davis answered. "He was here just fifteen minutes ago."

"Give me the details," Hadley ordered.

Davis, hoping he was not making a gigantic mistake, took a deep breath and continued, "He wanted to know what assets were available and when their next scheduled comm checks were. He selected one and gave me an Operational Immediate communications request."

"What asset and what location?" Hadley demanded.

"The USS *San Juan*, located approximately one hundred twenty miles north-northwest of São Miguel Island."

A worried look spread across Hadley's face. This had gone much further than he anticipated. He would have to have help and soon to prevent the catastrophe he feared was already in motion.

Hadley looked directly at Davis and spoke with an authority that left no doubt he meant exactly what he said, "Mister Davis, you are absolutely correct. I am giving you a direct order not to mention any of this to anyone. Am I clear?"

"Yes sir. Absolutely clear sir!" Davis acknowledged.

"Mister Davis, if you help me keep this under wraps, I promise you will be remembered," Hadley turned and hurriedly left the squadron duty office.

CHAPTER THIRTY-TWO

Sunday, March 29 – 0305 Eastern Daylight Time
Iron Forge Road
Walkers Mill, Maryland

Rear Admiral Charles Hadley lay awake staring into the darkness, unable to sleep due to the growing apprehension he felt. He had tossed and turned for over an hour. Exasperated, he decided to get out of bed rather than wake his wife, sleeping soundly beside him. He slid out from under the covers, felt his way to the door, and carefully eased it closed. Using the dim green glow from the nightlight at the end of the hall, he made his way into the kitchen. He pulled the refrigerator open, poured himself a small glass of milk, and headed for his office.

Admiral Hadley set the glass of milk on a coaster and sat in the swivel chair. Placing his elbows on the desk, he rested his chin on his hands. He was deeply worried about the sudden rash of suspicious deaths that had occurred. First, there was Commander Owen's urgent middle of the night request to help someone he thought to be long dead, escape from Europe with documents Commander Owen would not discuss, using off the record, backchannel assets. Second, there was an increase in submarine flash message traffic, initiated outside of normal channels. Third, the sudden alteration of a submarine's patrol route. And fourth, the rash of violent deaths of civilians and federal agents in proximity to one Zachariah Templeton.

Hadley was convinced something major was brewing. He had already complied with Owen's request for a backchannel escape plan. Owen was not an alarmist. If he said there was a major threat, he believed him without question. He also needed to protect Mister Templeton. For some reason, as yet unknown, Mister Templeton seemed to be at the center of whatever was going on. How was he going to protect Mister Templeton? "I know just the man," Hadley remarked, reaching for the phone on his desk.

"Yeah, who is it?" John Rodgers, Director of WITSEC, Witness

Security Program, answered on the fifth ring.

"John, this is Admiral Hadley. How are you?"

"Just fine Chuck," Rodgers huffed. "You do know it's the middle of the night don't you?"

"Yes, Yes. I'm sorry John," Hadley apologized. "It's very important. I need a favor. And I need it quick."

"At three in the morning?" Rodgers objected.

"Yes," Hadley shot back. "At three in the morning. It's that important."

"Okay, okay," Rodgers relented. "Go ahead. Ask away."

"I need a contact number for Bobby Joe," Hadley replied.

"No sir. No can do," Rodgers' responded without hesitation. "You know as well as I do I can't give out information about him."

"John, I know that," Hadley argued. "I assure you there is good reason. I wouldn't ask otherwise."

"I don't think …,"

"John, this is critical," Hadley continued, cutting Rodgers off midsentence. "I have a level four threat developing. I have good reason to believe it centers around a Mister Zachariah Templeton. Otherwise, I would not have called you."

Hadley waited. When Rodgers did not respond, he repeated his request, "I really need his number John."

"Ahh … I'll have to call you back," Rodgers replied.

"I need it right away," Hadley stressed. "Call me back on this number."

"Yes, Chuck. Give me five minutes," Rodgers said as he hung up.

Admiral Hadley sat in the dim light and waited. Six minutes later the phone rang. "John, do you have a number for me?"

"Yes I do," Rodgers answered. "You owe me big time. I had to tell some pretty big fibs to get this number, especially at three in the morning."

"Thanks John. I'll buy you the biggest, juiciest steak in town," Hadley said. "You just name the time and place."

"That's a deal Chuck," Rodgers agreed. "Oh, by the way his name is Norman Glover. I hope he agrees to help you. I'd be surprised if he even talks to you."

"I sure hope he does," Hadley added.

Hadley fished a small notebook out of the top drawer of the desk and wrote the phone number down as Rodgers called out the numbers. He thanked his friend profusely and hung up the phone. A jiggle of the mouse sitting on the desk, woke the computer from its sleep mode. He located a web site that listed area codes and searched for the area code he had written in his notebook. The area code was for southern Washington state. He closed the internet connection and looked at the clock. It was three twenty-nine a.m. in Maryland. That meant it was half past midnight in Washington state. Norman Glover would likely be in bed. *"Oh, well. What have I got to lose*," Hadley thought as he punched in the number.

In a small two bedroom ranch house on Northeast One Hundred fifty-ninth Street in Mount Vista, Washington, a telephone rang. After six rings, the house's owner grabbed the portable phone from the charger sitting on the nightstand and mumbled, "Hello, who is this?"

"Sorry to wake you Mister Glover. This is Rear Admiral Charles Hadley."

"Huh. Admiral who?" Norman Glover grunted, trying to clear the fog of sleep.

"Rear Admiral Charles Hadley from the Office of Naval Intelligence."

"Is this some kind of joke?" Norman growled. "What do you mean calling in the middle of the might?"

"I assure you this is no joke," Hadley replied. " I need your help."

"I don't know any Rear Admiral Hadley," Norman protested. "I'm going to hang up."

"No. No. Please don't hang up," Hadley begged. "Bobby Joe, I really need your help."

"How do you know that name?" Norman demanded.

"What's going on?" Norman's wife asked, awakened by his sudden shouting.

"Hang on a minute," Norman said, putting his hand over the mouthpiece. "Just go back to sleep honey. I'll take this in the other room." Norman slid out of bed, closed the door, and walked into the living room. He switched on a small lamp and sat down.

"Okay, explain to me how you found me."

"I got your number from Director John Rodgers," Hadley answered.

"I don't believe you," Norman blurted out. "He wouldn't do that. He promised."

"This is a special circumstance," Hadley countered. "I know your background. All the details. And I mean all the details. You are the only one that can help me. I begged Director Rodgers for your number."

"No sir! I'm done with that!" Norman shouted, visions of a former life swirling in his mind. Horrible, awful visions. "I walked away from that life. I vowed I would never return. I want no part of that life again, not ever!"

"I'm sorry," Hadley offered. "There is a disturbing situation developing. It requires someone with very specific skills, if you know what I mean."

"No sir. I said I don't do that anymore," Norman repeated.

"Mister Glover, it is absolutely imperative that you help me," Hadley exclaimed. "I need to have someone protected. It seems that a Mister Zachariah Templeton is smack dab in the middle of the situation. People around him are turning up dead, murdered without even a shred of evidence. They are professional hits."

Hadley waited for a response. He had played his one and only trump card. He hoped and prayed it would persuade Glover to agree to help him. No response. Just silence. Hadley asked again, "Mister Glover will you help me?"

"I can't believe I'm saying this," Norman moaned. "I agree. I will help you. When and where?"

"Thank you Mister Glover," Hadley chimed. "I'll have a plane pick you up at McChord Air Force Base in Lakeview at zero five hundred your time. Stop at the gate and show your ID. They will clear you in and take you directly to the flight line. As you might imagine, absolute secrecy is required. There is a very high level leak somewhere. You are to trust no one."

"Who will be my contact?", Norman asked.

"Your orders will come from me only. The pilot on the aircraft will provide you with an untraceable cell phone. Mister Glover, this is an off-the-books operation. If you get caught, I will not be able to help you."

"Supplies and equipment?" Norman questioned.

"Absolutely anything you need Mister Glover," Hadley answered, without hesitation. "Give a list to the guard at the gate. Everything you need will be waiting at your destination."

"Which is?" Norman asked.

"You will be told on the plane, after you take off," Hadley replied, hanging up the phone.

"What is it dear?" Norman's wife asked as she walked into the living room. "You look upset."

"They found me," Norman stammered. "I need to pack a bag."

"No Norman no! Not Again! You promised." his wife shrieked, following him into the bedroom.

CHAPTER THIRTY-THREE

Sunday, March 29 – 0803 Zulu
USS San Juan (SSN 751)
Sedlo Seamount; 40°13'N, 26°16'W
North of Azores Island

Commander Steven Richards, commanding officer of the USS *San Juan*, walked into the Conn, the command and control center of the boat, and observed the activities of the crewmen on duty. He glanced at the digital clock on the bulkhead. It was almost time for their routine scheduled comm check. He stepped over to the navigation table and asked Lt. Trent Hill, *San Juan's* navigation officer, where they were.

"Right here sir," Hill replied, making a pencil mark on the chart affixed to the navigation table. "Approximately seventy nine hundred yards north-northwest of Sedlo seamount."

"XO, what's our depth?" Richards asked.

"Quartermaster, Conn, what is our depth?" Lcdr. Edgar Dixon, *San Juan's* Executive Officer, relayed through the 1-MC.

"Conn, Quartermaster, current depth to keel is over thirteen hundred fathoms," Quartermaster First Class Gregory McCain answered.

Richards stepped up on the platform and spoke to the executive officer, "I have the Conn."

"Aye aye sir," Dixon acknowledged.

"Sonar, Conn, any contacts?" Richards inquired.

"Conn, Sonar, none sir. We hold no contacts at this time."

"Dive, Conn, five degree up bubble. Bring us to periscope depth." Richards ordered.

"Conn, Dive, five degree up bubble. Come to periscope depth aye," EM3 Kent Green responded, pulling back on the control yoke.

"Conn aye."

"Helm, Conn, ahead slow. Make turns for three knots," Richards ordered to prevent the periscope from making excessive noise as it sliced through the water.

"Conn, Helm, ahead slow. Make turns for three knots aye," EM2 Mike Hall answered.

"Conn aye."

The boat pitched slightly upward and began rising to the requested depth. When the boat reached periscope depth, Richards requested the periscope to be raised. He knelt down and put his eyes to the periscope, following it up to its full extended position, he made a full circle. Finding no surface ships or obstructions, he requested the periscope to be lowered.

"XO, raise the UHF SATCOM antenna," Richards ordered.

"Aye aye sir," Dixon answered. "UHF SATCOM antenna going up."

"Radio, Conn, UHF antenna is up. Commence scheduled comm check."

"Conn, Radio, commencing scheduled comm check," Radioman First Class Tim Bentley answered.

Bentley activated the UHF SATCOM radio link, watching the display intently. The display flashed "Acquiring" in bright green characters. After several seconds the display changed to "Ident", signifying the radio system had established a link with the satellite. The green flashing characters remained on the screen as the computer aboard *San Juan* communicated with the computer at the Navy's communication center. The flashing characters changed from green to red and the phrase "Flash Traffic" appeared on the screen.

Bentley reached up and thumbed the lever on the 7-MC, "Conn, Radio, comm system reports flash traffic sir."

"Conn aye," Richards acknowledged. "Receive the message, print it, and hold it. I will be there shortly."

"Receive, print, and hold aye," Bentley responded.

Bentley punched the appropriate commands into the computer system and waited while the message printed. The two computers had verified their respective identities and had transmitted the entire message in milliseconds.

"Conn, Radio, message complete sir," Bentley announced. "Message is designated Operational Immediate."

Richards acknowledged the message receipt and looked over at the XO, "Mister Dixon you have the Conn. I'll go find out what the flash message is all about."

"Aye aye sir. I have the Conn," Dixon answered to Richards' back as he disappeared down the passageway, sprinting toward the communication center.

"Coming down," Richards shouted as he started down the ladder to the lower level of the boat. Crewmen scrambled to get out of the captain's way. He hit the bottom of the ladder and ran down the passageway and stepped into the communication center. "Pass me the flash traffic message." Bentley did as ordered, handing him the message printout he was holding. Richards eyes widened as he read the message. He turned and ran back toward the Conn.

"Mister Hill you have the Conn," Richards panted, out of breath from the sprint back from the communications center. "Mister Dixon with me. Mister Hill notify all department heads to meet me in the wardroom. It doesn't matter what they are doing. I want them there ASAP."

Richards rushed to the wardroom with Dixon sprinting close behind. They entered the wardroom, Richards taking his usual seat at the head of the table with the XO immediately to his right. Richards was sweating from the exertion of running to the communication center and back to the Conn and then to the wardroom.

"What's up sir?" Dixon asked.

"Not yet," Richards said. "Wait till the department heads get here."

Richards pulled a handkerchief out of his hip pocket and wiped his face while they waited for the department heads to arrive. The department heads arrived over a two minute time span, each officer taking his assigned seat. Once all department heads had arrived, Richards nodded at Dixon, who got up and closed the door.

"Gentlemen, we have an extremely serious situation," Richards began. "We just received a flash traffic, Operational Immediate message from COMSUBLANT. It has been reported that USS *Providence* is now three comm checks overdue. As you would expect, COMSUBLANT is quite concerned about *Providence* being so long overdue. However, there is an even more ominous concern."

Richards looked up, waiting for the sudden chatter to cease, "Gentlemen if I may. The message goes on to say the captain of *Providence* is suspected of operating outside standard protocols. The message ..."

"There has to be a good reason why ...," Lt. Franklin Bishop, *San Juan's* Weapons officer, interrupted.

Richards' raised hand and icy stare silenced Bishop midsentence. Richards continued, "As I was saying. The message stops short of saying he has gone rogue, but the inference is definitely there. COMSUBLANT has ordered us to change course and intercept *Providence*." Richards hesitated, knowing the reaction the final paragraph of the message would illicit. He continued, "If we intercept *Providence* and she does not respond, we have been authorized to use whatever force necessary to stop her. Even if it means sinking her."

The officers sitting around the wardroom table were stunned, looking at each other in disbelief.

"They can't be serious," Lt. Alfred Patterson, *San Juan's* Engineering officer, sputtered.

"Dead serious," Richards affirmed as he slid the message printout to the center of the table.

Several of the officers got up from their chairs and gathered around to read the message for themselves. There were more gasps and exclamations of disbelief. Richards waited for the agitation to subside and for the officers to return to their seats.

"Gentlemen I don't have to tell you what this means," Richards pointed out. "Everyone, and I mean everyone, on this boat will have to be at their peak performance. We will go to our highest state of readiness. Four on, four off. When the men are not on duty, I want absolute quiet. Only critical activities will be performed, as quietly as possible. Am I understood gentlemen? Any questions?"

Each of the department heads acknowledged the captain. Since there were no questions, Richards ended the meeting, "Dismissed gentlemen."

Everyone left the wardroom except for Richards and the XO. The XO turned and looked at the Richards, "Sir, are you really going to sink *Providence?*"

"If I need to, absolutely!" Richards affirmed.

They both got up from the wardroom table and hurried back to the Conn. Richards arrived first, stepped up onto the platform, and announced, "I have the Conn."

"Aye aye sir," Lt. Hill acknowledged as he stepped down and returned to the navigation table.

Richards reached up, punched the "All Stations" button, and spoke into the 1-MC, "Attention all crewmembers, this is the captain. We have been notified by COMSUBLANT that USS *Providence* is overdue for three comm checks and is suspected of operating outside standard protocols. We have been ordered to locate her and to stop her using whatever measures necessary. We are going to readiness condition Alpha-One. If you have questions or concerns, speak to your department heads."

As expected, there were murmurs and whispers all over the boat. It would take some time for the shock to settle in. In spite of the crew's shock, Richards did not have the slightest doubt the crew of *San Juan* was up to the task.

Richards stepped down from the platform, stepped over to the navigation table, and studied the chart for several minutes. He stepped back up to the platform.

Richards keyed the 1-MC, "All Stations, rig for ultra-quiet. If you are not on watch you are to be resting, quietly. Critical activities only."

"Helm, Conn, left full rudder come to course one-three-two," Richards ordered.

"Conn, Helm, left full rudder come to course one-three-two aye."

"Conn aye."

"Helm, Conn, all ahead standard. Make turns for fifteen knots," Richards added.

"Conn, Helm, all ahead standard. Make turns for fifteen knots aye."

"Conn aye."

Beneath the professional exterior he displayed, Richards was also deeply stunned. He was close friends with Commander Chandler, commanding officer of the *Providence*, and knew him quite well. Chandler and his family had been guests at their house several times. He was having great difficulty believing Chandler could be guilty of what COMSUBLANT said he was. However, it was not his duty to question orders. It was his duty to follow them. And follow orders he would.

In spite of his commitment to follow orders, deep inside Richards asked himself if he could actually order the destruction of *Providence* and send her to the bottom of the ocean. Every fiber of his being hoped and prayed he would not be required to make that decision. But if the time came and the decision presented itself, yes, he would give the order to sink *Providence*.

Richards stepped off the platform and turned toward the navigation table, his singular objective: to hunt down and, if necessary, send an old friend to a watery grave.

CHAPTER THIRTY-FOUR

Zach had driven to the office early to try to make sense of the strange issues affecting the DOD microwave system in New Mexico. Fortunately for Zach, it was Sunday and there was no one at the office. When he arrived he was so upset he sat for a long time and just stared out the office window.

Zach felt miserable. He was exhausted and his head ached. The grief of losing his close friend, the strain of making funeral arrangements and attending to Rachael's needs, the arguments with Angie, and the data problems with the microwave system in New Mexico; were pushing Zach toward the brink of collapse.

He turned away from the window and stared at Fred's note. No matter how hard he tried, he simply could not make any sense out of them. He gave up and shifted his attention to the test data he had brought back from New Mexico. To be certain he did not lose Fred's notes, he took a small piece of tape and stuck them to the front of the computer monitor.

For two hours Zach poured over that data as he tried to determine a cause for the unusual data he had recorded in New Mexico. He tried every conceivable method of combining, filtering, and sorting the data. No matter what method he tried, the result was always the same. There was not even a clue as to the source of the interference.

He rubbed his tired, burning eyes. He desperately wanted to just quit and go home, but it was crucial he identify the problems and devise a solution to correct them. If he didn't, his company, Microwave Services Inc., was doomed.

"Why can't I solve this stupid problem?" he shouted out loud. In a sudden burst of anger his hand lashed out at the empty soda bottles sitting on his desk. The plastic bottles went flying and bounced across the floor of his office.

Needing a break and another shot of caffeine, he got up and went to the refrigerator. He grabbed another Mountain Dew and returned to his desk. Draining half of the bottle's contents, he set the bottle on his desk where the five empty bottles, now strewn across the floor, had been sitting. Many of Zach's friends thought his consumption of Mountain Dew bordered on addiction. He knew he was drinking far too much soda, but he did not care. Caffeine was all that kept him going.

No matter how he manipulated the data, he could not find even a shred of evidence that would account for the mysterious interference. Fred's note taped to the monitor nagged at his attention. He just could not keep his concentration focused on the data.

An automatic appointment alarm popped up on Zach's monitor. Zach double-clicked the icon and opened his appointment calendar. The appointment dialog box read, "Get items ready for Nevada trip on Monday, March 30."

Zach looked at the calendar on his desk and shook his head. He had completely forgotten about the trip scheduled for Monday. Fred's funeral was tomorrow. He would have to call the airline and change his reservation to Tuesday morning.

He was getting nowhere and his patience was wearing thin. Swiveling his chair toward the window, he stared blankly out the widow. The phone rang. Turning back toward the desk, he looked at the phone. Had it not been his personal line flashing, he would have ignored it.

Zach picked up the receiver and answered, "Hello, Microwave Services. This is Zach Templeton. May I help you."

"You don't know me but we need to talk," FBI Agent Benjamin Slater said.

"What are you talking about?" Zach asked.

"We need to meet. Today, if you can possibly manage it. It's very important," Slater insisted.

"I'm very busy," Zach answered. "I have a funeral tomorrow and I have to go out of town early the next day. It will have to wait until I get back. The office is closed tomorrow for a funeral. Call on Tuesday and make an appointment with the receptionist."

"It can't wait," Slater demanded. "Does a mysterious note capsule in Bimini ring any bells Mister Templeton?"

The mention of the note got Zach's attention. Yes, he remembered quite well. The memory of the dive in Bimini was very clear. Zach was startled and left speechless.

"Mister Templeton are you still there?" Slater questioned.

Zach hesitated for several seconds before answering. "Ah … Yes. I'm still here. Who are you?"

"That's not important right now," Slater countered. "We must meet today."

"Why should I trust you?" Zach questioned.

"I can assure you it's in your best interest," Slater advised. "You have no choice but to trust me."

There is always a choice Zach thought to himself, but he was curious and he wanted an answer as to why someone had passed him the note. "Okay. I'll meet you, but it has to be a public place," Zach replied.

"That's acceptable," Slater agreed. "You name the time and place."

Zach quickly went through the list of things he had to do. Gather up the test equipment for the Nevada trip, the meeting with the funeral home, pick up Pablo at Angie's apartment, pack a bag for the trip, Fred's funeral.

"I can't meet until later," Zach replied. "I have a lot of things to do. Meet me at Ricardo's Mexican Restaurant on Forty-first Street at six thirty."

"I'll see you at six thirty," Slater answered.

Zach went to the equipment room and gathered up several pieces of test equipment he would need. He stacked the items by the door and went back to his office to shut down his computer. The portable storage device containing the test data went into the top drawer of his desk. As he was locking the drawer, the phone rang again. He really did not want to answer it. Maybe the person on the other end would give up he thought to himself.

He walked to the door and was about to leave, but the phone continued to ring. He set the test equipment on the floor, hurried back into his office, and looked at the phone.

Zach picked up the phone and gave the standard company greeting, "Microwave Services. Zach Templeton. May I help you?"

"Zach. I'm glad I caught you," Angie exclaimed. "I wanted to ask you if you would go to church with me today."

"Sorry, I can't," Zach answered. "I was just gathering up some equipment for a trip to Nevada on Tuesday.

"Please Zach," Angie begged.

"Angie, I really can't," Zach apologized.

"It's always something isn't it Zach," Angie complained.

"Angie, everything's a mess," Zach offered in defense. "Especially with Fred's death. I'll have to carry the entire load by myself."

"I'm sorry about Fred," Angie answered. "His funeral is not until tomorrow. Surely you could afford a couple of hours."

"There are things you don't understand," Zach argued.

"What things don't I understand?" Angie asked, the irritation in her voice becoming obvious.

"I can't tell you," Zach stammered.

"What on Earth are you talking about Zach," Angie blurted out.

"Angie please," Zach pleaded. "I've said too much already. Let's just leave it at that."

"Fine," Angie snapped.

"I still have to pick Pablo up," Zach continued. "I'll stop by after a dinner meeting I have this evening. Around seven thirty or so."

"I'll be here," Angie answered coldly.

"I love ….,"

The connection went dead. He stood and stared at the phone. Very gently and deliberately he placed the receiver back in its cradle, fighting the urge to pick up the phone and slam it against the wall. He took a deep breath and let it out slowly.

His situation was becoming more bizarre and frustrating with each passing day. The strange phone call. And now this. He and Angie were growing even further apart. He did not know how much more he could take.

Zach remembered the meeting he had with the man from the funeral home at one o'clock. He looked at his watch. He had a couple of hours before lunch he could use to get the equipment and his clothes packed. He slung the laptop bag strap over his shoulder and hurried to the door. Hands loaded with the test equipment, he nudged the light switch with his elbow.

His mind was filled with a thousand questions as he ran toward the stairs that led to the basement parking garage. Perhaps the meeting that evening would begin to shed some light on the questions swirling in his head.

CHAPTER THIRTY-FIVE

Sunday, March 29 - 1827 Eastern Daylight Time
Chestnut Street
Chevy Chase, Maryland

Deputy Director Frank Porter's head bobbed up and down as he fought to stay awake. The sun glinting off the pool cast odd shapes and swirls on the ceiling of the enclosed porch covering the backyard patio. The dancing, swirling reflections had a calming effect making it difficult to fight off sleep. He rose from the chaise lounge he was laying on and padded barefooted over to the outdoor kitchen. Retrieving a pitcher from the mini-fridge, he poured himself another glass of lemonade. He set the glass on the table and climbed back into the chaise lounge.

Porter gazed out across his professionally manicured lawn, watching the late afternoon golfers hacking their golf balls down the fifteenth fairway of the Columbia Country Club. He had joined the club as part of the purchase of the house. He had tried his hand at golf, but quickly gave it up, telling everyone he just did not have time. More truthfully, he was a rotten golfer, and did not have the patience the game required.

He reached for the glass and took a large swallow of lemonade. The cell phone laying on the table began to buzz and dance around. He grabbed it, flipped it open, and spoke into it, "Yeah, what have you got," already knowing who was on the other end.

"We've got a new problem sir," Agent Williamson complained.

"Problems seem to be all you have," Porter grumbled. "Go ahead, tell me what the new problem is."

"The resource I have tailing Mister Templeton noticed someone else shadowing him," Williamson explained. "He tried to get close to the second tail but he lost him and he also lost Mister Templeton." Williamson held his breath, knowing what was coming.

"You idiot!" Porter bellowed. "What kind of lame-brain morons do you have working for you?"

"But sir he ...,"

"I refuse to listen to any more of your stupid, addle-brained excuses! Do you hear me?" Porter screeched.

"Yes sir. I hear you," Williamson answered. "I'll fly out there and take care of it personally."

"Yes, you most certainly will," Porter snapped back. "Do you have any guesses as to who it was or why someone else is following Mister Templeton?"

"No sir. I don't have any ideas?" Williamson replied.

"This is turning into a real mess," Porter croaked. "Shut down everything. Shut down the whole stinking mess."

"But sir ...,"

"I don't want to hear anymore," Porter interrupted. "It is over. Plain and simple. O – V – E – R!" Porter spelled out the last word for emphasis, continuing without giving Williamson a chance to speak, "Eliminate Mister Templeton and anyone else that could be considered a threat."

"I don't think that would be wise," Williamson protested. "We have stacked up a lot of bodies already. We'll never get away with it."

"I don't want your opinion!" Porter screamed, the veins in his neck bulging to the point of bursting. "You incompetent idiot! I want this mess cleaned up and I want it cleaned up now! I want every possible leak eliminated! Do you understand me?"

Williamson swallowed hard, "Yes sir. Understood sir."

"You had better understand. If you fail again, you had better find a deep, dark hole to hide in."

Porter was so angry he was shaking. He hurled the cell phone into the pool. It sputtered once and sank to the bottom. He closed his eyes and shook his head. He should have ended this mess a long time ago. Deep down he knew Williamson was right. They had stacked up too many bodies. It was time to put together an escape plan he could use if things went badly as he expected they soon would. He climbed out of the chaise lounge and headed for his upstairs office.

Once inside the office, he closed and locked the door. He dug in his pocket and pulled out a ring of keys, unlocked the bottom left-hand drawer of the desk, and pulled out a small lock box. The box required a different key. Inside the lock box was a selection of fake passports he always kept on hand. He selected one and locked the box, returning it to the desk drawer. He picked up the phone and dialed the American Airlines reservations desk.

"American Airlines," a female reservations specialist cooed. "How may I help you?

"I need a reservation, Washington National to Sao Paulo, Brazil, Saturday, early morning, April fourth." Porter replied.

"Let me check," the reservation specialist replied, tapping furiously on her keyboard.

"It looks like the seven-thirty flight is already overbooked." She continued, "There are two seats remaining on the nine-ten flight. It connects through Atlanta, arriving Sao Paulo at eleven thirty-five p.m. There are four seats on the six-fifteen a.m. flight connecting through Miami, arriving Sao Paulo at nine twenty-five p.m."

"I'll take the six-fifteen flight," Porter instructed. One-way tickets raised too much suspicion so he lied and requested a return flight. "I want a return flight anytime the following Saturday."

"There's a ten a.m. flight to Washington National, arrives at ten twenty-nine p.m.," she advised.

"Yes. Yes. That's fine," Porter replied.

"Name sir?" she requested.

Porter opened the fake passport and gave her the name shown inside. "Anthony Sterling," he lied.

"Okay Mister Sterling you are confirmed on the six-fifteen a.m. flight out of Washington National. How do you wish to pay for the ticket Mister Sterling?" she asked.

Porter read her the number from the credit card tucked inside the fake passport. He requested a will-call ticket be held for pick up at the airport.

He hung up the phone, walked over to the door, and unlocked it. A splitting, tension headache had developed, so he decided to go downstairs and grab a couple aspirins. What would he tell Mister Green he wondered as he padded down the stairs.

CHAPTER THIRTY-SIX

Sunday, March 29 - 1830 Central Daylight Time
Ricardo's Mexican Restaurant
Tulsa, Oklahoma

Zach worried and fretted over the upcoming meeting he had reluctantly agreed to as he drove from the funeral home to the restaurant. The warning contained in the capsule that had been passed to him, Fred's suspicious death, and the cryptic note Fred left combined to make Zach extremely distrustful of everyone. He pulled into the restaurant parking lot and went inside.

He stepped up to the hostess station and announced himself, "I'm Zach Templeton. I'm supposed to meet someone."

"Yes, Mister Templeton," the hostess said. "Your party is already here. Please follow me."

The hostess led Zach to a small table in the back of the restaurant. She waited while he sat down. "Can I get you gentlemen anything from the bar?" she asked.

"Light beer," Agent Benjamin Slater answered.

"Scotch rocks for me," Zach replied, knowing Angie would disapprove but, given the circumstances, he convinced himself he needed something to calm his nerves.

The hostess scribbled on a pad then left.

Slater held out his ID for Zach to see, "I'm FBI Field Agent Benjamin Slater. Sorry about your friend."

"Thanks," Zach replied.

"I guess you're wondering why I asked you to meet me," Slater continued.

"Yes. That thought did cross my mind," Zach answered. He was not going to offer any information until he found out exactly why Slater had asked for this meeting.

"Just some routine questions regarding Mister Hargrove's death," Slater lied.

"Why is the FBI interested in Fred's death?" Zach questioned. "He worked for the CIA and besides he quit almost a year ago."

Slater had suspected Zach would be too smart to fall for the standard FBI line, so he tried another ploy, "You only thought he quit. He was working undercover." Slater watched Zach's eyes to see what response his new ploy would provoke.

"What are you talking about?" Zach responded, his voice rising.

"Easy, Mister Templeton, " Slater urged. "Lower your voice. You have no idea of the risk I'm taking even being here with you."

"Let's drop the pretense," Zach snapped. "We both know Fred's death was no accident." Zach waited and watched Slater. It was his turn to make the other man squirm, to see what response his statement would elicit.

"I have no idea what you mean," Slater lied again.

"What kind of an idiot do you take me for?" Zach declared. "If this is the kind of games you're going to play, I'm leaving." Zach pushed his chair back from the table and started to get up.

"Wait. Wait," Slater pleaded.

"If you want me to stay, you had better start being straight with me," Zach warned.

"Okay, okay," Slater conceded. "But you have to promise me that anything I tell you will stay between you and me."

"I can't promise anything until I hear what you have to say," Zach remarked. He felt as if he was in the driver's seat and he intended for it to stay that way. Zach continued, "How was the water in Bimini, Agent Slater?"

"Huh, what on earth are you talking about?" Slater sputtered.

"Don't give me that, "Zach countered. "I recognized your eyes from behind the mask. I remember the dragon tattooed on the inside of your arm." Zach grabbed Slater's" arm and turned it over. A very distinct dragon revealed itself on the inside of his forearm.

Zach continued, "You had better give me some answers right now or I'm leaving."

"Yes. It was me that day in Bimini," Slater confessed. "Please believe me Mister Templeton. I don't have all the answers. Not yet anyway. Someone tried to kill you that day. If it hadn't been for me you would be dead."

"Kill me?" Zach blurted out. "What are you talking about? Why would anyone want to kill me?"

"I don't know that yet," Slater answered. "But if you help me, I believe I can find out." Slater knew he was taking a risk by revealing that information. If his superior found out, he would also be in extreme danger.

"I'm listening," Zach responded.

"I don't think we should talk here," Slater warned. "We need a place that is more private. Can you meet me somewhere tomorrow?"

"No. Not possible," Zach answered. "Fred's funeral is tomorrow. And then the family dinner. I'll be tied up all day. I'm going out of town early Tuesday morning. Won't be back for a couple of days. You'll just have to tell me now."

Slater opened his mouth to say something but stopped. He turned his chair to the left and whispered, "Don't say anymore. Someone came in and is watching us. Act outraged when I ask you to help us."

The waitress returned. They waited as she placed their drinks in front of them. Slater grabbed his beer and drained half of it. He sat the bottle down and wiped his mouth on his sleeve.

Zach picked up his scotch, sloshed the ice around, and took a large swallow of the golden liquid. The fiery liquor burned his throat as it went down. He took another, smaller sip and set the glass down. Already he could feel the warmth spreading from his stomach.

Slater continued, "Mister Templeton, we would like your help in clearing this matter up."

Zach had no idea why, but something inside urged him to play along with Slater. "No, Agent Slater. I don't think so," he answered, allowing his voice to rise a little.

"But Mister Templeton, we really need your help," Slater pleaded for effect.

"I said no! I want no part of it!" Zach said angrily, shoving his chair back. He hoped he was not overplaying his role. His voice had been loud enough that most of the people in the restaurant had taken notice and were watching.

Zach started to walk away, stopped, pulled out his wallet, and grabbed a couple of bills. Returning to the table, he dropped the bills on the table, winked at Slater, leaned over, and spoke directly in his face, "Don't bother me again." As he rose up, he whispered under his breath, "Call my office tomorrow. I'll make sure they can reach me."

Zach turned and exited the restaurant, uncertain of what he had just gotten himself into.

Zach unlocked his car and got in. He sat there staring straight ahead. Nothing made any sense. He had to be missing something. A sudden bright flash of light broke his concentration. To the North he saw the tell-tale flash of a thunderstorm approaching. If he hurried, he might get home before the storm arrived. He started the engine and raced out of the parking lot.

Arriving at Angie's apartment, his last stop, he punched the door bell and waited.

Angie opened the door. "Zach. Come in. I'll get Pablo's leash."

Zach heard Pablo's nails clicking on the floor as he came running out of the kitchen. He ran toward Zach and jumped into his arms.

"Hey Pablo. How are you boy?" Zach cooed.

Pablo was wiggling all over and licking Zach's face. Angie laughed at the hilarious sight when she returned to the living room.

"Did he get along okay?" Zach asked.

"He did just fine."

"I really appreciate your keeping him Angie," Zach managed to say between licks.

"Not a problem. I love having him around. It doesn't seem so quiet when he's here."

"Thanks again. Gotta run", Zach said reaching for the door.

"Why don't you stay awhile," Angie urged. "I think we should talk about the blow up earlier."

"Sorry, I can't," Zach apologized. "I have to arrange some final details for Fred's funeral tomorrow. And I've got some things to do at home tonight."

"There's always an excuse isn't there Zach," Angie declared, an accusing look on her face.

"Let's not do this tonight. Please," Zach begged. "I've been at the office most of the day. I still have some things to do to get ready for a trip to Nevada on Tuesday. Tomorrow will be a very trying day. I'm tired and I have to get up early in the morning."

"What excuse will it be next time Zach?" Angie taunted.

"After I get back from Nevada we'll talk," Zach promised.

"No we won't," Angie scolded.

Zach started to say more but thought better of it. There was so much he wanted to say, but his emotions were so enflamed he knew if he said any more it would turn into a full blown argument. And he did not want to involve Angie until he had more answers.

"Angie, do you want me to come by and pick you up for Fred's funeral?" Zach asked.

"No. I'll meet you at the funeral home," Angie responded coolly.

Zach leaned toward Angie to kiss her. She turned away and walked into the kitchen.

"See you tomorrow," Zach called out as he headed for the door. He hooked the leash to Pablo's collar and left Angie's apartment.

Zach opened his car door and put Pablo on the front seat. "Pablo, move over so I can get in," Zach complained.

Pablo leaped to the other side of the car, put his paws on the arm rest, waiting for Zach to roll the window down. Zach lowered the window several inches. Pablo stuck his nose out the window and sniffed the night air as Zach backed his car out of the parking space.

"Let's go home, copilot Pablo," Zach laughed.

Pablo wagged his tail furiously and barked at a passing car. He loved to ride in the car, often accompanying Zach on short trips. Half way home, Zach remembered he had forgotten to pick up the film from Fred's toolbox he had dropped off to be developed. He considered leaving it until he returned from his trip, but he was eager to see what was on the film.

He pulled into the left turn lane and made a u-turn at the next intersection. He backtracked and pulled into the drugstore's parking lot. It was after seven p.m. and the parking lot was mostly empty. He pulled into an empty parking space right in front of the drugstore.

As he got out of the car he patted Pablo on the head and said, "Stay. I'll be right back."

He went inside and picked up the photographs. When he came out of the drugstore, he walked to the small liquor store four doors down in the strip mall.

Zach strolled the aisles of the liquor store trying to decide what he wanted. His nerves were frazzled and he wanted something soothing. He selected a very old, and very expensive, blended, Canadian whiskey.

He carried the bottle to the counter, set it down, and fished out his wallet. "Hey Doug. Can a person get some service here?" he called out to the man restocking the wine rack. Zach almost always purchased his liquor from this store and had come to know the owner quite well.

"What's up Zach. Ain't seen you in a coon's age," Doug Blackwell, owner of the store responded. "I'll be right there. Let me finish stacking this case."

The owner finished placing the wine bottles on the rack, then walked over to the cash register. "Not the usual Zach," he observed.

"Felt like something different," Zach explained.

"Just heard about your friend. My condolences," Blackwell offered.

"Thanks," Zach responded.

The owner picked up the bottle of whiskey to check the price. "Mighty good stuff. Planning a big shindig?"

"No. It's been a long day and I need something soothing."

Blackwell rang up the price. Zach paid for the whiskey and left the store. He returned to the car and dropped the bottle in the back seat. As Zach started the car, Pablo took up his normal position on the passenger side arm rest with his nose out the window.

Zach backed out of the space, turned right onto the street, and drove the rest of the way home deep in thought. He pulled into his garage, punched the garage door opener, and waited for the door to close.

"Come on Pablo. Let's go get something to eat," Zach said as he opened the car door.

Pablo bounded out of the car, ran over to the door, and scratched at it, waiting for Zach to let him in. Zach retrieved the bottle of whiskey from the back seat and walked over to the door. He fished his house keys out of his pocket and unlocked the door. Pablo flew into the kitchen and immediately ran over and stuck his nose in his food dish. Finding his bowl empty, he turned and looked at Zach.

"Be patient," Zach shouted at Pablo. "Let me set these things down. I'll feed you in a minute."

Zach set the bottle and photos on the counter. He bent over and opened the cabinet door under the sink. "Okay, which one do you want?"

Pablo stuck his nose into the cabinet and sniffed every one of the cans. He selected a green and red can and pushed it over with his nose. Maybe it was the color of the label, or maybe he could smell it through the can. Zach was not certain how Pablo knew, but, when given the choice, he always selected his favorite Italian dog food.

Zach opened the can and spooned half the contents into his dish, while Pablo licked his mouth and ran circles around his feet. With Pablo busy eating, Zach grabbed a glass from the cabinet and dropped several ice cubes into it. He pulled the bottle from the sack, screwed the lid off, and poured a generous amount over the ice cubes.

He swirled the dark, reddish brown liquid around the ice cubes, held the glass under his nose, sniffing the whiskey's aroma. It had a heavy, sweet scent. He took a large sip and swallowed. The whiskey was strong and the flavor was deep. The fiery liquid burned as it flowed down his throat. He took another swallow.

Zach knew he should eat something as he had not eaten since breakfast. He opened the refrigerator and stared at its contents. Nothing interested him. He opened a pantry cabinet and surveyed the selection of canned items. He had not been to the grocery store in awhile and the selection was limited. Left with little choice, he opened a can of soup he really did not want, poured it into a pan, and set it on the stove. As he waited for the soup to heat up, he sat on a stool and watched Pablo finish his supper.

Zach finished his drink and poured another. By that time Pablo had finished his food and was licking the bowl around the kitchen. "Okay Pablo," Zach said. "You can stop now. You've licked the smell off." He bent over and picked up the bowl. He opened the dishwasher and dropped the bowl inside.

Zach went to the stove and checked on the soup. It was hot and starting to bubble. He poured the hot soup into a bowl, grabbed a bag of potato chips from the cabinet, and sat down at the table. Half-heartedly he ate several spoonfuls of the soup tossing every fourth or fifth potato chip to Pablo who would catch it in mid-air.

Zach gave up and set the bowl with the remaining soup on the floor for Pablo. After Pablo finished the soup, Zach picked up the bowl and put it in the dishwasher with the other dishes.

Zach picked up his drink and wandered around the house. He was edgy. He knew he should probably go to bed because the following day was going to be difficult and tiring. In a moment of weakness, he walked down the hall and opened the door to the master bedroom. It was a huge mistake to go into the room, but the liquor had dulled his senses and his resolve.

Two days after Angie moved out, Zach moved his stuff to the family room downstairs. He vacuumed the carpet in the master bedroom, closed the heater vents, and pulled the door shut. Not even once had he been back in the bedroom since.

He walked into the room. It was cold and empty except for a single chest of drawers sitting in the corner. Zach had never felt as empty and alone as he did at that moment. The room felt as cold and empty as his life. For several minutes he just stood there in the middle of the empty bedroom. Finally, he sat on the floor.

Pablo, having followed him into the room, jumped into Zach's lap and made him spill some of his drink. "Get off," he yelled, pushing Pablo off his lap.

Pablo scampered across the room, tail drooping. He laid down on the floor and watched Zach, sensing something was wrong. He made a pitiful sight laying there with his sad eyes. Zach instantly felt guilty for yelling at Pablo. None of this was his fault.

He sat his drink down and called Pablo, "Come here Pablo. I'm sorry boy."

Pablo jumped up, bounded across the room, and leaped onto Zach's lap, his tail waggling furiously as he licked Zach's face. If only people could be so forgiving Zach thought as he scratched Pablo's ears. He didn't know what he would have done without Pablo after Angie left. He was certain he would have gone crazy in the empty house all by himself.

"Come on. Let's go in the other room," Zach said, pushing himself up from the floor. He walked over to the door and took one last glance around as he pulled the door shut. Maybe Angie was right. Maybe it was time to pull the door shut on that part of his life and move on.

Zach went back to the kitchen and sat at the table. He opened the pack of photographs he had picked up at the drugstore and dumped them out. Exactly what he expected. All of the photographs were of desert landscapes. Zach was well aware of Fred's passion for photography. He flipped through the entire stack. Nothing unusual. Until he reached the last five photographs. The lighting was unbelievable. The colors were so vibrant. The photographs looked so real. Zach felt as if he should be able to feel the desert wind on his face.

"Oh, God. I'm going to miss you old friend," Zach whimpered out loud as he laid the stack of photographs on the table. He glanced at the clock. It was late. He must get to bed.

Zach got up from the table and stumbled off to bed. He slid under the covers and switched off the lamp. Pablo jumped up on the bed and licked Zach's face. Zach reached out and patted his head. "Good night Pablo", he said.

Pablo curled up beside Zach, satisfied his master was okay. He sighed and was asleep almost as quickly as Zach.

CHAPTER THIRTY-SEVEN

Monday, March 30 - 1036 Central Daylight Time
Clovis Avenue
Coral Hills, Maryland

Aronoff Porubsky, known as Agent Andrew Tiner to the FBI, sat on the couch in his small studio apartment switching disinterestedly through the TV channels. He had been through the entire list of available channels three times and he could not find a single program he wanted to watch. "Stupid American television," he complained, switching the television off

He picked up a magazine and started to flip the pages. "More stinking American garbage," he fumed. He threw the magazine across the room. It slammed against a kitchen cabinet, landing in the sink. "Why has Levka not called?" he grumbled. He was annoyed and tired of waiting. Another ten minutes passed before the bulky device, somewhat resembling a cell phone buzzed.

"Finally," Aronoff grumbled as got up and answered the device. "Yes, Levka. Why are you so late? I have been waiting for an hour."

"Sorry Aronoff," Levka began. "I have been talking with superiors. They are angry Aronoff. They hear bad things. Many bodies."

"I know Levka," Aronoff answered. "I barely got away with my life. I think our friend at the FBI is trying to interfere with our plan. He may be scared and ready to run."

"You know what happen if we fail Aronoff," Levka warned. "We die suddenly!"

"I know. I know Levka," Aronoff fretted. "We must do something."

"Superiors agree," Levka affirmed. "They ask if equipment ready."

"Yes it is ready," Aronoff confirmed. "At least the last time I checked it. Why did they ask?"

"Ismaylov wants plan go soon." Levka answered, his voice quavering. "Three days, four days, no later."

"What," Aronoff gasped. "That soon?"

"Ismaylov say no excuse," Levka replied. "Must be no later. He not make idle threat my friend."

"Why so soon?".

"He say they must have excuse to strike soon," Levka answered. "He say Kutepov's forces ready to seize control of Kremlin when US Navy responds. He take over all Russia, then he eliminate stupid American fools in giant fireball. He say we should do plan and leave quickly."

Aronoff's eyes grew wide with shock. "Are you certain Levka?"

"Da, my friend," Levka confirmed. "There no mistake."

"Okay, Levka," Aronoff advised. "I will input the final message soon and activate the equipment. The message should begin transmitting early Thursday. Inform our superiors."

"Da, I will tell Ismaylov plan is go," Levka agreed.

"Do zvidaniya, good friend." Aronoff broke the connection.

Aronoff switched off the device and headed for the closet to gather the items he would need. Fumbling around in the closet, he pulled out a small box and a beat up carryon bag. He stuffed the box and a change of clothes into the bag. Next, the communications device went into the bag. He would need it to call Vinogradov to help him leave the country.

Hesitating at the door, he wondered if he should take the time to eliminate traces of his identity. He shrugged, deciding it did not matter because in just a few days the apartment and everything within one hundred miles would be nothing but scorched earth and smoldering cinders.

He stepped into the hallway and pulled the apartment door shut without bothering to switch the lights off. Finally, all those years his parents had spent in deep cover would pay off. He would launch the revenge they had sacrificed so much to achieve.

* * *

Monday, March 30 - 1036 Central Daylight Time
Rose Hill Memorial Cemetery
East Admiral Place
Tulsa, Oklahoma

Zach walked around to the passenger side of his car, holding the umbrella for Angie as she climbed out. A steady rain had fallen most of the morning tapering off to a light drizzle as they arrived at the cemetery.

"Why did it have to rain today of all days?" Zach complained as he waited for Angie to get out of the car.

It was not particularly cold but the rain and the dark occasion made Zach feel cold deep inside his soul. He shivered uncontrollably when several drops of rain dripped off the umbrella and ran down his neck.

Angie looked at Zach and asked, "Are you okay?"

Zach did not answer.

Angie watched Zach very closely during the funeral. She watched him struggle desperately, trying to control his emotions. He nearly succeeded, keeping the tears at bay until the soloist got up and sang Fred's favorite song. It was then he could no longer hold back, tears streaming down his face.

Angie was very worried about Zach. Ever since his return from New Mexico he was increasingly distracted and irritable. She felt so sorry for Zach. The enormous grief he was suffering was painfully evident in his eyes. He took care of all the funeral arrangements and checked on Rachael several times a day. Angie was afraid he was taking on too much responsibility.

Angie reached out and took his hand. Still he did not answer. His hands were cold and clammy.

Angie nudged Zach's arm. "Zach! Zach, are you okay?"

Zach shuddered again. "Yeah, I'm okay. At least for now," Zach answered.

Ever since their return from the dive trip, Zach felt edgy and unsettled. Perhaps it was an inner sense learned in combat, or maybe it was just intuition. Whatever it was, Zach could not shake the feeling that something evil was shadowing him.

"Come on Zach. We don't want to hold up the service," Angie said, pushing Zach ahead of her. She squeezed Zach's hand hard as they headed for the grave site.

Zach opened his mouth to say something but stopped.

"What is it Zach? What do you want to say?" Angie questioned.

"Not now," Zach sniffled. "I'll talk to you later. Let's just get through this."

They walked the rest of the way to the grave site in silence. When they arrived at the grave site, Zach seated Angie in the second row and he took a seat beside Rachael. Turning and looking at her, he saw that her eyes were red and puffy, her face pale and strained. He patted the back of her hand, afraid to say anything. He refused to allow himself to break down now. He had to be strong for Rachael.

The minister arrived and took his place beside the casket. He looked at Zach. Zach nodded his head and the minister began the graveside service. He read several Scriptures and, thankfully, conducted a short interment service. At the conclusion, Zach signaled the honor guard to begin.

Assuming their position slightly to the left of the casket, the honor guard fired a twenty-one gun salute. Zach jumped as each volley was fired. The honor guard came to order arms as a lone trumpet played "Taps". Zach clenched his jaw and squinted as hard as he could, but his emotions simply refused to be controlled. In spite of his best efforts, tears formed and rolled down his cheeks.

Two members of the honor guard carefully and deliberately folded the flag that had draped Fred's casket. When they finished, Zach got up and received the flag from the honor guard. He turned and presented the flag to Rachael.

"I present you with this flag from a grateful nation in honor of this fallen soldier," Zach choked, through tears of grief. "Rachael, he was the bravest, most honorable man I ever knew. It was a great honor to have served with him; and a privilege to have been his friend."

Zach took one step back and saluted. He then made a crisp right-face and took a place with the honor guard. Even though Zach was not on active duty, the local commander of the Naval Reserve unit had secured special permission for Zach to wear his uniform and medals.

Zach stood at attention beside the honor guard until the crowd dispersed and only a handful of mourners remained at the grave site. He took two quick steps forward and did an about-face. "Honor guard, teeeen... huuuut. Dismissed," Zach barked.

Zach walked over to where Rachael and Angie were standing, just under the edge of the green tent the funeral home had provided. "How are you doing Rachael?" he questioned.

"Tired, but okay Zach," she answered. "I just need to go home and rest."

Zach motioned at Rachael's brother Randy and got his attention, "I think Rachael needs to go home and get some rest. How long are you going to stay?"

"Until Wednesday," he answered. "Then I have to return to Philadelphia. I wish I could stay longer, but I only had two days of vacation left to use."

"I'd come over, but I have to go back to the office for a while," Zach explained. "I discovered some serious problems while I was in New Mexico. If I don't get them corrected soon, I won't have a company to worry about."

"Zach, don't worry about it," Randy countered. "You've already done more than anyone could expect. I know how close you and Fred were. This can't have been easy for you either."

"You're right there," Zach agreed. "If you or Rachael need anything, and I mean anything, call me day or night. If you can't reach me call Angie. I'm sure she would be glad to help."

Zach returned to where Rachael and Angie were standing. "Randy's going to take you home now," he said. "I'll call you later to see how you're doing. I've instructed Randy to call me or Angie if you need anything. Don't worry about any of the details. I will see that everything gets taken care of."

"I don't know what I would have done without you Zach. Thank you so much," Rachael answered as she took his hand and kissed his cheek.

Zach watched as Randy took Rachael's arm and walked her to his car. He turned to Angie, "Let's go. I'll meet you at your apartment. Just give me a few minutes. I need to say goodbye."

Angie turned and headed for the car while Zach stopped at the casket. He stood there for several minutes, remembering the good times he had with his old friend. He leaned over the casket and laid his hand on its cold, damp surface. "Goodbye old friend. I promise you I will get the people who did this," he whispered. He straightened up and headed for his car.

A man deliberately bumped into Zach as he walked away from the casket.

"Act casual. Where will you be later? It's important," the man whispered, looking directly into Zach's eyes.

"I'll be at my office. Who are you?"

"Not important. We'll talk later. Don't say a word to anyone!"

The man continued walking, merging into the crowd.

Zach turned and continued walking toward the parking lot. He stopped, turning back toward the casket. For a few seconds, he watched as the men from the funeral home lowered the casket into the vault. It did not seem possible his friend was gone. He turned and walked over to the car where Angie was waiting.

"How are you holding up Zach?" Angie asked as she brushed a tear from Zach's cheek, the strain clearly evident in his face.

"I'm getting by," Zach answered. "I just need to stay busy."

"Who was that you were talking to?" Angie quizzed.

"No one in particular. He bumped into me by accident and offered his condolences," Zach lied.

Zach opened the door for Angie and waited for her to climb into the car. He walked around to the driver's side and got in. He settled into the seat and started the engine. Slipping the car into gear, he drove out of the cemetery, and headed for Angie's apartment.

The silence as they drove toward the apartment was charged with tension. Finally, Angie broke the silence, "Zach, how are you doing, really?"

Zach did not respond. She doubted if he had even heard what she said. She reached over and jabbed his shoulder, "Zach, I asked you a question."

Zach glanced over at her, "Sorry Angie, I guess my mind is elsewhere. What did you ask me?"

"I asked you how you are doing, really?"

"I feel numb. At times, I find myself refusing to believe Fred is really dead. Then I get angry and want to scream, but I know that won't help. Nothing seems to help. Angie, I don't know how I'm going to salvage the company without Fred!"

"It surely can't be that bad," Angie protested. "I liked Fred, but he was only one man."

"Yes, it can be that bad!" Zach snapped. "The system in New Mexico has serious problems. Fred discovered something and it got him killed."

Zach jammed on the brakes and pulled into the parking lot of a fast food restaurant. The car's tires squealed as he pulled into a parking space. He slammed the gear shift into park and turned toward Angie. The angry look on Zach's face scared Angie. So much so she did not say a word.

"Angie, I want you to promise me you will forget what you just heard," Zach ordered. "I'm depressed and angry. I lost control and said more than I should have. I'm not leaving this spot until you promise !"

"Zach what on earth are you talking about?" Angie demanded. "You're scaring me."

"Angie, I'm sorry, but I can't talk about it," Zach answered. "You have to promise me you will forget what you heard. Please. Promise me right now!"

The tone of Zach's voice and the fury in his eyes convinced Angie Zach was deadly serious. Never had she seen such a look in his eyes.

"Okay Zach," Angie agreed. "I can't possibly forget what I heard but I promise I will not mention it to anyone."

"You must swear you will mention it to no one!" Zach begged. "I mean no one! Not Rachael, not your minister, not you mother, no one! Do you understand?"

"Yes, Zach. I understand," Angie answered.

Zach slipped the car into gear, backed out of the parking space, and continued toward Angie's apartment. Neither one spoke a word until Zach pulled into an empty parking space in front of Angie's apartment.

"Zach, why don't you come in for awhile?" Angie asked.

"Sorry, I can't Angie," Zach answered. "I have to go back to the office for awhile."

Angie's anger flared up, "Can't you forget that stupid office just once. Especially at a time like this."

"I'm sorry Angie, but it's important," Zach explained. "The office is closed so I will be able to work in peace and quiet. I have to analyze the data I brought back from New Mexico. If I don't get that system corrected soon, I will lose the contract. If that happens, the company is finished."

"Well go then," Angie snapped as she got out of the car. She slammed the door and hurried toward her apartment.

Zach opened the door and called out, "Angie, don't get mad. I have to go."

Angie did not even turn around. She rushed into the apartment building, slamming the door behind her.

Zach got back into his car and slammed the door. "Why does everything have to be so hard?" he growled, jerking the car into gear and backing out of the parking space. He changed gears and stomped on the accelerator. His car roared out of the parking lot, tires squealing as he turned left onto the street.

Zach was furious, hardly noticing the traffic as he sped toward his office.

CHAPTER THIRTY-EIGHT

Zach drove straight to the office after his argument with Angie. Fortunately, there was no one at the office when he arrived. He was in such a foul mood he would have bitten the head off anyone who was unfortunate enough to speak to him.

For what seemed like an eternity, Zach poured over the odd data. Rerunning all the tests for a third time, attempting to find a common thread in the unusual data. He manipulated the data in every way he could imagine. No matter how he arranged the data, the results were always the same. There was not the slightest clue as to what caused the interference.

A bag of fast food sat on his desk untouched. To keep himself going, he had consumed one bottle of Mountain Dew after another. On his fourth trip to the mini-fridge, the supply had run dry.

Turning toward the office window he stared blankly at the scenery. Worry hung over him like a shroud. He feared he would be unable to determine the cause of the interference. If he could not determine the cause, he could not fix it. If he could not fix the issue, his company would lose the DOD contract for certain.

An automatic appointment alarm popped up on the screen. Zach double-clicked the icon and opened his appointment calendar. The appointment read, "Get items ready for Nevada trip."

"I would forget my head, if it weren't attached," he said, shaking his head. He had forgotten about the trip to Nevada again.

Zach pushed his chair back from the desk, stood up, and bent over to stretch the muscles in his back. Pushing himself back up to the desk, he positioned his hands above the keyboard. He looked at the data displayed on the computer monitor and shrugged, dropping his hands into his lap.

After pouring over the data for more than four hours, he could not force himself to look at it any longer.

"It's useless!" Zach moaned. "That's it. I can't take anymore. I'm done."

He drew his arm back about to take a swipe at the empty soda bottles sitting on the desk just as the phone rang. Had it not been for the odd exchange at the funeral he would have ignored it.

"Hello, Microwave Services. This is Zach Templeton. May I help you."

"I spoke with you earlier today at the funeral," a male voice answered.

"I remember. What do you want?" Zach asked, not in the mood for games.

"We need to meet," the man replied. "Today. It's very important,"

"I'm busy," Zach snapped. "I just buried my best friend and I have a trip tomorrow. I don't have time."

"I know what happened to your friend," the man offered as bait.

Warning bells rang in Zach's brain. Agent Slater had told him to trust no one. Zach did not answer.

"Mister Templeton are you still there?" the man asked.

"Yes. I'm still here."

"We must meet," the man demanded.

"Why should I trust you?" Zach asked.

"It is vitally important. I can protect you," the man replied.

He decided to agree to meet the man to buy himself some time.

"Ah … Do you know the Iron Skillet Restaurant on Highway 51?"

"I'll find it."

"Give me an hour to finish up here and I'll meet you there," Zach lied.

"One hour Mister Templeton. Don't be late," the man replied. The line went dead.

"Now what?" Zach exclaimed out loud. He would need a plan, and quick he thought to himself. It would not be safe to go home. The only thing he could think of was to check into a hotel near the airport instead of going home, but he would need clothes and the test equipment. He always kept an extra change of clothes at the office so that was covered.

But he did not have any test equipment. Without test equipment the trip would be wasted. Replaying the events of the previous day, he remembered he had loaded test equipment in the trunk of his car and had never taken it out because he was so focused on the arrangements for Fred's funeral.

He closed all the applications on his computer and switched it off. The laptop was powered down and stuffed into the laptop case. He went to the closet and grabbed the change of clothes and stuffed them into the laptop case. Uncertain it would be safe to take his own car, he called a taxi to pick him up at the north entrance of the Promenade Mall. He flipped open his cell phone and called Angie.

"Hello," Angie answered.

"Angie, it's me. I need your help." Zach pleaded.

"What do you need Zach?"

"Can you go over and pick up Pablo?" Zach replied. "I'm going to stay at a hotel near the airport. I'll be back in a couple of days."

"Why on earth are you going to stay at a hotel?"

"Angie, I can't tell you. You will have to trust me."

Zach waited but there was no reply. He spoke again, "Angie?"

"Zach, I need some kind of explanation," Angie insisted. "You have been acting strange for days. This has got to stop."

"Please Angie," Zach begged. "I promise I'll explain when I get back. It's really important. I wouldn't ask you otherwise."

"Well, okay," Angie agreed. "But you have to swear you will tell me what is going on as soon as you get back."

"I swear," Zach answered. "Thanks Angie. You're a lifesaver." He ended the call before Angie could say anymore.

He picked up the laptop case and slung the strap over his shoulder. In the parking garage, he grabbed the test equipment he would need from the trunk of his car. Exiting the parking lot by the rear door, he walked over to the north mall entrance.

CHAPTER THIRTY-NINE

Tuesday, March 31 - 0515 Central Daylight Time
Holiday Inn Express
Tulsa International Airport
Tulsa, Oklahoma

The phone on the night stand continued its incessant ringing. Zach struggled to wake himself from a deep sleep. The phone played a recorded message announcing the wake-up call he had requested the night before. He rolled over and peered at the clock, blinking several times to clear the dryness from his eyes. The red numerals on the clock indicated 5:10 a.m.

He wrestled himself out from under the blankets, slid his legs out, and sat up on the edge of the bed. "Why today of all days?" he complained as he stood up and shuffled off to the bathroom in the dark. Squinting in the bright light, he waited for his eyes to adjust.

He looked in the mirror, barely recognizing the face staring back at him. Eyes red and sunken. Dark circles under his eyes. He looked awful. The day had just started and already he felt tired. On top of that, the day ahead of him was going to be a long one. He wondered if the struggle to save his company was worth the price. At that moment he was no longer certain. He had lost his wife. He had lost his best friend. And he was in danger of losing his health. Perhaps it was time to give it up and throw in the towel.

He turned on the cold water and let it run until it was good and cold. Maybe the cold water would help clear the fog from his mind. He cupped his hands, let them fill with water, then splashed it on his face. Twice he repeated the process.

He straightened up and grabbed for a towel. Nothing. He felt on the other side of the sink. Nothing there either. "Good grief!", he muttered as he turned to grab the towel draped over the tub. His left foot slipped when he stepped in a puddle of water that had spilled onto the floor. Zach shifted his weight trying to avoid losing his balance.

Zach's other foot stepped on the edge of the towel he had left lying on the floor when he showered before going to bed. Both feet slid out from under him. He attempted to grab some-thing to stop his fall, but there was nothing to grab. Losing his balance, he twisted to avoid falling on his back. He over compensated, fell forward, and struck his head on the bathtub instead.

Pushing himself up from the floor, he grabbed the edge of the vanity to steady himself. His fingers gently touched his forehead just above his left eyebrow. "Ouch," Zach wailed, pulling his fingers away quickly. No blood on his fingers. At least he was not bleeding.

He touched the spot above his left eye more gently and looked in the mirror. A large goose egg was developing just above his eye, looking as if it was going to produce a nasty bruise. Already the edges were turning a deep reddish color.

"Good Lord!" Zach croaked. "What else is going to happen?" He grabbed a wash cloth from the basket and turned on the cold water, soaking the wash cloth. Gently he pressed the cold cloth against the goose egg, hoping the cold would help reduce the swelling.

Zach poured some water into the small one-cup coffee maker and ripped open one of the coffee packets. Still a little dizzy from banging his head, he tore the packet in the wrong place and ripped the bag of coffee inside, spilling coffee grounds all over the vanity. "Yeah, that's just what I needed," Zach growled. He tossed the ruined bag in the trash can and scraped the scattered coffee grounds into his hand, dumping them into the trash can as well. After selecting another coffee packet, he very carefully tore the top off and stuffed the coffee bag into the coffee maker. While waiting for the coffee maker to finish its brewing cycle, he examined the lump above his eye. The lump had already changed from red to angry purple.

He grabbed the coffee cup and went into the other room to gather up his stuff. A quick glance at the clock. The fiasco in the bathroom was going to cause him to be short of time. He hurriedly stuffed his dirty clothes into the laptop case, returned to the bathroom for his razor and toiletries, then returned and stuffed them into the case.

He gulped down the remaining lukewarm coffee from the plastic cup. Another glance at the clock. It was 5:45 a.m. "I sure hope Angie is awake," Zach said to himself as he picked up his cell phone and punched in her number.

"Hello," Angie's sleepy voice answered.

"This is Zach. Sorry to wake you," he apologized.

"That's okay. The alarm went off several minutes ago. I just haven't forced myself out of bed yet."

"Just wanted to remind you to feed and water Pablo while I'm gone. His food is under the kitchen sink."

"Yes Zach. I know where it is. Don't worry about it. I said I would take care of him."

"I should only be gone a couple of days. I'll call you when I know exactly when I'll be home.

"Thanks. I'll take good care of Pablo."

"Angie I.... I...," Zach stopped himself. He wanted desperately to tell her what he was going through but he just didn't have time. "I love you. Gotta go or I'll be late for my flight," Zach said as he hung up the phone.

Zach made a quick sweep of the hotel room to be certain he had not forgotten anything. His head was beginning to throb. He wished he could stop at the hotel's front desk and ask for some aspirins, but he did not have time. Only five minutes remained before the shuttle was scheduled to leave for the airport.

Fortunately, it was early and the traffic was light, allowing the shuttle to make good time. Twenty minutes later the airport shuttle discharged him in front of the airline ticket counters. He ran past the ticket counter, heading directly to the gate. After a quick trip through security, he ran up to the gate and handed his ticket folder to the gate agent. The gate agent quickly checked Zach, picked up the phone, and spoke with the flight attendant. The gate agent escorted Zach down the jetway.

One of the flight attendants escorted Zach to his seat. An already bad day got much worse when he realized he was stuck in a center seat. With no time left to argue, he took his seat and stuffed his laptop case under the seat in front of him. With a long sigh, he buckled his seat belt and settled in for the flight to Dallas, Ft. Worth where he would make a quick connection for the final flight to Las Vegas.

* * *

Tuesday, March 31 – 1842 Zulu
Marine Vessel Przeznaczenia
37°39'N, 21°41'W
310 Miles East northeast of Santa Maria Island

Having been cooped up in his small hidey-hole for what seemed like an eternity, Bill Morrison was overjoyed the long hours of hiding were nearly over. He had nothing to eat except the two candy bars he had purchased at the airport in Gdansk. There were only two swallows remaining in the one liter bottle of water he had carefully rationed. He gulped them eagerly.

He dug around in his duffel bag for his battery powered GPS device. For the fourth time in the last five hours, he turned the device on and waited for it to power-up. The device flashed "Searching" on the tiny screen display as it searched for a satellite signal. He waited. It began to flash "Acquiring". Twenty seconds later the device displayed the coordinates: 37°37'N, 21°39'W. Bill rummaged in the duffle bag and pulled out a map. He quickly located the coordinates on the map and made a pencil mark two miles from the upper end of the East Azores Fracture Zone, the rendezvous point his old friend had given him.

The time it would take for him to leave his hiding place, make his way up on deck, and retrieve the items the man on the dock had promised would put the ship within acceptable range of the rendezvous point. Bill shoved the GPS device and map into a plastic bag and squeezed the seals together. He stuffed the plastic bag and everything else into the duffel bag.

Bill listened intently for several seconds, hearing nothing but the muffled hum of the engines. He pushed the crate at the corner of the hiding place into the alleyway between the rows of crates. To conceal the hiding place, he pushed the crate back into place and set a carton on top of the crate.

Bill crept over to the ladder that led up to the cargo hatch door. He stopped and listened, again hearing only the hum of the engines. He hurried up the ladder two steps at a time and paused at the hatch. Pulling the metal hatch open a few inches, he listened. No voices or sounds of footsteps. He stepped into the passageway and pulled the hatch closed as quietly as he could. After dogging the levers tight, he ran quietly to the doorway that led out onto deck. Again he stopped and listened. No sound except for the wind rushing by the doorway. Once out on deck, he turned aft, heading for the row of lifeboats.

Quickly locating lifeboat 4C, two-thirds of the way down the row, he loosened the rope that secured its canvas cover and slipped his arm under the cover. A wave of relief rushed over him when he found the objects the man at the dock had promised would be there. He struggled into a lifejacket and secured the buckles. He reached his arm back under the canvas cover and located a small tubular package, attaching its lanyard to a "D" ring on the lifejacket. The handles of his duffel bag were attached to a second "D" ring on the life-jacket. Reaching under the cover one last time, he retrieved a small, one-man inflatable raft and re-tightened the canvass cover's rope.

Bill crept as far aft as he could, stepped over the railing, and gauged the direction of the waves. He jumped as hard as he could, praying he would land far enough away from the ship to avoid the propellers. He clutched the life raft tightly and took a deep breath as the icy water rushed up to meet him.

Bill's brain wanted to scream as he entered the frigid water. His kicking and the buoyancy of the lifejacket quickly brought him up to the surface. Kicking and paddling furiously he moved away from the ship as quickly as he could. It required an enormous effort due to the drag from the duffel bag and life raft he was clutching onto. Once past the wake of the ship, he moved away more quickly.

Far enough away from the ship to avoid being sucked into the propellers, Bill stopped kicking and watched as the ship grew smaller and it's lights grew fainter. He pulled the cord on the life raft and watched it inflate. He grabbed the safety line on the raft and tried to pull himself into the raft. He thrashed and kicked and pulled for several minutes before managing to haul himself up over the side and into the raft. Soaked and freezing, Bill laid in the bottom of the raft gasping for air, struggling to catch his breath.

It took several minutes for Bill to recover from the exertion. The duffle bag and the small tubular package were unclipped from his lifejacket and set in the raft. He broke the seal on the tubular package and withdrew a sonobuoy. After tying the lanyard to the raft's safety line, he tugged at it to be certain it was secure. Bill activated the sonobuoy, dropped it over the side of the raft, and played out the line until it was all in the water.

Bill prayed the rendezvous would be soon. There was nothing left to do but wait. He huddled in the bottom of the life raft, shivering uncontrollably.

CHAPTER FORTY

Tuesday, March 31 - 1207 Pacific Daylight Time
McCarren International Airport
Las Vegas, Nevada

Captain Tom Grantham cleared his throat and pushed the button to activate the intercom in the aircraft's cabin. "Good afternoon ladies and gentlemen. Las Vegas Approach Control has given us final clearance for landing. On behalf of the officers on the flight deck and the rest of the flight crew, we wish to thank you for selecting us for your flight today. We hope you will choose us for your travel plans in the future. Flight attendants prepare the cabin for landing."

Zach pulled his seat back to its full upright position and cinched his seat belt a little tighter. He had flown many hundreds of thousands of miles but he always got a little apprehensive when the plane landed. "Many more accidents happen during landing than during takeoff," a little voice whispered in his mind.

He looked out of the window at the desert below. The landscape was barren and empty for as far as he could see. Several roads snaked off into the distance and disappeared into nothingness. Zach never could understand why anyone had decided to build a city in such an inhospitable place.

The passenger on Zach's right tapped his arm. Zach turned and saw that the flight attendant was pointing at the glass in his hand. "Sorry," he said, handing the glass to her.

The flight attendants finished picking up items that had been passed out during the flight and made a final check of the cabin. Everything secure, they took their place in seats attached to the forward cabin bulkhead and fastened their seat belts. Zach felt the aircraft vibrate as the wing flaps were extended, making contact with the air rushing under the wings. The aircraft lurched slightly as the landing gear was lowered. The aircraft shook even more as the Captain extended the flaps to their full landing position. Several

187

equipment buildings painted in a red and white checkerboard pattern passed under the aircraft.

In spite of Zach's confidence in the flight crew, he looked forward and involuntarily held his breath, waiting for the wheels to make contact with the runway. Two thumps at almost the exact same instant as the aircraft touched down on the runway. The captain reduced the thrust and the nose wheel settled onto the runway. Zach felt himself pressed forward against the seat belt as the brakes and reverse thrust were applied.

The captain turned off the reverse thrusters and turned off the main runway onto a taxiway. One of the flight attendants came on the intercom and gave the standard arrival message. As they approached the gate, Zach saw the ground crew scurrying around getting ready to service the aircraft. A fuel truck ready to refuel the aircraft, a food service truck ready to restock the galley, and numerous baggage carts lined up ready to distribute the baggage to the baggage claim.

The aircraft stopped as it pulled up even with the jetway. Even before the engines had been shut down, passengers were getting up from their seats to retrieve carryon bags from overhead compartments. Zach remained in his seat, knowing it would be useless to get up. The forward hatch had not been opened yet and the aisle was already jammed full with passengers.

Zach waited as the crowd of passengers grabbed their belongings and left the aircraft. One passenger momentarily stopped the flow of passengers, stopping to retrieve a bag from an overhead compartment. Zach took advantage of the opportunity to climb out of his seat and head for the exit. He followed the crowd up the jetway and into the terminal.

The first thing Zach saw upon entering the terminal was rows and rows of slot machines. Several of the passengers had stopped and were already feeding coins into the glaring, one-armed bandits. Zach shook his head and continued on into the main terminal, searching for the rental car counter.

Zach spotted the counter on the far side of the terminal. He made his way through the throng of travelers and walked up to the counter.

"Zach Templeton. I have a car reserved," he announced to the rental agent.

"Let me check," the agent replied, tapping some keys on her terminal keyboard. She stared at the screen for several seconds before responding. "It seems we don't have any intermediate size cars left Mister Templeton. I can upgrade you to a full size for the same price. Is that okay?"

"That will be just fine," Zach answered.

"What credit card will you be using?" the agent asked.

Zach pulled a card from his wallet and slid it across the counter. The agent grabbed the card and ran it through the reader, turned it over and looked at the signature, and handed it back to Zach. She waited as the computer verified Zach's credit card and printed the rental contract. She tore off the contract and pushed it in front of Zach.

"Initial here, here, and sign here," she instructed.

Zach did as instructed and pushed the contract back to the agent. She tore off one copy of the contract, stuffed it into a rental folder, retrieved a set of keys from a peg board, and handed the folder and keys to Zach.

"Will you be needing a map or directions?" the agent asked.

"No. I've been here many times. I know exactly where I'm going," Zach answered.

"Your car is a gray Mercury Marquis. The shuttle bus will pick you up in front of the baggage claim. I hope you enjoy your stay in Las Vegas Mister Templeton."

Zach walked away from the rental counter and headed for the baggage claim. He exited the terminal through the automatic doors and waited for the shuttle bus. Fortunately, the shuttle bus had already left the remote parking area and he had to wait less than five minutes for it to arrive.

At the remote car parking area, Zach got off the shuttle bus and presented his contract to the lot attendant. The attendant pointed at a row of cars to his left. Zach walked down the row of cars until he came to the gray Marquis. He unlocked the door and dropped his bag in the back seat then started the engine, waiting for the air conditioner to blow cool air before closing the door.

Zach drove out of the parking lot, turning west on Sunset Road. Mid-afternoon traffic on Sunset Road was light, except for travelers leaving the airport. Zach spotted a convenience store two blocks ahead. He pulled into the right hand lane and turned in to the convenience store's parking lot.

Zach purchased a large Mountain Dew to drink during the drive to the microwave tower site. He jumped back into the car and screeched out of the parking lot, continuing west on Sunset Road. One half mile later he turned north onto Las Vegas Boulevard, north on Las Vegas Boulevard for a short distance, then west on Tropicana Road for one block, then left onto the entrance ramp for northbound Interstate 15. He always took the interstate rather than Las Vegas Boulevard to avoid the heavy traffic that clogged the streets around the casinos.

He drove north on Interstate 15 until it intersected with US Highway 95. He exited onto westbound Highway 95. As Zach left the rental agency's parking lot, a gray Jeep Cherokee with dark tinted windows had followed him. The driver of the Jeep Cherokee had been careful not to get too close. He did not want his quarry to get suspicious, especially while still driving in city traffic. The occupants intended to wait until Zach reached the remote radio site.

Zach absolutely hated the trip to the tower site on Stonewall Flat. It was dull, boring, and long. One hundred seventy miles from Las Vegas through dull, monotonous desert. There were only four towns to break up the monotony during the entire trip. Two of the towns were so small they were not listed on any maps.

During the first thirty-five miles of the trip, there were scattered houses as he passed through the outskirts of Las Vegas and then by Indian Springs Air Force base. From that point on there was very little to look at. The same gravely soil, occasional clumps of scrubby brush, and the ever present shimmering heat waves rising from the desert sand.

During the next fifty miles, he ran through the tests he intended to complete on the microwave equipment. He had no clue as to the cause of the mysterious interference. Hopefully the tests he had planned would reveal something. He went over the list of tests several times in his mind to be certain he had left nothing out. Every potential cause of interference would be examined. There was nothing left to do but endure the rest of the trip.

With nothing else to occupy Zach's mind, his thoughts drifted to the problems between him and Angie. He could come up with a thousand excuses in his mind, but none of them made any difference. No matter what he said, no matter what he did, nothing seemed to overcome the tension between them. It seemed their life together was over. He kept telling himself his dream was to build a company that could support itself so they could spend more time together. The things he had done while he was in the Navy had been to make her proud of him.

Everything Zach did was centered around her. Zach wondered why she couldn't see that? Angie was not cruel or heartless. He had to be missing something. But how could that be? Were the things Angie accused him of really true? He promised himself he would talk to her as soon as he returned to Tulsa. Maybe there was still hope.

Zach's concentration returned to the present. He looked down at the speedometer and realized he was driving eighty. A quick glance in the rear view mirror. No one close behind him. Nothing ahead as far as he could see. He decided to not slow down, wanting to get to the micro-wave site as quickly as possible so he could perform the tests and get home.

A weathered road sign announced that the Beatty and Highway 374 junction was three miles ahead. After the town of Beatty, there was only fifty-three miles left to go. Beatty, a small town with a population of less than seventeen hundred, had a small service station. Zach stopped, used the restroom facilities, and purchased another Mountain Dew.

Zach entered the Timbi-Sha Shoshone Indian Reservation and passed through Scotty's Junction, nothing more than a wide spot in the road. Why anyone wanted to live out here was a complete mystery to Zach. There was nothing for miles but rocks and gravel. Two miles past Stonewall Mountain, Zach turned off the highway onto a dirt road and drove the remaining two miles to the Stonewall Flat microwave site located at the southwestern edge of Mud Lake.

Zach opened the door to the equipment enclosure and switched the light on. He poked his head in carefully checking the interior of the building before entering. He walked over to the equipment racks, pulled the front covers off, and checked the indicators. Everything seemed to be okay. Due to the sporadic nature of the reported problems, he did not expect to find anything else.

He went back out to his car and grabbed the test equipment. Hurrying back to the equipment enclosure, he pulled the door shut to keep the cool air inside. If everything went as planned, the tests would take only an hour or so. Then he could check the two remaining tower sites at Springdale and Timber Mountain. If the tests at those sites also went well he should be able to finish before dark.

With the test equipment in place and functioning, Zach setup the equipment to monitor and record several critical test points. The recording equipment was set to begin recording the instant it sensed anything unusual. Zach watched the screen of the oscilloscope for fifteen minutes, glancing occasionally at the readout of the frequency counter. Nothing out of the ordinary. The uplink frequency was rock solid and the signal level at the output of the baseband channel group was exactly what it should be.

Impatient to find something, Zach decided to move the probe of the frequency selective levelmeter to a different test point. As he moved his arm, he noticed movement on the floor slightly to his right. The sound that filled the room made Zach to freeze instantly. The whirring buzz was unmistakable. No other sound in the world produced such instant fear. Zach allowed his eyes to shift toward the right in the direction of the sound. His worst fear was confirmed. A large rattlesnake was coiled just four feet from his right leg. It was shaking the large rattles on its tail violently, warning of an impending strike.

Zach was paralyzed with fear. Ever since he was a child he had been deathly afraid of snakes. He had tried to overcome the fear but had always failed.

Zach could taste the fear in his mouth. Large beads of perspiration formed on his forehead and ran down his face and into his eyes. He was frozen. Afraid to move. Afraid to even wipe his face. The perspiration burned his eyes. He blinked again and again, afraid that any movement might startle the snake, causing it to strike. The building's door was closed. Zach could not run. The snake could not get out. Zach had escaped death many times in the jungles of southeast Asia. Was he going to die in the desert because of a snake?

CHAPTER FORTY-ONE

Tuesday, March 31 – 2056 Zulu
USS Providence SSN 719
37°38'N, 21°39'W
195 Miles ENE of Santa Maria Island

Sonarman First Class Randy Jenkins had been staring at the sonar console screen for hours, watching for any sign of the unusual sonobuoy frequency the captain had ordered him to monitor. The highly sensitive sonar instruments were set in passive mode, listening for the slightest sound in the surrounding water. The sonar room was illuminated by blue light to help the technicians more easily read the sonar monitors and also to keep light away from the nearby Control Room. Even the soft blue light did not relieve his eye strain. He rubbed his weary eyes. After starring at the console screen for so long, he would not be surprised if his eyes had become square.

Jenkins stood up and yawned before turning back toward the sonar console. Gasping in surprise, "My God! There it is!" He threw himself into the chair and tuned the frequency adjustment to brighten the signal. For several minutes he stared intently at the waterfall display of the sonar screen as it painted sound waves picked up from the forward sonar array. Relying on his own skill rather than computer, he identified the sonobuoy's sound pattern from the surrounding background noise. Once the contact was identified, he looked horizontally across the screen to determine the bearing. He scribbled some numbers on a note pad, tore off the page, and ran out of the sonar room like the Devil himself was chasing him.

Jenkins ran down the passageway toward the officers berthing area. He stopped in front of the Captain Chandler's cabin and pounded on the door.

"Enter," Commander Chandler shouted.

Jenkins threw open the door and stammered, out of breath from his sprint from the sonar room, "Captain, I picked up the frequency! You know. The one you asked me to watch for."

"When?"

"Just now sir. Not even five minutes ago."

"Give me details Petty Officer Jenkins."

Jenkins took a breath and continued, "Sixty-five hundred yards sir. Bearing three-two-four relative."

"Good work Jenkins," Chandler said. "Go back to Sonar and keep your eye on that contact. We'll change course to intercept. Scan the area for any other possible contacts. If there is anything out there, I want to know about it."

"Aye aye sir," Jenkins acknowledged as he turned and ran for the sonar room. Chandler was right on his heels, heading for the control room.

"XO, I have the Conn," Chandler announced, stepping up on the platform. He did not even wait for the XO to acknowledge before he began barking orders into the 7-MC.

"Helm, Conn, left standard rudder. Come to course zero-nine-nine. Ahead standard. Make turns for eight knots."

"Conn, Helm, left standard rudder. Come to course zero-nine-nine. Ahead standard. Make turns for eight knots aye."

"Conn aye."

Three minutes later the 7-MC squawked to life. "Conn, Helm, steady on course zero-nine-nine. Making turns for eight knots."

"Conn aye," Chandler acknowledged. He made the mental computation in his head. Sixty-five hundred yards at eight knots would take just over twenty-five minutes. He clicked a stopwatch hanging around his neck and started the countdown. "Divers to the aft escape hatch. Prepare for rescue operations," Chandler barked into the 1-MC.

Chandler waited as the minutes counted off. When the boat had covered half the distance to the rendezvous point, he spoke into the 7-MC, "Helm, Conn, ahead slow. Make turns for three knots."

"Conn, Helm, ahead slow. Make turns for three knots aye."

"Sonar, Conn, report all contacts."

"Conn, Sonar, one surface contact dead ahead. No other close contacts."

"Dive, Conn, five degree up bubble. Come to periscope depth."

"Conn, Dive, five degree up bubble. Come to periscope aye."

The instant the diving watch reported the boat at periscope depth, Chandler looked over at the XO, "Up periscope." He knelt down as low as he could and met the periscope on its way up. Quickly spinning the periscope to zero degrees relative, he looked directly down the longitudinal axis of the boat, and ran the focus ring back and forth. In the dim light, he could just make out a small blob on the surface. He turned the periscope slowly clockwise until he had completed a full circle. "Down periscope," he ordered.

"Sonar, Conn, any other contacts," Chandler questioned.

"Conn, Sonar, no contacts except for the one surface contact dead ahead," Sonarman Jenkins responded.

During the periscope sweep, the momentum of the boat caused *Providence* to drift within two hundred fifty yards of the surface contact.

"Dive, Conn, surface the boat," Chandler ordered. No waiting for a response, he looked over at the XO, "Mr. Graham, you have the Conn. I'm going aft to supervise the recovery. I don't want the boat on the surface one second longer than absolutely necessary. As soon as the recovery is complete, I want you to take the boat to periscope depth and set course two-three-one. Once at periscope depth we will send a message to COMSUBLANT. Understood?"

"Understood Captain," Lcdr. Graham answered as he stepped up on the platform and assumed the Conn.

Chandler stepped down from the platform and ran aft toward the aft access hatch. When he arrived at the aft escape hatch, the divers were in their wetsuits and ready, waiting for the boat to surface. The XO notified Chandler that the boat was surfaced. Chandler shouted, "Open the hatch."

The lead diver un-dogged the aft access hatch and pushed it open. Cold water spilled down the escape trunk, splashing onto the floor. The lead diver scrambled out onto the rolling deck and waited. The next two divers shoved an inflatable raft up the escape trunk and struggled out on deck after it. Two more safety divers followed to assist with the launch and recovery. The lead diver pulled the cord to inflate the raft and let it down over the side of the boat. The first three divers out of the hatch slid down the side of the boat and dropped into the raft. The two safety divers on the deck let go of the safety rope and the divers in the raft immediately began to row toward the one-man raft bobbing on the ocean swells two hundred yards away. It took only a few minutes for *Providence's* divers to reach the small raft.

"Boy, am I glad to see you," Bill Morrison hollered against the wind, grabbing his duffle bag.

"I bet you are," the lead diver shouted back. "Come on. Hurry. The captain doesn't want to stay on the surface any longer than necessary."

The divers hauled Bill out of the one-man raft and into the larger one. With their guest safely aboard, one of the divers reached out and cut the sonobuoy's lanyard, sending it to the ocean floor six thousand feet below.

Bill hugged his duffle bag tightly while the divers paddled the raft back to *Providence.* One of the divers threw the safety line to the waiting safety divers standing on *Providence's* deck. The lead diver scrambled up the rope ladder hanging down the side of the boat, motioning for Bill to follow. Bill climbed up the ladder followed by the other two divers. The last diver up the ladder began to haul the raft up onto the deck.

"We don't have time," the lead diver shouted. "The captain wants to get out of here now! Just cut it and let it go."

The diver that had been hauling up the raft pulled a knife from a scabbard strapped to his leg and quickly jabbed three holes in the raft. He cut the safety line and let the deflated raft drift away. The divers directed Bill down the hatch and quickly followed. The last diver down the ladder slammed the hatch closed and dogged it down.

"Conn, recovery is complete," Chandler hollered into the 1-MC. He commended the divers on their speedy recovery and requested someone get some dry clothes for their guest.

CHAPTER FORTY-TWO

Tuesday, March 31 – 2127 Zulu
USS San Juan (SSN 751)
37° 36' 25"N, 21° 33' 10"W

"Conn, Sonar, mechanical transients, bearing two-four-nine relative," Sonarman First Class Roy Carter's excited voice announced.

"Sonar, Conn, can you determine what it was?"

"Conn, Sonar, still analyzing sir," Carter responded.

Carter reached up and readjusted his headphones for the fifth time. Even though the headphones were designed with soft, form-fitting earmuffs, they were horribly uncomfortable and pinched his ears. During his years serving aboard various submarines, he had logged hundreds of hours watching sonar displays and listening to the associated sounds picked up by the spherical sonar array. He reset the recording to the beginning and replayed the last five minutes. Adjusting the headphones yet again, he closed his eyes, concentrating on the faint mechanical sound. Three more times he reset the recording to the beginning, closing his eyes, listening intently . It was a metallic clang. It was definitely a hatch being closed.

"Conn, Sonar, sounds like a metal hatch being slammed shut."

"Sonar, Conn, do you have course and speed for the contact that produced the transient?"

Carter released the recording and focused on the current sonar display. "Conn, Sonar, we don't hold any contacts. Just the mechanical transient then nothing."

"Conn aye," Commander Richards acknowledged, wondering what had generated the transient if Sonar did not hold any contacts. The *San Juan* was approaching the area where the flash message had advised *Providence* was likely to be. His intension was to contact *Providence* if at all possible. However, to be prudent he would err on the side of caution. Richards decided to put *San Juan* on alert. He reached up and thumbed the 1-MC. "Man battle stations. Do it quietly. Rig the boat for ultra-quiet."

Two minutes later Carter's excited voice blared over the 27-MC, "Conn, Sonar, more mechanical transients. Hull popping. Submerged contact is changing depth. Bearing two-zero-nine, range nine thousand five hundred yards. Designate contact Sierra two-five."

"Sonar, Conn, do you have a designation on that contact?"

"Conn, Sonar, stand by." Twenty seconds later Sonar reported, "Computer confirms the contact is *Providence*."

A Los Angeles class submarine was extremely quiet at patrol speeds and should not have been detected. However, *Providence's* tonals and acoustic signature had already been entered into the sonar computer's memory. Because the computer knew exactly what to look for, it greatly narrowed the search, making it many times easier to detect and classify.

"Designate Sierra two-five as Master One," Richards announced.

"Conn, Weapons, load tubes one and two. Flood tubes one and two. Open outer doors."

"Weapons, Conn, load tubes one and two. Flood tubes one and two. Open outer doors aye."

"Conn, Weapons, Firing point procedures. Keep the firing solution constantly updated. Be ready to fire immediately."

"Firing point procedures. Weapons aye."

"Sonar, Conn, Set up the WQC for underwater communications."

"Conn, Sonar, Set up the WQC for underwater communications aye."

The AN/WQC-2, also called Gertrude, is an underwater telephone used on all Naval submarine and surface ships. It uses sonar hydrophones to transmit through the water.

"Helm, Conn, ahead standard, make turns for eight knots. Right standard rudder, come to course two-zero-nine."

If *Providence* did not respond or initiated threatening action of any kind, *San Juan* was fully prepared to engage. Richards grabbed the WQC microphone and took a deep breath.

He pressed the microphone transmit button and spoke slowly and distinctly, "United States submarine *Providence*. This is USS *San Juan*. Do not fire. Repeat, do not fire. USS *Providence* you are overdue for comm checks. State your status and intention."

Richards waited one minute and then repeated the message.

* * *

Tuesday, March 31 – 2132 Zulu
USS Providence SSN 719
37° 37' 40"N, 21° 36' 35"W

In *Providence's* control room Lcdr. Graham had ordered the boat to periscope depth as he raised the UHF radio mast. He had ordered the radio room to prepare to send a message to COMSUBLANT confirming the recovery of the package.

"Conn, Sonar, new narrowband contact, submerged. Designate Sierra 71. Bearing zero-two-nine, range nine thousand five hundred yards!" screamed Sonarman Jenkins' excited voice.

"With me," Commander Chandler barked, grabbing Bill Morrison's arm and dragging him forward. He and Bill ran down the passageway toward the control center as the deck of the *Providence* pitched downward. The XO had ordered the boat to go deep, attempting to slip away from the new contact. Chandler and *Providence's* new guest ran puffing into the control center.

Chandler guided Bill to one side of the control room and said, "Stand right here. Do not move. And hang on."

"Mr. Graham, I have the Conn," Chandler shouted as he stepped up on the platform.

"Conn, Radio, outgoing message is incomplete."

"Radio, Conn, very well. XO, lower the UHF radio mast."

"Sonar, Conn, where did that contact come from?"

"Conn, Sonar, don't know sir. It just suddenly appeared. It had to have been sitting dead in the water until we submerged sir."

"Sonar, Conn, develop a track as soon as you can and keep me appraised of course and range."

"Conn, Sonar, receiving underwater comm," blared the 27-MC.

"What?", Chandler exclaimed, a puzzled look on his face. "Sonar, put the comm on the speaker."

"Sonar aye."

All eyes in the control room turned and looked at the speaker. For a few seconds there was only static, then came the distorted but understandable message, "United States submarine *Providence*. This is the USS *San Juan*. Do not fire. Repeat, do not fire. USS *Providence* you are overdue for comm checks. State your status and intention."

Lcrd. Graham looked at Chandler. "What do you think Captain?"

"They're lying," Chandler answered. "It's a trap. The flash message advised we should expect a scheme of this sort. Battle Stations XO!"

Bong, bong, bong reverberated throughout the boat as Graham reached up and sounded the general alarm. He thumbed the transmit lever on the 1-MC, "Battle Stations! Battle Stations! This is not a drill! Battle Stations! Battle Stations!"

"Weapons, Conn, load tubes one and two. Open outer doors."

"Conn, Weapons, load tubes one and two. Open outer doors aye."

"Sonar, Conn, get me a range and bearing quickly."

"Sonar, Conn, aye."

CHAPTER FORTY-THREE

Tuesday, March 31 – 2133 Zulu
USS San Juan (SSN 751)
37° 36' 25"N, 21° 33' 10"W

Sonarman First Class Roy Carter nearly had a heart attack when he heard the tell-tale ringing of the general alarm as *Providence* went to battle stations. "Conn, Sonar, general alarm sounding. Contact is going to battle stations. Mechanical transients. Torpedo tube outer doors being opened."

"Helm, Conn, ahead full make turns for fifteen knots. Right full rudder come to course two-zero-nine."

"Conn, Helm, ahead full make turns for fifteen knots. Right full rudder come to course two-zero-nine aye."

Commander Richards had expected a verbal response from *Providence*. He certainly had not expected them to go to battle stations and prepare to fire upon *San Juan*. Attacking *Providence* was an action that filled him with revulsion, but he would not jeopardize *San Juan* and her crew.

"Weapons, Conn, as soon as we steady up on course and have a range and bearing, we will fire."

"Weapons aye."

Waiting for *San Juan* to steady up on the ordered course, Richards had visions of one hundred thirty brave sailors dying in the cold Atlantic waters. In his mind, he could hear their horrified cries as the submarine filled with water and sank. The face of his friend, Commander Chandler, stared back at him in disbelief. How could he unleash certain death on the crew of *Providence*. The voice of the helmsman snapped his attention back to the duty at hand.

"Conn, Helm, steady on ordered course two-zero-nine."

"Conn aye."

"Sonar, Conn, range and bearing to Master One."

"Conn, Sonar, range nine thousand six hundred yards."

"Weapons, Conn, report status."

"Conn, Weapons. Firing solution entered and locked. Weapons ready in

199

all respects."

Richards grimaced and gave the order he had hoped he would not have to give, "Fire tube one."

The boat shuddered as the torpedo was impulsed from the tube. The weapons department rapidly vented the torpedo impulse tanks and refilled them to supply water for the second torpedo loaded in tube two if necessary.

All ears in the control listened as the sonar room reported the progress of the torpedo just launched. "Own unit in the water, running normally." A few seconds later, "Torpedo turning to preset gyro course. Switching to high speed."

* * *

Tuesday, March 31 – 2138 Zulu
USS Providence SSN 719
37° 37' 40"N, 21° 36' 35"W

"Conn, Sonar, change in aspect sir. Course one-four-zero. Speed increased to fifteen knots. Contact is turning toward us. Range nine thousand five hundred yards."

"Conn aye."

"Conn, Dive, level at four hundred fifty feet."

"Conn aye."

"Helm, Conn, all stop."

"Conn, Helm, all stop aye."

"Attention all hands. This is the Captain. Rig for ultra-quiet. If you aren't on watch, don't move."

"Sonar, Conn, are there any thermoclines?"

"Conn, Sonar, yes sir. We passed through one at two hundred fifty feet."

"Conn aye. Report any changes on the contact. Quietly."

"Sonar aye."

Crewmembers throughout the boat instantly stopped whatever they were doing, remaining as quiet as they could. All unnecessary machinery was switched off. Everyone stood motionless and waited, muffling coughs or sneezes with handkerchiefs or shirt tails.

Bill stood pressed against the starboard bulkhead mesmerized by the array of lights, displays, and controls. He watched in awe as the crew of *Providence* prepared for battle.

The crewmembers in the control room sat motionless, barely breathing as the seconds ticked off.

"Conn, Sonar, outer doors opening. Range nine thousand three hundred yards. Course steady. Speed steady at fifteen knots."

"Conn aye."

Slowly the seconds ticked off. Crewmembers shifted uncomfortably in their seats. Some twisted their heads from side to side. Others rubbed stiff shoulder muscles.

"Conn, Sonar, high speed screws! Torpedo in the water! Range nine thousand one hundred yards. Bearing one-one-five," Sonarman Jenkins screamed

"Conn aye."

Commander Chandler made a mental computation of how long he had to take evasive maneuvers. It would take slightly under three minutes for the torpedo to close the distance between them. Even if he ordered an emergency course change and flank speed, it would be impossible for *Providence* to outrun the torpedo screaming toward them.

"Helm, Conn, right full rudder come to course one-one-five. All back emergency."

"Conn, Helm, right full rudder come to course one-one-five. All back emergency aye."

Commander Chandler knew their only hope was to turn toward the incoming torpedo and present as small a target as possible.

"Launch port and starboard countermeasures," Chandler shouted.

Hopefully, the two countermeasures canisters would create enough noise and disturbance in the water to mask *Providence's* propeller noise. If *Providence* could open enough distance from the countermeasures and if the incoming torpedo was fooled into targeting the counter-measures, they just might survive. The only thing left for them to do was pray.

Everyone in the control room was riveted in place. All eyes, except those responding to the ordered course and speed change, were on the captain.

The seconds ticked off like hours.

CHAPTER FORTY-FOUR

Tuesday, March 31 - 1510 Mountain Daylight Time
Stonewall Flat Microwave Tower Site
Forty-Two miles south of Tonopah, Nevada

Zach had absolutely no idea how long he had been standing there paralyzed by his fear of the snake coiled behind him. He knew he had to do something. Neither he nor the snake could get out of the building. The rattle decreased in frequency. Very, very slowly he turned his head. Out of the corner of his eye he could see the snake, still coiled, about six feet behind him.

He estimated the snake to be maybe five feet long. If the snake did strike, it would not be able to reach him. He hoped. But what if he was wrong and the snake was seven feet long? It really did not matter. He simply had no other option.

If he jumped to his left, the equipment rack might shield him from the strike. But then what? He had no weapons. How was he going to kill the snake? He knew a snake could not strike if it was stretched out. If he jumped to his left, the snake would strike. Then he could rush it and stomp on its head. "Not much of a plan, Einstein," Zach thought to himself. It was risky, but it was all he could think of.

Zach took several deep breaths. He would get only one chance. One more deep breath. "Now!" he shouted out loud.

Zach jumped to his left. The snake struck but came about two feet short. Zach ran over to the snake while it was still stretched out and stomped on its head. The heel of his shoe landed directly on the snake's skull. Zach's first effort, powered by sheer terror, had landed with such force the snake's skull was completely crushed, but Zach did not care. He stomped at the snake again, and again, and again, until his foot hurt. The snake's head was completely un-recognizable. It was a bloody pulp at the end of the snake's body. Zach opened the door to the equipment building and grabbed the still writhing snake. He rushed outside and hurled the snake as far as he could.

He went back inside the building and closed the door. He staggered over to the toolbox and sat down, shaking like a leaf. His shirt was soaked with perspiration. Even the top three inches of his trousers were soaked. After ten minutes of deep breathing, Zach finally calmed down enough to be able to function.

How had the snake gotten inside the building. The specifications for the construction and installation of the equipment buildings were quite specific about being varmint proof. Zach got up and went over to the equipment rack. He pulled the lower cover off the rack and inspected the floor where the utility cables entered the building.

"What's the....?" Zach exclaimed, dropping to his knees for a closer look. The foam insulation that was supposed to seal the access hole in the floor had been pushed out and an extra black cable ran up into the equipment cabinet. Zach tugged on the cable. It ran down through the floor and disappeared under the building.

He pulled all the covers off the equipment rack and traced the cable up through various bundles and raceways. The cable ran behind the receiver sections and entered the transmitter section. Zach grabbed a small wrench from his toolbox and removed the internal cover of the transmitter multiplier section. The cable led to a small circuit board hidden inside the multiplier section. Zach looked the board over very carefully. It appeared to be a signal injector of some kind. The output pin of the circuit board was capacitor coupled to the input of the final multiplier circuit of the transmitter. Somebody was injecting a signal into the microwave system.

Zach grabbed a small notebook from the toolbox and made a detailed drawing of the circuit board and its components. He setup the small oscilloscope he had brought with him and tested several points on the circuit board. No activity. The circuit board seemed to be dead, but what would be the point.

He decided to go outside and see if he could determine the cable's course. He grabbed a flashlight from the toolbox and walked around the building looking for evidence of tampering. It did not take long to find what he was looking for. Whoever had tampered with the microwave system had been very sloppy. They had not even bothered to smooth the dirt out where they had dug under the north edge of the building.

"What's e ah doin?" Angus asked.

"Don't know. He's walking around the building," Frenchie responded.

The same two men that had murdered Fred Hargrove had followed Zach as he left the airport in Las Vegas. Had they not been certain where their quarry was headed, it would have been impossible to follow unnoticed. The highway was flat and traffic that far from Las Vegas was nearly non-existent. Even one vehicle would have been noticed.

Frenchie and his accomplice, Angus, had turned off the highway several miles behind Zach and had driven to a north side of Stonewall Mountain where they could watch him with binoculars.

"He's poking around under the building!", Frenchie exclaimed. "He must have found the receiver. We'll have to shut him up before he can tell anyone."

"Angus, get in the Jeep. We'll pick him up when he comes back to the highway."

Zach got down on his knees and peered under the building very carefully not wanting a repeat of the snake incident. Pointing the flashlight toward the point where the utility cables entered the building, he followed the path of the extra cable. It was attached to a small metal box just two feet in from the edge of the building.

Zach reached under the building and dragged the box toward him. There was enough slack in the wire to get the box close enough to examine it. A small access plate, secured by screws, was visible on the side closest to Zach. He laid the flashlight on the ground and went back into the building, returning with a screwdriver. He removed the screws and dropped them in his shirt pocket. There was nothing unusual inside the box, just more electronic circuits.

A short antenna on top of the box indicated it was a receiver of some type. The rest of the circuitry was a mystery. A remote controlled device certainly could explain the intermittent nature of the system failures. It would also explain the fact nothing could ever be found to identify the interference. Zach had seen enough. He replaced the access plate and pushed the box back to its original position. Using his foot, he smoothed the dirt around the building as best he could.

Back inside the building, he threw the tools back in the toolbox and replaced all the covers on the microwave equipment. The purpose for the tampering was a mystery, but he was certain it was related to the recent incidents plaguing his life. He did not have time to worry about the purpose behind the tampering. His main objective was to get back to Tulsa as quickly as he could and contact someone in Washington. The warning he had received that day on the dive trip finally made sense. There was only one person he could trust. He would call his old friend, Senator Mark Bradfield.

Toolbox in hand, he stopped at the door and made one last check of the building. Satisfied everything was as he found it, he pulled the door shut and dumped the toolbox in the back seat of his rental car. He jumped in the front seat, started the engine, and sped back down the dirt road toward the highway.

When Zach reached the highway he slowed slightly, checking traffic in both directions. There was nothing as far as he could see. He turned onto the highway and pressed his foot to the floor. When the speedometer reached eighty, he eased back on the accelerator and pushed the cruise button. He was in a hurry but he didn't want to risk getting a ticket. Two miles down the road the gray Jeep Cherokee turned onto the highway and followed him. Zach did not notice, his attention focused on the events of the past week. Some of the pieces were beginning to fall into place but something was still missing. He hoped he would be able to find the key to the puzzle when he got back to Tulsa and spoke to his friend.

The Jeep Cherokee followed close behind as Zach sped toward Scotty's Junction.

"We ah gettin close to Scotty's Junction boss. We gonna 'ave to do something soon," Angus said.

"Yeah, I know," Frenchie answered. "I guess now's as good a time as any."

Frenchie accelerated and pulled up close to Zach's rental car.

"Is there anyone behind us?" he questioned Angus.

"No, I donna see nobody."

"Hang on!" Frenchie yelled.

Frenchie accelerated again and pulled slightly ahead of Zach. He jerked the wheel to the right and cut in front of Zach's rental car. Startled by the sudden movement Zach jerked the wheel to the right and his car began skidding toward the ditch. Unable to stop, the rental car ran off the highway into the ditch.

Zach sat there staring out of the windshield. His heart was beating wildly from the adrenalin his system had released into his blood stream. When his heart rate had slowed somewhat, he released the seat-belt and climbed out of the car and walked around it, looking for damage.

He had been extremely lucky. He could find no apparent damage. No flat tires. No body damage. The sand was dry but not too deep. He should be able to simply drive back onto the highway and continue on his way.

"Crazy moron," Zach muttered as he walked back around to the driver side of the car.

Less than a mile down the road, Frenchie and Angus had pulled off the road and had watched as Zack examined his car for damage.

"What we gonna do now boss?" Angus asked.

"I don't know. Shut up and let me think," Frenchie hissed.

Frenchie sat there watching Zach, trying to decide what to do. "We'll have to kill him. If he gets into town, we'll lose him."

Frenchie slammed the Jeep Cherokee into gear, squealed back onto the highway, and headed toward Zach's location. "Get your gun ready," Frenchie shouted as they sped down the highway.

Another car appeared, heading toward Scotty's Junction. The driver noticed Zach's car off the side of the road and screeched to a stop. He jumped out and ran over to where Zach was standing. "Are you all right?"

he asked.

"Yeah, I'm fine," Zach answered. "Some blasted idiot ran me off the road. Looks like the car is okay though. If you could hang around until I see if I can get it back on the highway, I would really appreciate it."

"Be glad to," the driver of the car said.

"Some stupid fool stopped to help him," Frenchie screamed. "No matter. We'll just kill them both."

Zach opened the door and was about to get in when he noticed the approaching Jeep Cherokee. It was the same car that had run him off the road. Someone in the back seat had his arm out of the window. When Zach realized he was holding a gun, he dived for the interior of the rental car as the first shot hit the passenger window shattering it into thousands of tiny shards. The next shot hit the driver that had stopped to help him. He fell sideways and disappeared from sight.

Zach was sorry for the man but he could not wait around to help him. He started the engine and was about to slam the rental car into gear when the Jeep Cherokee skidded to a stop in front of the rental car, blocking his escape.

Frenchie and Angus jumped out of the Jeep Cherokee. Angus ran to the passenger side and pointed his gun through the shattered window while Frenchie ran around to the driver's side and pointed his gun directly at Zach.

"Out of the car!" Frenchie bellowed. "Get to the back of the Jeep now!"

Left with no choice, Zach complied. Frenchie poked the gun in Zach's back and followed him. When they reached the back of the Jeep, Frenchie shoved Zach roughly against it. Angus took a position beside Frenchie.

In an abandoned gas station further down the highway a man dressed in desert camouflage held his eye to the scope mounted on his M21 sniper rifle, a modified version of the old M14. The man, an expert in military firearms, knew the 7.62mm projectile would rise slightly for the first two hundred yards before it began to drop. He estimated the distance to the target to be just under one hundred fifty yards. Easing the scope's crosshairs down about two inches, he took a steadying breath and gently pulled the trigger. The 7.62mm projectile covered the distance to the target in less than two tenths of a second and slammed into the target dead center between the shoulder blades.

Zach stared in amazement as a bright red stain began to form in the middle of Angus' chest. He slumped to his knees and fell face first. Two seconds later a bright red stain formed one inch below the base of Frenchie's neck. Frenchie's knees buckled and he fell beside Angus. The only sounds Zach heard were the sickening thumps of the bullets hitting the bodies. Zach crouched and looked in the direction from which the shots would have originated. Nothing. Several derelict mobile homes and an abandoned gas station over one hundred yards away.

No telltale gunshots, two center-mass hits from who knew where, and only two seconds apart could mean only one thing. A highly trained sniper. Whatever was going on Zach elected not to find out what it was. He ran around the Jeep and dived into his rental car. In the abandoned gas station, the man dressed in desert camouflage placed his semi-automatic, M21 sniper rifle back into its case. The M21 was the number one choice of U. S. Army snipers because it weighed only twelve pounds with a fully loaded, twenty round magazine and was accurate to over three hundred yards. Its current user could happily attest to its deadly accuracy.

Zach's rental car roared up onto the highway and sped south toward Las Vegas. Two miles down the road Zach looked down at the speedometer. The needle was sitting on ninety. He eased up on the accelerator, holding the speed steady. Zach glanced in the rear-view mirror. The highway was empty. No one was following him. Zach held the speed at ninety for ten more miles. Another glance in the rear-view mirror. Still no one following. Zach slowed to eighty, maintaining that speed all the way to Las Vegas.

Zach reached the outskirts of Las Vegas where the highway turned into a controlled access highway. Another glance in the rear view mirror. He thought about taking the next exit but there was nothing close. Overtaking several cars, he changed lanes and roared past them. As soon as he was past the lead car, he pulled back into the right lane and watched for the next exit.

The highway curved to the south. One-quarter mile ahead he saw another exit with several businesses close by. A large building resembling a hotel sat just one hundred yards or so north of the highway. Zach decided it was his best opportunity to get off the highway.

Zach kept his speed until he was right on the exit. He slammed on the brakes and turned onto the exit ramp. If anyone was following him, he hoped they would not notice him exit the highway. Roaring up to the stop sign, he slowed only as much as necessary, and turned left. The building he had spotted was a hotel. He turned into the parking lot and pulled into the first empty space he found. The equipment would have to be sacrificed. The only thing he dared not lose was his briefcase. He reached over the seat, grabbed the briefcase, and ran for the hotel lobby.

He would call a taxi and abandon the rental car. A taxi was discharging a passenger just as he reached the lobby. His good fortune was almost too good to be believed. Waving at the cabby, he hollered, "Taxi! Taxi!"

The cabby slammed on his brakes and waited as Zach threw open the door and jumped inside.

"Where to?" the cabby asked.

"I don't know. Let's just get out of here. Someone is chasing me. I've got to get out of here before they find me," Zach panted, out of breath from his sprint toward the lobby.

The cabby dropped the flag and sped out of the hotel driveway, turning toward the highway.

"No!" Zach shouted. "I just came from that way. Go the other way. Take the long way into town. That will give me some time to think."

"Okay. Okay," the cabbie replied as he turned the other way, heading north.

Zach knew it was too late to catch a flight back to Tulsa. He would have to wait until morning. Whoever had tried to kill him had known exactly where he was going to be. It would be too risky to go to his normal hotel. Instead he would find a small hotel by the airport, but first he would need a few things.

"Is there a hotel by the airport with a mall or shopping center close by?" Zach asked the cabbie.

"Yeah, there's one with a mall three or four blocks away, but it is not by the airport," the cabbie answered.

"Ah ... That's okay. Drop me there," Zach said.

Zach sat in silence, formulating a plan for the return trip to Tulsa and what he would say to Senator Mark Bradfield. In view of the events of the past two weeks, he would need to be careful what he said to the Senator.

Every few blocks Zach glanced behind the cab to see if anyone was behind them. There was no one following them. It appeared his quick action on the highway had been successful.

The cab pulled up in front of Arizona Charlie's Hotel and Casino. Zach grabbed several bills from his wallet and tossed them over the front seat. The amount was more than double the fare amount on the meter.

"I would really appreciate it if you forgot you ever saw me," Zach said as he climbed out of the cab.

"You bet. Never saw you in my life," the cabbie responded, scooping up the bills and heading for his next fare.

Zach went inside the hotel lobby and paid for a room in cash using a false name. He walked to the door, poked his head out, and checked the street in both directions. Seeing no sign of suspicious activity, he left the hotel and hurried to the mall to purchase a change of clothes and something to disguise his appearance.

CHAPTER FORTY-FIVE

Tuesday, March 31 – 2126 Zulu
USS Providence SSN719
37°37'35"N, 21°36'33"W
ENE of Santa Maria Island

"Rig for impact!" Commander Chandler shouted over the 1-MC when the XO's count down to the torpedo's impact reached thirty seconds. Every member of *Providence's* crew sucked in their breath. Many prayed, waiting for what they expected would be certain destruction.

The XO continued counting down the seconds to the torpedo's estimated impact, "Five, four, three, two, one, impact!" Nothing. Everyone waited. Six seconds later a violent shockwave impacted *Providence's* bow, reverberating throughout the boat. Several systems went offline due to the violent vibrations. The seal on one small water line gave way and began spraying water in the engine room. The engine room crewmen sprang into action and had the leak controlled in less than two minutes. Crewmen elsewhere in the boat were already in the process of rebooting systems that had gone offline.

Fortunately, the torpedo had targeted the countermeasures and detonated four hundred yards before reaching *Providence*. Commander Chandler asked for and received damage control reports from all departments. The damage was surprisingly minimal and all necessary repairs were underway. The next course of action would be to decide if they would engage their attacker or leave the area quickly and quietly.

"Helm, Conn, left full rudder. Come to course three-zero-three. Make turns for three knots."

"Conn, Helm, left full rudder. Come to course three-zero-three. Make turns for three knots aye."

"Dive, Conn, ten degree down bubble. Make your depth nine hundred fifty feet."

"Conn, Dive, ten degree down bubble. Make your depth nine hundred fifty feet aye."

"Sonar, Conn, Report."

"Conn, Sonar, contact has slowed to five knots. Course and depth steady."

"Conn aye. Report any changes immediately."

"Sonar aye."

For some unknown reason the contact broke off the attack. Chandler had no idea why but he was going to find out who was responsible. He assigned the Conn to Lt. Flanigan. Chandler stuck his head in the sonar room and asked, "Petty Officer Jenkins, what can you tell me about the contact that fired that torpedo?"

"Analysis just coming out now sir," Sonarman Jenkins replied, ripping the page off as it ejected from the printer. A startled look spread across his face as he scanned the computer's analysis of the contact. "Computer says it was the *San Juan* sir."

"What?" Chandler gasped. "One of our own shooting at us? That can't be. There has to be some mistake."

"No sir. There is no mistake," Jenkins affirmed. "Computer identifies the contact as the *San Juan* with ninety-nine percent accuracy."

"Give me the analysis," Chandler ordered as he turned and headed back to the control room. He entered the control room and walked over to the Conn. "Mr. Flanigan you still have the Conn. Mr. Graham come with me."

Lcrd. Graham followed Chandler to an isolated area of the control room. Chandler handed the sonar computer's analysis to Lcdr. Graham.

"This can't possibly be correct," Graham exclaimed, shaking his head as he handed the printout back to Chandler.

"Computer estimates ninety-nine percent accuracy," Chandler countered.

"But why?" Graham asked.

"Your guess is as good as mine, Mr. Graham," Chandler answered. "I know Commander Richards, skipper of the *San Juan*, very well. He wouldn't fire on another US submarine without direct orders to do so."

"But that still doesn't answer why," Graham protested.

"I suspect it has something to do with our guest," Chandler hinted.

"Should we phone this in?" Graham asked.

"No," Chandler answered. "I did not share the entire content of the earlier flash message we received. It directs us to maintain absolute radio silence unless we receive a pre-designated code. The message said it was imperative we deliver our guest to Norfolk Naval Station ASAP. Once we are safely out of the area, we will return to base course and rise above any haloclines or thermoclines and extend the long wire antenna."

"What about our guest?" Graham questioned.

"I left our guest standing in the control room with orders to not move," Chandler replied. "Mr. Graham, go round him up. Get him some fresh clothes and assign him a place to bunk."

"Aye sir," Graham replied.

While Graham went to take care of *Providence's* guest, Chandler returned to the control platform. "Mr. Franklin, I have the Conn."

"Conn, Dive, level at nine hundred fifty feet."

"Conn aye. Helm, Conn, all stop."

"Helm, Conn, all stop aye."

Chandler reached up and thumbed the 1-MC, "All stations, this is the captain. Rig for ultra quiet. Put all non-essential systems in standby mode. Switch off all fans and ventilation systems. Wherever you are, stop and sit. I don't want any sound whatsoever. I want this boat so quiet I could hear a gnat fart."

Immediately, systems all over the boat were either switched off or put in standby mode. Nobody spoke a word. Even the crew's breathing slowed. The boat became eerily still.

On the *San Juan*, the sonar room operators were puzzled when *Providence's* sonar trace faded out. There were no sounds of a hull breaking up and no machinery noise. No mechanical transients or tonals. It was as if *Providence* had vanished.

For the next twenty minutes, crewmen in *Providence's* sonar room watched the traces on their sonar screens as *San Juan* made sweeps across the area, listening for flow noises or tonals of any kind. Jenkins saw a track change, indicating *San Juan* had changed course to the northeast. He slipped his sneakers off and tiptoed silently into the control room. Stopping short of the platform, motioning at Chandler.

"What is it?" Chandler whispered.

"Contact has changed course to the northeast, speed 8 knots," Jenkins said as quietly as he could. "I think they've lost us and are widening their search pattern."

Chandler gave Jenkins a "thumbs up" signal and crept silently over to the helmsman. "Ahead dead slow. Left standard rudder. Come to course two-six-two."

"Aye sir," EM2 Connaly whispered.

The ordered course was nearly opposite that of *San Juan*, which would increase the distance between them. Twenty minutes later, *San Juan* faded off *Providence's* sonar screen.

"All stations, this is the captain. Secure from ultra quiet. Restart ventilation. Return all systems to full operating mode."

"Helm, Conn, ahead standard. Make turns for ten knots."

"Conn, Helm, ahead standard. Make turns for ten knots aye."

All over the boat there were sighs of relief. *Providence* had avoided certain death.

CHAPTER FORTY-SIX

Admiral Beckwith gathered up the communications briefs he was working on and locked them in the file cabinet. He straightened the items on his desk and slipped some unclassified documents into his briefcase. The phone rang as he was about to walk out the office door.

"Yes, this is Admiral Beckwith."

"Sir, I have message traffic from *San Juan*," the duty communications officer announced.

"Go ahead. What is it?"

"Sorry Sir. I can't read it over the phone. The message is classified. You will have to come to the communication center to view it."

"Very well," Beckwith grunted into the phone, not wanting to make the long walk to the communications center. He was tired and looking forward to a drink and a quiet night at home. With briefcase in hand, he pulled the office door closed and headed for the communication center.

Twenty minutes later Beckwith walked into the communication center, pulled out his ID badge, and displayed it for the duty communication officer, "You called and notified me there was message traffic from *San Juan*."

"Yes sir," the duty communication officer replied, comparing the Admiral's face to the photo on the ID badge. Satisfied Beckwith was who he said he was, he slid a clipboard in front of Beckwith, pointed to a blank line near the bottom of the page, and said, "Sigh here, sir."

The duty communication officer reached under the counter and pressed a button, releasing the lock on the door into the communication center. He directed Beckwith to a secure room and offered him a chair. The duty officer stood in front of the file cabinet to shield his activity as he spun the combination lock. A folder with a diagonally striped security seal was placed in front of Beckwith.

"Buzz me when you are done," the duty officer said as he closed and locked the door.

Beckwith opened the folder and began reading.

YYYY DE XXXX 012/34
YYYYXXXX RUCBXXX3456 17118855-UUUU-RMFRSUU.
ZNR UUUUU
P 221510Z JUL 14
FM: USS SAN JUAN SSN751
TO: COMSUBLANT
BT
CLAS //N02120//
1. USS SAN JUAN DETECTED USS PROVIDENCE 180 MILES EAST NORTH-EAST OF SANTA MARIA ISLAND @ 2120 ZULU, 31 MARCH.
2. USS PROVIDENCE IMMEDIATELY COMMENCED EVASIVE MANUEVERS.
3. USS SAN JUAN WITHIN FIRING RANGE
4. FIRED ONE MK48 ADCAP TORPEDO
5. IMPACT CONFIRMED, NO FURTHER CONTACT.
BT
2021

Beckwith shook his head as he finished reading the message. His earlier communication sent to *San Juan* was intended to create a firestorm not a single shot then nothing. There was not enough time to create another incident in the North Atlantic. The earlier decision to move up the timetable also had not produced the results he had hoped for. He slid the message back into the folder and buzzed the duty communications officer. He passed the classified message back to the duty officer and headed back to his office.

Another brisk twenty minute walk back to his office left him winded. He entered his office and locked the door. A number was punched into an untraceable cell phone. Wiping his face with a handkerchief, he slumped down in his chair, waiting for an answer.

"Yes," Director Porter answered.

"Success in moving up the timetable has become critical," Beckwith declared. "I need to know that you have done as instructed."

"Yes sir," Porter lied. "Everything is in place."

"It had better be," Beckwith warned. "If you fail, prison will be the least of your worries."

"I understand," Porter acknowledged.

Porter immediately flipped the cell phone back open and punched in a number. After twelve rings, he slammed the cell phone closed and punched in a different number. Again the phone on the other end rang and rang. He glanced at his watch. It was five p.m. in Nevada. Why did neither of the idiots he had hired answer their phones. They had been instructed to answer the cell phones he had provided them no matter what time he called.

If the two idiots in Nevada had failed, Templeton would be alerted. If that happened, Admiral Beckwith would also be alerted. Porter ran through all the possible scenarios. His resources were dying like flies. He would need someone he could trust implicitly to go to Tulsa and end the mess once and for all. That person would never answer a call from an unfamiliar number so he picked up the phone on his desk and punched in a number.

"Yes," a female voice answered.

"I need to talk to you but not on this phone. I will call right back."

"I'll be waiting."

Porter hung up the landline and punched a number into the cell phone.

"Yes," the female voice repeated.

"I have a situation that I need help cleaning up."

"Sorry, I'm kind of busy."

"This can't wait. I will pay three times the normal price."

"I'm listening."

"I need you to fly to Tulsa as soon as you can. A loose end needs to be tied up."

"I don't know. Out of town and on short notice. That's a lot of trouble and extra expense."

"Okay. I will add a five thousand dollar bonus."

"Done. Wire the money to the Cayman account."

"Agreed. How soon can you begin.?"

"I always have a bag packed darling. I'll leave on the first available flight."

"Great. I'll send a photo and details to the usual email. Advise me when it's done

"Don't I always darling."

Porter flipped the cell phone closed and laid it on the desk. He logged onto his computer and signed into his private, online banking account. A transfer of the agreed to amount was scheduled to a numbered account at a bank on Grand Cayman. He logged into his secret email account and typed in an email address from memory, attached a photo of Zach Templeton, typed in the location of Zach Templeton's office, and some other necessary details, then clicked send. He signed out of the email account, powered down the computer, and went to the study to mix himself a stiff drink and plan his next move.

* * *

Wednesday, April 1 - 0445 Pacific Daylight Time
McCarren International Airport
Las Vegas, Nevada

Zach tossed several bills over the seat to the driver and climbed out of the taxi. Quickly crossing the sidewalk, he entered the airport terminal through a large sliding door. First he needed to sit for a few minutes and collect his thoughts.

A group of chairs tucked into a corner next to a small gift shop would give him a good vantage point. Selecting a chair in the row against the wall where no one could come up behind him, he had full view of the airport entrance.

The previous night he had made a quick trip to the mall adjacent to the hotel and had purchased some items to disguise himself. A completely different set of clothes, a dark brown wig, a baseball cap, new shoes, a pair of wraparound sunglasses, a canvass carryon bag, and even some makeup to darken his skin color. Everything about his appearance was different, a whole new look. No one would recognize him, not even his friends.

In spite of his disguised appearance, Zach was not going to take any chances. The pieces of the puzzle did not fit together yet, but he knew for certain someone had tampered with the microwave system. That someone knew he knew and wanted him dead. Until yesterday Zach had a strong suspicion Fred's death had been no accident. There was no longer any doubt in his mind. Yesterday's events provided all the proof he needed.

Zach looked at his wristwatch and compared it to the large clock on the wall. To avoid unnecessary exposure, he would go to the gate at the last minute. Twenty minutes remained before he needed to head for the gate. While waiting for the time to pass, he watched the entrance to see if anyone suspicious entered.

Time passed slowly. Zach was anxious to get home, call his old friend, and begin the process of identifying Fred's killer. He watched all kinds of travelers passing through the sliding doors, business men rushing for flights home or to meetings in distant cities, elderly ladies possibly off to visit grandchildren, women with children in tow, probably heading to meet arriving husbands, couples arm in arm; all heading somewhere.

Zach's attempt to analyze the events of the last several days was mostly unsuccessful. Way too edgy and absorbed watching everyone entering the airport terminal, he was unable to concentrate. Everyone that entered within Zach's field of vision seemed to be nothing more than an ordinary traveler. Satisfied he could do so safely, Zach got up and headed for his gate.

Still wary and watchful, he blended in with the flow of passengers passing through the security checkpoint at the entrance to the concourse. He dropped his carryon bag on the x-ray machine's conveyor belt as he stepped through the magnetometer. He passed through cleanly without any alarm, having put anything metal in his carryon bag before leaving the seating area. Proceeding to the gate as quickly as possible and without any undue attention was of utmost importance.

He grabbed the carryon bag as it slid down the chute from the x-ray machine and headed for gate thirty-one. Another quick glance at his watch. His timing was perfect. The flight should start boarding just as he arrived at the gate. Walking slightly past gate thirty-one, he crossed to the other side of the concourse and walked back toward the gate. The general boarding process had not started, so he ducked into a small gift shop and pretended to browse for a gift. A small glass bell caught his attention. It was unique. He was certain Angie would love it. He snatched it from the shelf and hurried over to the cash register. The sales clerk punched the price into the register and placed the item in a small sack. As Zach dug in his pocket for some cash, he heard the gate attendant announce the boarding process for American Airlines flight three sixty for Dallas. He dropped a couple of bills on the counter. "Keep the change. They're calling my flight. I've got to run", Zach called out to the clerk as he hurried out of the store.

Zach merged into the line of passengers heading for the jetway door. He handed his ticket to the gate attendant who tore off the boarding stub and handed it back to him. Breathing a sigh of relief, he walked down the jetway toward the aircraft. Once settled into his seat, he would have plenty of time to go over events of the last few days. He was determined to have a plan when he arrived in Tulsa. Somebody had murdered his friend and they were going to pay. No matter what it cost him personally, they, whoever they were, were going to pay. And pay dearly.

CHAPTER FORTY-SEVEN

Wednesday, April 1 - 1305 Central Daylight Time
American Airlines Flight 3521
28,000 feet over Northern Oklahoma

A warm breeze blew across Zach's body, the hot tropical sun warming the bronze skin of his back. It felt good laying there in the sun with Angie beside him. A hand nudged at his arm. "Angie, don't. It feels so good here in the sun."

"Sir. Wake up," the flight attendant urged. "We're about to land."

"Huh," Zach mumbled, struggling to wake up. Gradually the fog of sleep cleared and Zach remembered where he was.

After a short connection in Dallas, he had boarded flight 3521 for Tulsa. Even though the flight was short, Zach was so tired he quickly drifted off to sleep. The sand, the breeze, the sun; it had all seemed so real. Everything was good. Very good. Hopefully, he would be able to recapture the dream later.

He straightened himself in the cramped seat and pulled his seat belt a little tighter. The whirring of the electric motors driving the flaps indicated they would be on the ground soon. He stared out the window and watched the patchwork fields as the aircraft approached Tulsa's north-south runway. Zach was anxious to be on the ground and put the plan he had devised into action.

The final approach and landing were uneventful. Even before the aircraft had parked at the gate, Zach had unfastened his seat belt and had retrieved his carryon bag from under the seat. A lot of things needed to be done and he wanted to leave the airport as quickly as he could. Whoever was behind the attempt on his life would certainly have someone watching the airport. It was imperative he slip through the airport quickly without being seen.

As usual, passengers clogged the aisle of the aircraft waiting for the cabin door to be opened. Zach edged his way into the aisle behind a very large woman and her two children, hoping to appear as if he was with them.

Gradually the line of passengers began moving. He stayed close to the woman and her children as they made their way out of the aircraft and up the jetway into the terminal.

Throngs of people milling around the gate, waiting for family and friends to deplane, would make it easier for Zach to slip through unnoticed. Fortunately, no one was waiting for the woman and her children. She dragged her children through the crowd and headed for the baggage claim area. Zach stayed as close as he dared as they walked down the concourse.

As they exited the concourse and entered the terminal proper, Zach split off from the woman, walking hurriedly toward the exit. He stopped abruptly by the door and set his bag on a chair, pretending to be fumbling for something inside. Glancing in all directions, he did not see anyone that appeared to be following him. He zipped the bag shut, exited the terminal, and flagged down the first taxi he saw. Before the driver could get out, Zach opened the rear door and climbed inside, sliding down in the seat.

"Forty-first and Hudson. Quick. I'm in a hurry," Zach shouted to the driver.

"You got it," the driver responded as he slipped the car into gear and stomped on the accelerator. Tires squealing, the driver pulled away from the curb and moved into the center lane. "Anyplace in particular?" the driver questioned.

"No. Just drop me at the northwest corner," Zach answered.

Zach's car was parked in the long-term parking lot, but he couldn't take the risk of picking it up. Someone would almost certainly be watching his car and waiting for him to do something stupid. He would call Angie as soon as he could find a quiet place.

Zach made frequent glances out the back window of the taxi, but never saw anything suspicious. It appeared he had gotten away cleanly from the airport. It was time to put his plan into motion.

"That'll be twenty-six-fifty," the driver said as he pulled over to the curb on Hudson Street close to the intersection of Forty-first Street.

"Keep the change ," Zach said, handing the driver two twenty dollar bills.

Zach climbed out of the taxi and walked to the intersection. He turned right on Forty-first Street and headed for the Panera Bread store just past the corner, hoping it would be quiet this time of day.

Zach entered the store and purchased a soda, needing the energy boost the sugar and caffeine would give him. At the back of the store, he sat at a small table and drank half of the soda while rehearsing what he was going to say to Angie. If there was anyone else he could trust, he would not get Angie involved. He would do his best to not frighten her, but he had to get her full attention. It was vital he could depend on her to do exactly as he asked.

The store was nearly empty. It was time to get this over with. He took a deep breath and punched Angie's work number into his cell phone.

The phone rang twice. Zach heard Angie's voice, "Hello. This is Angie, may I help you?"

"Angie. Its Zach. How's your day going?"

"Fine, Zach. I didn't expect you back this soon."

"Yeah, I know. I had planned to be gone two or three days, but I had trouble with the equipment. Decided to come home early."

"Zach I thought you ..."

Zach cut Angie off, "How did Pablo get along?" Zach asked.

"He did just fine. Zach I ..."

Zach cut Angie off again, "Sorry to cut you off again but I'm in a hurry. I need to talk to you. It's really important. I'm in trouble. Meet me at five-thirty. Favorite place. You know where. I'll explain then. I love you." Zach hung up before Angie could ask any questions. He hated to be so short with Angie but he could not risk giving out information on the phone. It was highly possible her phone could be tapped. He could only hope she would do exactly as he had asked.

Zach left the Panera Bread store and headed for his office two blocks west on Forty-first Street. He would have to be extremely careful. Surely the people behind the incident near Las Vegas realized what had happened. To be safe, he would have to assume they would also have set up surveillance on his office building.

* * *

Wednesday, April 1 – 1412 Central Daylight Time
Southroads Shopping Center
Forty-first Street and Hudson Avenue
Tulsa, Oklahoma

An average looking woman with dark brown hair dressed in a light green business suit was sitting in a parked rental car at the shopping center. She had watched Zach Templeton as he exited the taxi cab and entered the Panera Bread store. The photo emailed to her secret email account matched in height and build. In spite of Zach's disguise, she was convinced the man she watched was the target she had been sent to Tulsa to eliminate. She exited the shopping center and drove west on Forty-first Street, parking her rental car in the Promenade Mall parking lot. She selected an empty space in a row close to the street because it had an unobstructed view of the stores in the shopping center.

To most observers, she appeared to be an ordinary, well-dressed woman sitting in her car waiting for someone at the mall. Far from ordinary, she was a very highly skilled assassin and deadly as a cobra. Those that knew her called her Black Death and remarked she must have ice water running through her veins. She was merciless, cold, and totally without feeling. She would murder anyone if the price was right. Her targets were just that — targets. Nothing more. Nothing less. A job to be done for a price.

After parking her rental car, she opened the expensive leather briefcase lying beside her on the front passenger seat and slipped out the Ruger Mark II .22-caliber automatic, her weapon of choice for up close and personal jobs. The grip plates had been removed to reduce the automatic's weight and also to lessen the bulge it made under her suit jacket. She screwed on the sound suppressor, pushed in the clip, and pulled back the slide to make certain it was loaded and ready. The sound suppressor seriously reduced the bullets accuracy. Accuracy was of little concern because the kill shot would be delivered at skin-touch range. What little sound the suppressor did not muffle, would be soaked up by the flesh of the target. Lifting her jacket out of the way, she shoved the automatic into a shoulder holster modified to accept the sound suppressor. She buttoned her jacket and checked the profile. It fit perfectly. No one would notice.

She waited for her target to exit the store he had entered. After fifteen minutes of watching and waiting, she got edgy and climbed out of the car and strolled down the street toward the mall entrance. Walking leisurely past the entrance to the mall, she turned back toward Forty-first Street. Upon reaching Forty-first Street, about to turn back toward the parking lot, she saw her quarry exit the Panera Bread store and start down Forty-first Street in her direction. She watched her target stop in the middle of the block, wait for a break in the traffic, and sprint across to the south side of the street.

Her target turned west, continuing in her direction. She entered a fast-food restaurant situated at the intersection, slipping into a booth by the window. She watched her target walk past the multi-story building directly across the street from the mall. Her target turned south at the intersection, walked past the building, and stopped beside a bus stop bench. He leaned down and tied his shoe. She continued watching as her target straightened up, turned around, and hurried into the basement garage of the building.

She exited the fast-food restaurant and hurried across the street. Inside the front entrance, she located the elevator and watched the floor numbers light up in succession as the elevator descended from the eighth floor. The elevator passed the first floor and stopped in the basement which meant her target had likely summoned the elevator from the basement. She reached out, punched the up button, and waited for the elevator to stop at the first floor. A closer examination of her target would allow her to assess his size and strength.

CHAPTER FORTY-EIGHT

Once in the parking lot of his building and out of view of the street, Zach fished a building access card out of his pocket as he headed for the elevator. He jammed the card into the reader and pushed the door open. "Please be waiting," he whispered as he pushed the UP button. Only then did he look up at the floor number display and notice the elevator was starting from the ninth floor. The elevator stopped on nearly every floor, adding to his impatience. Finally, the door slid open and Zach stepped inside. He pushed the button for the floor above the one on which his office was located, jabbing repeatedly at the door close button trying to hurry the door closed.

Zach stared at the floor indicator intently, hoping no one else was waiting for the elevator on another floor. "Just great!", Zach muttered under his breath when the elevator stopped at the first floor. He leaned against the back wall and observed two people getting onto the elevator. A man in a dark gray pinstripe suit carrying a very expensive looking briefcase and a woman in a light green business suit fiddling with a bank deposit envelope. A bank located on the first floor of the building always accounted for a lot of traffic up and down the elevator, especially near the end of the day as people hurried to get extra cash before the bank closed.

The man with the brief case got off on the third floor. The man seemed somewhat familiar. Probably a member of the law firm that rented the north half of the third floor. Zach had likely passed him countless times coming and going from the building without even giving him a second thought, but today he scrutinized minute details of everyone he saw. Anyone not familiar could be watching or following him.

He had not been nearly as careful as he should have been the past several days. All that changed after the incident on the highway near Scotty's Junction in Nevada. Determined to not make any more careless mistakes, he would use techniques he had learned in the Navy during his

SEAL training, the most highly trained and feared military combat unit in the world. His drill instructor had trained him to not miss a single sight, sound, smell, or feeling. And especially people's eyes. "Watch their eyes," he had drilled into their minds incessantly. A person's eyes always gave them away.

Zach watched the woman as she stared at the floor indicator. She was very well dressed. Even though she was rather ordinary looking, her hair was immaculately styled, her shoes matched her business suit perfectly. Everything was perfect. The way she carried herself bespoke a woman that knew she was important and not afraid to show it. Probably another lawyer Zach thought. But even from a distance, her perfume was overpowering. It was much too heavy and sweet for his taste.

For the briefest instant, he noticed her eyes glance in his direction. Zach really did not give her much thought. The first rule of stalking someone was to never call attention to yourself. Blend in. Be average. Be just another face in the crowd. This woman's perfume would be a dead giveaway. It would attract attention before she even got close. Zach almost laughed at the thought of her being a "spy" or a professional "killer".

Zach was relieved when she got off on the sixth floor. Even after she left the elevator, her scent lingered. He felt sorry for the poor souls that had to work in close proximity to her.

After the woman stepped out of the elevator and the doors slid closed, she slipped a cell phone out of her purse, punched a speed dial button, and waited for an answer.

"Hello," a male voice answered.

"He's here," the woman said.

"It's still a go," the voice on the other end said.

"Consider it done," she replied, punching the end key. She turned around, walked back to the elevator, and punched the down button, her work done, at least for the moment.

Zach, completely unaware of what had taken place on the sixth floor, got off the elevator on the ninth floor and walked toward the end of the hall. Seeing and hearing no one in the hallway, he slipped into the stairwell, carefully closing the door behind him. He hurried down the flight of stairs and inserted his key into the door lock. Opening the door just a crack, he listened to see if anyone was in the hallway. Voices coming in his direction. Quickly he pulled the door shut and stood there listening, unable to make out what was being said.

Somewhere a door slammed and all became quiet. Again he opened the door a crack and listened. Silence. He pushed the door open a little further, stuck his head into the hallway, and glanced in both directions. Empty. He pushed the door open and ran for the back door to his office, key already in hand. Quickly he slipped inside and pulled the door shut. Standing there in the darkened hallway for several minutes, he listened for any sounds. He crept quietly down the interior hallway and slipped into his office. It was not completely dark, the drapes letting in some filtered light. He walked over to his desk and switched on a small desk lamp.

Janine jumped when the phone on her desk buzzed. It had been deathly quiet in the office all afternoon and she had been daydreaming about her date later that evening. She stared at the phone wondering who could be using the intercom. There was no one else in the office other than Monica and she was busy in the map room. Zach was out of town at least until the end of the week so who could it be?

Janine was puzzled and a little frightened as she picked up the receiver. "Yes," she said, a slight waiver in her voice.

"Janine, this is Zach. Don't be alarmed. Don't say a word. I'm in my office. Whatever you do, don't let anyone know I'm here. Make up some excuse and come in here. I need to talk to you."

Janine laid the receiver back in its cradle and hollered at Monica, "Monica. Come here I need you to watch the phone."

Monica poked her head out of the map room. "You need something?" she asked.

"Yes," Janine answered. "Watch the phone for a few minutes. I just remembered that I was supposed to fax something to the hotel where Zach is staying. I almost forgot. I have to go into his office and hunt for the document."

"Sure. No problem," Monica chimed. "I was getting tired of sorting maps anyway. I needed a break,"

Janine pulled the top drawer of the desk open, grabbed her ring of keys, and called out over her shoulder, "May take me a few minutes. I'm not sure exactly where to look." She turned and headed for the door to Zach's office, making a pretense of unlocking the door.

"Zach what on earth is going on?" she whispered as soon as she had closed the door.

"Come over here and sit down," Zach said, pointing to one of the leather chairs sitting in front of his desk. "We need to be quiet. I can't tell you much. I don't want to get you involved any deeper than is absolutely necessary."

"But Zach .....,"

Zach held up his hand and cut Janine off, "Don't say anything. Just listen. You've been with me since I opened this office and I know I can trust you, but you have to swear you will keep everything I tell you to yourself. You cannot tell a single soul that I'm back from Las Vegas. My life may depend on it."

Janine eyes widened. She wanted to ask questions, lots of them, but she did as Zach had asked, and just listened.

Zach continued, "You know about the problems we have been having with the microwave systems in New Mexico and Nevada. Well, I discovered something while I was at the tower site near Tonapah, Nevada. The problems we have been having are the result of tampering. I'm not exactly certain why, but someone has been tampering with the systems. Then on the way back to Las Vegas someone tried to kill me." Zach stopped talking, waiting for Janine's reaction to what he had just told her.

"Zach, you're kidding!" Janine exclaimed, a look of disbelief on her face.

"I'm as serious as a heart attack," Zach replied. "I'm only telling you this so you will understand why it is so important to keep quiet. Absolutely no one can know I'm here, except for Angie. I've already talked to her."

"Zach, you should go to the police," Janine suggested.

"There's more. I am convinced Fred was murdered and it was made to look like an accident. I didn't say anything when I got back from New Mexico because I wasn't certain then, but I am now."

"But why would anyone want to kill Fred?" Janine blurted out.

Zach continued, "I still don't know who or why, but I promise you I intend to find out. That's where I will need your help. If anyone, and I mean anyone, asks about me, you have not heard from me. As far as you know, I am still in Las Vegas. There are only two people I will talk to, Angie or Benjamin Slater, the man that called on Monday. Janine, this is very important. I am going to find whoever murdered Fred and I am going to see to it that they pay."

"I understand Zach. Just tell me what you want me to do."

"Can you stay an extra hour or so tonight?" Zach asked. "I have some things I want to work on and I can't answer the phone."

"No problem Zach," Janine answered. "I'll be glad to help however I can."

"Thanks Janine. I really appreciate your help. When you go back to your desk, tell Monica she can leave early."

Janine nodded her head in agreement as she got up and headed for the door. Remembering the excuse she had given Monica for coming into Zach's office, she stopped and grabbed several sheets of paper from the credenza before leaving the office.

As soon as the door was closed, Zach reached down and switched on his computer. He stared blankly at Fred's notes, still stuck to the monitor's case.

The note to Rachael was clear but the other note just didn't make any sense. Zach gave up on the notes for the time being turning his attention to the data he had been analyzing before he left for Las Vegas. He started up the data analysis application and opened the file he had copied to his flash drive while at the tower site in New Mexico. Starting at the beginning, he recalculated all the numbers. Transmitter frequencies were well within tolerance. Power output levels all okay. Receiver input signal levels all okay. Page after page, all the numbers were exactly as expected.

Zach was getting frustrated. No matter how much he looked at the data, there was simply nothing there to indicate any problems. But there had to be something. The cryptic note proved Fred had been trying to tell him something. Zach stared at the note. Nothing. He recounted the events in New Mexico and in Nevada. How did these events tie together? What was he missing?

His attention returned to the test data displayed on the monitor. He sorted the data. He rearranged the data. He reversed the columns and rows. He recalculated the data for the third time. Still nothing. Always nothing. He swore at the computer.

Zach rearranged the data and repeated the analysis steps again, trying all possible permutations and arrangements he could think of. No matter how much he massaged or manipulated the data, nothing unusual presented itself. There could only be one answer. The simplest answer. There was simply nothing in the data to find. Deciding any further effort would be wasted, he gave up on the data analysis and powered the computer down. He punched the power switch on the monitor and pulled off the cryptic note that Fred had left inside the microwave equipment and leaned back in his chair.

"What are you trying to tell me Fred?" he asked himself out loud, staring at the note. He ran his fingers over the letters as he remembered his old friend. He did not really believe that touching the letters would reveal their meaning but he was stymied and he would try anything. Why had Fred used such seemingly meaningless words?

"Chou Nezhoni Mosai," Zach read the words aloud, hoping their sound might reveal something. Again and again he read the words. Changing the accent. Changing the tone. Changing the speed with which he read the words. Anything he could think of. It was as if the words themselves refused to reveal their meaning. Zach knew there could be no doubt Fred was the one that had left the note buried inside the equipment where only he would find it. That also meant that Fred had expected he would be able to figure out the note's meaning.

"What do they mean? What do they mean? What do they mean?" Zach shouted.

Tired and frustrated, he knew there was no point in continuing, and it was nearly time to head for the mall and the meeting he had arranged with Angie. He stuck the notes back on the monitor and picked up the phone.

"Janine, I've had it for today. I'm going to leave by the back door. Hang around for another ten minutes or so, then you can leave. I really appreciate your hanging around."

"Glad to help Zach," Janine responded. "I hope you find whoever's responsible for Fred's death."

"You can bank on it," Zach promised. "If it's the last thing I do in this life, I will see that they pay. I'll be back in the morning. Remember, no one is to know I'm here."

Zach dropped the phone back in its cradle, switched off the lamp, and left by the back door. Retracing his earlier route, he entered the stairwell and went up one flight of stairs to the ninth floor. He slipped into the hallway and walked to the elevators and punched the DOWN button.

Impatient and fidgeting, he punched the down button several more times, knowing it would not make the elevator come any sooner. It was something almost everyone did. He felt relief when the elevator finally opened and it was empty. He stepped inside and pushed the button for the basement parking garage, eager to get to his meeting with Angie.

The elevator ride to the basement was quick, the elevator passing each floor without stopping. When the elevator passed the first floor, Zach moved up against the door and stepped through the instant it opened wide enough to allow him to slide through. He pushed the door to the parking garage open and hurried for the street.

Zach's mind was fixed on the meeting with Angie and what he was going to say to her. Had it not been for his SEAL training he would probably not have noticed the slight odor drifting his way. The events of the past few days left him suspicious and edgy, rekindling those heightened senses. The combat-trained portion of his brain produced a sense of awareness of minute details that would normally have escaped his attention. The smell of perfume was slight but detectable. Instantly, Zach remembered the smell of that heavy, sweet perfume. He slowed, already stiffening before the movement to his left registered in his brain.

About to duck sideways, he felt a cold gun muzzle pushed against his neck. Suddenly, the gun pulled away from his neck. Pffftt, whack. A bullet whizzed past Zach's left ear and smacked into the concrete ceiling of the parking garage, sprinkling small bits of concrete on his head. Before the assailant could get off another shot, Zach heard two more muffled pops similar to the first one. Zach heard something clatter to the floor then a thump as a woman in a light green suit hit the floor. He glanced down and saw a gun lying near his feet. An automatic with a cylindrical extension on the barrel. A sound suppressor. This was not a mugging or a robbery. Only professionals used suppressors.

A hand gripped Zach's shoulder, as a dark red stain spread across the back of the woman's green suit.

A voice behind him spoke, "Mister Templeton, do not turn around. Stand perfectly still while I tell you exactly what you are going to do. Do you understand?"

"Yes," Zach answered

"Good," the voice answered. "I saved your life in Nevada and again here. You are going to forget what just happened here. You are going to walk straight to the exit door and you are going to leave without turning around. Is that clear?"

"But I …."

The voice interrupted, "Mister Templeton, I will take care of everything here. No one but you and I will ever know what happened. I will dispose of the body as soon as you leave. You must do exactly as I told you quickly before someone comes down the elevator. I really do not want to hurt an innocent bystander, but I will if I have to. Leave now, Mister Templeton. I will be watching"

The man lifted his hand off Zach's shoulder. Zach ran to the exit door, threw it open, and rushed outside. Once outside he walked as fast as he could to the mall. He retrieved a cell phone from his pocket and called for a taxi.

Norman Glover rolled the woman over. A dark red stain also discolored the front of her dress. He felt her neck for a pulse. Nothing. She was dead. It was definitely the woman he had seen tailing Mister Templeton. He knew it would be a waste of time to search her for clues. She was a professional and would not be carrying anything that would divulge her identity or link her to the people she worked for. Who had ordered the hit on Mister Templeton he wondered? Norman pulled a cell phone from his pocket, snapped a photo of the woman's face, and forwarded it to the email address Admiral Hadley had given him.

He dragged the body over to the rental car he had parked in the garage earlier. Norman dumped the body on a plastic tarp he had placed on the floor of the trunk. A quick search of her pockets produced only a cheap throw-away cell phone. He grabbed the briefcase she had been carrying, dumping its contents and the cell phone into a small bag. The items would be discarded later when he was far away from the building. The tarp was wrapped around the body and secured with rope. Norman pulled off his gloves and dropped them into the small bag

He climbed into the rental car and drove out of the parking lot as if nothing had happened. After exiting the parking lot, he turned north onto Darlington Avenue.

Zach walked out of the mall just in time to see a car exit the underground parking garage and speed up Darlington Avenue. It turned east onto Forty-first street and disappeared. Zach walked several blocks and waited for the taxi to arrive. He wondered if Angie would believe any of the wild tale he had to tell her.

A yellow taxi cab pulled up to the curb and stopped. "Woodland Hills Mall and hurry. I'm late," Zach shouted to the driver as he climbed inside.

CHAPTER FORTY-NINE

Wednesday, April 1 – 1730 Eastern Daylight Time
Office of Naval Intelligence
Suitland, Maryland

Rear Admiral Charles Hadley reached into the inside pocket of the uniform jacket hanging over the back of his chair and retrieved a ringing cell phone. He flipped it open and answered, "Yes."

"Sir, this is Norman."

"What do you have to report?" Hadley questioned.

"It's not good sir," Norman Glover answered. "I observed two men try to kill Mister Templeton after he left the tower site in Nevada. They have been eliminated."

"Did he see you? What was his reaction?"

"No, he didn't see me. His reaction was exactly what you would expect. He jumped into his car and sped off to Las Vegas."

"What about the bodies?"

" I didn't have time to sanitize the area, so I just left them lying in the desert. I had to get back to Las Vegas and see if I could locate Mister Templeton."

"Did you locate him?"

"No. He never returned to the hotel where he was registered. He must have checked into a different hotel. I knew he would head back to Tulsa, so I had the pilot fly me back to Tulsa and waited for him to show up at the airport there."

"Did he show up at the airport?"

"Yes. He was disguised, but I recognized him. He hailed a taxi. I followed the taxi to a shopping center near his office building. He got out and went into a store."

"What else …."

"Wait there's more," Norman interrupted. "He spent some time in the store and then he came out, ran across the street, and walked past his office building twice. It was obvious he was watching to see if anyone was following him. He turned and ducked into the building's underground parking garage."

"And."

"Oh, it gets even better," Norman added. "I noticed someone else watching him. A well-dressed woman. She rushed into the building as soon as he ducked into the garage."

"Did you follow her?" Hadley asked.

"No. I was unable to get into the building quickly enough to follow her. I assumed Mister Templeton would exit the building through the parking garage, so I opted to watch for him there."

"Go on. I'm listening."

"I waited for about an hour. I saw Mister Templeton exit through the elevator door and then the woman I saw earlier stepped out of the shadows and shoved a gun against his neck. I stepped out from where I was hiding and grabbed her. She fired, but missed. I put two quick rounds into her. She's dead."

"Did Mister Templeton see you?" Hadley gasped.

"No. I grabbed him and warned him to not turn around. Told him to leave the garage and not look back."

"Did he?"

"Yes sir. He did exactly as instructed."

"Do you have any idea who the woman is?"

"No sir. She was carrying a Ruger Mark II, .22-caliber automatic with a sound suppressor. I searched her and the briefcase she was carrying. No identification of any kind. It's obvious she was a professional. I snapped a photo of the woman's face and sent it to the email address you gave me."

"Stand by," Hadley instructed, turning toward his computer keyboard.

Norman heard the tapping of keys.

Thirty seconds later Hadley returned to the conversation, "I don't recognize her either. I sent the photo to the analytics department to run through the facial recognition software. Hang on while I give them a heads-up."

Norman heard the Admiral's muffled voice as he talked to someone from the analytics department.

"I told them to call the instant they had something," Hadley advised. "Is there anything else?"

"I dumped the body in the trunk of my rental car and wrapped it in a tarp. I neutralized the blood stain. Nobody will know anything happened."

"Where is the body now?"

"Still in the trunk. I will dump the body where it will not be found for a long time. I ..."

"Hang on Norman," Hadley interrupted, turning to answer his office phone.

After a lengthy delay, Hadley returned to the phone call, "You are not going to believe this. The analytics department says she is one of *our* special operators," Hadley said, emphasizing the word "our".

"What does that mean exactly Admiral?" Norman questioned.

"It means someone from the FBI or CIA is behind this," Hadley snapped.

"If someone from our own government would risk trying to kill Mister Templeton, there must be something major going on."

Hadley hesitated, not certain how much he should share with Norman.

"Admiral, are you still there?"

"Yes I'm still here. I don't know how much I should tell you."

"You tracked me down Admiral," Norman protested. "You woke me in the middle of the night and sent me on a mission that has resulted in me killing three people. I think you owe me some answers."

"Yes, I suppose you're right," Hadley agreed. "I have uncovered what I believe could possibly be a scheme to start a war. There is also a leak at a very high level."

"You're kidding!"

"Not in the least. It's a very serious threat. There has already been a serious incident in the North Atlantic. I was asked by someone I trust implicitly to assist in helping a deep, under-cover operative escape from Europe with materials he claims will expose the scheme and whoever is behind it."

"How soon will this operative arrive with the materials?" Norman asked."

"Five or six days."

"The way people are dying I don't think we have that long Admiral."

"I agree. How long will it take for you to dispose of the body?"

"No more than an hour or two."

"I will formulate a plan to get the materials here ASAP and make the necessary arrangements. Take care of the body. As soon as it's done return to the airport and make contact with the pilot. I will contact him with the details."

"Understood Admiral," Norman replied, ending the call and focusing on the task of dumping the body where it would remain hidden for a very long time.

CHAPTER FIFTY

Wednesday, April 1 - 1731 Central Daylight Time
Woodland Hills Mall
Tulsa, Oklahoma

Zach arrived at the mall fifteen minutes before his scheduled meeting with Angie. To kill time, he purchased a soft drink from in the food court and selected a table in an isolated section of the seating area. He was still edgy from the attack in the parking garage and hardly able to sit still.

After what seemed like an eternity, the time came to make his way to the store where he had arranged to meet Angie. Zach got up from the table and strolled through the food court toward the south end of the mall.

He walked over to the escalator and stepped on. At the bottom of the escalator he turned to his right and entered the store where the meeting had been arranged. A quick glance around revealed Angie had not yet arrived. He walked to the back of the store and began browsing the unique items sitting on the floor and displayed on various shelves.

It was Zach's and Angie's favorite store. Before they separated, they came here often to look at the hand-crafted items imported from all over the world. All types of creatures carved from parasite wood, hand-carved Buddhas from India, carved animals and plants from Africa, polished stones, brass and wooden containers, and all manner of items from third world countries where labor was cheap. The heavy odor of incense in the air was the one thing Zach did not like. Even a few minutes in the store gave him a headache.

Zach picked up a small oblong box carved from some kind of stone and was examining it when he saw Angie walk through the door. She strolled through the store browsing the various items like any other shopper, just as she had been instructed. He placed the box back on the shelf and walked in Angie's direction.

Moving to a spot beside her, he picked up a small hand-carved, mahogany Buddha, pretending to examine it.

"Angie, it's Zach. Don't look at me," he whispered softly. "Just keep looking at the carvings. Don't acknowledge me."

"Zach, what is this all about?" Angie asked, glancing briefly in his direction.

"I can't talk here," Zach answered. "Let's go back to your apartment and I will tell you as much as I can."

"Okay. Let's go," she responded, setting the item she had been examining back on the shelf.

"You go ahead. Act like nothing is going on. Window shop as you leave the mall," Zach instructed.

"Why all the cloak and dagger?" she asked.

"Please, just trust me," Zach pleaded. "I'll explain later. Wait for me at the exit. When you see me coming, leave the mall, get in your car, and wait."

Angie started to say something but Zach interrupted her, "No more questions please. I need to get out of here. Right NOW!" Zach commanded.

Angie did as instructed. She left the store, pretending to look in store windows as she strolled toward the exit. She selected an empty bench by the mall exit and sat down. Unable to imagine what was making Zach act so strangely, she was becoming deeply concerned.

Several minutes later she spotted Zach making his way toward the exit. She watched him stop and look in several store windows as he approached the exit. When she saw Zach look in her direction and wink, she got up and left the mall. She walked slowly toward her car, making certain Zach saw the row she was walking down.

Stopping beside her car, she deliberately spent some time fumbling in her purse for her keys, then unlocked the door and got in.

She waited for Zach to show up, glancing several times in the direction of the mall exit. Even though she was expecting Zach, she jumped when she heard tapping on the rear passenger window. She pushed the unlock button. Zach opened the rear door and slid in on the seat.

"Let's get out of here," Zach urged. "Take a different route to your apartment. Keep an eye on the rear view mirror to see if anyone is following us."

"Zach, this is crazy. Tell me what is going on!" Angie demanded.

"Not now," Zach begged. "Please Angie, wait until we get to your apartment. I apologize for the secrecy. I promise I'll explain."

"Okay Zach, but it had better be good," Angie protested. She started the car and backed out of the parking space. Following the mall's perimeter road, she turned west on Seventy-first Street and headed the opposite direction from her apartment. She drove west for several miles then turned left onto a major street and drove south.

"Zach, do you mind if I stop and pick up some sodas?" Angie asked. "I don't have anything at the apartment."

"Sounds fine. Just be careful," Zach answered. "Make certain no one is following us."

Angie continued driving south for several miles before turning into a small strip mall, and pulling up in front of a convenience store. "Cream soda for you?".

"Scotch would be better, but cream soda is okay," Zach answered.

"Be right back," Angie said.

Angie returned from the store in less than ten minutes. She sat the bag she was carrying on the floor, started the car, and left the strip mall. As she continued on the indirect route to her apartment, they remained silent.

"Zach we're at the apartment," Angie said as she pulled into her assigned parking space. "What do I do now?"

"Are you certain no one followed us?"

"I'm positive," Angie replied. "I made frequent checks in the rear view mirror just like you asked. I never saw anyone that appeared to be following us."

"Good. Go on into the apartment. I'll follow along in a few minutes."

"Zach this is ridiculous. I'm not going to ...."

"Angie please," Zach interrupted "This really is necessary. You'll understand when I explain."

"Okay Zach," Angie agreed as she climbed out of the car and started for her apartment. She returned to the car and grabbed the bag of sodas and said, "Your explanation had better be good."

Zach listened as Angie's footsteps faded out in the distance. Two cars passed by during the ten minutes he laid there waiting. Deciding there was no reason to wait any longer, he took off the ball cap he had been wearing and slowly inched his head up toward the window. A quick survey of the parking lot revealed no activity. He fished his cell phone out of his pocket and dialed Angie's number.

"Hello."

"Angie, it's me," Zach whispered. "Go to the window and check the parking lot. Do you see anyone, and I mean anyone? Standing, walking, or sitting in a car?"

"Wait, I'll check," Angie answered, annoyance evident in her voice.

Zach saw the edge of the curtain in Angie's apartment draw back and her face appear in the window.

"I don't see anyone in the parking lot Zach," Angie huffed when she returned to the phone. "Is all this really necessary?"

"Yes, Angie, it is. I'm coming in. Be at the door waiting," Zach said.

He opened the rear passenger door and slipped out. Carefully pushing the door closed until it latched, he listened. Silence. It would take him less than one minute to get inside the main door to Angie's apartment building.

He simply could not afford to be seen. Angie was likely in some danger already. If he was seen going into her apartment they could both end up dead. Once inside her apartment, he would wait for the cover of darkness.

One last time he listened and scrutinized the parking lot. Still no sounds or movement. He straightened up and headed for the apartment building door, glancing in all directions as he hurried for the door. He ran the last few steps and threw the door open and leaped inside, scrambling up the stairs three at a time.

Angie already had the door open a crack. She pulled the door the rest of the way open when she saw Zach reach the top of the stairs. He rushed inside and pushed the door shut.

He could not resist hugging Angie. "Thanks for being so understanding," he beamed as he let go of her, the delicious scent of her perfume lingering in his nostrils.

"You're welcome. Now, I need that explanation you promised," Angie demanded as she stepped back and looked at Zach.

"How about something to drink first," Zach suggested. "That will let me catch my breath and calm down a little."

Angie turned and headed for the kitchen. Zach found a chair in the living room and waited for Angie.

Zach could hear clinking as Angie dropped ice cubes into two glasses. Then hissing as she popped open two soda cans. Momentarily, she appeared in the doorway with two glasses in hand and walked over to where Zach was sitting and handed him a cream soda. She selected a chair across from Zach and looked directly at him.

"Well, let's have it."

"Give me a minute," Zach stammered, lifting the glass to his lips and taking a big gulp of the fizzy liquid. "I need to compose myself and decide where to start."

Zach took a deep breath and began, "Angie, you are probably not going to believe what you hear, but I swear every single word of what I am about to tell you is true. Just listen and try to believe me."

Another sip from his soda, then he continued, "Someone tried to kill me twice in the last two days, once in Nevada and once here in Tulsa. And Fred's death was no accident either. I think ...."

"You've got to be joking!" Angie blurted out, a look of utter amazement on her face. "You run a communications company. Why on Earth would anyone want to kill you?"

Zach held up his hand, "Angie, please don't interrupt. Let me finish. Once you've heard the whole story, you can ask questions."

Before Angie could object, Zach continued, "I was suspicious even before I went to New Mexico but what I found at the radio site convinced me something was wrong. The first clue was the fact that all of Fred's camera equipment was missing from the rental car. Fred never went anywhere without it. When I was using his tool box at the radio site, I found a roll of exposed film mixed in with the jumbled tools, so I know he had it with him."

Zach took another sip of soda and continued, "The next clue was a note Fred left hidden in the radio equipment exactly where he knew I would find it. The note contains three coded words that I haven't been able to decipher as yet. When I tried to use his laptop computer, I found it had a virus on it. The virus erased the entire hard drive."

Zach took a deep breath and continued, "There is no doubt in my mind that Fred discovered something at the radio site and it got him killed. Whoever killed Fred must think I found out what Fred knew and now they are trying to kill me. When I was on my way back to Las Vegas from a tower site, someone deliberately ran me off the road. Then they turned around and blocked my car and murdered a motorist that stopped to help me. They dragged me out of the car and were going to shoot me, but before they could someone else shot them. I did not hear a single gunshot and I did not see anyone. I didn't stick around to find out what was going on. I jumped in my car and drove to Las Vegas as fast as I dared. I don't know if the shooter followed me or not. I dumped the rental car in a parking lot at the first hotel I came to. From that hotel, I took a taxi and checked into a hotel close to a mall."

Zach took another long gulp of his soda and continued before Angie could say anything. "When it got dark, I picked up a disguise at the mall. The next morning I caught a flight to Tulsa. I left my car in the airport parking lot and took a taxi to the office. I sneaked into the office through the back door. I was absolutely certain no one followed me, but when I left the office, someone shoved a gun against my neck in the parking garage. She fired a shot but it hit the ceiling. I heard two muffled pops and the woman fell at my feet. A man grabbed me from behind and told me to leave the garage without looking back. I did exactly what he told me to do. Angie, the woman that jumped me was a professional killer."

Zach took out the gun he had picked up from the floor of the garage and laid it on the coffee table. "This is the gun she was carrying. Do you notice anything unusual?" Zach questioned.

"Is that a silencer?" Angie gasped.

"More accurately, a sound suppressor, but yes, it certainly is," Zach answered. "Look there. The serial number has been filed off. There's no doubt, she was a professional killer."

"But Zach, why you?" Angie blurted out. "What are you involved in?"

Again Zach held up his hand as he continued, "It has to be related to whatever Fred found out while he was in New Mexico. Remember, I said whoever is responsible for Fred's death must think I know something.

While I was at the tower site in Nevada, I found evidence of tampering. Fred must have found the same kind of tampering as I did. I don't know how all these things tie together but I believe they must be related to the trouble we have been having with the DOD microwave systems."

Zach looked directly at Angie and spoke with all the authority he could muster, "Angie, I am not going to rest until I find out who is responsible for killing Fred. He was my best friend and I owe him my life. I don't care how long it takes. I am going to find out."

Zach got up from the chair and walked over to the window. He carefully pushed the curtain aside and scanned what he could see of the parking lot. He turned around and walked back over to the chair he had been sitting in and raised the glass to take another drink of soda but the glass was empty.

"Angie, how about another half glass," Zach said, lowering himself back into the chair.

"Sure. I could use a refill myself," Angie responded, taking the glass from Zach's hand.

While Angie busied herself in the kitchen, Zach rehearsed in his mind how he was going to tell Angie about the mission he and Fred had been on together, the one that had nearly cost Zach his life.

"Thanks," Zach said as Angie handed him the glass of soda. He took a swallow and slumped back in the chair and thought about how to begin.

He fiddled with the glass, watching a small bead of moisture that had condensed on the glass as it ran down the side and dripped onto his leg. He continued to stare at the glass deep in thought, trying to find the right words to tell Angie about his past.

"Come on Zach, I'm waiting," Angie prodded, impatient to hear the rest of Zach's story.

"Angie, you absolutely have to promise what I am about to tell you will stay between us. You must not tell anyone. Absolutely no one. Do you understand?"

"No Zach, I don't understand," Angie snapped. "Why all the secrecy? None of this makes any sense."

"It will make sense if you just listen to what I'm about to say," Zach shot back in frustration. "I'm sorry Angie," Zach offered in defense of his sudden outburst. "I'm under a lot of strain. You are the only one I can talk to. Please. Just listen."

Zach looked up and studied Angie's eyes. He was not certain if the look on her face was disbelief or irritation. "Oh, well. Just as well get it over with", Zach told himself.

"Angie, what I'm about to tell you happened several years before I got out of the Navy. I was instructed by someone very high up in the chain of command to never tell anyone about the mission. I was warned that if I did, I would be charged with treason and desertion under fire."

"Fred and I were on a mission together conducted under the utmost secrecy. The mission was a death trap. We completed the objective but our unit was ambushed before we could get to the extraction point. Fred and I were the only survivors. During the fire fight, I got hit by shrapnel from a mortar. If it hadn't been for Fred, I would have died in the jungle like the rest of the unit."

Zach took another swallow of soda and continued, "Fred dragged me down a stream and into a clump of trees. We hid there until the enemy unit left the area. Fred dragged me through the jungle for three days until we made it to the extraction point."

Retelling the story of the mission brought back memories of Fred and how much he owed him. Zach choked back the flood of emotion threatening to overwhelm him.

"Angie, I owe Fred my life," Zach stammered, on the verge of tears. "I don't know what I'm going to do without him."

"You told me you were injured on a training exercise. So, you lied to me for all those years," Angie accused.

"Angie, I didn't have any choice. The people responsible for the mission were serious about the threats they made. I was also afraid that if I told you, your life would be in danger."

"Zach, you've got to be kidding," Angie interrupted.

"No. Not even a little bit," Zach protested. "The people responsible for the mission were dangerous and powerful. They would not hesitate to eliminate me and you if it met their purpose."

Angie started to say something but Zach continued before she could get the words out, "The mission was alleged to be a routine reconnaissance mission. Angie, Fred knew the real reason for the mission. He overheard a coded transmission. He was able to decipher the message because he knew the Navajo code they were using. There are extremely few non-Navajo people in the world that understand the code. Only two people knew that Fred and I had been trained in the Navajo code language for a special op two years earlier."

Zach drained the last of his soda and continued, "Angie, the ambush was no accident. It was deliberate. It had been planned from the very start. The entire unit was supposed to have died. Then the ugly secret would have died with the unit."

"Fred told me about the message. We agreed on a story that would make everyone believe we were convinced the enemy discovering our unit was just bad luck. Fred and I also promised each other to never speak of the mission. We knew we would never be able to prove what we had learned. The mission was never mentioned again."

"I never saw or heard anything regarding that mission or the Navajo language code again. Until six days ago, that is. Remember the morning on the dive trip when we were diving on the "Wreck of the Sipona"?"

Angie nodded her head in agreement.

"I went ahead of you and rounded the bow end of the ship so I could get a photograph of you. While I was waiting, a strange diver approached me. He handed me a capsule and wrote a message on an underwater slate. It said I was in great danger. He turned around and swam toward the north and disappeared.

The next morning we were so busy getting packed and clearing customs I didn't even think about the capsule until I felt it in my pants pocket during the ride to the airport. When we got to the airport and received the news about Fred, the capsule became the furthest thing from my mind."

"Later, on the flight to Albuquerque, I remembered the capsule after I awoke from a short nap. I went to the lavatory and opened the capsule and read the note. My blood ran cold when I read the Navajo code word - Beshlo. Angie, other than myself, no one, except Fred and one other person from my SEAL team, had ever even heard of the Navajo code let alone knew the special code word Fred and I used to warn each other of imminent danger. The note repeated the diver's warning that I was in great danger. The note said to memorize the phone number on the note and then to destroy the note. I memorized the number then tore the note in tiny pieces and flushed it."

"Angie, the note's warning was certainly true. Fred was murdered, twice someone has tried to kill me, and someone has been tampering with the microwave systems. Somehow all these things must tie together, but I haven't been able to find a link between any of them."

"Zach, I want to believe you, but this is all a little crazy," Angie confessed. "Why would someone want to kill you if you have been silent all these years?"

"I don't know yet. It must have something to do with what Fred discovered in New Mexico and the tampering I found in Nevada," Zach explained. "First, I have to figure out what Fred's note means. If I can figure that out, maybe I can put the rest of the puzzle together. I left the note stuck on my monitor at the office. I need to go back to the office and work on the test data I brought back. Maybe while I'm doing that, I can figure out what Fred's note means."

"If you're in such great danger, how do you expect to get back to the office?" Angie asked, disbelief in her voice.

"I'll need your help," Zach replied, looking at Angie's face to see what her reaction would be.

"That depends on what you need help with."

Zach continued, hoping Angie would agree. "I need you to help me sneak back into the parking garage. I need to see if the body is still there."

"Zach, you can't be serious!" Angie blurted out. "Why don't you just call the police and explain what happened?

"That would be the worst thing I could do," Zach exclaimed. "I have already been contacted by someone claiming to be with the FBI. Something about the agent's questions and the way he acted just didn't seem right."

"Zach, this whole thing is unbelievable," Angie blurted out.

"Angie, you've got to trust me," Zach butted in. "There is something very wrong. Angie, there is only one person that I can trust to help me get to the bottom of this. I've got to get to Washington before ..."

"No Zach," Angie interrupted. "You said you were through with the sudden disappearances and the secrecy. When you left the Navy you said it was over." Anger was visible on Angie's face as she got up from her chair and stormed into the kitchen.

Zach got up and followed her. He tapped her shoulder. "Angie, please trust me," he pleaded.

Angie turned around and faced him. "Why should I?" she snapped.

"Because my life depends on it," Zach replied. "The person that tried to kill me was a professional. I can't prove it but I think someone important is involved. Probably someone very high in political office or even in the FBI itself."

"That is ridiculous!" Angie sneered. "Now you're talking nonsense."

"Now, maybe you can understand the nightmares. I have relived that horrible mission a thousand times in my sleep. It is as if the souls of those dead comrades have been crying out for justice all these years. I felt like a coward. I failed the memory of those brave soldiers. They sacrificed their lives for a lie. Every day I have been haunted by their faces. Faces crying out for justice. And now Fred's dead too. Angie, I don't know where to turn."

Angie saw the tears forming in Zach's eyes, in spite of his battle to keep his emotions in check. The pain of those memories was clearly evident on his tormented face. She was angry Zach had lied to her for all those years. But still she felt compassion for him. Something stirred deep inside her. She couldn't begin to grasp the horrible anguish he must be feeling. At least, she finally understood why he and Fred had been so close.

Angie desperately wanted to hold him. To tell him everything was going to be all right. To comfort him. To love him. But should she? Was there still love for him or did she just feel sorry for him? Did she even want to love him anymore. She was afraid to answer those questions, even to herself. Now was not the time to ponder those questions. Zach was under such tremendous stress it would not be fair to give him hope where there might be none. But he was in such turmoil she could not just turn her back on him. What was she going to do?

Before she could answer, Zach asked again. "Angie, I need your help. I have to get back into the parking garage unseen and see if the woman's body is there. If it is we will have to dump it where it won't be found. We will wait until after dark."

Angie could scarcely believe the words that came out of her mouth as she agreed to help Zach with his insane plan. "Okay Zach. I'll help you. But what happens after that?"

"I'll try to figure out what Fred's note means. Beyond that I can't say. I don't want to get you any more involved than you are already."

"Any more involved?" Angie blurted out. "Are you kidding? I just agreed to help you dump a dead body."

"I know. I know," Zach agreed. "I can't risk telling you more. I wish I hadn't had to ask you to help me at all, but with Fred gone there is simply no one else I trust."

"How will I get in touch with you? How will I know if you're all right," Angie asked.

"You won't," Zach replied. "I will contact you. That's all I can say."

"But Zach ..."

"Angie that's it. I'm not going to say any more. Let's not talk about it anymore. How about a little something to eat before we go," Zach offered, trying to lighten the mood.

"Sure. Okay. What would you like?" Angie asked as she got from her chair, heading toward the kitchen.

"Something light. A sandwich and chips would be fine," Zach replied.

Angie busied herself in the kitchen while Zach sat in the living room staring vacantly at the wall. His mind was busy trying to sort out the pieces of the insane puzzle he had fallen into. None of it made sense. Fred's death, the tampering he had found at the tower site, the mysterious note from the diver, professional killers, the woman assassin, the FBI, ... On and on the unanswered question went.

Zach massaged his temples. The stress of the past few days had given him a ferocious headache. He felt dead tired and he desperately needed a good night's sleep. Maybe Angie would agree to let him spend the night. In her apartment, watching her busy in the kitchen, he felt safe, relaxed, and comfortable. If only he could turn the clock back a couple of years to a happier time.

Zach got up from his chair and walked to the kitchen doorway. He leaned against the door jam and watched Angie preparing the sandwiches. How beautiful she was. She was tall with beautiful auburn hair just touching her shoulders. He remembered the exact day he had fallen in love with her some twenty years earlier. From the first instant he saw her, he knew he loved her. Never once had he even imagined being with someone else. And she had loved him. He was certain of it. But what had happened? He still loved her. What had he done to make her stop loving him? Why couldn't he fix it?

Angie turned to get something from the refrigerator and was startled by Zach standing in the doorway. "Why are you staring at me?" she questioned.

"Just remembering how much I love you," he answered.

"Zach, now is not the time. There's enough going on already. Let's not start that," Angie scolded, opening the refrigerator and grabbing a bowl of fruit.

Zach took the bowl from her hand and set it on the counter. He put his hands on her shoulders and looked into her eyes. "I wish I could make all this go away. I wish I could turn the clock back to a time when we were happy but I can't. I.... I ..." Zach stammered, not knowing what else to say. "Thanks for not shutting me out completely," he said as pulled her close and held her.

Angie did not resist him. She put her arms around Zach and held him gently. She could smell the lingering scent of his cologne. She felt the strength in his arms, and the warmth of his body. It felt good. She too remembered a time when she had loved Zach. Part of her wanted to give in. But why did she want to give in? Was it because she was lonely. Was it because she felt sorry for Zach or was it just because they were comfortable together?

Zach released his hold on Angie and stepped back when he felt her arms go limp. "I'm sorry," he said, grabbing the plates and heading for the table.

"That's okay," Angie answered, taking her place at the table.

But it was not okay. Zach could tell by the expression on her face as he sat down across from her. There was already more than enough tension between them, so Zach decided to let the matter drop.

They picked at their sandwiches and fruit in silence, neither of them eating much. Zach was the first to break the silence. He walked to the window and pushed the curtain aside to see if it was dark yet. "Looks like about thirty minutes before it will be dark," he observed, glancing at his watch.

He was worried about involving Angie in this awful mess but he had no choice. There was no one else he could trust.

He was convinced either the data he had recorded in New Mexico or Fred's cryptic note had to be the key. He could not explain how he knew. He just knew. He was determined to unravel the mystery and take the first step toward making the people that murdered Fred pay. Before he could do that, he had to see if the body was still lying in the parking garage of his office building.

Zach became more edgy and nervous with each passing minute. Something frightening was growing around them and he had put Angie right in the middle of it. He got up from the chair and stretched. Now was not the time to get sloppy. He had been careless earlier in the day and it had nearly gotten him killed.

Zach hollered at Angie, still in the kitchen cleaning up, "Angie, we need to go. It will be dark by the time we get to the office and I want to get this over with."

"Okay. Be right there," Angie yelled from the kitchen.

"I'm going to grab the shower curtain in case we need something to wrap the body in. I don't want anything to contaminate your car."

He took down the shower curtain, folding it into a small rectangle. When he returned to the living room Angie was waiting.

"I don't know about this," she fretted, worry clouding her face.

"Everything will be fine as long as we're careful," Zach reassured her. "There shouldn't be anyone at the office at this time of night and it shouldn't take more than four or five minutes tops."

"I hope you're right."

"I'll go out first and walk around behind the building. Give me a couple of minutes then you come out. Turn right at the corner. I'll get in the back when you stop at the crosswalk."

Zach opened the door and left. Angie paced nervously, waiting for the minutes to pass. She waited three minutes, turned off the lights, and left the apartment. She got in her car, backed out of her parking space, and turned right at the parking lot's exit, stopping at the crosswalk like Zach had instructed.

Zach stepped from behind a tree and got in the back seat and slid down out of sight. "Let's go. Take the quickest route to the office," he instructed.

Zach knew whoever the female assassin took orders from would become suspicious if she did not check in. They likely did not have much time to dispose of the body. It surprised him that he had gotten this far.

They arrived at the office building and drove into the parking garage. All was quiet. "Park over there," Zach directed, pointing to an empty space near the door to the elevator. Grabbing a flashlight from the glove compartment, he climbed out and ran over to the spot where the attack had taken place. Angie came up behind him. She watched Zach search frantically for the body.

"It happened right here. She fell right there!"

"Are you sure?" Angie questioned.

"Right there! There was blood on the floor! I saw it! Right there!" Zach shouted, pointing at the floor.

"Zach, keep your voice down," Angie urged.

"Maybe it was over here," Zach sputtered, running to look between the few cars parked close to the elevator. He looked between them. He looked in front of them. He looked under them. There was no body. There was no blood.

"I don't understand! She was right there!" Zach wailed.

"There is no body," Angie asserted "Let's get out of here."

"I don't ..."

"Let's go Zach," Angie repeated, shoving him toward her car.

Inside the car in the dark parking lot Zach continued, "Angie, I swear to you. There was a woman's body lying there just a few hours ago. I watched her fall. I saw the blood."

"Well, where is she? If someone found a dead body, the garage would be swarming with police cars."

"It had to be the guy that killed her. He took the body and he cleaned up the blood."

"How could he. And why would he? Zach, this is becoming more and more unbelievable."

"Angie you have to believe me."

"I don't know what to believe."

"Oh, my God. What's happening?" Zach moaned, leaning forward with his face in his hands.

The gun in his pocket banged against his hand. He yanked the gun out of his pocket, "What about this? Did I just dream this into existence? Huh, did I?"

"Zach, calm down," Angie pleaded.

"But Angie you have to believe me. Tell me you believe me."

"Okay, okay, I believe you. What do we do now?"

"I can't go to the office now. I'm too frazzled. I'd be wasting my time. I can't go home. Think Zach think," he commanded, thumping himself in the forehead again and again.

"I know," he exclaimed. "Take me to the La Quinta hotel. I'll stay the night and calm down. Then I'll sneak back into the office in the morning and work on the data."

Angie started the engine and drove out of the parking garage. A few blocks from the office building, she pulled up to a stop in front of the hotel Zach had mentioned. He climbed out and stuck his head back into the car.

"Stop and pick up Pablo on your way back to the apartment. Watch your mirrors closely to see if anyone follows you. If anyone does, pretend you don't notice. When you get home call me."

He kissed her and said good bye.

Angie watched as he hurried into the hotel lobby. What on earth was he involved in. And what had she become involved in she wondered as she drove away.

CHAPTER FIFTY-ONE

Wednesday, April 1 – 1850 Central Daylight Time
Office of Naval Intelligence
Suitland, Maryland

"A plan. I need a plan," Rear Admiral Hadley muttered.

A steady rain drummed against the window of his office as he paced back and forth. He had told Norman Glover he would devise a plan to get the undercover operative and his materials back to the United States as soon as possible.

Head down, hands clasped behind his back, he paced back and forth going over possible scenarios. If the rendezvous had occurred as scheduled, USS *Providence* was already steaming back toward Norfolk Naval Base with the operative on board. No other naval assets, that he could safely divert, were within range of *Providence*. Options. He needed options. There were always options. But what were they?

Tired of pacing, Hadley turned and walked over and stood in front of his desk. A brightly colored map of the North Atlantic Ocean was spread out across his desk. Printed on the map, in stunning detail, were various underwater features: continental slopes, sea mounts, abyssal plains, fracture zones, the lengthy Mid-Atlantic Ridge, underwater plateaus, and islands.

"That's it! That's exactly what I need!" Hadley exclaimed, as he rushed around the desk, slamming himself into his chair. He yanked the middle drawer open and tore through its contents until he located a pair of dividers, a protractor, and a navigational "measuring stick". With the pencil he made a horizontal mark where the rendezvous was supposed to have taken place. He extended a course line from the rendezvous point in the general direction *Providence* would most likely have taken to arrive at Norfolk Naval Base.

A quick mental calculation determined the rendezvous had occurred twenty-six hours earlier. Travelling for twenty-six hours at twelve to fifteen knots would mean *Providence* would have traveled between three hundred ten and three hundred ninety miles. Admiral Hadley positioned the "zero" point of the "measuring stick" at the rendezvous point and made a crosshatch mark on the course line he had drawn at three hundred fifty miles, halfway between the two possible distances.

"Perfect. That will work. That will absolutely work," Hadley assured himself, pushing the map off the desk to uncover the computer keyboard. He jiggled the mouse to wake the computer up and pulled up a blank template for a flash message. Furiously he typed in the body of the message to USS *Providence*. After a quick proofread, he clicked "Print". The printer sitting on the credenza began to whir and clunk, finally spitting out a single page.

Hadley grabbed the message sheet from the printer's output tray and reread the message. In his last message to *Providence*, he had instructed the captain to respond only to one specific designated EAM (Emergency Action Message) code that had been contained in that message. He had also instructed the captain of *Providence* to deploy the long-wire antenna whenever possible. Only a small window of time existed before *Providence* would have traveled too far for the change of plan to work.

He grabbed his briefcase, stuffed the flash message into it, and locked it. Upon reaching the door, he decided he should notify the pilot waiting at Tulsa International Airport to be waiting for a change in plans. He set the briefcase on the floor and called the pilot.

"Yes sir," pilot Kip Johnson answered.

"Might be a change of plans. What is the range and speed of the Gulfstream?"

"The G550 has a range of six thousand seven hundred nautical miles. Max cruising speed is five hundred thirty knots."

Hadley thought for a moment, "Great. That will work. As soon as you hang up, call Mister Glover and have him return to the airport immediately. Depart as soon as he arrives."

Hadley and the pilot discussed the specifics of the plan Hadley had concocted. The pilot agreed. He informed Hadley the plane had been fueled, the pre-flight had been performed, and it was fully ready for takeoff. He said he would load up Mister Glover as soon as he reached the airport and report "wheels up" on departure.

* * *

Wednesday, April 1 - 2002 Eastern Daylight Time
JCS Conference Room ("The Tank")
Pentagon - Corridor 9, E Ring
Washington, DC

Hushed conversations filled the Joint Chiefs of Staff Conference room. Invitees that had already arrived carried on private conversations while they waited for the emergency meeting's organizer to arrive.

The JCS Conference Room was called the "presentation" room when it was first organized. However, it soon became known as "The Tank." The popular explanation of the nickname came from the fact the entry to the conference room was down a flight of stairs through an arched doorway. All those entering the room said it gave them the feeling of entering a tank. Even though the conference room had moved several times, the nickname stuck.

Interrupted conversations and the sound of scuffling of chairs being straightened and pulled up to the large conference table preceded the entrance of Fleet Admiral Douglass Bennington, the emergency meeting's organizer.

"Gentlemen, if you would have your aides leave the room," Fleet Admiral Bennington announced.

Several of the invitees had brief whispered exchanges with their aides before they left the room. Standing at the head of the table, Bennington watched as the last aide exited the room. He nodded to his aide who closed the conference room door and assumed his post in front of the door to prevent anyone from entering.

Bennington picked up a small remote and turned on the video projector suspended from the ceiling. The video projector warmed up and the image on the wall screen brightened and came into focus. A bright blue glow filled the room, cast from the image of the North Atlantic Ocean displayed on the screen.

One bright yellow icon appeared on the screen.

"That gentleman was the reported position of USS *Providence* when she was fired upon by a Russian Navy submarine," Bennington disclosed.

Stunned looks and murmurs filled the room.

"Gentlemen, please," Bennington shouted, banging the remote on the table. "No questions until I finish."

"But Adm …."

The words died in his throat when Bennington turned and shot an icy stare directly at Major General James Radford, US Air Force Chief of Staff.

"Thank you General." Bennington continued, "As I was saying, *Providence's* sonar computer confirmed the submarine that fired the torpedo as a Russian Akula class submarine, more specifically, the K-391, *Bratsk*. *Providence* further reported a second surface contact, classified as a Kirov class battlecruiser, the *Pyotr Velikiy*. The battlecruiser launched multiple anti-submarine helicopters with dipping sonar."

"Upon detection of high speed screws, *Providence* commenced evasive maneuvers and fired countermeasures. The inbound torpedo locked onto the countermeasures and detonated with no harm to *Providence*. *Providence* immediately assumed firing-point procedures and developed a target solution on the *Bratsk*. She then fired two Mark 48 torpedoes. Target kill was confirmed by primary and secondary explosions and by hull popping as the *Bratsk* broke up and sank into deep water. *Providence* concluded an attack on the surface ship would be foolhardy and departed the area."

"While this information is disconcerting enough by itself, even more disturbing is the report from *Providence* that the contacts were dead in the water until commencement of the attack. *Providence's* captain is convinced the Russian ships were waiting for them. That is all I have gentlemen."

General William Danvers, US Army Chief of Staff, was the first to speak, "Admiral, is there any suspected motive for the attack? Any intelligence chatter? Anything at all that would explain the attack?"

"Nothing that I am aware of General," Bennington answered, turning and looking at Matthew Tyler, the National Security Advisor.

Tyler shook his head, "Absolutely nothing sir."

Major General James Radford spoke next, "Anything on diplomatic channels?"

Bennington looked at Tyler again. Another shake of the head.

"What's our next step Admiral?" Brigadier General Andrew McCune, Marine Corp Chief of Staff asked.

"Without any communications from the Russians or conformation of a reason for the attack, I believe we have no choice but to maintain our current state of readiness."

"Admiral I think ...."

"Gentlemen, hold your questions and comments," Bennington interrupted. "I have another matter to discuss. But before I start, I must advise you this matter is extremely sensitive. You will discuss it with no one. Not even your aides. You will not even discuss it with each other, unless we are meeting in this room. Understood?"

All meeting attendees agreed. Bennington reached out and pulled the Polycom Conference Phone over in front of him and punched in a number.

After three rings, a voice answered, "Yes, this is Rear Admiral Hadley."

"Admiral Hadley, Fleet Admiral Bennington here."

"Good evening Admiral. What can I do for you?"

"I am calling from the JCS Conference Room. All the Joint Chiefs are here plus the National Security Advisor. I would like to discuss the matter you called me about earlier."

"Yes, Admiral. I was expecting your call."

"Gentlemen, do you all know Rear Admiral Charles Hadley, Director of Naval Intelligence?"

Receiving nods of agreement from everyone in the room, he continued, "Admiral Hadley called me earlier and revealed a most distressing situation. Gentlemen, sensitive intelligence information is being leaked from a very high-level source. Admiral Hadley has strong suspicions it may be part of a scheme to start a war between the United States and one or more countries in Europe."

"What?" gasped all the Joint Chiefs in unison.

General Radford regained enough composure to speak, "This is General Radford. You can't be serious Admiral Hadley."

"I am absolutely serious General Radford."

"Well then Admiral, who's behind it?" General Radford countered, more than a little skepticism evident in his voice.

"I won't say at this point General," Hadley answered. "There is not adequate proof as yet. I won't risk destroying someone's career until I am certain."

General McCune spoke up, "General McCune, Admiral. How do you suggest we proceed? If, as you suggest, there may be a threat of war, we can't just sit idly by and do nothing."

"General, I believe we have insufficient intelligence at this time to warrant any increase in DEFCON status. We must maintain absolute secrecy regarding this matter. It is vital we identify the threat and eliminate it. If the perpetrator suspects we are on to him, he may panic and start World War Three before we have a chance to react."

"I agree," Bennington affirmed. "I have already instructed everyone in the room regarding the need for absolute secrecy. Anything else Admiral Hadley?"

"I believe we should contact all Combat Commands and advise them to cancel pending leaves, recall critical personnel, and be alert. However, they should remain at their current readiness condition. Admiral Bennington do you concur?"

"I concur," Bennington agreed without hesitation.

"That's all I have for the group," Hadley announced. "But I have a private matter I need to discuss with you."

Bennington addressed the group, "I don't believe there is anything further we need to discuss until we have more intelligence on this matter. I repeat my earlier caution, this matter is not to be shared or discussed outside of this room. Gentlemen, Admiral Hadley and I have something to discuss privately. This meeting is adjourned."

One by one the Joint Chiefs got up from their chairs and filed out of the conference room with looks of shock and bewilderment on their faces. Bennington remained seated with his finger on the mute button. When the last Joint Chief left, Bennington's aide pulled the door closed.

"Everyone is gone Admiral Hadley. What is it you need?"

"The situation seems to be escalating. There have been multiple attempts to silence a man responsible for a DOD microwave communication system. I assigned someone to protect him. If he hadn't intervened, that individual would be dead. The last attempt was executed by a well-dressed female. A photo of her was identified by our facial recognition software as a known contract assassin. Even worse, Admiral, she is a "black ops" asset used by the FBI on numerous occasions. So far, four or more suspicious deaths can be linked to people directly or indirectly involved in this matter. Admiral Bennington, I think someone may be getting scared. Perhaps scared enough to provoke an incident we will not be able to contain."

"Given you are correct, how would I be able to help?"

"I was contacted by someone that must remain nameless. Someone I trust implicitly. He requested I develop an escape plan for a deep-cover operative in Europe to bring out evidence of the scheme to start a war. The operative claims the materials he has in his possession are irrefutable. Under the plan I devised, he will not arrive in the United States for another four of five days. That is not nearly soon enough. I need your help in shortening that time to less than twenty-four hours."

"That's a rather short timeframe. What exactly are you suggesting?"

"Admiral, I need use of a Navy Amphibious Assault Team right now. More specifically, I need a Naval Special Warfare, Special Boat Team. The window of opportunity for the plan to work is less than two hours."

"Admiral Hadley you are asking a lot. Activating a Special Boat Team on such short notice would require special authorization. I don't think I can authorize that on suspicion alone."

"Admiral, I have four dead bodies, possibly more, and a man that says he has absolute proof. I know him personally Admiral.

"Who is this man you trust so highly?"

Even though he did not want to, Admiral Hadley knew this was not the time to withhold information. "Bill Morrison. Formerly Lieutenant Bill Morrison of SEAL Team Four."

"What? That's not possible. He's dead. The entire team died in the jungles of Southeast Asia, except for two men and he was neither of them."

"I assure you he is alive. He has been working a deep undercover assignment in Europe. Only three people were aware he is still alive. Furthermore, one of the four dead bodies I mentioned was one of the survivors of SEAL Team Four. The other survivor of that team, Zach Templeton, is the man responsible for the DOD microwave communication system. There have been two attempts on his life in the last two days."

Persuaded by the new information, but with some reluctance, Bennington agreed to the "off-the-books" operation as explained by Admiral Hadley.

Details of a highly unusual, and exceptionally dangerous, operation to intercept Bill Morrison and return him to the United States in less than twenty-four hours was discussed by Hadley and Bennington, emphasis on speed being stressed by Hadley.

To shorten the time required to activate the Special Boat Team and to reduce the possibility of further intelligence leaks, Bennington agreed he would personally make the call to the Naval Special Warfare group.

CHAPTER FIFTY-TWO

Thursday, April 2 - 0118 Local Time
US Naval Base
Azores, Portugal

Lcdr. Glen Ewing, Command Duty Officer for US Navy Squadron One, hung up the phone and whistled out loud. Never, in his career had he spoken directly with a Fleet Admiral. During the conversation, he spoke very little. Mostly, he frantically scribbled notes on a pad to make certain he did not miss a single detail of the operation the Admiral outlined. He picked up the phone and dialed the number for the Amphibious Assault Team duty office.

"Assault team duty office," Boatswains Mate First Class Brian Draper announced.

"Scramble the team. Now!" Ewing barked. "This is a priority one alert. I repeat, priority one alert!"

"Yes sir. Scramble the team. Priority one alert sir," Draper repeated.

"Have Lieutenant Moore call me at the base duty office the instant he is awake and dressed."

"Yes sir. As soon as he is awake and dressed sir."

"Now petty officer. Now!" Owen yelled.

"Yes sir!" Draper acknowledged, literally throwing the receiver at its cradle, as he ran from the assault team duty office, heading for the team's duty bunkroom.

Draper entered the duty bunkroom, switched on the light and shouted, "ATTENTION! Priority one alert. ATTENTION! Priority one alert."

The assault team members were awakened either by the shouting or the noise created by other team members jumping from their racks and clambering into their uniforms. Draper located Lieutenant. Conrad Moore, the assault team leader, and ran over to him.

"Sir, the CDO called and issued a priority one alert. He requested you call him the instant you are dressed."

"Any details Petty Officer?"

"No sir. Just the request for you to call the base duty office."

"Very well."

Moore grabbed his fatigue pants, slipped on one leg, and hollered, "Senior Chief."

"Yes sir," Senior Chief Gunner's Mate Robert Tucker answered from the far side of the bunk room.

"Muster the team in the equipment bay Senior Chief. Full turn out gear. No mission details as yet. I will call the base duty office. When I have the mission parameters, we will gather any additional equipment we might need."

"Aye aye sir," Tucker acknowledged as Moore disappeared out the door.

Sliding to a stop in front of the duty watch desk, Moore grabbed the phone and punched in the number for the base duty office.

"Command Duty Office, Lieutenant Commander Ewing,"

"Lieutenant Moore, Amphibious Assault Team Two. You have a priority one alert."

"Yes, Mister Moore. Direct from Washington. Fleet Admiral Bennington called personally. This is as hot as it gets Mister Moore."

"A Fleet Admiral called personally?"

"That's what I said Mister Moore. You are to assemble a four-man assault team and proceed to a point seven thousand yards from Ponta Delgada at a bearing of one-seven-five degrees. You are to take a submarine communications buoy. When you arrive on station, lower it over the side and squawk ident 1161. Set the transmit range to twenty-five thousand yards and squawk the ident code twice on three minute intervals. When you receive an acknowledgement, you will transmit a coded message. The duty runner is on the way to your location with the coded message text."

Moore made notes on a small waterproof slate as the CDO described the mission.

"Anything else sir?"

"Yes. You will retrieve a package. Return immediately. Transportation for the package will be waiting."

"Is that it?"

"Yes Mister Moore. You will instruct your team to never speak of this mission. It never happened."

"Yes sir. Never happened sir."

Moore hung up the phone and sprinted to the assault team equipment bay. All team members were assembled and sitting on the floor beside their gear, waiting.

Sounds of scuffling feet echoed in the equipment bay when Senior Chief Tucker saw Lieutenant Moore entering the equipment bay and shouted, "Attention on deck."

"As you were men," Moore ordered. Pointing out four team members, he added, "I need you four team members. The rest of you may fall out and return to your bunks. Sorry for rousting all of you. I just got the mission parameters from the base duty office."

Moore waited for the dismissed team members to gather their gear and leave the equipment bay. When the last excused team member left, Moore spoke to Machinist Mate Second Class Miguel Sanchez, the team's demolition expert, "Petty Officer Sanchez, close the door and see that no one enters."

Moore discussed the mission parameters with the team members he had selected, stressing the vital importance of their mission and the need for secrecy. Being a US Navy Special Forces team, they were accustomed to being instructed the mission on which they were about to embark did not exist.

The five team members making final preparations for their mission were all highly trained SEALs, waterborne commandoes, trained to respond at a moment's notice and to carry out dangerous missions on any terrain – sea, air, or land. Tonight their mission was in the hazardous, cold waters of the North Atlantic.

Their current mission had room for only four team members, requiring one of the members to be left behind. Sanchez, selected as the one to be left behind, would be assigned to the communications shack to monitor the team's progress and to summon additional resources should the team encounter trouble.

Final checks of equipment complete, the four-man team, dressed in full wet suits, double-timed it to the pier and quickly stowed their gear aboard the waiting MK V STC, a Mark V Special Operations Craft. The Mark Five with a speed of forty-five knots, was fitted with several types of weapons to provide suppressive fire for operations in hot pick-up zones. Its angular design and low silhouette reduced its radar signature, making it harder to detect. The Mark Five is used to initiate safe extraction of Navy SEALs in low to medium threat environments.

"Safety checks complete?" Moore queried.

"Yes sir," came the response from each team member.

Moore released the mooring line, dropped into his seat, and cinched up his safety belt. Turning toward the Mark Five's pilot, Moore nodded and said, "Seven thousand yards, bearing one-seven-five. Light er up."

The pilot backed the Mark Five away from the pier and turned toward open water. He idled the Mark Five between the channel markers for several minutes to clear shallow water in the harbor and then mashed the throttles all the way to the stop. The Mark Five's twin 12-cylinder TE94 Diesel engines roared to life. Because of the boat's V-hull and shallow draft, it remained low in the water and produced a much smaller rooster tail than other boats its size.

Even though the V-hull design gave the Mark Five good handling in rough water, it slammed hard into the crossing waves as it sliced through the notoriously rough seas of the North Atlantic. The assault team members gave little notice to the rough seas, having been through similar missions many times before.

Five minutes later the Mark Five's pilot pulled back on the throttles and reduced their speed. He idled the boat for thirty seconds and then cut the engines completely. One of the boat's crewmen scurried to the bow and heaved a drift sock, a type of sea anchor, into the water to reduce the boat's drift.

Moore removed a hand-help radio from a watertight box and depressed the transmit button twice.

"Badger One, this is Cobra. Confirm on station," Sanchez, inside the communications shack, spoke into the microphone.

Moore clicked the microphone transmit key once.

"Put the submarine comm buoy in the water Senior Chief," Moore ordered.

Tucker nodded at Engineman Second Class Scott Hardman to give him a hand deploying the submarine comm buoy. Together they released the locking clamps on a long, narrow crate and removed a cylindrical object. Hardman eased the object over the side of the boat and into the water while Tucker held the tether. Tucker let the tether cables slide through his hands until a yellow band around the cables reached the water. He secured the tether with the buoy suspended one hundred feet below the boat. As soon as Tucker plugged the free end of the tether cable into the controller, Hardman pressed the "ident" button, waited five seconds, and pressed the "ident" button again.

Watching the soft green glow from the tritium dial of his Navy Diver's watch, Hardman repeated the ident process at precisely three minute intervals. Eight times the interval was repeated before an acknowledge ident code was received, decoded, and the "Safe to Transmit" indicator illuminated. Hardman pressed the "Transmit" button and the encrypted message, keyed into the controller during the transit, was sent. Two seconds passed. The "Transmission Complete" indicator illuminated.

The submarine communications buoy was hauled back aboard and stowed in its container. There was nothing left to do but wait, the first phase of their mission completed.

CHAPTER FIFTY-THREE

Thursday, April 2 - 0213 Local Time
USS Providence SSN 719
East Azores Fracture Zone; 37° 30' 00"N, 25° 43' 20"W
South of Azores Island

"What on Earth," Radioman First Class Brett Easley exclaimed when the inbound message alarm sounded. "Hey Mike, are we due for a comm check?"

"No Brett," RM3 Mike Hall, junior radioman aboard *Providence*, answered. "Remember. Captain said no communication without his direct authorization."

"Oh, yeah. Right. Well then, I wonder what this inbound message is?" Easley questioned as he reached over to the communications panel and pressed the print button. Bent over the printer, his eyes flicked back and forth as he followed the print head across the paper.

"Holy moly!" he cried, pulling the paper up and tearing if off the printer. "Mike, watch the radio. I have to get this to the captain ASAP."

Before Hall could answer, Easley had already vanished from the radio shack and was running down the passageway toward the captain's cabin. Panting from the long sprint, Easley's sneakers screeched on the floor as he slid to a stop in front of the captain's cabin door.

"Captain, Captain," Easley shouted as he banged on the door.

"What is it?" Commander Chandler hollered, scrambling out of his bunk, grabbing for his uniform.

"Radioman Easley sir. I have an inbound encrypted message sir."

Dressed only in his trousers, still unzipped and hanging loosely around at his waist, Chandler pulled the door open. "Enter. Let's have it."

"Here sir," Easley stammered, handing the message to Chandler. He stood rigid in front of the Captain as he read the message.

"Petty Officer Easley, find a runner and send him to my cabin now!"

"Conn, this is the Captain. Change course to zero-one-one. Increase speed to eighteen knots."

"Change course to zero-one-one. Increase speed to eighteen knots aye,"

Lt. Flanigan, the current Duty Officer, acknowledged.

Chandler grabbed a fresh uniform shirt from a hanger, threw it on, and began stuffing it into his trousers.

Another knock on the door. Chandler opened the door and motioned EM3 Hall into the cabin.

"Find the COB. Wake him if you have to. Have him round up our two best swimmers. Tell them to meet me on the mess deck. Then go wake up our guest and escort him the mess deck."

"Yes sir. Right away sir."

"Conn, this is the Captain. Rig for red."

"Rig for red, aye sir," Lt. Flanigan replied.

"Conn, I'll be on the mess deck. If anything comes up, find me."

"Aye aye Captain."

Chandler stepped over to the wash basin and splashed some cold water on his face. He dried his face, straightened his uniform, and headed for the mess deck.

Dodging crewmen in the narrow passageway, Chandler made his way aft to the midships ladder. "Down ladder. Make a hole," he shouted, sliding down the handrails without touching a single step. He ran onto the mess deck just as the COB and the swimmers were taking a seat at one of the tables. RM3 Hall arrived with Bill Morrison in tow.

"Clear the room," Chandler barked. As soon as the last crewman left the room, he continued, "No time for pleasantries gentlemen. We just received a coded message from a close-aboard, surface contact. The message has been verified as authentic."

Chandler looked directly at Chief of the Boat, Master Chief Michael Mazetti, "COB, we have been ordered to transfer our guest to the surface contact."

"Mister ... Ah... I don't know your name," Chandler said, looking at *Providence's* newest passenger.

"Bill Morrison sir."

"Mister Morrison, have you ever used SCUBA gear?"

"No sir. Why?" Bill asked, a frightened look spreading across his face.

"As you know, we were recently fired upon making it far too dangerous to surface. You and the two divers seated beside you will exit through the escape trunk and make contact with a Navy assault team on the surface."

"No sir! No way! I can't ...."

"There is no alternative Mister Morrison," Chandler interrupted. "The orders came direct from Washington. The divers will get you into a wet suit and give you the basic instruction you need. They will lead you to the surface and deliver you to the assault team."

Shaking his head, Bill repeated his disagreement, "No sir. I can't. I don't know a thing about diving"

"You will do as ordered Mister Morrison," Chandler bellowed. "I will not risk this boat because you are afraid of a little swim."

Bill started to protest again, but the captain's raised hand stopped him. Bill shrugged his shoulders and gave in, realizing he had no choice.

"COB, take Mister Morrison and the divers and get them suited up. Have the divers instruct him in the basics then stand by at the aft escape trunk until we reach the transfer point. Make certain the materials Mister Morrison is carrying are packaged in a watertight bag. Tape the bag to his skin under the wet suit. They must not be lost or destroyed."

"Aye aye Captain," Mazetti acknowledged, sliding off the bench and guiding Bill toward the equipment locker.

Bill wondered what he had gotten himself into as he was dragged aft.

Chandler hurried back up the midships ladder and ran into the control room.

"I have the Conn," he announced, stepping up onto the platform.

"Aye aye Captain," Lt. Flanigan responded, stepping down.

"Sonar, Conn, Report all contacts."

"Conn, Sonar, No contacts at this time."

"ATTENTION ALL HANDS! BATTLE STATIONS! BATTLE STATIONS! THIS IS NOT A DRILL." Chandler shouted into the 1-MC.

All normal activities aboard *Providence* stopped immediately as crewmen dropped what they were doing and rushed to their assigned battle stations. Crewmen not specifically assigned to a battle station went to their bunks and stayed out of the way.

"Weapons, Conn, load tubes one and two and open outer doors."

"Conn, Weapons, load tubes one and two and open outer doors aye."

"ATTENTION all hands. This is the Captain. We are going shallow which will make us an easy target. I want the boat rigged for ultra-quiet and I want everyone alert and ready for action."

"Conn, Weapons, weapons systems report ready in all respects."

"Conn, Aye. Dive, Conn, Five degree up bubble. Make your depth two hundred feet."

"Conn, Dive, five degree up bubble. Make your depth two hundred feet aye."

Everyone in the control room braced themselves as the boat pitched slightly upward. Drops of perspiration glistened on foreheads, everyone concentrating intently on their assigned duty. Chandler studied the crewmen in the control room. The crew of the most lethal weapons platform in the world was ready. If a contact appeared and so much as turned in their direction, they would blow it into oblivion.

Chandler stepped down from the control platform and walked over to the navigation table. "Mister Flanigan how far to a point seven thousand yards from Ponta Delgada on a bearing of one-seven-five?"

Flanigan grabbed a protractor and drew a bearing line of one-seven-five degrees from Ponta Delgada, grabbed a pair of dividers, and set the distance between the two points equal to seven thousand yards. He placed one point of the dividers at Ponta Delgada and made a mark on the bearing line at the other point. After setting the width of the dividers' points equal to the distance between the mark he just made and *Providence's* current position, he held the dividers to a navigation rule.

"Approximately thirteen thousand, three hundred yards sir. At our present speed of eighteen knots we should arrive in twenty-two minutes."

"Very well," Chandler said as he clicked a stopwatch and stepped back up onto the control platform.

"Sonar, Conn, Any contacts?"

"Conn, Sonar, No contacts."

"Conn aye."

The only sound in the control room was the soft humming of machinery and an occasional muffled cough as the minutes ticked down. At the fifteen minute mark, Chandler reached up and toggled the 1-MC, "Helm, Conn, Ahead slow. Make turns for three knots."

"Conn, Helm, ahead slow. Make turns for three knots aye."

"Dive, Conn, come to periscope depth."

"Conn, Dive, come to periscope depth aye."

One minute passed.

"Conn, Dive, at periscope depth."

"Conn aye."

Nodding to the XO, he crouched as low as he could and met the periscope on the way up. He adjusted his cheek to the eyepiece and spun the focus ring back and forth. Making a slow three hundred sixty degree circle, he searched the ocean surface for any possible ships or obstructions. Satisfied all was clear, he ordered the periscope lowered.

"Dive, Conn, three degree down bubble. Make your depth one hundred thirty feet."

"Conn, Dive, three degree down bubble. Make your depth one hundred thirty feet aye."

Two minutes passed.

"Conn, Dive, on depth at one hundred thirty feet."

"Conn aye. Helm, Conn, all stop."

"Conn, Helm, all stop aye."

"Mister Graham, you have the Conn."

"I have the Conn," Lcdr. Graham answered.

Chandler rushed out of the control room, heading for the aft escape trunk. The two divers and a very frightened looking Bill Morrison were waiting at the hatch to the escape trunk.

"Okay gentlemen, time to go. The assault team should be approximately one hundred yards off our starboard quarter."

"But sir," Bill protested, hoping to find a way out of what he believed was death in the frigid water.

"Don't worry," Chandler said. "Our divers do this all the time. The deck is only one hundred feet from the surface."

"What? One-hundr…"

Bill's protest was cut off as Hull Technician Second Class Ben Whitman shoved him into the escape trunk and stepped in behind him. Hull Technician Third Class Andy Baldwin, the second diver, stepped in and pulled the hatch closed with a loud clunk.

Whitman scrambled up the ladder into the escape chamber and motioned for Bill to follow. Bill climbed up the ladder with Baldwin right behind him. Baldwin pushed the lower hatch closed and spun the locking wheel.

Whitman punched Bill on the arm to get his attention, "Your ears will pop when Andy opens the seawater valve and the air in the chamber equalizes to the outside seawater pressure. Swallow hard to clear your ears."

Whitman grabbed Bill's shoulder and turned him so they were facing each other. "Get a grip man. Calm down. It won't be that bad. The water will be cold when it first soaks into your wet suit but it will warm up quickly and then it won't feel all that bad. Just be sure to keep the regulator in your mouth. Andy will keep a tight hold on your vest. He will be right beside you if you have any trouble."

Whitman nodded at Baldwin to open the seawater valve to flood the escape chamber. Hissing sounds filled the escape chamber as water flowed into the chamber and the air pressure equalized to that of the sea pressure outside the boat.

Bill shuddered violently as the cold salt water climbed to his knees, then his waist, then to his chest. Absolute horror spread across his face as the water splashed at the glass of his mask, then covered it completely. Bill's every instinct told him not to breathe. Expecting that very thing, Whitman gently punched Bill in the stomach, causing him to suck in a breath, followed by three more rapid, terrified breaths. He tapped the glass of Bill's mask to get his attention. Bill's brain finally realized he wasn't drowning. His breathing slowed somewhat and the panic subsided enough to allow him to follow instructions.

The two divers flashed the "OK" sign to each other. Whitman ascended up the escape tube, pushed the outer hatch open, and swam outside, utter blackness enveloping him. He located a small underwater lantern tethered to his vest, switched it on, and waited for Baldwin and the "newbie" to join him.

Baldwin pushed Bill up the escape trunk, following close behind. Whitman grabbed Bill's vest as soon as his head emerged from the hatch and hung on to him while Baldwin exited and secured the hatch. Whitman spun Bill around to face him, looked into his eyes, and gave him the "OK" signal. Bill shook his head up and down in agreement. Whitman turned his charge over to Baldwin and gave him the "thumbs up" signal.

Slowly they ascended up through the cold dark water. Keeping a close watch on his depth gauge, Whitman tapped Baldwin's leg when they reached thirty feet. Stopping their ascent, Whitman grabbed the lantern and pointed it upward. He waved it back and forth several times, then switched it off. No response. The three men hung there in the inky blackness, waiting. Whitman repeated the signal with the lantern. Still nothing. Bill was teetering on the verge of full-blown panic. A third time Whitman repeated the signal.

A light appeared in the darkness sixty yards away. Bill had started to thrash around. Andy grabbed Bill's head and turned it toward the light suspended in the water. Once Bill saw the light and stopped thrashing, they started swimming horizontally in the direction of the light. When they reached the light, they ascended straight up, surfacing no more than ten feet from the assault team's boat.

"We've been waiting for you," Senior Chief Tucker called out as he threw a line to the three men bobbing in the water.

Whitman reached out and snatched the line floating on the water and pulled the group over to the boat and then around to the stern.

"This is the package," Whitman called out to the men on the boat.

Several hands reached over the edge of the boat and hauled Bill on board. Bill slumped down on the floor of the boat panting, completely exhausted from the frightening ordeal.

"Wait. Wait," Bill croaked, scrambling to get up with the heavy SCUBA gear on his back. Managing to get up onto his knees, he hung his head over the edge of the boat. "Ben, Andy, thanks guys. I promise you I will never forget this experience."

"Glad to be of assistance," Whitman shouted back. He shoved the regulator back into his mouth and sank out of site.

Bill turned around and plopped down on his backside. He stuck out his hand and introduced himself, "I'm Bill Morrison. Thanks for meeting me."

"Glad to meet you, Mister Morrison," Lt. Moore chimed, reaching out to shake Bill's cold, wet hand.

Moore looked over at the pilot, "Back to the barn, Captain."

While the assault team sped away, the two divers scrambled back into *Providence's* escape hatch. With the divers safely back on board, *Providence* changed course and headed for deep water.

On the Mark Five Special Operations Craft, Bill shivered as the boat raced back toward the safety of the harbor.

CHAPTER FIFTY-FOUR

Wednesday, April 1 – 2310 Pacific Daylight Time
Stonewall Flat Microwave Tower Site
42 miles south of Tonopah, Nevada

A soft green glow suddenly illuminated the darkness under the equipment building at the Stonewall Flat microwave tower site. Underneath the floor, a hidden receiver received a valid access code and switched into the active mode. Three miles away a similar green glow illuminated the darkness inside a dark blue SUV parked fifty yards off the road. The "Active" indicator on the device in Aronoff Porubsky's hands indicated the two devices had acknowledged each other and were communicating.

Aronoff had keyed the final message into the device as soon as he arrived in Las Vegas. The final message had been delivered to him several weeks earlier. At the eastern edge of Las Vegas, Aronoff had picked up a sandwich and a drink at a fast food restaurant and had waited for darkness.

Complaining more with each passing mile, Aronoff had driven only as close to the tower site as he had to. He had stopped twice before, but both times his device's signal had been too weak to reach the device hidden under the equipment building. He would be glad to get this over with and call his friend to arrange a rapid exit out of the country.

Aronoff pressed the "Send" button on his device which immediately began to transmit the coded message to the device three miles away. The device at the tower site received the message, stored it in its internal memory, and transmitted an acknowledgement code. Darkness returned under the equipment building as the device returned to the "sleep" mode, waiting for the preset time to insert the message into the microwave system.

Relief flooded over Aronoff when he saw the "Message Complete" indicator light up. He switched the device off and tossed it on the passenger seat. Engine already running, he slammed the SUV into gear and headed back for the highway.

The tires of the SUV screeched in protest as he roared up onto the highway and mashed the accelerator. Fighting the urge to drive as fast as he could, Aronoff forced himself to stay just under the speed limit. His was the only car on the highway. He did not wish to be stopped and questioned by the authorities.

He reached down, picked up the cell phone sitting on the slide-out tray, and pressed a speed dial number.

His old friend, Vinogradov, answered on the fourth ring, "Do zvidaniya, my friend."

"It is done."

"All is okay?"

"Da, Everything went as planned."

"Very good. How I help you?"

"Let our superiors know the plan is complete."

"Da, I will tell Ismaylov."

"I need a vacation," Aronoff added, letting his friend know he wanted to execute the escape plan."

"Soon?"

"As soon as you can arrange it."

"Da, I arrange for tomorrow."

"You should go also. It's going to get very hot here."

"Da, I will."

"Same meeting place?"

"Da."

"Do zvidaniya, good friend," Aronoff said as he flipped the cell phone shut, breaking the connection.

Aronoff twisted the cell phone back and forth until the two sections separated. He threw both pieces out the window, a large smile spreading across his face as he thought about the glorious retribution that would be visited on the lazy Americans he hated so much. He would also very much enjoy the million dollars he had been promised and the warm island sun on the other side of the world where he would soon be headed.

* * *

Thursday, April 2 – 0645 Local Time
João Paulo Airport
Ponta Delgada, Azores, Portugal

With only a small carryon, containing the materials he had risked his life for several times and one spare change of clothes, Bill Morrison walked through the sliding glass doors of João Paulo Airport in Ponta Delgada, located on the island of São Miguel.

The Navy assault team that had picked him up the previous night, had been most gracious. A comfortable bunk and a surprisingly good breakfast had been provided. Over and above anything Bill could have expected, the team compared his size to the members of the assault team. Two of the team members were roughly his size and had volunteered one change of clothes each. One he was currently wearing, the other was stuffed in the carryon hanging from his left shoulder. The team had even provided transportation, dropping him right at the entrance to the airport.

Bill turned and looked both ways, locating the security entry point to his left. He walked down the highly polished, white tile floor and dropped his carryon on the x-ray machine's conveyor belt. Removing his shoes, he placed them in a plastic tub and set it on the belt. He passed through the magnetometer without incident and collected his belongings.

Bill stopped a passing security guard, "General aviation terminal?"

"That way. End of hall," the guard answered, pointing to Bill's right.

"Muito obrigado," Bill thanked the guard. At least he hoped he had said thank you, knowing only a few phrases in Portuguese.

Turning in the direction the guard had indicated, Bill walked to the end of the hallway. A sign above the door on the left said "General Aviation". He pushed the door open and walked in.

Already waiting in the passenger lounge, the pilot of the Gulfstream G550 got up and hurried over to where Bill was standing and stuck out his hand, "Kip Johnson. You must be Bill Morrison."

"Yes, Mister Johnson, that's me."

"Come on," the pilot urged. "Let's go. Some mighty important folks are eager to talk to you."

The pilot pushed the door open to the general aviation ramp and waited for Bill to walk through. Motioning to the right, the pilot said, "Big white one over there. November-four-six-Mike-Lima. The one with the dark blue stripe down the fuselage."

"Wow, nice plane!" Bill commented, as he stopped and gazed at the huge eighteen passenger private jet.

Urging him to hurry, the pilot shoved Bill toward the waiting plane and drawled, "Come on. We gotta saddle up and skidaddle."

Bill climbed the three stairs and stepped into the lavishly appointed cabin, stunned by its elegance. The passenger cabin had been reconfigured by removing the eighteen standard seats. Along the starboard side of the cabin there was one plush forward-facing seat near the front of the cabin and one double, rear-facing and one double, forward-facing seat at the over-wing emergency exit. On the port side of the cabin there was a luxurious couch and a burled walnut credenza. In the rear of the cabin there were two forward-facing and two rear-facing seats on either side of the cabin. Four large oval windows on either side of the cabin let in an amazing amount of light.

A single individual sat in the rear of the cabin, swirling a drink in his hand. He got up, placed the drink on the credenza, and walked forward.

"I'm Bill Morrison," Bill offered, sticking out his hand.

"Glad to meet you Bill. My name is Norman Glover. Can I fix you a drink while we wait for clearance to take off?"

"A drink, you bet. After what I've been through I could use a dozen. I'll have whiskey, neat."

"Tell me about it."

"Long story. Maybe later."

Norman slid one of the doors of the credenza open, selected a bottle of very old whiskey, and poured a generous amount into a tumbler. Bill picked up the tumbler and took a generous sip and let the warm, brown liquid flow down his throat. Finally, he felt as if he could relax.

Norman pointed at the single seat near the front of the cabin and said, "Sit." Norman took a seat on the couch on the opposite side of the cabin. Once Bill was comfortably seated, Norman continued, "I understand you know a Mister Zach Templeton. I was asked by Rear Admiral Hadley to look out for Mister Templeton. I personally witnessed two attempts on his life."

"Two? Is he okay?" Bill asked.

"Yes. A little shaken, but fine. I interceded and eliminated both threats. I dare say, they will not be bothering him again, if you catch my drift."

"Who is Admiral Hadley?"

"Close friend of Commander Owen Patterson. I believe you asked him for help."

"Yes. If he hadn't agreed to help, I would never have gotten out of Europe alive. I …."

Bill was interrupted by the pilot's announcement they were ready for departure and should fasten their seat belts.

"We'll talk later," Norman smiled, taking Bill's glass and walking back to the credenza. He dumped the contents of both glasses, and stowed them. He took one of the seats in the rear of the cabin and buckled his seat belt.

In the cockpit, Kip Johnson had completed the pre-flight check and the necessary paperwork. He pressed the transmit button on the yoke, "Ground control November-four-six-Mike-Lima requesting clearance for taxi to active runway."

"November-four-six-Mike-Lima hold. There is cross-traffic on the taxiway behind you."

"Roger ground control."

Two minutes later the radio crackled to life, "November-four-six-Mike-Lima. Traffic behind you has cleared. You are clear to taxi. Taxi to runway three-zero and hold."

"November-four-six-Mike-Lima roger."

Kip Johnson pushed the throttles forward, twisted the steering yoke to the right, and slowly eased the Gulfstream toward the taxiway. He straightened out the steering yoke and increased the throttles slightly. The Gulfstream bounced slightly as it rolled down the taxiway. Kip taxied the plane to the far end of the taxiway and stopped short of the active runway.

Kip keyed the intercom, "Gentlemen, one plane inbound on final and we are next."

Both passengers leaned forward in their seats to watch the plane as it landed. A Boeing 767 jumbo jet flared over the threshold of the runway and flashed by the small private jet. Tires screeched and puffs of smoke rose into the air as the jumbo jet settled onto the runway.

"November-four-six-Mike-Lima, you are cleared for takeoff. Fly runway heading and report to departure control at two thousand."

"November-four-six-Mike-Lima roger."

Kip eased the throttles forward, steering the Gulfstream onto runway three-zero. Lined up on the centerline, he set the brake and pushed the throttles all the way forward, waiting for the twin Rolls-Royce BR710 engines to spool up. Upon reaching seventy percent thrust, he released the brake and the sleek Gulfstream began its take-off roll. Kip scanned the gauges and indicators as the Gulfstream accelerated toward V1, the decision speed where a pilot can still abort a takeoff . Everything normal and no warning indicators. At VR, rotation speed, he pulled back on the control yoke and the nose wheel lifted off the ground. A few seconds later, the Gulfstream reached V2, safe take-off speed. The rear wheels lifted from the runway and the jet began its climb-out into the early morning sky. At two hundred feet, Kip retracted the landing gear.

At precisely two thousand feet, Kip thumbed the transmit button and contacted departure control, "Departure control, Gulfstream November-four-six-Mike-Lima, out of two for ten. Request VFR clearance for flight path to Tulsa, Oklahoma."

"November-four-six-Mike-Lima, climb to flight level three-one, heading two-seven-nine. Contact Boston ATC enroute."

"November-four-six-Mike-Lima roger."

Kip keyed the intercom, "Gentlemen, it is safe to move around the cabin. It will be a beautiful day for flying. Enjoy the ride."

Norman unbuckled his seat belt and fixed another drink for himself and one for Bill. He handed one drink to Bill and sat on the couch beside him. They settled in for the long flight to Tulsa and began a long conversation.

CHAPTER FIFTY-FIVE

Thursday, April 2 – 0515 Central Daylight Time
Microwave Services Communications Lab
Tulsa, Oklahoma

Wearing the same disguise he had used in Las Vegas, Zach crept through the early morning darkness. Two attempts on his life in two days made him as jumpy as a cat. The awareness of being hunted was reasserting Zach's SEAL training. Eyes constantly on the move, scanning everything and everyone in his field of vision. Not missing a single movement, sound, or smell, he stayed close to buildings, bushes, or other objects to minimize his profile.

Picking a point as far from street lights as he could, he ran across Forty-first street. Racing around his office building, he ducked into the underground parking lot, jammed his access card into the card reader, and waited for the elevator. As soon as the elevator doors opened, he stepped in, and pressed the button for the floor his office was on. As early as it was, no one else would be in the building.

Zach stepped out of the elevator and leaned against the wall, listening for the slightest sound. Hearing nothing, he ran straight to the front door of his office, unlocked it, and stepped inside. Standing in the darkness, he allowed his breathing to return to normal. He felt his way along the narrow hallway to the door to his personal office. Once inside his office, he stepped over to the window and pulled the blinds closed.

He switched on a small desk lamp, adjusting the flexible neck until the bulb was close to the computer keyboard. He punched the power buttons on the computer and the monitor. While the computer went through its boot-up sequence, he made his way to the kitchen and grabbed a bottle of Mountain Dew. Returning to his office, he closed and locked the door.

For three long, tedious, and grueling, hours Zach poured over the data he had recorded and brought back with him. Every conceivable method of rearranging, sorting, comparing, and aggregating the data had been tried at least twice. Some methods had even been tried three or four times. At his wits end, he decided to make one last attempt at unraveling the mystery. He selected one of the aggregation routines, entered a different key attribute, and launched the process. Rather than sit and stare blankly at the screen while the process ground through the data, he shoved himself away from the desk, and headed for the kitchen and another soda. He turned the lock carefully and eased the door open slowly, knowing Janine would already be at her desk in the lobby.

Leaving the door open, he tiptoed down the hall and into the kitchen. He pulled the refrigerator door open and reached in for a bottle of Mountain Dew. As his hand closed around the bottle, someone spoke, "Zach?"

"Huh, what? Ouch …," Zach wailed as he jerked upright, slamming his head into the upper rack. Several bottles of water, knocked of balance, fell off the rack, thumped against the lower rack, and went spinning wildly across the kitchen floor.

"Zach, are you okay?" Janine cried out.

Zach turned around and saw Janine approaching from the corner of the kitchen where a small table was situated. "Oh, hi Janine. I was so careful being quiet, I didn't even see you," Zach chuckled, rubbing the top of his head.

"Zach what are you doing here so early?"

"Been here for over three hours. Trying to find an answer to the problems with the DOD microwave system."

"Have you found anything?"

"Nada, zip, zilch. Not a blasted thing so far."

"What are you going to do?"

"Nary a clue at this point. If I don't find something soon, we'll lose the contract for sure."

"Is your head okay?"

"Yeah, its fine. Well, back to work," Zach said, bending over to pick up the wayward bottles of water.

Zach put the water bottles back in the refrigerator and headed for the kitchen door. Halfway through the door, he turned back toward Janine, "Janine, just like before. Nobody except Angie is to know I'm here."

"Okay Zach."

Zach returned to his office and plopped down in his chair, the message "No Discernible Pattern or Groupings Found" glaring at him. It was as if the computer was mocking him. "Arrrgggh!" Zach snarled, slamming his fist down on the computer keyboard. Three keys from the left side of the keyboard flew off and bounced across the floor. "It hopeless! What's the use!" he snapped, swiping at the keyboard causing it to slide off the desk and bang against the side of the desk, swinging back and forth on its cord.

He reached over the desk and grabbed the keyboard and set it back on the desk in front of the monitor. He noticed three keys were missing, but he just didn't care. Leaning back in his chair, he rubbed his tired eyes. "Now what, Mister Microwave Expert?" he chided himself.

Realizing any further effort would be wasted, he shut down the computer, drained what was left of the Mountain Dew, and tossed the empty bottle in the trash can. Not certain what to do next, he sat there staring into space.

About to get up and go home, the phone on his desk rang. He glanced at the display and recognized Rachael's number. It rang twice and stopped. The line one button glowed solid, indicating Janine had picked it up at the reception desk. It glowed solid for several seconds and then started flashing. Immediately Zach's personal line started ringing.

"Yes, Janine. What is it?"

"Its Rachael. She sounds frantic. Something about Fred's computer. I don't understand what she's talking about. She's not making any sense"

"Okay. I'll take it."

Zach punched the button for line one, "Rachael. How can I help you?"

"Zach, I didn't mean to…. I don't know what to do. It's crazy. Oh, Zach I don't …"

"Calm down Rachael. Take it slow. Tell me what happened."

"I went into Fred's study. I wanted to straighten things up a little. I picked up a pile of papers and was going to put them in a drawer. I guess I bumped the mouse. Anyway, the computer woke up and there was a message on the monitor. Zach, someone dialed into Fred's computer the day he died."

"What? Who?"

"I don't know. I have no idea how to operate this thing. The little box thing on the screen says 'Inbound call received 1227, Wednesday, March 25'. And it has a little button that says 'OK'. Zach, what does it mean."

"Exactly what it says Rachael. Fred's computer received a call at the time in the little box."

"Was it someone from your company?"

"No. I don't think so."

"What should I do?"

"Just leave it alone. I'll come right over and have a look and see if I can determine who called the computer."

"Okay Zach. I'll leave it alone."

Zach pressed his finger on the release button then pressed the intercom button for the receptionist's desk.

"Yes Zach."

"Janine, can I borrow your car. I need to run over to Rachael's house and have a look at Fred's computer. There is something very suspicious."

"Sure Zach. Anytime."

"Thanks. I'll be right out."

He dropped the handset back in the cradle and turned to shut down his computer. As he turned, his eyes fell on the note Fred had left hidden in the microwave equipment. If the situation Zach was caught up in had been a cartoon, a little light bulb above his head would have lit up. Suddenly the little note made sense.

Not waiting to shut down the computer, he raced out of his office and ran down the hallway. Halfway to Janine's desk he hollered, "Janine, keys! Now!"

"Hurry!" Zach urged, standing halfway out the door.

Janine dug the keys out of her purse and threw them to Zach. He caught them one handed and rushed toward the elevator, anticipation and worry building in his mind.

CHAPTER FIFTY-SIX

Thursday, April 2 - 0856 Central Daylight Time
Rachael's House
East Forty-eighth Street,
Tulsa, Oklahoma

In Janine's borrowed car, Zach raced down Forty-eighth Street toward Rachael's house. He jammed on the brakes, sliding ten feet past her driveway on loose gravel in the gutter. He threw the car in park, rushed up to the door, and reached out to push the doorbell.

Rachael pulled the door open before Zach's finger made contact with the doorbell, "Zach, come in. I've been waiting."

"Came as quick as I could," Zach offered.

"Somebody called Fred's computer the day he died. Why would someone do that?" Rachael wailed, obviously distraught.

"Calm down Rachael," Zach urged. "I'll have a look and see if I can figure out who called and why."

"Fred's study is that door over there," Rachael said, pointing to her left. "Can I get you something while you work?"

"Coffee would be great," Zach answered, knowing it would be best to keep Rachael busy doing something.

Zach opened the door to Fred's study and walked over to his desk. Stacks of papers and books littered the surface of the desk, neatness never having been one of Fred's strong suits. Zach rearranged some of the papers and made two stacks of books to clear enough space for the note pad he pulled out of his laptop case. A shake of the mouse and the screen came back to life. There was the dialog box just as Rachael had described it. It revealed only that an inbound call had been received at 12:27 p.m. on Wednesday, March 25. Zach scribbled the time and date on the note pad and clicked the OK button. The dialog box disappeared. Nothing of interest presented itself on the screen. Just the standard desktop wallpaper with various icons arranged in vertical columns. Perhaps the communications software would provide a clue as to who had called.

Zach double-clicked the communications software icon and waited while the program started up. Once the program's main interface screen appeared, he opened the activity log and scrolled down to the last entry. "Hmmm, there it is," Zach mumbled, noting that the time and date matched what he had scribbled on the note pad. He double-clicked the last entry and the call detail screen opened up. The detail screen provided the originating phone number of the call, which Zach wrote on the note pad under the time and date. Below the time and date, a text box indicated a file named "jcyxxzt.zip" had been received. The cryptic file name provided no clues. Zach wrote the cryptic file name under the phone number and exited the communications software.

A quick scan through a phone number list Zach always carried revealed the originating phone number was a dedicated test number used at the radio observatory in New Mexico. Zach opened a command window and started a recursive search for the file name just as Rachael walked into the room with two steaming cups of coffee.

Zach reached out and took one of the cups from Rachael, "Thanks. Smells great." He blew across the steaming liquid and took a sip.

"Have you found anything yet?"

"Yes and no. The computer definitely received a call at the date and time you mentioned. So far, I found out the call came from a test line at the observatory in New Mexico. No one from MSI was in New Mexico except Fred. I have to assume it was Fred sending something home for safe keeping."

"Why would he do that?"

"Angie and I were on vacation. The call came in around noon. I'm guessing he couldn't reach anyone at the office, so he sent the file here as a backup."

"I guess ..."

"Huh," Zach sputtered, interrupting Rachael. Zach stared at the message returned by the search process - "No File(s) Found". He set the coffee cup down, verified he had the spelling of the file name correct, and repeated the search process.

"What is it Zach?"

"The file search I just ran said it could not find the file. Has anybody else been here?"

"No. Absolutely no one. Except you and Angie."

"Well then. The file has to be here."

"I don't get it," Zach snapped when the second search returned the same message. "The file's not here."

"How can that be? No one's been here and I haven't been in this room until today."

"I don't know. Maybe the file transfer failed. No, that can't be it. The communications software wouldn't have saved the log entry if that was the case. The file search runs through all subdirectories. Unless…"

Zach turned away from the computer and dug through the front pocket of his laptop case. His hand located the flash drive he always carried containing various utilities to analyze computer problems. Turning back to the computer, he stuck the flash drive into an empty USB port and launched a specialized search utility. After selecting options to only list hidden and system directories, he clicked the Start button. One by one, hidden and system folder names scrolled by as the utility searched through the computer's entire hard drive. Much too long a list to read from the screen, Zach clicked the print option from the menu bar.

Whirring and clunking sounds filled the room as the printer exited its sleep mode and began spitting out sheets of paper. Zach grabbed the three page listing from the printer's output tray and began scanning the list of directory names. Halfway down the second sheet, he eyes stopped on a folder named – "Fred's Stuff", identified as a hidden, system folder, which would have masked it from the earlier search. He grabbed a pen and circled the folder name.

Returning to the command window, he changed to the directory he had circled and requested a list of files in the directory. Only one file was listed, the file the comm software indicated had been received. Zach sent a copy of the archive file to his flash drive for safe keeping.

Every attempt to open the archive file failed. It was encrypted and password protected. Zach tried every password he could think of. Fred's birthday, his and Rachael's anniversary date, Rachael's birthday, their names backward, their address, anything and everything he could think of. Nothing worked.

Needing a break, he pushed himself away from the desk and walked into the kitchen. Rachael had tired of watching Zach working at the computer and had returned to the kitchen. Zach found her chopping vegetables for a soup she intended for lunch.

"Got any more of that coffee?" Zach asked.

"Yes, right over there," Rachael answered, pointing to the coffee pot on the counter behind her. "Help yourself. Did you have any success finding the file?"

Pouring a fresh cup of coffee, Zach looked over his shoulder and answered, "Yes I did. It was hidden, but I can't get it to open."

"Why not?"

"It's password protected. Do you know any of the passwords Fred used?"

"No. He never shared those with anybody. You know how Fred was about security."

"Yeah, I remember."

"Didn't you say Fred left you a note? Was there anything on it? A clue or some kind of key?"

Zach jerked upright, spilling his coffee. "That's it! Why didn't I think of that," he exclaimed' racing back to Fred's study without giving the spilled coffee a second thought.

In the password block he typed the letters: Ba-Ha-Ne-Di-Tinin, the Navajo word "Key", a password they had often used for passing secure messages when they served as members of SEAL Team Four.

When the archive file opened, it contained only three files: a text file, a large data file, and an analysis file. Zach extracted the three files onto the flash drive. First, he would have a look at the text file.

A look of total disbelief spread across his face as he read down through the file.

The more he read, the more astonished he became. Had Fred lost his mind? What he had written in the text file was unbelievable. Surely it could not be true.

Needing hard facts to verify what Fred had written, he opened the analysis file and lined it up alongside the text file, comparing it to Fred's explanation. What Zach saw left no doubt. Fred's analysis was spot on and absolutely correct. The frequency variations could be converted into a binary coded message. While random frequency variations might occasionally translate into letters, it was extremely unlikely they would translate into words. And they absolutely would never translate into the same series of words, repeating over and over.

The odd circuitry he found under the equipment building in Nevada suddenly made sense. Fred's conclusion that someone had tampered with the DOD microwave system to piggyback a message on it was true. To determine if the microwave system was still being tampered with, he launched a remote control utility and selected the Sanchez tower site in New Mexico because it was the only site that allowed remote access to the DOD microwave system.

Username and password entered and accepted, the monitor in front of Zach displayed a remote image of the control and analysis screen at the New Mexico site. Zach watched the frequency and power indicators. They were rock solid. No variations whatsoever. Everything seemed perfectly normal. For ten minutes he sat motionless, staring at the display. About to give up, a sudden dip in frequency caught his attention. The frequency began to vary from normal, first above normal, then below normal. He quickly activated the data capture feature of the remote control software and let it run for fifteen minutes.

Zach archived the data capture file and transferred it to Fred's computer. After creating a new analysis file using the newly transferred data and repeating the steps in Fred's analysis, he examined the resulting message.

"Oh my God!" Zach exclaimed.

The series of words the analysis produced were not the same as those in Fred's analysis. They were much, much worse.

Without hesitation, Zach remotely disabled the entire microwave system, attempting to prevent the message from being sent. Unknown to Zach, it was too late. A thousand miles away a bright flash lit up the darkness under the tower site west of Las Vegas. The hidden device self-destructed, leaving nothing but melted components and a severely charred circuit board, having already transmitted its stored message for the final time.

Zach printed the analysis results and saved the new analysis file. He removed the flash drive and stuffed it into his front pants pocket. Someone needed to see what he had just uncovered and soon, but who? Senator Mark Bradfield would know. Fishing his cell phone out of his pocket, he called his old friend.

"Senator Mark Bradfield's office," the receptionist drawled.

"Is he in? This is Zach Templeton."

"Zach. Haven't heard from you in a coon's age. How y'all doing?"

"Sorry Judy. I'm in a hurry. This is important."

"Okay Zach. I'll see if he'll take your call."

Soft music played while Zach waited.

"Zach, old boy. Judy said it was important."

"Yes sir it is. It's very important. I need a name. Someone you can trust. Absolutely."

"What's this about Zach?"

"I'd rather not say. It's way too sensitive."

"What kind of name?"

"Someone appropriate for a serious threat to national security."

"Zach, are you serious?"

"Mark, I don't have time to debate. I need a name now," Zach insisted, his voice rising in pitch and volume.

"Okay, okay. I would suggest Rear Admiral Charles Hadley."

"Thanks Mark. Please don't tell anyone why I called. My life may depend on it."

"Stay on the line. I'll have Judy pick up and give you the Admiral's cell number."

"Thanks again Mark," Zach replied as the senator put the line on hold, the soft music returning. A few seconds later Judy came back on the line and gave Zach the Admiral's personal cell number. He thanked her and ended the call before she had a chance to say anything. Immediately he flipped the phone back open and dialed the Admiral's number.

"Admiral Hadley. Who is this?"

"Admiral Hadley, this is Zach Templeton. I need your help. Someone's been ..."

"Mister Templeton, I've been meaning to contact you," Hadley interrupted.

"Huh. Contact me? What for?"

"I know someone has tried to murder you."

"How do you know that?"

"I have someone watching you. He stopped a woman in Tulsa and two really bad men in Nevada."

"What? Why are you watching me?"

"Mister Templeton, you have no idea what you are involved in. You are ..."

This time it was Zach who interrupted, "Admiral, I just found evidence of tampering on the DOD microwave system in Nevada. Someone has connected external circuitry to the transmitter section to allow a piggybacked message to be placed onto the system. You won't believe what I just decoded."

"Can you tell me what you found?"

"No sir. No way. Not over the phone. It's too sensitive. You need to see it. I have proof it's real."

"Way ahead of you Mister Templeton. How soon can you get to the general aviation terminal at Tulsa International Airport?"

"Maybe thirty minutes or so."

"I'll notify my pilot. When you get to the terminal look for a man named Kip Johnson. He will fly you to Washington."

"If I'm going out of town, I need to make a stop first."

"No, Mister Templeton. Absolutely no stops. Do not mention this conversation to anyone. You must leave for the airport immediately."

Zach was going to protest, but Hadley continued, "Anyone you tell about this will also be in grave danger. The well-dressed woman in the parking garage of your building was a contract assassin, likely hired by someone in the FBI."

"The FBI? After me? That's crazy."

"I'm dead serious. Someone is watching your every move."

"Let me think," Zach blurted out to give himself time to decide if he wanted to follow the Admiral's instructions. His mind was reeling. Events were spinning out of control. Events he did not understand. Events he could not control.

"Mister Templeton, are you still there?"

"Yes. I ah ... I ah ...," Zach stammered.

"Mister Templeton you must listen to me. If you do not, I may not be able to help you."

"Uh ... Okay. I'll leave for the airport right now."

"Good. The pilot will be waiting," Hadley said as he broke the connection.

Zach powered down Fred's computer and stuffed the data analysis that would prove his allegations into his laptop case. Grabbing the laptop case and slinging the strap over his shoulder, he headed for the kitchen to tell Rachael he was leaving.

"Rachael, gotta go," Zach announced, poking his head in the kitchen.

"But Zach, I was fixing lunch for us."

"Sorry Rachael, I discovered something. I have to go."

"Discovered what?"

"Please forget I said that. Can you pick up Janine at the office?"

"Sure, but what …."

"Tell Janine her car will be at the general aviation terminal at the airport. The keys to the company car are in the middle drawer of my desk. She can use it until I get back"

Rachael tried to ask Zach another question, but he had already raced out the front door and was sprinting toward Janine's car.

CHAPTER FIFTY-SEVEN

Thursday, April 2 – 1015 Central Daylight Time
General Aviation Terminal
Tulsa International Airport
Tulsa, Oklahoma

Zach pulled up to the parking lot entrance adjacent to the general aviation terminal on the northwest side of Tulsa International Airport. Leaning out the window, he grabbed the parking ticket and parked in the first empty space he found. He grabbed the laptop case from the rear seat and sprinted toward the terminal's entrance. Once inside the terminal, he stopped at the security checkpoint.

"I'm Zach Templeton, I was told to meet a private pilot named Kip Johnson at the general aviation terminal," Zach panted.

The security guard consulted a sheet of paper lying on the podium in front of him containing a list of pre-authorized individuals. "Ah, yes. Here's your name Mister Templeton. Put your bag on the conveyor belt and step through the magnetometer please. General aviation is down the hall to the left."

Zach followed the security guard's instructions. After passing through security, he turned left, hurried down the hallway, and entered the waiting area for general aviation. Scanning the waiting area, he spotted a man seated on the far side of the waiting area with epaulets on the shoulders of his shirt. Seeing Zach heading his way, the man got up and met Zach as he came around the last row of seats.

"Kip Johnson," the man said, sticking out his hand. "I assume you're Zach Templeton,"

Zach shook his hand and nodded. "Yes. I'm Zach Templeton. Admiral Hadley said I was to meet you here."

"Correct. The Admiral called me and told me to be expecting you. Come on. Let's go. The Admiral said it was important we get back to Washington ASAP."

Outside on the ramp, the pilot pointed to the Gulfstream, "White jet.

On your right. November-four-six-Mike-Lima. The one with the dark blue stripe down the fuselage."

Zach was impressed by the sleek, white jet sitting on the tarmac. A lot of activity surrounded the aircraft. A fuel truck had just finished refueling the aircraft and was pulling away. Someone from a catering service was busy restocking the galley while a maintenance man cleaned the cockpit windows.

Thirty minutes earlier, the Gulfstream had landed in Tulsa after its return from Ponta Delgada, Azores. Bill Morrison sat in the passenger cabin waiting. Norman Glover had instructed both the pilot and Bill to not mention him and then had moved to the cockpit. It would be best for him to remain out of sight and unknown to Zach for the time being.

The pilot climbed up the pull-down stairs and stepped into the Gulfstream's passenger cabin. Zach followed and stepped into the cabin. He was just beginning to admire the sumptuous interior of the Gulfstream when his eyes settled on the face of the man sitting in the first seat.

Recognition was instantaneous, even though Zach had not seen that face in many years.

"What? How?" Zach sputtered.

Bill Morrison got up from his seat, walked to the front of the cabin, and stood directly in front of Zach.

"Zach, long time," Bill offered, holding out his hand, fearful of what he expected would follow.

Anger instantly boiled up inside Zach. "You ... You are supposed to be dead!" Zach snarled, barely able to hold his anger in check.

"Zach, I'm sorry. I ..."

"Sorry! Sorry!" Zach shot back, grabbing Bill's shirt nearly pulling him off his feet and pinning him against a row of seats. "Sorry doesn't cut it pal. Not even close. How could you? How could you let all of us believe you were dead? You good-for-nothing, stinking scum bag. You rotten, lowlife weasel. I watched your wife sobbing at your memorial service."

The pilot was shocked by Zach's sudden outburst. He felt uncomfortable observing what was obviously a very private matter. Wanting to hear no more, he ducked into the cockpit and pulled the door shut.

"Zach stop," Bill protested, teetering on his tiptoes. "Hear me out please. Give me a chance to explain."

"Why should I?"

"Because you don't know the whole story."

Zach released Bill's shirt and stood there with his fists clenched, deciding to hear him out. "I'm listening. It better be good."

"After the shelling started we got separated. Remember? Whoever was directing the ambush dropped three mortar rounds right on our position.

Everyone was killed instantly. Except for me. I was unconscious. I have no idea how long. When I woke up, I was in a four by four cage. I never figured out who kept me prisoner. I heard voices but I could never make them out. I don't even know how long I was kept prisoner. Maybe weeks. Maybe months. I just don't know. Zach, somebody must have substituted a body and falsified the body count. Somebody didn't want anyone to know I survived the ambush. One night, a man in camouflage broke me out of that cell. He always kept his face hidden and to this day I still don't know who he was."

Bill stopped to take a drink of water. Zach stood motionless, waiting for him to continue.

"After four days in the jungle the man turned me over to three men dressed in civilian clothes and disappeared. The three men claimed they were CIA. They convinced me I could never go home. Not ever. Miriam still doesn't know I'm alive. The men said they knew who was behind the ambush but couldn't prove it. They said someone would kill Miriam if I so much as talked to her. I ..."

Zach interrupted, "She never did remarry. Do you know that?"

"Yes, I know. Someone passes me information occasionally. I still carry her picture. Every single day I look at it." Bill pulled out his wallet, flipped it open, and showed Zach a tattered photo of Miriam.

"Go on."

"Well, the three men got me to the coast and turned me over to someone else. After that, I was trained to be a deep undercover operative. For the last three years I have been involved in an undercover operation in the Czech Republic. I never did find out who was behind the ambush. That is until a few days ago."

"'What? Who?" Zach roared, he eyes burning with rage.

Bill motioned Zach toward the rear of the passenger cabin.

Checking the cabin to be certain they were alone, Bill tipped a large manila envelope up and slid several documents out onto one of the seats. Zach reached out and turned one of the photographs around to get a better look. A look of utter disbelief spread across his face as he stared at the photograph.

"No. That can't be." Zach gasped.

"Have a look at this," Bill said, handing him a document. "Read the handwritten message at the bottom."

The jaw muscles in Zach's face clenched even tighter. "I will rip the skin from his body and shove it down his throat!"

"Zach, this is way bigger than the ambush. Here, have a look at this," Bill added, handing Zach another document.

"Are you sure about this?"

"Absolutely Zach. No doubt whatsoever."

Bill took a step toward Zach with deep sadness in his eyes, "Zach, I'm so sorry. Please forgive me. I had no choice."

"Fred's dead," Zach declared. "Murdered. And someone has tried to kill me. Twice."

Before Bill could respond, Zach turned and started toward the cockpit, "We've got to get those materials to Washington as quickly as we can."

Zach was about to knock on the cockpit door when it opened and the pilot stepped out with a cell phone.

"Mister Templeton, Admiral Hadley says he needs to talk to you."

Zach took the cell phone and placed it to his ear. He listened for several seconds and then stepped off the aircraft. When he finished the conversation, he climbed back onto the aircraft.

"What a crock. Admiral Hadley must think I'm some kind of idiot. Stupidest thing I ever heard. Its utter nonsense. I'll not have any part of it."

Zach turned and looked at the pilot. "I need to make another phone call," Zach said as he stepped off the aircraft a second time. This time he walked away from the aircraft and stood by the terminal. The pilot watched Zach, animated and obviously very angry, as he talked on the cell phone. Zach slammed the cell phone shut and headed back to the aircraft.

"Let's get to Washington and get this ridiculous nonsense over with," Zach barked, tossing the cell phone to the pilot.

"Yes sir," the pilot responded, as he ducked back into the cockpit and pulled the door shut.

"What was that all about?" Norman Glover whispered.

"I have no idea. The Admiral obviously shoved a burr under that boy's saddle. A really big one."

Kip settled down into the pilot's seat and buckled himself in. He slipped the headset on, stuffed the earpiece in his ear, and adjusted the boom mike so it was directly in front of his lower lip. Kip started the aircraft's engines. Once the engines were up to speed and he had checked all the gauges, he keyed the transmit button on the control yoke.

"Tulsa Ground, November-four-six-Mike-Lima request taxi clearance."

"November-four-six-Mike-Lima, Taxi via taxiway Alpha, hold short of Charlie."

"Taxi via taxiway Alpha, hold short of Charlie roger."

Kip eased the throttles forward and the Gulfstream began to roll. He steered the aircraft away from the parking ramp and turned right onto taxiway Alpha. The aircraft rolled past the commercial gates as it headed toward the south end of the airport, stopping at the intersection with taxiway Charlie.

"November-four-six-Mike-Lima, Contact Tulsa Tower, one-one-niner-point-one."

"Contact Tulsa Tower, one-one-niner-point-one roger."

"Tulsa Tower, November-four-six-Mike-Lima request take off clearance."

"November-four-six-Mike-Lima, Runway Three Six Right, hold short Runway Three Six Right, inbound traffic on two and one-half mile final, be ready for immediate."

"Hold short Runway Three Six Right, inbound traffic on two and one-half mile final, be ready for immediate roger."

Bill and Zach watched out the windows as a large Airbus A320 completed its final approach and landed on the runway with a loud screech and a cloud of blue smoke from the landing gear.

"November-four-six-Mike-Lima, clear for takeoff. Fly runway heading. Climb and maintain two thousand."

Kip released the brakes, eased the throttles forward, and steered the Gulfstream onto Run-way Three Six Right. Lined up on the centerline, he set the brake, pushed the throttles all the way forward, and waited for the engines to spool up. At seventy percent power, he released the brakes and the Gulfstream gained speed as it raced down the runway.

When the Gulfstream reached V2, safe take-off speed, the rear wheels lifted from the run-way, and the jet began its climb-out to the north.

At two thousand feet, Kip thumbed the transmit button and called departure control, "Tulsa Departure, Gulfstream November-four-six-Mike-Lima, request VFR clearance for flight path to Washington DC."

"November-four-six-Mike-Lima, climb to flight level three-three, turn right heading zero-eight-five. Contact Kansas City Center enroute."

"November-four-six-Mike-Lima roger."

Twelve minutes later, Kip thumbed the passenger cabin intercom button, "Gentleman, you may safely move about the cabin now. We should arrive in Washington D.C. in approximately two hours and twenty-five minutes."

Releasing their seatbelts, Zach and Bill climbed out of their seats and stretched. They stepped over to the mini-bar hidden in the credenza. Bill poured himself a bourbon and coke and Zach opened a diet coke. With drinks in hand, they moved to the seats in the rear of the cabin and sat across from each other. First came small talk and more apologies from Bill, then they began the process of reviving a long-lost friendship.

CHAPTER FIFTY-EIGHT

Thursday, April 2 – 1150 Eastern Daylight Time
JCS Conference Room ("The Tank")
Pentagon – Corridor 9, E Ring
Washington, D.C.

Nervous conversations filled the Joint Chiefs of Staff conference room. All the Joint Chiefs were nervous and edgy. A serious threat had to have developed to precipitate a second emergency meeting of the Joint Chiefs in just sixteen hours.

As usual, Fleet Admiral Douglas Bennington, Chairman of the Joint Chiefs, was the last member to arrive. As he entered, he signaled the aides to leave the room. Holding a single sheet of paper in his hand, he stood at the head of the table and waited for everyone to end their conversations.

"Gentlemen, our intelligence department has intercepted and decoded a very ominous message. If this message is legitimate, and our best analysts believe it is, an extremely serious threat to our national security now exists. The message, between too very high ranking officials, indicates Russia is planning a preemptive strike against the United States. The timing of that attack is not completely clear at this time. However, recent Russian troop movements and repositioning of Russian Naval assets would seem to suggest a timeframe of twenty-four to forty-eight hours. "

Admiral Bennington stopped and waited for the sudden outburst from several of the Joint Chiefs to subside.

Admiral Bennington glared directly at Brigadier General McCune, the most impatient and outspoken member of the Joint Chiefs, and continued, "If I may finish General. We know a member of the old communist hardliners, one General Anatoly Kutepov, a Russian Army division commander with strong ties to Chechen separatists, has been pushing for an overthrow of the current ruling party for a long time. Our intelligence analysts believe this would be the exact catalyst he would need to eliminate what little resistance remains. Intelligence on General Kutepov reveals he has long supported a preemptive strike against the US. Even more alarming, he enthusiastically advocates the use of nuclear weapons."

General McCune spoke up immediately, "Admiral, this can't be true. The Russians can't be that stupid."

Vice Admiral Beckwith stood up and interrupted, "Admiral Bennington, if I may?"

"Go ahead Admiral Beckwith," Bennington agreed, taking his seat.

"Our intelligence department has been watching developments amongst General Kutepov's followers for months. Over the past several years they have become increasingly radical. There is clear evidence they are planning a takeover of the Kremlin. Be assured gentlemen, General Kutepov will use nuclear weapons to get what he wants. We ..."

"But Admiral Beckwith," General William Danvers, US Army Chief of Staff, interrupted. "It is just one intercepted message."

"Gentlemen, we pulled that message off our own communication system. Somehow, someone has managed to infiltrate a secure communications system. We must then also assume they would have the ability to disable that system." Beckwith turned and stared directly at General Danvers, seated on his left, " If that is the case General, we would be totally blind. How long do you think we would last then General?"

"Admiral Beckwith, I will not ..."

"Gentlemen, Gentlemen," Bennington shouted. "This is not the time to argue. Considering this message, the tampering of our communications systems, the intelligence we currently have on General Kutepov, and let's not forget the unprovoked attack on *Providence* a few days ago. I believe we have more than sufficient cause to increase our threat level. General Beckwith what say you?"

"What we have uncovered represents an extremely serious threat. I suggest we go to DEFCON TWO."

General Danvers stood up, "DEFCON TWO? You can't be serious Admiral. Do you want to start a war?"

Beckwith had to work hard to suppress a smile. Yes, he really did want to start a war, but he could not reveal that to the men in the conference room.

"Gentlemen, this threat is real. If we do not put our military forces on alert immediately, we will not be able to respond quickly enough."

Beckwith listened as the Joint Chiefs discussed the appropriate readiness level. General Danvers was the last Joint Chief to finally agree DEFCON TWO was the proper response.

Bennington stood and addressed the group individually, "General Radford, I want B-52s in the air ASAP with appropriate targeting packages. Generals McCune and Danvers, put all ground forces in Europe on heightened alert. I will order our Naval surface fleet to high alert and I will order our SSBNs to Battle Station – Missile."

Bennington walked to the door and held it open, "Gentlemen, get to your offices and begin making notifications now."

* * *

Thursday, April 2 – 1352 Eastern Daylight Time
Gulfstream G550
33,000 Feet above Virginia

Kip Johnson, piloting the Gulfstream G550 on a heading of zero-eight-four, keyed the passenger cabin intercom, "I'm sorry gentlemen but there is going to be a thirty minute or so delay due to weather in the Washington, D.C., area. We are currently in a holding pattern over Harrisonburg, Virginia. Once Air Traffic Control releases us, we will start our descent into the Washington D.C., area and should be on the ground twenty minutes after that."

Only Zach heard the pilot's announcement, looking up from the magazine he was browsing disinterestedly. Bill was snoring softly, sound asleep, exhausted by his harrowing adventure at sea and the long flight back from the Azores. Used to weather delays aboard aircraft, Zach shrugged and went back to his magazine.

Twenty minutes later the radio in the cockpit crackled to life, "November-four-six-Mike-Lima, weather around Washington has cleared. Turn right, heading zero-niner-one, descend and maintain flight level two three."

"Turn right, heading zero-niner-one, descend and maintain flight level two three roger."

Kip thumbed the intercom button, "Gentlemen, return to your seats and fasten your seatbelts. We have been cleared into the Washington area and are beginning our descent."

Zach climbed out of his seat, walked back to the rear of the cabin, and punched Bill on the arm. "Hey Bill, we're starting our descent. Pilot says to buckle up."

Just as promised, twenty minutes later, Kip had the Gulfstream lined up for a visual approach to Washington National Airport. The aircraft was flying just west of the Potomac River on a heading of zero-zero-four, right down the centerline of Runway One. As the Gulfstream approached the threshold of the runway, Kip eased back on the throttles to reduce the aircraft's speed. When the end of the runway and the horizon line converged, Kip pulled back on the control yoke and allowed the aircraft to settle smoothly onto the runway. He braked the aircraft and turned left off of Runway One onto taxiway N1. At the intersection with taxiway K, he turned left again, following taxiway K all the way to the south end of the airport. An airport ramp service worker guided the aircraft to an open spot on the general aviation parking ramp. Kip set the parking brake and shut down the engines.

"Stay here," he instructed Norman Glover, opening the cockpit door and stepping into the passenger cabin.

Zach was already out of his seat and standing at the front of the passenger cabin, waiting for the pilot to open the exit door.

"Welcome to Washington National gentlemen," Kip greeted, opening the door and extending the stairs.

Zach exited the Gulfstream and stood on the tarmac. Bill followed close behind and came up beside Zach. "Zach, let's go get …."

Zach held up his hand to silence Bill, "I need to make another phone call." Zach walked over beside the Gulfstream's exit door and leaned his head inside. "Hey Kip, I need to make another phone call. Toss me your cell phone please."

"Stay here," Zach instructed, catching the cell phone Kip tossed his way in one hand and heading for the terminal. Once inside the terminal, Zach found a quiet, isolated spot and called Admiral Hadley. They talked for several minutes. Zach closed the cell phone the pilot had tossed him, fished out his own cell phone, and called a different number.

Twice Zach stopped talking when people walked by. Zach had to swallow hard to control his anger. He slammed the phone shut and stormed off toward the Gulfstream.

When Zach got back to the Gulfstream, Kip was standing on the tarmac beside Bill. "Stupid moron," Zach sneered. "Admiral Hadley promised a car would be waiting. Is it ready?"

"Yes it's ready," Kip answered. "Follow me."

Kip led Zach and Bill out through the terminal building to an adjacent parking lot. They walked part way down the fourth row of cars to a light brown Cadillac. "The brown one," Kip said, pointing at the Cadillac. He tossed Zach a set of keys.

Zach unlocked the car and tossed his laptop case in the back seat. "Is the stuff I asked for here?"

"Yes. It's locked in the trunk. In the spare tire compartment."

Punching the trunk lid release on the key fob, Zach leaned sideways to avoid the trunk lid as it opened and poked his head into the trunk. Reaching his hand under the carpet pad, he felt around the spare tire compartment for the object he was looking for. He withdrew a 9mm automatic and pulled the slide back to load a round into the chamber. After thumbing the safety on, he stuffed the automatic under his jacket and climbed into the car.

"Come on Bill, let's go," Zach shouted through the closed windows.

Climbing into the passenger seat, Bill asked, "Where are we headed?"

"Not here. Wait til we're out of the parking lot."

Zach started the engine, backed out of the parking space, and sped off toward the airport exit and their next destination.

Once they were on the airport perimeter road and approaching the exit, Zach hollered at Bill, "In my laptop case. Side pocket. Grab the GPS unit. Type in Ben Brenman Park and feed me the directions."

Back in the airport, Kip walked through the general aviation terminal and met Norman Glover standing beside the Gulfstream.

"Where are they headed?" Norman asked.

I don't have a clue."

"You must have some idea."

"No. Mister Templeton didn't say a word. They just jumped in the car and roared out of the parking lot."

Norman grabbed another set of keys from Kip and headed for the parking lot. With nothing else to do until Admiral Hadley requested him to fly someone somewhere, Kip headed for the snack bar to get something to eat. He had not eaten for over twenty-four hours and he was starving.

Zach and Bill exited the airport and merged onto the George Washington Memorial Highway and then onto southbound Interstate 395. As they drove toward their destination, Zach shared with Bill all the details of his two phone calls at the airport. Bill's eyes grew wider and wider with each new revelation. At the end of the revelations, Zach looked at Bill and said, "Well?"

Bill gave him a very short and succinct answer.

"I'm in!"

CHAPTER FIFTY-NINE

Thursday, April 2 – 1530 Eastern Daylight Time
Ben Brenman Park
Alexandria, Virginia

Slowly Zach drove south on Somerville Street to the second entrance into Ben Brenman Park in Alexandra, Virginia, and turned left onto Brenman Park Drive. He drove between the north ball diamond and the lake, continuing to the end of the street where it ended in two parking lots. Pulling the Cadillac into the first parking space of the south lot, he parked adjacent to a large pavilion.

Bill and Zach climbed out of the Cadillac and walked over to the pavilion, selecting seats that would not be visible from the street.

Completely out of sight, flying high above them, a helicopter had watched the Cadillac pull into the park and come to a stop at the pavilion. The pilot radioed the Cadillac's final destination to someone on the ground, turned and flew west, disappearing from sight.

Pulling the collar of his jacket up around his neck, Zach shivered as a steady, cold wind whipped around the walls of the pavilion, scattering little swirls of dust along the rows of metal benches. Even though Spring was only three weeks away, dark gray clouds threatened snow from a late winter storm.

The sound of tires crunching on gravel echoed through the pavilion. Zach stiffened and waited. A black Chevy Tahoe slowly pulled around the pavilion and parked beside the Cadillac. A single individual dressed in a long black overcoat climbed out of the Tahoe and walked briskly toward the pavilion.

"I assume you're Mister Templeton," the man announced.

"Yes, I'm Zach Templeton."

"I can't say I'm pleased with the way you threatened me. And I really don't like the demands you're making."

"Well, that makes us even," Zach snapped back at the man. "I don't like that my company is being destroyed. And I really don't like it that someone tried to kill me. Twice!"

The man stood silent, assessing the situation. He glanced at Bill but did not recognize his face.

Zach continued, "I know about the sabotage to the DOD microwave system. I know about the piggybacked signals. I decoded them and I know what's going on, you traitorous pig."

"What! You ... You ... You can't talk to me like that."

"I can. And I just did!" Zach shouted in the man's face.

"I know something else. Does SEAL Team Four ring any bells?"

"I ...."

"Just shut up and listen. We know you were responsible for the ambush in the jungle and we know who put you up to it. You are either going to get the needle or you are going to prison for a long time. A very long time."

"You can't threaten me," the man shrieked, the veins bulging in his neck. "Do you know who I am?"

"It doesn't matter who you are. You are guilty and you are going to pay."

"That's a lie," the man blustered. "You can't prove any of that. Nobody will believe you."

"Oh yeah," Zach bellowed. "Bill, bring that photo over here."

Walking over to where Zach and the man were standing, Bill pulled an eight by ten photo from a manila envelope and held it out for the man to see.

"The man who took that photo has verified it was you," Zach declared. "How about the other face in the photo? Recognize him?"

The man shook his head.

"Come on. Don't be stupid. Of course you know him. You and he served together. You both got a hero's welcome when you returned home."

"One photo doesn't prove anything," the man protested.

"Oh, there's more," Zach asserted. "We have documents detailing your involvement and I have hardcopy proof of the microwave tampering. You won't be able to weasel your way out of this."

The man started to protest again but Zach silenced him and continued. "My company has been destroyed along with my credibility. I demand to be compensated. I want half a million dollars sent to an offshore account in Grand Cayman. And I want another half million dollars sent to an account for Mister Morrison. We get the money and the photos and the documents go away. All of it. Gone."

"That's preposterous. I don't have that kind of money."

"Don't give me that. If you're half as important as you think you are, it should not be a problem. The money or prison. You choose."

Zach stood there waiting for the man to respond.

"Fine," Zach said, turning and walking toward the Cadillac.

The three men had been so busy arguing and watching each other they had not noticed Norman Glover sneak around behind the west side of the pavilion.

After leaving the airport, Norman had called Admiral Hadley who scrambled a helicopter to track the Cadillac. Following the Cadillac had been as easy as child's play because a tracking device had been placed inside the trunk before it was parked at the airport parking lot. The helicopter pilot had kept Norman informed of the Cadillac's position and its final destination at Brenman Park.

Entering the park five minutes after the black Tahoe, Norman had parked at the far end of the north parking lot and had crept up behind the pavilion. He had watched and listened to the entire exchange between the three men. Norman was stunned, hardly able to believe what he had heard. Zach Templeton was a traitor, attempting to blackmail the other man. He would have never believed it had he not heard it with his own ears.

After reaching the Cadillac, Zach put his hand on the door handle and started to open the door when the man, rushing across the parking lot, called out.

"Wait, Wait," the man hollered as he ran over between the Cadillac and the Tahoe.

When the encounter moved to the parked vehicles, Norman quickly moved to a hiding place behind a large pine tree not more than eight feet from the two parked cars.

Standing beside Zach, Bill watched and listened as they argued back and forth about the amount of money. Then they argued about the timing and the method of payment. Finally, reaching an agreement suitable to both of them, Zach made the fatal mistake of looking over at Bill, momentarily taking his eyes off the man. The man jerked his hand out of the pocket of his overcoat. Clutched in his hand was a large, black automatic.

"Turn around Mister Templeton. Very slowly," the man warned, patting Zach's jacket and feeling the lump in the small of his back. Slipping his hand under the jacket, he removed Zach's 9mm automatic and laid it on the Tahoe's hood. He reached in his back pocket and tossed a set of handcuffs to Bill.

"Open the door, put your arms around the door post and put those on. As for you Mister Templeton, I think I will just kill you right here. Save the taxpayers some money. And I think I'll kill your stupid friend too. Enjoy the afterlife Mister Templeton."

"Not so fast Director Porter," Norman Glover threatened, slipping up behind the man and placing his gun against the man's head. Even if Zach Templeton was a traitor, he would not allow him to be murdered.

"Huh, I ...."

"Flinch. Please." Norman snarled, hoping for an excuse to put a bullet into the brain of the traitorous scum standing in front of him.

Porter stood perfectly still as Zach turned around and ripped the gun from his hand. About to say something to the man, Zach turned to see who had saved his life. His arms went slack and dropped to his side. The gun slipped from his fingers and clattered on the pavement.

His mouth hung open, moving, words refusing to come. He felt paralyzed. Images from the past swirled in his mind: ghosts, scraped knees, a frightened little boy.

"How …, how …," Zach stammered. "It can't be."

"I'm truly sorry Zachman," Norman said.

"It's true! It's not a trick!" Zach's subconscious screamed at him. Nobody had called him by that name in a very, very long time. Not in over forty years.

Standing right in front of him was his father, James Templeton.

More images from the past flooded into his mind: the disbelief and horror when the police knocked on his door, the months of waiting and not knowing, the grief and tears at the memorial service. Anger replaced shock. Zach needed answers.

"How could you?" Zach croaked. "I want …"

"Not here. Not now," James Templeton interrupted. "There are far more important issues that must be settled first."

"No. I want answers now!" Zach protested.

"Not now!" James Templeton shouted. "You will get your answers. I promise. Just not now. End of discussion!"

James Templeton grabbed Porter's arm and swung him around, looking him directly in the eyes and placing the barrel of a gun directly on the tip of his nose. "You will go back to your office and you will do exactly as Mister Templeton asked. If the money is not in the Grand Cayman accounts within two hours, we will expose you. If you are lucky, you will spend the rest of your life in a federal prison. If not, you will be executed."

The three men watched as Porter scrambled into the Tahoe like a scared rabbit and roared out of the parking lot.

Turning toward his father, Zach opened his mouth and started to say something. But before he could say anything, his father repeated his earlier injunction. "Still not the time Zach." James Templeton glanced at his watch and pointed at the Cadillac. "Get in. Zach, you drive. We've got to be somewhere in no less than twenty-five minutes."

Climbing into the driver's seat, Zach did as instructed. When his father said end of discussion, especially in the tone he had used, it meant just that. Further attempts at conversation would be wasted. Answers, something he desperately needed, would have to wait for another time. Zach backed the Cadillac out of the parking space and headed for the park exit.

As Zach steered the Cadillac onto the entrance for northbound

Interstate 395, James Templeton pulled a cell phone out of his pocket, punched in a number, and waited for someone to answer.

"Yes."

"Twenty minutes," James responded. He ended the call and instructed Zach to take exit 8C.

CHAPTER SIXTY

Thursday, April 2 - 1642 Eastern Daylight Time
Pentagon - Corridor 9, E Ring
Washington, DC

Six men sat in a small anteroom adjacent to "The Tank", the Joint Chiefs Conference Room.

Zach Templeton, James Templeton, and Bill Morrison sat on one side of a large, antique mahogany table. On the other side of the table sat Fleet Admiral Douglass Bennington, Rear Admiral Charles Hadley, and National Security Advisor Matthew Tyler.

Hadley was the first to speak. "Gentlemen, we are here to discuss a deadly serious matter. As you know, just five hours ago the Joint Chiefs, with the President's concurrence, agreed to raise our military forces' readiness level to DEFCON2. The Air Force Global Strike Command scrambled their long range strategic bombers, including B-52 and B-2 bombers, with updated targeting packages and authority to deliver their bombs as part of operation Brushfire. They are currently in the air and are on their way toward their assigned targets."

Hadley took a sip of water and continued, "Our military ground forces in Europe have been put on high alert and both COMSUBPAC and COMSUBLANT have ordered their SSBN submarines to assume Battle Stations – Missile. As I said, the bombers are enroute and the SSBNs are weapons free. Gentlemen we are teetering on the brink of World War Three. Some new information has just come to light. First, let me introduce Mr. Bill Morrison. He has just completed an arduous escape from Europe with some very enlightening information. Mister Morrison, you may begin."

Bill rose and walked to the front of the table. Before revealing any of the information inside the manila envelope lying on the table in front of him, he briefly explained how the materials had come into his possession and the risk he had taken to return them to the United States. Not leaving out a single detail, he told them about his friend Leuka's murder, the attempt on his life by Leuka's nephew, and finally, the attempt to kill him on the train to Gdansk. The details were necessary to establish the authenticity of the materials and the lengths someone would go to prevent them from being seen.

"There is a traitor in your midst," Bill declared as he slid the material onto the table and spread the photos and documents out for everyone to see. He selected one particular photo and pushed it in front of Admiral Bennington. "Do you recognize those two faces Admiral?"

"You bet I do," Bennington exclaimed, his lips tightening into a thin line.

"Here, read the note at the bottom right," Bill added, shoving another document in front of the Admiral.

"Holy ...," Bennington gasped, the final word dying in his throat.

Before Bennington could disagree, Bill continued, "Yes Admiral. I know it's hard to believe, but it is absolutely true. There is no doubt whatsoever."

Bennington slid the photo to Rear Admiral Hadley on his left. After a quick scan of the photo, he passed it on to Matthew Tyler. The document with the hand-written note followed, having the same effect on Hadley and Tyler as it had on Bennington. After gathering up the photos and the other documents and sliding them back into the manila envelope, Bill handed the envelope to Hadley. "I believe you will want to secure these Admiral. They must not be lost because there are no other copies."

As Bill returned to his seat, Hadley picked up a telephone and buzzed the aide sitting outside the door.

"Yes sir," Captain Aaron Carpenter replied, sticking his head into the room.

Hadley motioned him over to the table. Handing him the envelope, he instructed the captain, "Take this envelope. Make copies of the contents. Seal the originals in a Top-Secret security pouch and lock them in my safe. Hold the copies at the desk until we are finished. And Captain, absolutely no one is to touch these."

"Yes sir. Right away sir," Carpenter snapped as he hurried out the door.

Zach's father punched him on the arm. It was Zach's turn to share his discovery. As he stood and took a spot at the head of the table, he addressed Bennington "It would be easier if I display this on the screen Admiral."

Swinging around in his chair, Bennington opened the top draw of a credenza sitting against the wall. He grabbed a remote for the video projector and slid the remote down the table toward Zach. "Laptop is on the table behind you."

Zach picked up the laptop and transferred it to the table. A jiggle of the wireless mouse awakened the laptop from its sleep mode. He dug the flash drive out of his front pants pocket and stuffed it into an empty USB port. Selecting the appropriate application, he opened the analysis file, and paged down to where the frequency variations began. With the frequency variation on one side of the screen and the decoded message on the other, he explained the methods he had used to decode the message.

Everyone in the room agreed the frequency variations could not be accidental. With that concurrence agreed to and spoken out loud, he concluded his presentation with one final screen. "Here is the entire message displayed on the screen by itself. As soon as I decoded the full message, I disabled the entire microwave system. However, I suspect the message may have already completed. If that's true, disabling the system will have had no effect."

"Good God man!" Bennington bellowed. "We've got to turn those bombers around now! We will reduce the threat level to DEFCON3 for now. Mr. Tyler do you concur?"

"Absolutely Admiral. Let me confirm with the President." Tyler dialed the direct line to the President's desk. After a quick conversation he handed the phone to Bennington. Bennington listened for a few moments then hung up and announced. "The President concurs."

Bennington turned toward the other side of the table and spoke, "Admiral Hadley you call COMSUBPAC and COMSUBLANT and have them issue a Launch Termination Order immediately! I will call the Air Force Global Strike Command and have them recall the bombers and return them to base."

Immediately, there were hurried phone calls to the aforementioned military commands to pull the United States back from the brink of war. Zach, James, and Bill sat silently listening to the frantic phone calls.

Bennington leaned back in his chair and wiped his face with a handkerchief. "Mister Templeton, that message is the exact same one delivered to the Joint Chiefs of Staff meeting five hours ago. Mister Tyler what was the source of the earlier message?"

"Admiral Beckwith told me he personally retrieved the message from the Defense Intelligence Agency Communications Center."

"Mister Templeton, is there the slightest possibility that message could have made its way to the DIA Comm Center?"

"Absolutely not Admiral. That is an encrypted system. It's simply not possible."

As Bennington reached for the telephone, James Templeton spoke up, "Wait Admiral. There is something else you need to hear." Templeton pulled a small voice recorder out of his pocket and set it on the table. As he pushed the play button he said, "Get a load of this."

The entire conversation, every incriminating detail, between Zach Templeton and Director Frank Porter had been recorded, using a highly sensitive boom microphone. The other meeting attendees, those that had not witnessed the scene at Ben Brenman Park, sat and shook their heads in disbelief.

Bennington reached for the telephone and punched in the number for the Pentagon Police, who had exclusive jurisdiction within the Pentagon Reservation.

"Pentagon Police, Sergeant Wilbur Solis."

"Sergeant Solis, this is Fleet Admiral Bennington. I need a detail at my office ASAP."

"Yes sir. On our way," Solis responded.

"Admiral Hadley, I assume you would like to take care of our friend, Director Porter."

"Yes sir!" Hadley exclaimed. "It will be my pleasure."

"Before you leave Admiral Hadley," Zach interjected. "I want everyone here to know that none of this would have been possible were it not for Fred Hargrove. Fred, a former member of SEAL Team Four, was the senior technician for my company. He is the one who first discovered the interference and determined what it was. And it cost him his life. He was murdered by the stinking scum behind this evil scheme. I would like to ask that something special be done for his widow, Rachael."

"You can count on it," Bennington affirmed. "I will see to it personally."

There was a knock on the door. Bennington got out of his chair and opened the door. Standing just outside the door, was Sergeant Solis and three uniformed officers.

"Let's go Sergeant. We have a traitor to arrest," Bennington snarled, starting out the door. He hesitated, looking back at Zach. "Would you like to join us?"

"You bet I would," Zach answered. As he headed out the door to catch up with Bennington and the Pentagon police, he tapped Hadley on the arm. "Don't forget that other little thing we talked about."

"Already in progress Zach."

It was only a short walk down the corridor to the Navy Executive offices. With Sergeant Solis close on his heels, Bennington barged into the outer office of the Director, Joint Staff and walked across the office to the door to Admiral Beckwith's private office. The Admiral's personal assistant rose to block entry to the Director's private office, but shrank back immediately when she realized who was standing in front of her.

Full of indignation, Beckwith jumped up from his desk to complain to whomever dared interrupt his meeting unannounced.

Bennington looked at the two men seated in front of the desk and yelled, "GET OUT. NOW!"

Scrambling out of their chairs and grabbing their briefcases, the two men literally ran out of the office. Bennington kicked one of the overturned chairs out of the way and yelled out to Sergeant Solis, "Arrest that stinking traitor!"

As the Pentagon Police grabbed Beckwith and put him in handcuffs, he thought about protesting, until he saw Zach Templeton's face in the doorway. He knew it was over. His only reason for living vanished in an instant. Never would he feel the sweet revenge he had dreamed about for so long. Instead, he would spend the rest of his life in prison. But it really did not matter. Whatever the punishment was, it paled in comparison to the blinding pain he had lived with every day.

"Get that slimy traitor out of here," Bennington sneered. On his way out of Beckwith's office, Bennington stopped and laid a hand on Zach's shoulder. "Mister Templeton, the country is deeply in your debt. Without your help, we would likely have been at war within a few hours. I promise you there will be something very special for Mrs. Hargrove. I will make certain you are given the details."

Nine miles away at the office of the Deputy Director of National Clandestine Services at CIA headquarters in Langley, Virginia, Admiral Hadley and a contingent of Federal Police kicked in the office door. It was obvious the Director had already come and gone, clearing out anything of value. The wall safe stood open, stripped of everything that had been inside. Papers were strewn about the floor. Desk drawers hung open. Whoever had been here had no intention of ever returning.

Hurried calls were made to alert all local and federal law enforcement agencies and to put out APBs for Deputy Director Frank Porter. Unfortunately, all efforts to locate and apprehend Porter would prove to be unproductive because he was long gone.

While the meeting at the Pentagon had taken place, Porter had entered his office and had taken only a few minutes to gather the things he needed. He was already sitting on a private plane that would take him to an intermediate destination. The fake passport and credit cards in his pocket identified him as Anthony Sterling. When he arrived at the intermediate destination, he would connect with a commercial flight to the country where he had already transferred his secret account. He would never be able to go home again, but he did not care. He would live a life of luxury surrounded by money and all the things it could buy. Or would he?

CHAPTER SIXTY-ONE

Thursday, April 2 – 1825 Eastern Daylight Time
Washington National Airport
General Aviation Terminal
Washington, DC

Tipping up his coffee cup, Bill Morrison drained the last swallow of the dark, bitter liquid just as the pilot's cell phone rang. Pilot Kip Johnson answered his cell phone, listened for a few seconds, then handed it over to Bill.

"Now?" Bill protested. He listened for a few more seconds. "Okay sir. Will do," he groaned as he ended the call and handed the phone back to the pilot. Pushing his chair back, Bill stood up and said, "Sorry. Gotta go. They didn't give me a choice. I have to attend a debriefing."

Rounding the table to where Zach was seated, Bill stuck out his hand. Zach rose, took his hand, and pulled Bill toward him. The two men embraced and slapped each other's backs, promising each other they would get together soon as parting friends always do.

"We have a surprise for you," Zach added as they released each other. Kip was standing by the entrance to the coffee shop. He nodded to someone out of sight. Bill's eyes widened and immediately filled with tears when he saw Miriam, his wife, walk into view. They raced into each other's arms and hugged and cried, and hugged and cried. Many eyes in the coffee shop observed the tearful reunion, having no idea of the years or horrible events that had separated Bill and Miriam.

After giving them several minutes, Kip tapped Bill's shoulder. "Admiral Hadley has a car waiting out front. Miriam can ride in the car with you to the debriefing. The Admiral promised to make it as short as possible. After the debrief, he has arranged a suite for an entire week at the Miami Beach Resort all expenses paid. I'll show you to the car. The Admiral is waiting."

Kip escorted Bill and Miriam through the general aviation terminal to a long, black limo waiting outside at the curb. "It was a pleasure and an honor to meet you. If you ever need a lift, call me," Kip smiled, giving Bill a wink.

Zach and James Templeton were left sitting alone in the coffee shop after Kip escorted Bill and Miriam to the limo. Both of them were staring at the table, avoiding the subject neither of them wanted to bring up. It was Zach who finally summoned the courage to ask the question. "Will I ever see you again?"

With a sad look in his eyes, James shook his head and answered, "Probably not. It would be far too dangerous. For all of us. You, me, your mother. And Angie. As you might expect, I cannot tell you why your mother and I had to disappear. You will just have to accept that it was absolutely necessary."

"It was you in the parking garage wasn't it?" Zach asked.

"Yes."

"And in the desert in Nevada?"

"Yes. That was me too."

"Great shooting. Two dead-center, kill shots from over one hundred yards and two seconds apart."

"Some skills left over from a former life," James laughed.

Zach had more questions but James refused to answer them, knowing it would only create more confusion for Zach. Silence again filled the air as they sat staring at the table, each knowing a difficult goodbye was coming.

Kip walked back into the coffee shop and stopped beside James. Leaning over, he whispered something into James' ear. He straightened up and left the coffee shop, giving father and son some space.

"Follow me," James said as he got up and grabbed Zach's arm, directing him toward an isolated spot in the terminal's passenger waiting area. He put both hands on Zach's shoulders. "Zach, I can't begin to tell you how proud I am of you. You have always done the right thing no matter what the cost. You have likely stopped a war and have saved countless thousands of lives. After all these years, when I look at you, I still see my little Zachman."

Tears filled Zach's eyes as he wrapped his arms around his father. That was the first time he had ever heard his father say he was proud of him, something he had longed for his entire life. They held their embrace for a long time, until James spoke, "Zach, I have to go. If we say any more, it will only get harder."

Zach released his grip and stepped back a step and started to say something, "Dad, I ...."

"Don't say any more. I know you love me. I have always known. Tell Angie your mother and I love her too. But tell her she must never speak of this to anyone but you. Not ever."

Withdrawing an object from his pocket, James reached out and dropped the object into Zach's hand. Taking a step backward, he came to attention and saluted smartly and said, "Hooyah, Senior Chief Templeton." James Templeton turned away and walked directly to the exit without looking back and climbed into a waiting black SUV with darkened windows. Zach followed several steps behind and watched the SUV speed away from the loading zone and disappear from sight.

Zach turned his hand over and looked at the object his father had placed in his hand. There in his hand was the pocketknife he had given his father for his birthday. Zach remembered the day like it was yesterday. He had been only six years old when his mother had taken him to the hardware store to select the birthday gift himself. He had been so excited he could hardly wait till his father's birthday came. His father had loved the pocketknife and had carried it everywhere he went. In fact, Zach could not remember a time when his father had not had that pocketknife. After all these years, he still carried that simple little gift Zach thought as he clutched the pocketknife tightly in his hand. An enormous weight lifted off Zach and a mixture of joy and relief flooded over him. A decision he had been dreading became crystal clear as he headed for the exit to the aircraft parking ramp.

"Hey Kip, I need to make a phone call," Zach hollered as he reached the stairs to the waiting Gulfstream.

"No problem, Mister Templeton," Kip answered. "Just board the aircraft when you're done and holler at me. I'll be in the cockpit."

Zach punched the speed dial number for Angie's apartment and waited.

"Zach, where are you?" Angie asked, recognizing the number displayed on the caller ID. "I've been waiting to hear from you."

"Not important," Zach answered. "How's Pablo doing?"

"He's doing just fine. Laying on the couch snoring as usual. Are you all right? Are you going to be home soon?"

"I'm fine. NO, I'm great actually. Better than I have been in years. I'll be home really late tonight. Angie call in sick tomorrow. I need to talk to you."

"Zach, you know I don't like to call in sick if I'm not really sick."

"Please Angie. I have a whopper of a story to tell you. You aren't going to believe it."

"What is it?"

"Not on the phone. It's way too long a story. Come on Angie. Please, please, please."

"Okay Zach. I'll call in sick. Do you want me to meet you somewhere?"

"No. I have a couple of things to arrange first thing in the morning. I'll swing by your apartment. Say around ten-thirty."

"That's fine. I'll be here."

"I love you," Zach bubbled as he severed the connection and headed for the Gulfstream. He scampered up the stairs and stepped into the passenger cabin. Poking his head into the cockpit, he chimed, "Light 'er up Mister Pilot. Let's get back to Tulsa."

CHAPTER SIXTY-TWO

Friday, April 3 – 1015 Central Daylight Time
Angie's Apartment
Tulsa, Oklahoma

Zach Templeton walked up to the door to Angie's apartment and pushed the doorbell.

Angie pushed the curtain aside and peered out the window to see who was at her door. "Zach, come in," she said, pulling the door open.

"Hey Angie," Zach said as he stepped inside and pushed the door shut. He reached out and pulled Angie close to him. Hugging her so tightly she could hardly breath. She cried out for him to let go. He nuzzled her neck, his warm breath spilling out against her skin.

She shuddered and moaned, "Ooooo, Zach don't do that." Pushing him away, she stepped back and looked at his face.

"What's gotten into you? You have the strangest look on your face. What happened?"

"Boy, you have no idea," Zach chuckled. "How about some coffee before I tell you."

Zach and Angie engaged in some small talk while Zach sat at the breakfast bar and Angie busied herself in the kitchen. Pablo heard Zach's voice and came bounding out of the bedroom and leaped into Zach's arms. Zach hugged him and scratched his ears while Pablo proceeded to give Zach's face a thorough washing. He tried to put Pablo down on the floor but he would have none of that, whining and scratching at Zach's leg. Back on Zach's lap he went, returning to licking Zach's face, until Angie set some cinnamon rolls on the counter. Pablo's attention was immediately diverted to the delicious smelling rolls. He made an attempt to grab one of the rolls which resulted in a quick swat on his rump and being put down on the floor with a stern warning to stay there.

Angie poured a cup of coffee for each of them as Zach began explaining the events of the past day and a half. Several times Angie tried to interrupt but Zach convinced her to let him finish. Twenty minutes later Zach finished recounting the unbelievable events he had just lived through and took a large swallow of his coffee.

Angie sat there stunned, not certain she could believe the tall tale Zach had just told her. "That's a lot to take in Zach. It sounds more like a fairy tale."

"How about this?" Zach asserted, sliding the pocketknife across the counter. "My father handed me that pocketknife less than eighteen hours ago. He said he and Mom love you very much. Angie, my father's existence must stay between us. You must never mention it anyone other than me"

"I don't know what to say," Angie stammered. "All those years. How could they let you believe they were dead? And me! I loved them too. What about me?"

"There are things, horrible things, that go on in this world. Things you would not believe. I have seen them. I believe him when he said he had no choice. He told me he was proud of me. He called me his little Zachman. Angie, nobody has called me that in over forty years. I felt like the little boy sitting on his lap again. All of it, the whole ugly thing, was worth it for just that last five minutes with him. I can't begin to explain the weight that was lifted off my shoulders."

Angie saw Zach's eyes get red and fill with tears. "I'm glad for you Zach. I truly am. What do we do now?"

"I have another surprise for you," Zach announced. "Let's go grab a late breakfast."

"Okay, let me put these thing away," Angie replied, gathering up the cups and taking them to the sink. She switched off the coffee pot and grabbed her purse from the closet.

Reaching down and patting Pablo on the head, Zach cooed, "We'll bring you something special from the restaurant boy. Go get in your bed." Ears drooping, Pablo scurried across the living room and hopped into his box. He spun in a circle and curled up on the soft pad lining his box.

Pulling the apartment door shut, Zach grabbed Angie's hand as they headed for his car.

Sitting in a booth in their favorite restaurant, Zach ordered his favorite breakfast, an omelet with bacon and hash brown potatoes. As the server was leaving, he added a short stack to his order. For the first time in months, he had slept like a baby. Having left the house early to get some things started, he had not taken time for anything, not even coffee, and he was famished.

Between bites, he answered most of Angie's questions, filling in some details he had left out during his earlier account of the events of the past several days, withholding the classified details that could put her in danger. His finger made swirls in the condensation running down the side of the glass of ice water sitting in front of him as Angie expressed her concern for

Zach. Reassuring her as best he could, he drained the last of his coffee and grabbed the check.

"Let's go," Zach called over his shoulder, heading toward the cashier's station to pay for their breakfast. He paid for their breakfast and held the door open for her. They exited the restaurant and climbed into Zach's car. Zach drove out of the parking lot and headed for his office.

Realizing where they were heading Angie asked, "Why are we going to your office?"

"Just hang on," Zach urged. "It's a surprise. A really big surprise."

Somewhat annoyed that Zach felt it necessary to drop by the office considering all he had been through, she rode the rest of the way in silence. Zach pulled into the underground parking garage and parked in his usual, assigned spot.

"Come on. Let's go," Zach urged.

"Alright, alright, I'm coming."

They stepped into the elevator and waited while it rose to the eighth floor. Shock and surprise spread across Angie's face as she stepped off the elevator and saw the commotion in Zach's office. Two men with Midwest Moving stenciled on the back of their coveralls were covering pieces of furniture with moving blankets and wrapping them with stretch film. Two other men were taking down decorations and artwork and packing them in boxes. Janine was pulling papers out of cabinet drawers and placing them in file boxes. And lastly, she saw a man scraping the lettering off the office door. All that remained on the door was – "Microwa----". After a couple more quick scrapes even that was gone.

"Zach, what on Earth is going on?" Angie asked, a very puzzled look on her face.

"Seems the National Radio Observatory was serious about their complaints," Zach explained. "And when I disabled the entire microwave system to stop the fake message and the system was down for two entire days, Jameson blew a gasket and cancelled the contract. Without that contract, there's not enough cash flow to keep the business running. I decided that was it, all she wrote, over, done, kaput, el finito."

"Oh, Zach. I'm so sorry."

"Not to worry. I don't care anymore. I really don't."

"But I thought the company was so important to you."

"After yesterday, I realized it was a just a dream. Angie I'm serious. It really doesn't matter. After all, I have you don't I."

Before she could answer, he leaned in and gave her a kiss, grabbed her hand, and said, "Let's go celebrate. I'll stop at the store and grab some vanilla ice cream and sodas. We'll make ice cream sodas, eat cookies, and watch a movie. I'll even make one for Pablo."

"Come on," Zach urged, nearly knocking Angie off her feet as he pushed her through the door. As the door swung shut, Zach rubbed the glass where the company name used to be. "Well, it was worth a shot," he thought to himself, smiling and turning away from the door.

Waiting for the elevator, Zach kissed Angie again. When the elevator arrived and the doors opened, he dragged her inside and chortled, "Hubba, hubba," raising his eyebrows up and down several times, giggling like a silly schoolboy.

Unable to resist the infectious smile spread across his face, she grabbed him and hugged him, harder and more affectionate than she had in a very long time.

Zach sighed and buried his face in Angie's neck.

Yes, he was going to be fine. Just fine

EPILOGUE

Anthony Sterling, formerly known as Director Frank Porter, strolled along east side of the Plaza de la Independencia, the central square in the Old Town section of Quito, Ecuador.

Quito had been selected for his new life primarily because of Ecuador's extremely restrictive, and secretive, banking laws. Other reasons were the warm climate and the low cost of living. The funds he had transferred to a bank in Quito would last him a very long time, even though he lived a lavish lifestyle.

The streets surrounding the Old Town's inner plaza were lined with regal, colonial mansions. Anthony had settled on a sumptuous apartment in one of those regal mansions to serve as his new residence.

As he did every day, Anthony Sterling selected a table in an outside courtyard at one of the many small coffee shops lining the street. A young woman with a heavily stained apron wrapped around her waist approached the table. He ordered a large coffee and an empanada.

Anthony unfolded a copy of El Migrante Ecuatoriano, a local newspaper, and began reading. To improve his limited knowledge of the local language, he read Spanish newspapers and spoke with locals as much as he was able.

The server returned with his order and set it on the table. Anthony picked up the cup and took a careful sip of the dark, steaming liquid. "Mmmm," Anthony murmured. The coffee was rich and dark, just the way he liked it. He took another sip and went back to the paper. Twenty minutes and another cup of coffee later, he laid the paper on the table and leaned back in the chair. The sun, shining brightly, in a cloudless sky felt good on his face. Smiling to himself, he was convinced he had made an excellent decision. He was going to like his new home very much.

Despite his seemingly good mood, Anthony's smile quickly faded and his face clouded with anger. Never more than a single thought away, he remembered the dimwitted moron that had discovered and thwarted his plan for revenge. Years of planning and painstaking preparation, destroyed by one man. Anthony's chair scraped the floor as he lurched forward. Furious, seething anger boiled inside him as hot, burning acid rose in his throat, agitating his growing ulcer. He reached into his jacket pocket, pulled out a bottle, and shook two antacid tablet into his hand. He grimaced as he chewed the chalky tablets.

He so desperately wanted revenge. A plan to exact the revenge he craved on Mr. Zach Templeton was already forming in his mind. No matter how long it took, no matter how much it cost him, he was going to put a bullet in that man's brain. Someday soon he would laugh in the face of the man that he destroyed everything he had worked for.

Anthony folded the paper, stuffed it under his arm, and headed for his apartment, savoring the image of sweet, satisfying revenge he had planned for the man he hated.

* * *

Saturday, April 4 – 0820 Central Daylight Time
Zach Templeton's House
Tulsa, Oklahoma

"Stop. Stop. Pablo stop," Zach protested when Pablo stuck his cold, wet nose on Zach's neck and started licking furiously. Having spent the entire evening with Angie, Zach had arrived home late, happy, contented, and full of hope for the future. He and Pablo had crawled into bed and both had fallen asleep almost instantly. Zach would have been able to sleep longer, but Pablo was desperate to go outside.

As Zach straightened the covers, Pablo jumped off the bed and ran in a circle, barking impatiently.

"Okay, okay, I'm coming. I'm coming." Zach smiled, watching Pablo's antics and wondering what he would have done without his loyal companionship the last few months. Zach padded barefooted into the kitchen, finding Pablo already waiting and scratching at the door. He pushed the sliding door open and Pablo flew out into the yard. While waiting for Pablo to return, Zach started the coffee pot and ducked out the front door to grab the morning paper. As expected, when he returned to the kitchen, Pablo was already scratching at the door to be let in.

Immediately, Pablo ran over to the cabinet under the sink, nosed the door open, and pawed at a can with a green, white, and red label. The can tipped over and fell out of the cabinet, rolling to the center of the kitchen floor.

"Well, Fabrizio's Italian it is," Zach laughed. Digging a can opener from the drawer, Zach opened the can of dog food and dumped it into Pablo's dish. "How bad do you want it?" Pablo immediately sat up and barked loudly, drool dripping from his tongue. Zach sat the bowl on the floor, poured a cup of coffee, and busied himself reading the morning newspaper while Pablo devoured his dog food.

Thirty minutes later, Zach folded the paper and dropped it into the trash basket beside the kitchen table. He felt relaxed and at ease, finally relieved of the tension of a struggling company and a dying marriage. The company had been closed permanently and was no longer a worry. His marriage finally seemed to be on the mend, at least he hoped it was. The one remaining thing threatening his new-found happiness was the lack of closure surrounding his best friend's death. He desperately wanted the man that was responsible for Fred's death to pay for his crime. The despicable traitor, Frank Porter, had slipped away without a trace. Zach was not certain he could ever feel complete resolution of the terrifying nightmare he had endured until that man was caught and brought to justice.

Wandering through the house, he stepped into his home office. About to press the power button on the computer, he realized there was not any reason to turn the computer on. Microwave Services Incorporated was defunct and closed permanently. All the furniture and equipment had been removed, the sign had been scraped off the door, and Zach had handed the keys to the landlord. Slumping down in the office chair, he stared vacantly out the window, an odd feeling sweeping over him. He had absolutely nothing to do. For months, every waking moment had been consumed by his attempts to salvage his company and his marriage.

"Holy crow!" Zach squawked, as an unsettling thought entered his mind. "What am I going to do for a living? How am I going to pay my bills?" There were only enough funds in his bank account to last a month or two, and only if he was careful. After that, it would be the bread line. He pulled a yellow, ruled tablet from the desk drawer and laid it on the desk. "I'll make a list of people to call next week," he said, grabbing a pen. He sat staring at the blank page, unable to think of a single name to write on the paper. Deep in thought, he flinched when the phone on his desk rang.

"Hello, this is Zach Templeton."

"Zach, Admiral Hadley here. How are you?"

"Surprisingly, better than I've been in a long time Admiral. What can I do for you?"

"I promised you I would do something special for Rachael Hargrove. Well, it's all arranged. President Cantwell wholeheartedly agreed. Fred will be posthumously awarded the Presidential Medal of Freedom. Rachael will be flown by private jet to Washington to receive the award for him. The President and all Joint Chiefs of Staff will be there to personally thank her for what Fred did."

"Wow! That's great Admiral. I can't thank you enough. Rachael will be thrilled."

"There's more. Zach, you will also be honored at the awards ceremony."

"Huh...what? No, Admiral. I didn't do that much."

"Come on, Zach. Your actions saved countless thousands of lives. The paperwork is already completed and signed. You and your wife will accompany Rachel to Washington for the award ceremony. All expenses paid and the finest hotel in Washington. I told the President it was the least we could do."

"I am truly overwhelmed Admiral."

"One more thing, but you must keep this to yourself. Your mother and father will be flown in secretly to observe the ceremony."

Admiral Hadley could not see the tears welling up in Zach's eyes. "You just made my day, Admiral Hadley."

Zach and the Admiral talked for a few additional minutes before ending their conversation. The rest of the day was a blur as Zach tried to absorb the good news Admiral Hadley had shared with him.

Zach was happier than he had been in a long, long time. The following day he spent time reading the Sunday paper and playing with Pablo. Sunday evening he and Angie had a great meal at their favorite Italian restaurant. After dinner, they spent several hours at her apartment talking. When he climbed into bed he felt contented and full of hope for the future.

He had no idea the madman that had slipped away, was conjuring up a plan that would plunge Zach into yet another nightmarish encounter with wicked men. An encounter so horrifying and unthinkable, it would threaten to plunge the United States into a global war.

Sleep peacefully Zachariah Templeton. Soon the peace and hope you dream of will be crushed like eggshells.

ABOUT THE AUTHOR

Keith Hoar is a writer and former IBM Certified Business Intelligence Expert who consulted for numerous Fortune 100 companies. He designed executive suite business intelligence reporting systems and software subsystems for companies such as: Motorola C&E, Cigna Insurance, Hyundai Motors NA, Continental Airlines, Sprint Wireless, Wells Fargo, and others.

Keith also owned his own consulting company that designed custom software systems and sophisticated data-driven reporting systems.

Keith proudly served his country in the United States Navy for ten years. At Naval Submarine School, New London, Connecticut, his duties included: setup of training scenarios, input of attack center maneuvering orders, monitoring of firing point procedures, and tracking outcome of weapons launch.

Keith is a PADI certified SCUBA diver with 100+ dives all over the Caribbean. Keith has published two novels, *Edge of Madness* and *RAGE*, edge-of-your-seat, hold-your-breath thrillers. He has also published a nonfiction book, *DECEIVED The Assault of Revisionist History*.

Thank you for taking the time to read about the author. He is most grateful for fans of his books, and would love to correspond with readers like you. Sample Prologues and Chapters for all his books can be viewed on his website at WWW.Zhetosoft.com. You are welcome to reach him through his email at author@zhetosoft.com.